This Other Eden

Skimmerdale
(Book 1)

Sharon Booth

Typesetting and Design Fabrian Books – fabrianbooks.com.

About the author

Sharon lives in East Yorkshire, and is the author of two other novels, *There Must Be an Angel* and *A Kiss from a Rose*, and has also written for *People's Friend.*

She is one tenth of The Write Romantics, has a love/hate relationship with chocolate, is a devoted Whovian, and just a little obsessed with *Sherlock, The Musketeers* and *Poldark.* She freely admits that she would write more books if there weren't so many gorgeous men on television. The situation has recently become critical since she was given a DVD of *Outlander* for Christmas.

You can find out more about Sharon at http://sharonbooth.co.uk/

Other books by this author

The Kearton Bay Series

There Must Be an Angel

A Kiss from a Rose

For Steve

"Love you most"

XXX

CHAPTER ONE

'Don't look now, but that couple over there appear to have a stalker,' Eden said, glaring at Fiona when she immediately turned to peer at the pair in question. 'What part of *don't look now* didn't you get? Talk about making it obvious.'

'Are you for real?' Fiona tutted in disgust and began wiping down the bar, scrubbing at an obstinate beer stain with a cloth that had definitely seen better days. 'Are you seriously telling me you don't know who those two are?'

Eden frowned as she tried to stare at the couple without actually looking at them, which wasn't easy. 'I think he looks vaguely familiar,' she admitted eventually.

'Vaguely familiar? Honestly, how old are you? That's Troy Troughton.'

'Troy ...?'

'Troughton! The lead singer of Tuna Sandwich.'

'Who the hell are *Tuna Sandwich*?'

Fiona stopped cleaning and gaped at her. 'You really don't know, do you? Tuna Sandwich are the hottest band in Britain, right now. And that fella over there is the hottest member of the hottest band in Britain.'

'He is?' Frowning, Eden peered over at a youth with a very average appearance, who looked as if he should still be in school. 'Crikey. You learn something new every day.'

'Yeah, I don't get it, either. He's been in all the papers lately. He's just got engaged to Trixie Much. I expect you don't know who she is, either.'

'Well …' Eden scrutinised Troy's companion, who seemed to be hanging onto his every word, 'I should think she's about twenty years old, pretty, with long blonde hair and a simpering expression on her painted doll face.'

'You'd be very wrong, then.' Fiona grinned. 'Trixie is

the dark and sultry lead singer of Verity. That girl over there is *not* his new fiancée.'

'But they've been whispering sweet nothings into each other's ears all evening. And they've kissed!'

Fiona giggled at her obvious outrage. 'You are funny, Eden. And naive. You obviously don't recognise *her*, either. That's Honey Carmichael. You know, the spoilt little princess daughter of Cain Carmichael? And if you tell me you've never heard of him, I'm going to rub this disgusting cloth in your face.'

'Of course I've heard of Cain Carmichael.'

Hadn't she just! He was a seventies rock legend, and she'd grown up listening to his albums, which her father had insisted on playing at full volume every time they went out in the car—much to her mum's disgust, since she was more of an Abba girl.

Cain Carmichael lived in a village about twenty miles away from Lowminster, and Gavin, landlord of the town's worst pub, The Red Lion, where Eden and Fiona worked, lived in hope that, one day, his pub would be honoured with a visit from the man himself. So far, though, Cain had avoided the place—not surprisingly, given the grubby state of it—but it appeared his daughter wasn't so choosy.

So, that was the only child of the seventies superstar and his beautiful ex-wife, Freya Barrows? Had she been his second wife or his third? Eden couldn't remember. She knew they were divorced and had been for many years. Cain had vowed never to marry again, after Freya won a very bitter court case and walked away with a fortune. He never had, too, but it didn't stop him from having a string of relationships, some with women who didn't seem much older than Honey herself. Eden could almost feel sorry for her, but seeing her fawning all over the newly-engaged, fickle-hearted singer, her sympathy was draining away fast.

'Well, then,' said Fiona, 'is there any wonder they've

got a stalker? The papers will be all over this, and if they've got photos, well, that's Troy's engagement over. Trixie doesn't take any crap, I'll give her that.'

'Oh, he's got photos all right.'

They watched as the stalker lifted his mobile phone and took another shot. He'd sat some distance from the lovesick couple, so it was no wonder they hadn't noticed him. Although, with his sunglasses perched on his nose and a flat cap on his head, he wasn't exactly blending in.

'That picture will be in the tabloids tomorrow,' said Fiona, with some satisfaction. 'Trixie will hit the roof, Troy's manager will wipe the floor with him, and I shouldn't think Cain Carmichael will be too thrilled that his little princess is finally making headlines of her own, either.' She glanced around. 'Where's Gavin?'

Gavin was nowhere to be seen, which was unusual. He normally kept his beady eye on them all evening. He liked to find fault with everything they did, and they'd lost count of the number of times they'd been threatened with the sack. He prided himself on running a tight ship, although obviously, he was happy to let it slacken off immeasurably when it came to cleanliness and hygiene, in spite of Eden's best efforts. It was frustrating how, after just one or two days off, the kitchen would revert back to its former grubby state and Eden would have to start scrubbing and mopping and disinfecting before she could even begin to cook. How The Red Lion hadn't been closed down was a complete mystery to everyone who knew Gavin. He liked to inform people his bar was bang on trend, being a homage to shabby chic, but it was actually just shabby. Eden often thought the sooner she found another job, the better. Cooking in that kitchen was a thoroughly depressing experience.

'No idea,' Eden said, in answer to Fiona's question. 'He'll be absolutely livid that he's missed out on seeing his hero's daughter right here in his pub.' The thought cheered her up no end.

They watched as Troy stood up and headed to the toilets. Once alone, Honey sat back and closed her eyes.

Immediately, the stalker took more photos.

'Why is he photographing her? Shouldn't his real target be Troy?' asked Eden.

Fiona shrugged. 'He's probably going to do a hatchet job on her. Maybe going for the angle of the heartless other woman who's destroyed the engagement of our latest celebrity couple. Reckon Honey's going to cop for the lot. Bet he's a fan of Trixie. Serves her right, I suppose.'

'She's just a kid,' Eden murmured, her feelings towards the girl softening as she watched her reaching into her handbag and pulling out a vanity mirror.

Honey examined her mouth, pulling back her top lip with obvious anxiety, and Eden realised she must be worried some of the salad leaves she'd picked at earlier had stuck in her teeth. Maybe she was only human, after all, although Eden had wondered at first. She'd ignored all the dishes on the main course menu and ordered a side salad and mineral water, while Troy had tucked into Hunter's Chicken. It had thoroughly annoyed Eden, who took great pride in her culinary skills. Even so, it didn't seem fair that a lowlife reporter was watching her every move and preparing to tear her to shreds in the tabloids.

Troy returned, and, after murmuring something to him, Honey stood up and made her way to the ladies.

'Where are you going?' Fiona demanded, when Eden headed out from behind the bar.

'Won't be a moment,' she whispered, and followed Honey into the toilets.

She found the young woman picking at a bit of watercress in her teeth with one of her beautifully manicured nails, and when their eyes met in the reflection of the mirror, Honey flushed slightly and began to rummage in her bag.

Eden took a step closer. 'Honey?'

She raised an eyebrow. 'What? I don't do autographs, sorry.'

Autographs? Why the hell would she want Honey's autograph? Honey hadn't done anything special. Unless she counted having a secret relationship with an engaged man, obviously.

'I don't want an autograph. I just came to warn you that a man has been watching you for ages, and he's been taking photographs of you on his mobile phone.'

'Has he?' Her eyebrows shot up as glee sparked in her eyes.

Eden had a feeling she hadn't grasped the implications of her situation. 'You need to get out of here. You do realise this will probably be in all the papers tomorrow?'

'Gosh.' She leaned against the basin, her gaze dreamy, like she was visualising glamorous photos of herself being admired and talked about on programmes like *Lorraine*.

Time for a reality check. 'Honey, Troy is engaged. His manager isn't going to be happy if he gets caught with his pants down, so to speak, and Trixie will be furious. This will really damage his career. And you'll be branded a scarlet woman. Trixie's so popular, you'll be torn apart in the press. You know they always blame the other woman. Do you really want that?'

'Shit!' She drummed her fingers on the sink and considered the matter. 'What do I do?'

'I'm not sure there's much you *can* do, to be honest. Maybe you should go home and ask your dad's advice. He may know someone who can work on some damage limitation.' *God knows, Cain Carmichael must have experience of heading off damaging stories in the press*, she thought.

'What about Troy?'

'Oh, bugger Troy,' Eden said.

As far as she was concerned, it was his own fault. Jumped up little tosser. Honey wasn't much more than a kid, for God's sake.

She opened the toilet door and scanned the room for the reporter, jumping when she spotted him hovering just to the side of her. She shut the door and turned back to Honey. 'He's outside,' she said. 'Wait there.'

She headed back into the bar and walked over to Troy. He looked terrified when she sat opposite him, but Eden had no time for introductions.

'See that bloke with the sunglasses and the flat cap, over by the ladies' toilets? Yeah, the one who's pretending to be looking at the crappy picture on the wall. He's been taking photographs of you and Honey all evening, and now he's lurking outside the toilets waiting for her to come out. I reckon he's going to start firing questions at her.'

Troy's skin turned grey. Almost as grey as the tea towels in the kitchen of The Red Lion, but not quite. 'Christ! I've had it. I thought we'd be safe here. No one ever comes to this dump.'

Eden bristled for a moment then mentally shrugged. He was right, after all. 'Yes, well, you thought wrong. You need to go, and so does Honey.'

'If Trixie finds out, she'll have my balls for Christmas tree decorations.'

'Hmm, yes, well, I was thinking you could —'

She gaped when Troy jumped up from his seat and ran to the door. He'd torn out of the pub before Eden could even begin to suggest he speak to the reporter, offer some sort of bribe, or a deal. She had no idea how those things worked, but the man had been taking photos for a good while and would already have a story, so damage limitation seemed to her to be the only option left. Unfortunately, Troy didn't seem to share her opinion. For him, obviously, it was all about escaping and making the most of his testicles while he still owned a pair.

There was only one thing for it. Eden rushed over to Fiona. 'Distract him.'

'Distract him. How?'

'How should I know? I need to get Honey out of here, and I can't think of any other way to—'

'Leave it to me,' Gavin barked, marching past them.

Eden hadn't even noticed him come in. To be fair, she hadn't noticed him go out, either.

He strode over to the reporter and tapped him on the shoulder. 'Right, sunshine, what do you think you're up to, hanging round the ladies' toilets?'

Eden and Fiona exchanged a glance before following their boss.

The reporter gulped. For a hardened tabloid journalist, he was a bit of a wimp. Eden could see him trembling from where she stood. 'I can assure you, I'm not hanging round the ladies' toilets.'

'Oh, no? So, what does that sign say?' He indicated the door, the only thing protecting Honey from the media shark—although the way he was opening and closing his mouth soundlessly, he was acting more like a goldfish than a shark, in Eden's opinion. 'Well?'

'Er, it says ladies' toilets.'

'Exactly. And are you, or are you not, standing right beside them?'

'Yes, but—I was just admiring this painting.'

They all turned and stared at the painting on the wall. It was a cheap print of a view of Lowminster, painted by a local artist and sold to Gavin at a car boot sale for less than a tenner. Van Gogh it wasn't.

'Wanna take your sunglasses off and have a proper look?' asked Gavin.

The journalist tentatively hitched up his sunglasses, perching them on the top of his head, and peered at the painting. A look of horror crossed his face as he evidently realised how awful it actually was, and he gulped.

Gavin folded his arms. 'Wanna try again?'

'I, er, I think I should leave.'

'I think you should, too,' said Gavin.

The man began to move away, and Eden took her opportunity. She stepped in his path and held out her hand, glaring at him. 'Not 'til you've shown me the photos on that mobile phone.'

'What? Certainly not. It's private.'

'He's been snapping away all night,' she told Gavin. 'We can't let him leave with all those pictures.'

'Hand it over,' said Gavin.

'You can't make me. I'll call the police,' said the intrepid reporter.

'Do what you like, mate. Invasion of privacy, that's what it is. I won't have my guests harassed in my own pub. Now, if you want to call the police, feel free. I shall tell them all about your perverted behaviour, hanging around the ladies' toilets and leering at the women as they go in. Disgusting. You wanna get yourself some counselling.'

'Now, look here!'

Gavin whipped the phone from his hand and began scrolling through the photographs. The reporter was almost crying as he protested his innocence and begged Gavin to leave at least some of the pictures intact.

While they argued, Eden pushed open the door of the toilets and beckoned Honey out. Fiona took the chance to tell the journalist what she thought of men like him, distracting him beautifully while her colleague led Honey into the kitchen and out through the back door. They ran through the car park and onto the main street.

'Gosh, that was exciting,' Honey said. 'Can you slow down a bit? These heels are killing me.'

'We need to get you home before he leaves the pub. I'll get you a taxi. Have you got any money on you?'

'No, but it doesn't matter. Once they know where I live, they let me off with everything,' she said confidently. Obviously she'd tried it before.

'If you say so. I've left my bag in the pub. Have you got a mobile on you?'

She gave Eden a withering look. 'Of course I have. By the way, what about Troy? Is he still in there?'

Eden hesitated, but Honey deserved to know. 'I'm sorry. He did a bunk as soon as he knew what was going on.'

She held her breath, hoping there wouldn't be any tears, but Honey merely rolled her eyes and scrambled in her bag for her phone. 'Might have known he'd leg it and leave me in the shit. Utter knobhead. What that Trixie Much sees in him, I'll never know. Well, I can hazard a guess. It must be money, because it sure as hell isn't the size of his dick, I can tell you that much.'

Eden's mouth fell open in shock. How old was this girl? She looked like a Disney princess, but she was obviously more experienced than she'd given her credit for.

She was about to tell her it really didn't matter why Trixie was engaged to Troy, the point was she *was* engaged to him, and Honey really ought to have respected that, but her words were cut off by the screeching of tyres, and she found herself standing beside a magnificent Rolls Royce.

A gravelly voice yelled, 'Is that reporter still in there? Get in!'

'Oh, shit. That's all I need.'

'Who is it?' Eden said.

'Yes, he is, and I can get a taxi!' Honey pouted and turned her back on the car.

Eden watched, amazed, as Honey began to walk away, but the door opened and a man yelled, 'I said, get in this bleeding car now!'

Honey actually stamped her foot.

Eden gaped at her. She looked like a toddler having a tantrum, and Eden made the mistake of laughing.

The man who'd climbed from the car turned to her. 'And who the bleeding hell are you?'

It took less than a second to realise she was being glared at by none other than the legendary Cain Carmichael, and Eden's face heated until it burned. Her dad would be so proud to learn his daughter was being sworn at by his hero. 'I'm Eden Robinson,' she said. 'Not that it's relevant.'

'Oh, really? I'll be the judge of that.'

'Leave her alone, Dad. She's just saved my bacon,' said Honey.

He looked at Eden with new respect. 'Really? Get in.'

'Pardon?'

'Look, what is it with you two? Get in the bleeding car before that sodding reporter comes out, because if I see him, I won't be able to keep me hands to meself, and we all know where that will lead.'

Honey gave a dramatic sigh and grabbed Eden's hand. 'Come on, get in.'

'What? No, I can't. I've got to—'

Honey shook her head and pushed her into the car. Eden hardly had time to gather her thoughts before Honey jumped in beside her, Cain got in the front seat, and they were driving away from the pub.

'How did you know about the reporter?' demanded Honey. She folded her arms, her expression sulky.

'Landlord of this gaff telephoned Snarler to tip me off.'

'At the house? How did he know our number? We're ex-directory.'

'Turns out he plays cards with Snarler, and he called his mobile and explained the situation. Good job. I told Snarler to call him back and tell him to make sure you got out of there safely, and I'd come and get you. Reckon he thinks I'll be going inside the pub to thank him. Fat chance. It looks a proper dive. What the hell were you thinking?'

'Troy said it would be private. No one ever goes in there.'

'No bleeding wonder! What a shithole.'

'Who's Snarler?' Eden said, though she didn't know why. It hardly mattered but it was all she could think of to say.

'Chauffeur,' said both Cain and Honey automatically.

'What the hell were you doing with that tosser, Troy Troughton?' demanded Cain. 'You can do better than that. Bet his balls haven't even dropped yet.'

'If Snarler is the chauffeur, why are you driving?' Eden asked.

'He's got a hangover,' they both answered.

'Of course Troy's balls have dropped. Believe me, he's all man,' snapped Honey.

What a fibber, Eden thought. That's not what she'd been saying ten minutes ago.

'Do you mind?' Cain said. 'You do realise he's practically a married man?'

'Oh, that wedding won't happen. Trixie's only after the publicity. She doesn't really care about him.'

'Trixie doesn't need the publicity. Verity are a great little band.'

'Oh, pur-lease.' Honey sneered. 'They sound like the Spice Girls on helium.'

'At least Trixie can sing, which is more than that daft twat can. Troy bloody Troughton. Sounds like he should be piloting a Thunderbird.'

'Oh, bugger off,' snapped Honey.

'Well, that's charming. What a delightful daughter you are.'

'Is there any chance I can get out of this car now?' Eden asked.

'And how the hell did that reporter know where to find you? That's what I'd like to know. Did you tip him off?'

'Why would I tip him off?' demanded Honey.

'I wouldn't put anything past you. You're becoming a proper pain, just like your bleeding mother. You want to be in the papers, and you don't care how you get there, you stupid little tart.'

Fancy saying that to his own daughter! Eden tried to imagine her dad having this sort of conversation with her. The most they ever argued about was who'd finished off the Cheerios, and the worst name he'd ever called her was 'Bossyboots'. He'd be seeing Cain Carmichael in a new light when she relayed this conversation to him.

'To be fair,' Eden said, 'I really don't think Honey knew the reporter was there. She only realised when I tipped her off.'

Cain glanced at her in the rear-view mirror. 'Who are you, anyway?'

'I told you. I'm Eden Robinson. I work at The Red Lion. At least, I did, but since I've just abandoned my post without warning, I've probably been sacked.'

'I'm sure your boss will understand,' said Cain.

'That's all you know,' Eden said. 'Understanding isn't the word I'd use to describe Gavin. And you've made it ten times worse by not going in the pub to thank him. The fact that I'm in this car with you right now will be the final straw. I reckon I'm for the chop.'

'Bugger. I'm sorry.' At least he sounded genuine.

Eden shrugged. 'It doesn't matter. It was a crap job, anyway. Look, not that I don't appreciate the experience of riding in a proper Rolls Royce, but do you think you can drop me off now? My bag's back at The Red Lion, and I live three miles in the opposite direction from the pub, anyway. It's going to take me forever to get home at this rate.'

Cain watched her through narrowed eyes for a moment

before speaking 'How old are you?'

'Twenty-three. Why?'

'Look, come back to our gaff for some supper. I want to talk to you.'

'Jesus, Dad, you can't shag her!' Honey looked as appalled as she sounded. 'She's practically staff.'

'Do you mind?' Eden gasped. 'You're one spoilt, rude little brat, aren't you?'

Honey looked stunned by that summing up of her character, though Eden found it hard to believe no one had told her before. Or maybe no one had, and that was the problem.

Cain laughed. 'That's told her. Look, love, I ain't after shagging you. You needn't worry on that score.'

'Oh.' Eden wondered whether to feel relieved or offended. He wasn't exactly known for being choosy, after all.

'I may have a job for you.'

'What sort of job?' Honey and Eden spoke in unison, then looked equally appalled by the fact.

'Looking after her,' he said, nodding at Honey's reflection.

'Looking after me? Are you insane? I'm nineteen years old and perfectly capable of looking after myself.'

'Oh, yeah, we can see that. Made a right balls-up of tonight, didn't you? Left to your own devices, you'll be in rehab before you're twenty-one. Nah, you need someone to watch you, and I haven't got the time.'

'What do you mean, watch her? You mean like babysitting?' Eden had visions of making Honey hot chocolate and toast, then tucking her up in bed, before plonking herself in front of the telly to watch a horror film and make illicit phone calls on the house phone, which was what her previous babysitting experience had consisted of. 'No thanks.'

'Honey's a young woman now. She needs to start

making her way in the world, earn her own living. She's had it too easy, for too long. I'm setting her up in a little shop in the village, but she'll need help. You work behind the bar, so you obviously know how to handle a till. You can be trusted with cash.'

'Excuse me,' said Eden indignantly. 'I'm not just a barmaid, you know. I went to catering college for three years. I'm the chef.'

'Even better. You can cook us some decent grub now and then. Look, darls, you can deal with the public. More than that, you looked out for her tonight. I won't forget that. We owe you, and this job will be well paid.'

Eden had been about to tell him thanks but no thanks, but the last part of his speech caught her attention. 'How well paid?'

'Whatever your previous salary was, I'll double it.'

'Hmm.'

'Plus, there'll be a room for you at our house. You can live in. No bills, no rent. All inclusive. What do you say?'

Honey had observed the conversation with a look of dumbstruck horror on her face, until she finally found her voice. 'She says no. Of course she bloody says no. And I say no. I don't need anyone to help me in the shop. I want to do things my way, and this sodding barmaid isn't going to tell me what to do, that's for sure.'

'Listen, kiddo, if you want this shop you'll do as you're told or you can whistle for it. I wouldn't trust you with a toy post office, never mind a real business, especially after today's performance.'

'Oh, but you'd trust a random stranger?'

Cain shrugged. 'I'll need a criminal record check and a character reference,' he said to Eden's reflection. 'Would that be a problem?'

'No, but—'

Honey glared at Eden. 'You're not seriously considering this? I don't need you, so don't think you're worming your way in here. I do things my way.'

It was as if Cain hadn't heard her. He raised an eyebrow and surveyed Eden through the mirror. 'Well?'

Honey looked at her in fury. 'Tell him no!'

Eden leaned back in her seat and folded her arms. 'Triple the salary, and you've got a deal.'

Honey shrieked.

Cain grinned. 'Deal.'

And that was how Eden Robinson's life collided with that of Honey Carmichael.

CHAPTER TWO

Three years later.

'Where the hell is she?' Cain's face purpled with rage, as he stormed towards the triple garage, waving his iPhone in the air. 'Little git isn't answering my calls. When I get me hands on her, she's dog food.'

'Charming as ever,' Eden muttered, climbing out of the car and preparing to face her furious employer.

In the driver's seat, Joshua tried valiantly to suppress a whimper.

'Stay there and keep quiet,' she instructed.

Cain stood in front of her, his bloodshot, watery blue eyes boring into hers. 'Well?'

'Well, what?'

'Don't give me that. Where's Honey? I suppose you know all about it. What's the stupid little git gone and done now? Don't even try to pretend you don't know what's going on. I don't pay you to—who the bleeding hell are you?' He looked at Joshua menacingly, and the poor man visibly shrivelled.

Eden couldn't blame him. Cain in a temper wasn't a pretty sight. Cain at any time wasn't a pretty sight, really. God knows how he managed to attract so many beautiful women. Okay, strike that. You only had to look at his fabulous house, collection of cars, and pretty impressive stack of platinum credit cards to realise he had plenty to draw women to him, even if he did look as handsome as … well, as a sixty-six-year-old man with bleached blond hair and a penchant for leather trousers.

'This is Joshua,' she informed him.

'And who the bleeding hell is Joshua? More to the point, what's he doing in the driving seat of Honey's car?'

'It's all right,' Eden said hastily. 'Honey asked Snarler to clean it, but he's got a hangover, so I said I'd do it for him. I was showing Joshua the interior. He loves cars, but I wouldn't let him drive it.'

'I should hope not. That's nearly thirty grand's worth of car, there, mate. Keep your greasy mitts off it. Who are you, anyway?'

'Joshua's my, er ...' Eden's voice trailed off. She'd been about to say boyfriend, but realised that wouldn't be strictly true, given that she'd just told him she was finishing with him. After a pathetic two weeks of dating, it had become strikingly obvious that the only thing about her that really excited Joshua was the fact that she worked for the Carmichaels and lived in their house. Without them in the equation, she doubted very much she'd be able to raise a smile from him, never mind anything else. The last fortnight had been nothing but a crippling blow to her ego, and she'd had enough.

He hadn't taken it as well as she'd hoped. He'd assured her the Carmichaels didn't matter a jot to him, and that it was Eden he was interested in and not them. Eden might have believed him, if his eyes hadn't kept straying longingly to Cain's Rolls Royce, which was parked on the driveway in front of a bright yellow Volkswagen Beetle Cabriolet. The latter had been a present for Honey's twenty-first birthday last year from her mother, who'd been away skiing at the time and so was unable to actually visit her daughter to share in the celebrations. Joshua had obviously found the Beetle irresistible, too, as he couldn't seem to make up his mind which one to drool over the most.

When Eden had told him there was no going back, she'd been shocked when his eyes filled with tears. She hadn't known he cared, until he'd murmured forlornly, 'I never even got to meet Honey,' and she realised he didn't bloody care.

'For God's sake,' she'd snapped. 'Tell you what, why don't I let you sit in her car for five minutes as a consolation prize?'

God knows, she hadn't expected him to accept her sarcastic offer.

Cursing her own kindness, she'd unlocked Honey's car door and watched, as he climbed in.

'It's perfect,' he said, touching the steering wheel with reverence and gazing in awe at the dashboard. 'I can just imagine Honey sitting in here.'

As if he hadn't bruised her self-esteem enough, he'd nodded towards the vintage Rolls Royce, just beyond the Beetle's windscreen. 'I don't suppose there's any chance we could sit in that, too?'

'Don't push it, Joshua,' she said. 'Anyway, there's no chance. Cain guards it with his life. Only he and Snarler are allowed to drive that, depending on who hasn't got the hangover. No one else touches it. You should be grateful you're in the Beetle.'

'May I start it? Just to hear the engine?' So stunned by his cheek, Eden merely nodded, and he beamed in delight as he turned the key in the engine. 'Who's Snarler, anyway?'

Eden watched him run his hands over the upholstery of the Beetle with a great deal more interest than he'd ever paid when running his hands over her, and any guilt she'd felt for finishing with him melted away. 'Snarler used to be Cain's roadie, about a million years ago,' she said, 'They had a high old time together—literally. Now he works as their chauffeur. No way would he trust that Rolls to anyone but him.'

'Shame. Still, this car is pretty special, too. Purrs like a kitten.'

'Er, okay.' Eden rolled her eyes. Boys and their toys.

They'd only been in the car a couple of minutes when Cain had stormed out, full of fury. He didn't even seem to be listening to her, so Eden didn't have to find an explanation for who Joshua was, after all.

'When she gets back from wherever it is she is—and Gawd knows, I dread to think where that is—you tell her from me that I want to see her. A.S.A.P.! I'll be in my den. Get it?'

'Got it.'

'Good.'

He threw Joshua one last look of contempt, then strode back into the house, slamming the door behind him. Within seconds, the screaming vocals and grinding guitar music from one of his biggest hits was blasting through the open window and polluting the peaceful Cotswolds air. Not a good sign. Cain only played his own music when he was in a foul temper.

Joshua shivered, as Eden climbed back into the car beside him. 'Is he always like this?' he asked, his eyes wide and full of fear.

'Pretty much,' she said.

He sighed. 'It seems to be my day for shattered dreams.'

She was about to suggest that he head home, when there was a sudden screech of tyres and the slamming of a car door. Eden watched through the wing mirror, as Honey paid off a taxi driver, who obviously wasn't going to waive his fee no matter who her father was, then stamped to the front gates. She punched in the key code and marched into the drive as the gates swung open. She looked about as happy as her father.

'It's Honey!' Joshua moony-eyed the girl like he'd died and gone to heaven.

'I'd shut up and stay still, if I was you,' Eden said. 'With any luck she won't notice us. The mood she's in, you'll be mincemeat if she catches you in here.'

His fear made another appearance, and he jumped so hard he almost banged his head on the roof, when Honey suddenly bent down and banged furiously on the car window.

'Who the fuck are you, and what are you doing in my car?'

'Stay there and say nothing,' Eden told him, seeing that he looked as if he was about to have a panic attack. She climbed out of the passenger seat yet again and shut the door behind her, going around the car to stand beside Honey.

'Who is this moron?' Honey demanded.

'Joshua.'

'Joshua who? Oh, you mean the eunuch?'

'Shut up! I never called him that.'

'You said he wasn't interested in sex.'

'That doesn't make him a bloody eunuch. It makes him a gentleman.' Eden was growing more annoyed by the minute, not least by the fact that Honey's rudeness was forcing her into defending Joshua.

'Yeah, right. He looks like a eunuch.' She peered in at poor Joshua, who stared steadfastly ahead of him.

Even from outside the car, Eden could see the beads of sweat on his upper lip. She wondered why she'd thought he was so good looking when she first met him.

'Although, I suppose it could be that he just doesn't fancy you,' Honey continued. 'Who knows, with another woman he could be a demon lover.' She gave a sarcastic laugh, and Eden decided it was time to bring her down a peg, or two.

'Never mind all that. Your father's on the warpath. He wants to see you in his den—now.'

She sighed. 'Guessed as much, with him playing that God-awful racket at full blast. How the hell he sold any of that garbage, I'll never know.'

'He's been trying to ring you,' Eden said.

Honey grinned and waved her iPhone at her, just as Cain had done moments before. 'I know. I've been counting the missed calls. I was, er, busy.'

'Please don't tell me you were with Crispin.'

She shrugged. 'Okay, I won't. Best go and smooth the waters with dear papa, then.'

'Honey!' Eden grabbed her arm. 'This is serious. You told me you'd called it off with him. You said it was a brief fling and didn't mean anything. You promised.'

'I told you what you wanted to hear.' Honey wrenched free of Eden's grasp and glared at her, eyes flashing with anger. 'You did your duty. You told me to behave myself, and I salved your conscience. That's how it works, isn't it? If you hadn't been snooping on me you'd never have known and wouldn't have had this dilemma. Your own fault, really. You should know by now, Eden dear, no one tells me what to do. Least of all you. You're nothing but a glorified shop assistant, and it's time you realised I'm twenty-two years old and I do whatever the fuck I like.'

'Fine,' Eden yelled as Honey walked away. 'Go and face the music, then. And good luck with it, because Cain looks ready to kill you.'

Waving a hand airily, Honey didn't even bother to look round before disappearing into the house—a seven bedroomed neo-Georgian abode that was only beaten in Cain's affections by his car.

Eden stood there for a second, furious with her and furious with herself for being so stupid as to take the job in the first place. Three years of Cain raging and Honey behaving like a spoilt brat, while she struggled to keep the peace between them. No wonder her life felt so empty.

Joshua's window slid open silently, and he popped his head out. 'All clear?'

'Oh, bugger off, Joshua,' she said. 'Turn off the engine and get the hell out of here. War's about to break out.'

He swallowed. 'What do you mean?'

'I mean, Cain's about to explode, and it's not going to be pretty. If you want to get out of here intact, I'd scarper.'

He looked horrified. No doubt he remembered the tales of Cain's wild behaviour back in the day, and the many court appearances he'd had for wilful damage and assault. Of course, he'd either been stoned or drunk back then, and he hadn't behaved in that manner for decades, but Joshua wasn't to know that.

'Shit.' His head drew back and he began fumbling around. She was about to tell him to get out and she'd put the car away, when it suddenly shot forward.

There was a moment when everything seemed to be moving in slow motion. She wanted to shout out, but she was frozen.

Then there was a mighty crunching sound and an eerie silence.

Rooted to the spot, Eden stared at the Beetle—which had its front end firmly wedged in the boot of the Rolls Royce.

'Dear God. I'm dead.' Had she said that out loud?

'Oh, no, no, no.' Joshua appeared beside her, his head in his hands. 'I'm going to die, aren't I? He's going to kill me.'

For the first time in three years, Eden was glad Cain was playing his terrible music at full blast. At least he wouldn't have heard the crash.

'What did you do?' she murmured. 'How did you manage that?'

'I don't know. I swear I don't know. I meant to turn off the engine. My foot must have slipped. I was panicking. I wasn't thinking straight. I don't know how it happened.'

'How *could* it have happened?' It didn't make sense. The car hadn't even been in gear. Had it? She glared at him. 'You put the car in gear.'

'No! No, I didn't. Well, maybe I did. I was playing around. I never meant to go anywhere, I swear. What am I going to do?'

'Run.'

'What?'

'Seriously, Joshua. Luckily for you, Cain and Honey

are a bit preoccupied at the moment, but it won't take long before they find out what's happened, and they'll both be gunning for you. Go home. You don't want to face them when they're in this mood. Give them a chance to calm down. Go on, run!'

He didn't need telling twice. Stupid man was almost crying.

Eden hurried down the drive with him and let him out through the gates. There was no need to tell him not to come back. She knew she'd never see him again. Thank God.

After making sure the gates were shut behind him, she headed towards the house, casting a last rueful look at the cars. Knowing what Honey had been up to, she wasn't looking forward to the showdown, because no doubt Cain would blame her, and he'd be right. She should have told him about Honey's illicit meetings with Crispin Cavendish. It was part of the job and she'd let him down. Moreover, she should never have allowed Joshua to sit in the car, never mind turn on the engine. It had been irresponsible, and she'd seriously messed up on both counts.

Eden would be lucky if she still had a job by the end of the day.

CHAPTER THREE

Completely unafraid of her father, Honey headed up the solid oak staircase to freshen up. Combing her hair while standing in front of the mirror in her luxurious en suite bathroom, she studied her reflection for a moment, a smile of satisfaction on her face. She'd had a fun time, and knowing she had the adoration of a rather important man was a huge boost to the ego.

Crispin was putty in her hands. Everything could all work out hugely in her favour. She just had to make sure that no one—least of all her father—put a spanner in the works. She'd have to make sure his damn wife kept out of the way, too, although that would soon be taken care of.

Yes, things were going very nicely, thank you very much.

Slipping her comb into her bag, she left the bathroom and walked confidently down the stairs, sauntering into Cain's den with a big smile on her face as if to demonstrate that, no matter how he raged and yelled, it would have no effect on her. He'd never raised a finger to her, and Honey knew that, deep down, it was all hot air. She'd realised that from a very early age. Even so, it had been a long time since she'd seen him so angry—not since she'd posted pictures on Facebook, showing him in the middle of having his hair dyed. That hadn't gone down too well, at all, though those particular photos must have broken some sort of record, with the amount of likes and shares they'd generated.

Honey had been adamant he should be grateful for any sort of publicity at his age and refused to apologise. In revenge, he'd given away her thousand-pound television and laptop to the local charity shop, but after two days he'd gone out and bought her even better ones, so she wasn't bothered. She'd informed Snarler, from the moment he'd loaded the goods into his car, that it would be to her advantage, and she wasn't wrong. Her father was so predictable it was laughable.

Shutting off the music, he turned to face Honey, his face stony.

A weight creaked the stairs, giving away Eden in her attempt to sneak up to her room. Cain was evidently having none of that, because he threw open the door of the den and yelled, 'You! In here!'

Eden crept reluctantly into the room and seemed annoyed to see Honey sprawled on the sofa, where she casually filed her nails as if she hadn't a care in the world.

'Did you know?' Cain's voice was deceptively quiet, and Honey watched as Eden swallowed hard.

'I discovered she'd been on a couple of dates with him,' she admitted. 'She promised me it was over. She swore.'

'I'll bet she bloody did. And you were stupid enough to believe her? Why the hell didn't you tell me?'

'Because she said it was nothing—a meaningless fling. I didn't want to worry you for nothing.'

'I pay your bleeding wages! You tell me everything. That was the deal. Now look what you've gone and done.'

'What do you mean? I haven't done anything. Don't start yelling at me, when it's Honey who's been doing whatever it is she's been doing.'

'And what *have* you been doing?' he demanded, glaring at his daughter.

Honey shrugged. 'You tell me. You seem to have all the information. Obviously, you've been spying on me like the saddo you are. You ought to concentrate on your own love life instead of worrying about mine.'

Cain gripped the desk and visibly struggled to keep his temper. Honey noticed Eden sinking into the chair. It was probably a wise move. This could take a while, and she was actually trembling. Honey wondered why. Not like Eden to let such trifling matters bother her. Surely, she'd figured out by now that Cain was all wind and water?

Realising her father was ranting, Honey made some attempt to look interested.

'I haven't been spying on you, though Gawd knows, maybe I should have been. I was tipped off. Got a bleeding Facebook message, can you believe? Bin in me inbox for over a week, but I hardly ever go on there, do I? Should have checked more frequently. Some tit calling himself Romeo Lovegod has sent me a private message, telling me my own darling daughter has been having it away with Crispin Cavendish. I mean, Crispin bleeding Cavendish, of all people! What the hell are you thinking?'

'I'm thinking that if my own father is stupid enough to believe anyone calling themselves Romeo Lovegod, then he deserves the heart attack or stroke that's coming his way any moment now, judging by the way his face has turned that peculiar shade of purple.'

Cain took a deep breath. 'Maybe I wouldn't have believed it, if he hadn't given me times and dates of your meetings, not to mention the places you'd met. And then there was the photo.'

Honey put down her nail file. 'Photo? Someone's been photographing us?'

'Yes, Honey. Someone's been photographing you. Now do you see the crap we're in? Do you never learn? Did all that stuff with Troy sodding Troughton teach you nothing? That's how you wound up with your babysitter there,' he added, waving a dismissive arm at Eden.

'Thanks very much,' she said, looking offended.

He rubbed his forehead. 'You've got no right to be upset, Eden. This is all your fault! So much for keeping an eye on her. Oh, if I ain't sick of her antics. She winds me up something chronic!' He glared at his daughter. 'You got away with it last time. Don't ask me how no one found out about you and that popstar idiot. For some reason, that journalist kept his trap shut.'

'It would hardly have mattered if he hadn't,' said Honey. 'In fact, it would probably have done Troy a favour, since the marriage lasted less than eighteen months and she did that horrible story on his crap sexual technique in the papers.'

'Which you said was entirely true,' Eden pointed out.

'That's not the issue. Wonder how much she got paid for that? If she'd found out about me and Troy, she wouldn't have married him, and he wouldn't have had to go through that awful custody battle.'

'I didn't know he had kids,' Eden said.

Honey looked at her pityingly. 'For the Chihuahua, you idiot. Honestly, sometimes I think you never read anything decent like *All the Goss*. Too busy wasting your time with that Jane Eyre woman's books. What is it you're reading now? Sense and Senility?'

'That's right,' Eden said. 'And when I've finished that I'm going to read Emily Bronte's latest. Apparently, she's just finished it, and it's a really funny romcom. Almost as hilarious as Withering Tights.'

Honey tutted. 'Very funny. Everyone knows it's Withering Heights. You must think I'm stupid.' She turned back to her father. 'Can I go now?'

Cain dropped down into his big leather chair and stared at her from across the vast expanse of his mahogany desk. Honey was aware that sitting there made him feel important. He considered his den to be his domain. The walls were decorated with gold records in black shiny frames, and photographs of himself in his heyday, getting drunk with the likes of The Rolling Stones and staggering out of nightclubs with his arm around some doe-eyed blonde or other. He'd even framed newspaper clippings of his court appearances, kiss and tells by various sexual partners, and the infamous article, written by a born-again Christian in America, claiming Cain was the evil son of Adam and Eve, reincarnated to bring hell and destruction to mankind. Cain had apparently found that one particularly hilarious, especially as he'd actually been registered at birth as Jeffrey Dennis Moggs, a fact he didn't like to dwell on. Neither did Honey, come to that. Honey Moggs simply didn't have the same ring to it. Thank God for deed polls.

The room itself was strictly off limits to all but his nearest and dearest. The rest of the house looked like something found in an edition of *Country Life*. The only photographs on display in the other rooms were strictly respectable ones. Cain with his loving children; Cain with his late mother and father; Cain shaking hands with the prime minister after taking part in some charity event for sick children; Cain laughing uproariously at some joke the Prince of Wales had made at a country show; Cain proudly showing off the brace of pheasants he'd bagged while on a shoot at one of his showbiz pal's country estates.

Oh, yes, the twenty-first century Cain Carmichael was an entirely different animal to the long-haired, out-of-control lout portrayed in the pictures looking down on the three of them. He was a changed man.

The door opened, and Roxy, his latest bit of stuff, popped her head round, giving him an uncertain smile. 'I heard shouting. Is everything all right, Cainey?'

Honey rolled her eyes.

Cain tutted. 'It's family stuff. Nothing to do with you, Rox. Get out, and I'll come and find you when I'm done.'

Hmm, maybe he hadn't changed that much, after all.

Roxy withdrew, closing the door behind her.

Honey scowled at her father. 'Can I go now? I'm bored.'

'Bored? How dare you? Do you have any idea of the damage you can cause by having it away with Crispin Cavendish?'

'His poor wife will be devastated,' Eden said.

'Honestly, Honey, you are selfish.'

'Never mind his wife,' said Cain. 'What about the Party? Crispin Cavendish is hotly tipped for a top spot in the next cabinet reshuffle. The prime minister is very impressed with him, and he's got the backing of everyone that matters. I won't have you jeopardising our Party for anyone.'

'*Your* Party? I didn't know you had a seat in the cabinet,' said Honey, her voice dripping with sarcasm.

'I may not have a seat in the cabinet, young lady, but I've donated enough bleeding money to pay all their wages for years.'

Honey looked at him and wondered, not for the first time, how the tearaway kid from the council estate in south London, with a libido the size of Tower Hamlets and a mouth as wide as the London Eye, had ended up living in a twee Cotswolds village, hunting, shooting and fishing, being invited to tea by royalty, and calling the bluest of Tory politicians his friends. It beggared belief.

It was almost as weird as her mother, a woman born into luxury and privilege, with a title and a family home that made Downton Abbey look like a weekend retreat, claiming to be a socialist and going on all those ridiculous rallies and marches in aid of various causes. Honey was pretty certain that it was mostly done to wind her father up. There was no other explanation.

'You won't see him again,' Cain ordered. 'Do you understand? Not ever.'

Honey laughed. Her father could be most amusing when he chose.

'I don't see what's so bleeding funny. Crispin is too important to us. You're not going to ruin this for him. If the press get a whiff that he's not squeaky clean, his career will be over. Can you imagine what people will say? I'll be ruined. They'll never forgive me. My knighthood will be flushed down the bleeding pan, and all the crappy charity events I've attended, and all the cash I've handed over, will count for nothing. I'm not having it, do you hear me? I want my knighthood. I've earned it. You're not going to spoil this for me.'

'I've never heard anything so pathetic,' said Honey. 'What do you want a knighthood for, anyway? Just 'cos your poncy showbiz pals have got one.'

'Yes, they have! And why? Gawd knows, because I outsold them all at my peak.'

'You outsold Paul McCartney?' Eden failed to keep the amusement from her voice. She must have had a death wish.

Cain gave her a look of pure venom. 'Well, maybe not old Macca, no. You'd be amazed, though. And I wouldn't look so bloody amused, if I were you. Remember, all those record sales are paying your wages, lady.'

'This is all because Rex Scotman got the OBE last year,' said Honey, breaking the taboo of mentioning her father's massive rival from his rock star days.

'It's got nothing to do with it. I couldn't give a monkey's toss what happens to that moron. An OBE, my arse. For what? For inflicting a voice that sounds like fingernails running down a chalkboard on the world for the last thirty years? He should have been put in the Tower of London for high treason, not given a bloody medal.'

'He's done an awful lot for charity,' Eden mused. 'He's raised hundreds of thousands for that educational programme in Africa and—'

'We've all done a lot for charity,' snapped Cain. 'I even bought one of his records once, and if that's not helping the aged, I don't know what is.' He turned back to Honey. 'Are you going to stop seeing him?'

'Who?'

'You know who! Crispin bleeding Cavendish, who else?'

'Nope. I care about him. He's rather sweet.' She picked up her nail file again and smiled angelically at him. 'So, now that's settled, can I go?'

'Right. If you won't listen to me, I'm calling in the big guns.'

Honey and Eden exchanged glances. Who exactly were the big guns?

Cain picked up his iPad and gave it a couple of taps. Honey frowned. What was the old goat up to now? After a moment or two, he gave a triumphant smile. Then they heard a familiar upper class voice.

'Cain! What in God's name do you want? I'm in the middle of lunch with my friends.'

Honey giggled. 'Really? Big guns? Surely you can do better than Mother?'

'Was that Honey? What's she up to now?' There was a big sigh. 'Honestly, this is too much. Will you excuse me, ladies, I'll have to take this in the drawing room.'

Honey began to file her nails again. 'Well, if that's the best you can do, I think it's safe to say I'll be meeting Crispin for dinner tomorrow night, as planned. We have a lot to discuss. His wife is going abroad for the summer break, leaving him behind. He can't do sunshine. He burns. So we're going to spend the summer together with her safely out of the way. Try to stop me, and I'll go to the papers and tell them everything, and don't think I won't. I've got nothing to lose.'

'Crispin has,' Eden said. 'And you said you cared about him.'

'I do. He'll get another job. He's bright enough.'

'Honey, you really don't understand what he's risking here,' Eden said. 'This isn't just a job. This is his career. His life's work.'

'You sound like my father.'

'God forbid. Hell would freeze over before I'd vote for that bunch of b—'

''Bout time.' Cain, who hadn't been paying attention to their conversation, turned the iPad so they could all see his ex-wife's face. As always, she was made up immaculately, her blonde hair in a chic topknot, showing off the diamond studs in her ears. 'Are you ready now, Freya? Comfortable, are we? Good. So would you like to hear what our darling daughter's been up to now?'

Freya sighed. 'Not really, but I don't suppose I have a choice. Go on.'

'She's been having it away with a married man.'

Freya faked a yawn. 'Big deal. Bit of a hypocrite, aren't you? I mean, you were a married man when we got together. And you were married to me when you were shagging that scrawny little scrubber, Lucinda Farquhar. And a scheming little Farquhar she was, too.'

'Never mind all that. This particular married man is strictly off limits.'

'God, you'd think I was shagging the Pope,' said Honey.

'The Pope would hardly be a married man,' Eden said.

'Why? Is he gay? They can get married, too, now, you know. Honestly, you must start reading the tabloids, Eden.'

Eden gaped at her. 'How much did her private education cost you, Cain?'

Cain was too busy glaring at Honey's mother to notice.

'Go on,' said Freya. 'Surprise me.'

'She's been shagging Crispin Cavendish.'

There was a silence for a moment while that sunk in. Then there was a shriek.

'*What*? Honey, how could you?'

'Mother, don't try to pretend that you care about Crispin's chances of becoming the next leader of the Conservatives, or whatever,' said Honey.

'Of course I don't care,' snapped her mother. 'But you're screwing a Tory, for God's sake!'

'Makes a change from them screwing us,' Eden said, foolishly trying to lighten the mood.

'How could you do something so disgusting?' Freya looked furious. 'When my friends find out you're sleeping with the enemy, my life won't be worth living.'

'Oh, you and your socialist pals.' Cain laughed. 'Now, who's the hypocrite?'

'What do you mean by that?' she demanded. 'I have very strong socialist principles. I always have had. I believe in a fairer society, where everyone is treated equally and given the same opportunities to succeed. Not like you lot, with your *I'm all right, Jack* mentality.'

A loud crash and a wail came through the iPad, and Freya disappeared.

'What happened?' Eden said, peering at the screen.

Honey shrugged. 'Another drama for my mother to enthral me with in one of her tedious weekly texts.'

Freya reappeared, her brow furrowed.

'Looks like your Botox is wearing off,' said Cain helpfully. 'What was that about?'

'The stupid maid dropped the tray with my Emma Bridgewater teapot. Well, that's a tenner a week from her wages. Thank God it wasn't my Gien. She'd have been paying that back for months.'

Cain threw his hands up. 'Same old Freya. Champagne socialist. Priceless. Anyway, what are you going to do about Honey and Crispin?'

'What do you mean, what am I going to do? What do you expect me to do?'

'Well, you're her mother, aren't you?'

'And you're her father. You've had her under your roof for the last five years, for God's sake. Why is it my responsibility all of a sudden?'

'Typical of you. Pass the buck. Wash your hands of her. Well, if you want all your communist pals to know that your daughter is doing the deed with a true-blue Tory boy, that's up to you. Your credibility as a fully paid-up member of the Labour party will be obliterated. You won't be able to face them ever again, once they know you have a traitor in the midst. Up to you, like. No pressure.'

'Oh, shit. This is all your fault. If you'd been firmer with her, if you'd been a proper father to her, instead of chasing the next bit of skirt, this would never have happened.'

'How dare you say that? You only palmed her off on me in the first place so you could bugger off to all your wealthy lovers' holiday homes in the sun. Funny how you never shag anyone who's skint. They don't call you Freebie Freya for nothing.'

Honey stood up. 'Well, while you two are reliving the halcyon days of your marriage, I'm going upstairs to change. Nice to see you, Mother. Look forward to chatting again. In about six months.'

She headed out of the room, paying no attention to the shrieks of protest from her mother or the angry shouts from her father. She hesitated in the hallway as, behind her, she heard Eden's voice.

'I'll go after her. You two need to stop bitching at each other and think of a way to stop her. While you're arguing about who's going to be humiliated the most, there's a marriage at stake here. I don't see why Crispin's wife should be hurt and embarrassed so Honey can score points in this weird family game you've got going on.'

'Crispin's wife? Hurt and embarrassed? You've obviously never met Lavinia Cavendish,' she heard her mother say.

'She's right,' said Cain. 'We need to sort this, pronto. Go on up, Eden, and try to talk some sense into her, while I do the same with my dear ex-wife. Least you can do since it's all your fault.'

Honey rolled her eyes and went up the stairs. Between her mother and father, it was a miracle she'd turned out so nice and normal.

****

Sitting on her bed, Honey flicked through the latest issue of some glossy magazine. She didn't even look up when Eden walked into her room.

'Save your breath,' she said. 'I'm not listening. Have those two shut up, yet?'

'Thought you weren't going to listen,' Eden said, sinking down onto the bed beside her. 'Listen, Honey, I know you think we're all nagging at you, but it's really important that you end this now. I don't know what point you're trying to prove, but it's going to end badly. Not just for Crispin, but for you, too. There's nothing the press loves more than to destroy a woman who's wrecked a politician's marriage. It's not worth it.'

'Who says it isn't worth it?' she demanded. 'For your information, it will be totally worth it.'

'Really?' Eden frowned. 'Are you saying you actually love him?'

She shrugged. 'Maybe. Like I said, he's sweet, and he's so much better in bed than Troy was. Power is such an aphrodisiac, don't you think? Anyway, this is my big chance.'

'Your big chance? For what?'

'To make a name for myself, without being known as Cain Carmichael's daughter. This could lead to modelling contracts, magazine features, an advertising campaign. I could get my own reality show.'

'You're not serious?'

'Why shouldn't I be serious? I'm not going to be stuck in that poxy little shop for the rest of my life.'

'The shop was your idea! You made your father pay for it, and you stock it with all the stuff you like.'

'It's boring. Besides, I'm sick of being stuck in there every day. It's incredibly restrictive, having a nine-to-five job.'

'Nine-to-five job? You have to be kidding me. If you turn up for three hours, it's a miracle. You don't even bother to come in at all on Saturdays, which is the only day we get any real trade, by the way. You're hardly chained to the till.'

'Look, it's all right for people like you,' Honey said. 'Shop work is your sort of thing, but I'm not cut out for that life. I need more. Crispin could be my ticket to better things.'

'Like being branded a marriage wrecker and a slut? Thanks. I'd rather be a shop girl.'

'I'm sure you would,' Honey said, in a tone that didn't sound at all complimentary.

'Can't you, for once, do something nice?' Eden asked.

Honey flung the magazine aside and stood up. 'You're getting as bad as my father,' she announced, heading to the window to gaze moodily outside. 'I'm sick of being told what to do. I'm sick of being controlled. I'm sick of—fucking hell! What the fuck happened to the cars?'

Eden went cold. She'd forgotten Honey's room had a view over the drive.

Honey threw open the window and leaned out. 'Holy crap. How did that happen? Dad's going to explode.' She turned to Eden. 'Was this something to do with the eunuch?'

'Please don't tell your dad,' Eden pleaded. 'If Cain gets hold of him, he really will end up a eunuch.'

'Oh, this is a hoot.' She threw herself back on the bed, surveying Eden with a big grin on her face. 'I think my little escapade with Crispin will pale into insignificance, when he cops an eyeful of his precious Roller. You'll be for it. The mood he's in, you'll be lucky if you get away with being fired. And the eunuch will be sued to within an inch of his life. He'll be stripped of every asset he possesses. Supposing he has any assets. I couldn't see much evidence when I looked at him.'

'Leave Joshua out of this,' Eden said. 'I'll take the blame. It was my fault. I shouldn't have let him sit in the damn car. I was trying to be kind, since I'd just dumped him.'

'Really?' Honey looked at her with something that unnervingly approached respect. 'Good for you. Oh, hell, here he comes. Round two. Ding, ding.'

CHAPTER FOUR

Triumphantly, Cain threw open the bedroom door, still carrying the iPad. He was barely able to wipe the grin off his face. 'Right, young lady. We've sorted it.'

'Really? What are you going to do? Buy me a chastity belt?'

'Nope. Tell her, Freya.'

'Yes, Mother. Do tell me.'

Cain passed her the iPad. Behind him, he felt Eden peering over his shoulder.

'Do you remember my cousin, Jemima?' Freya asked Honey through the iPad.

Honey shook her head. 'Nope. Next question.'

'Don't be rude.' Freya scowled, confirming Cain's suspicions: her Botox really was wearing off. 'Jemima was the daughter of your Great Uncle Sebastian. You met her once, when you were a little girl. She was like you. A real rebel. Kept doing things to annoy her parents. She went a bit further than you, though. She actually married her lover.'

'Oh?' Honey looked suddenly interested. 'Was there a scandalous divorce?'

'What divorce? The man she married was single.'

'Oh, well, what was so rebellious about that?' demanded Honey.

'Eliot wasn't—shall we say—one of us.'

'You mean, upper class.' Cain tutted in disgust. 'So much for equality.'

'Dad is hardly upper class,' pointed out Honey. 'It didn't stop you marrying him.'

'That was different,' Freya said hurriedly.

'Yeah. I was loaded and could keep her in the manner to which she'd like to become accustomed. Her dad may have had the family tree, but he was pretty short on dosh.

I think the entire family benefited from my success. My *Greatest Hits* album paid for a new roof on their west wing. Ungrateful bleeders.'

Freya obviously chose to ignore him—much as she had throughout their entire marriage, Cain thought ruefully. Pretty she may have been, and a lady she most definitely was, but she was a prize bitch and no mistake. She could have won the champions cup at Crufts.

Anyway, Jemima met Eliot Harland when she was on holiday in Yorkshire,' his ex-wife said, her cut-glass tones still having a disturbing effect on him. He was a sucker for the gentry. 'She was staying at the estate of my other cousin, Lucas. They'd gone to a country show, and Eliot was showing some sheep, or something. Freya thought he looked rather handsome and remarked as much. Of course, the family immediately told her to stay away from him, which was like a red rag to a bull. Within half an hour, she'd introduced herself to him and was flirting outrageously. He fell for her, of course. Why wouldn't he? She was stunning. Anyway, the family disapproved most strongly. She was on the verge of becoming engaged to someone far more suitable, you see, so they banned her from seeing the sheep farmer, but she took no notice. She was totally in love with him. They married secretly and she went off to live with him.'

'Very romantic,' Eden said.

Freya peered from the screen. 'Who's that? Oh, it's the babysitter again.' She looked most put out that Eden was party to the conversation. Her sense of social justice and equality for all didn't stretch to being polite to the hired help, obviously. 'Cain, why is she still here? I thought this was private family business. It's not for staff to listen in on.'

Cain felt indignant on Eden's behalf, in spite of the fact that she'd let him down. 'Eden's not just staff,' he said. 'She's looked out for Honey for the last three years, which is more than you've done, so shut up moaning and get to the point.'

Freya bristled. 'Well, really. Is there any wonder our marriage didn't last?'

'The wonder is, I married you in the first place.'

'Never mind all that,' said Honey. 'Finish this story, will you? It's Christmas in five months.'

Freya tutted. 'For goodness sake. Well, the marriage was successful. Eliot and Jemima were very much in love and had three children. They would still be together now, but there was a terrible accident. Poor Jemima was killed in a car crash two years ago. It's a terribly tragic story.'

'It's a terribly pointless story,' said Honey.

Eden wiped away the tears from her eyes and sniffed. 'How can you be so heartless?'

'Why should I care if some woman I met once, years ago, snuffed it? Don't be such a drip, Eden. What's all this got to do with Crispin and me, anyway?'

'Oh, please,' said Cain, stepping forward with a smirk on his face, 'let me tell her.' Frankly, he could hardly wait. Serve the little git right.

'Very well,' said Freya, graciously.

'Tell me what? What's going on?' Honey sounded nervous, to his satisfaction.

'This Eliot bloke's been well and truly landed in it. I mean, poor bugger's stuck out there on the Yorkshire moors —'

'The Yorkshire Dales,' interrupted Freya.

'Yeah, the Yorkshire Dales. Anyway, he's stuck out there with only sheep for company, grieving for his lost wife and trying to cope all alone with three motherless children.'

Honey shrugged. 'So, what?'

'Poor man,' Eden murmured. At least she had some compassion, even if his own daughter appeared to be sadly lacking in that department.

'Poor man indeed,' said Cain. 'And, of course, the school summer holidays are coming up. How's he going to cope, eh? Three kids not at school, running wild in the house, no one to take care of them while he's stuck out on the mountains.'

'Mountains?' asked Eden.

'Well, as good as. Very hilly in the Yorkshire wotsits. And no one around for miles. Reckon them sheep are his only friends.'

'How disgusting,' said Honey.

'Point is, he's a busy man, and he's all on his own with the little ones. How's he gonna manage?'

'Same as he managed last year and the year before, no doubt.'

Really, Honey was all heart. Eden was in tears, but his own daughter obviously couldn't give a flying fig for the poor bloke's predicament. Well, he'd soon shut her up.

'Well that's just it,' he said smugly. 'He won't have to manage. Not this year. Because he'll have help.'

After a stunned silence, Honey stood up, shaking her head furiously. 'Oh, no. You can't be serious! You think I'm going to go to Yorkshire, to look after three snotty children and Old MacDonald? Forget it!'

'It's all arranged,' said Freya brightly. 'I've spoken to Eliot. It was very lucky, actually. I got his number from Jemima's sister, Juniper.'

'Juniper? Seriously?' Eden giggled then looked embarrassed.

Freya ignored her, which didn't surprise Cain. Well, Eden was only staff, after all. 'I managed to get through on the landline. Apparently, there's hardly any mobile phone signal where he lives.'

'What?' Honey paled.

'And the internet is pretty unreliable, too,' said Cain gleefully. 'What a bugger, eh?'

'How did you manage to contact him, then?' Eden

asked. 'Why would a farmer be home at this time?'

Honey looked suddenly hopeful. 'Exactly! You didn't, did you? You're bluffing. This is all a big joke to teach me a lesson, right?'

'Nope.' Cain shook his head. 'Eliot's youngest child was sick, so he's been stuck in, caring for him. He's been tearing his hair out. So he's over the moon that he's going to get some free childcare.'

'Free childcare? Are you mad? I'm not going.'

Honey was almost in tears, a sight Cain had never seen before. He wondered if he could bear it, then remembered his knighthood. 'You are going, so you can save the hysterics for someone who cares. You've gone too far, this time. If you won't end it with Crispin, I'll make damn sure you're well out of his way.'

'I will end it with Crispin, I promise.'

'Never try to kid a kidder,' said Cain. 'Your promises are worth diddly squat. You had your chance, and you blew it. You're going to Yorkshire for the entire summer. That will keep you out of Crispin's way until his wife gets back from her holiday.'

'You can't make me.' Honey seemed to be struggling for composure. He'd never seen her rattled before. It seemed he'd finally outsmarted her. 'I'm twenty-two years old. I won't go.'

'If you don't go,' said Cain, 'I will stop your allowance immediately. You won't get another penny from me.'

'I have the shop,' she said. 'I don't need your allowance. I can support myself.'

Cain laughed and turned to Eden. 'Tell her.'

Eden went red. 'Really?'

'Really. Tell her.'

She gulped. 'The shop is running at a massive loss, Honey. You haven't made a profit, ever. You've never actually broken even. Your dad's been subsidising the business from the start.'

'I don't believe it. You said we were doing well.'

'He told me to tell you that. He wanted you to believe you were doing well. He said success bred success, and if you believed you could do it, you eventually would. I'm sorry.'

'This is your fault. You're in charge of the shop. You should have made it work.'

'How could she make it work?' demanded Cain. 'The stupid crap you sell there doesn't appeal to anyone but you. I mean, it's just any old tat that takes your fancy.'

'It's pretty stuff. I'd buy it. It's not my fault people round here have no taste.'

'You're supposed to study the market. Stock your shop with stuff people will actually buy. You have no business sense whatsoever. It's been a silly little hobby. Well, it stops now. The shop closes. I'm getting rid of it, so it seems to me you've got no choice but to go to Yorkshire for the summer, because if you don't, not only will I cut you off without a penny, I'll chuck you out of here, too.'

'You don't mean it.' Honey was actually in tears. 'You wouldn't do that. Not to me.'

'Really? Watch me. I told you, I want that knighthood, and you're not going to stop me.'

Freya giggled.

Honey glared at her. 'It's not funny!'

'What, your father with a knighthood? Oh, it is funny, darling, let's be honest. Well, at least that nasty business is sorted at last. Do you mind if I return to my guests? Lunch is ruined, of course. I'll have to get the cook to make me something else.'

'Of course.' Cain bowed to the iPad. 'Thanks for your help. You'll be in touch with the details?'

'I'll email Honey the directions to Skimmerdale as soon as I have them. I can't believe we actually outfoxed her. Amazing. Congratulations, you wizened old goat.'

'Cheers, you plastic old tart.'

'And now, leave me alone, for pity's sake, at least until Christmas. All right?'

'Fine by me. See you, Lady Muck. Enjoy your lunch.'

She was gone, and Honey stared at the blank screen in bewilderment. 'This can't be happening.'

'I think it is, and I think you're finally going to learn your lesson.' Cain patted her on the head. 'Now, if you'll excuse me, I have a rather tasty blonde waiting for me downstairs.'

****

Honey wasn't the only one in shock. As Eden heard Cain's footsteps on the stairs, and his cheery whistle as he headed off to celebrate his triumph with the lovely Roxy, it occurred to her that she was probably unemployed and homeless. If Cain was closing the shop, there wouldn't be anything for her to do. He could hardly justify keeping her on as a babysitter to Honey, especially as Eden hadn't exactly managed to keep her out of trouble so far. Although, really, what was she supposed to do? Cain had let his daughter go to his charity events, and she'd been bound to meet rich young men at them. Trust Honey to make a beeline for the married one.

'This is a catastrophe,' Honey wailed. 'My life is over.'

'Your life is far from over,' Eden assured her. 'You're talking eight weeks of minor inconvenience. Whereas I'm now out of a job and a home.'

Honey wiped away tears. 'You don't have to look after three brats and a Neanderthal. And you'll still have your mobile phone.'

Eden tutted impatiently and jogged downstairs. She had to see Cain and clarify the situation.

She knocked twice on the door of his den. When there was no response, she headed to the living room. As she walked in, she recoiled in horror. Roxy was lying on the sofa, dress pulled back to her thighs, her legs wrapped around Cain's waist as he writhed on top of her.

Eden knew she should have backed away, but she somehow managed to utter an appalled squeak before she could do so.

Roxy shrieked and lowered her legs immediately. Cain didn't move at all. He looked mildly annoyed.

'If you've come to talk me out of this, forget it. She deserves it and—'

'Never mind Honey,' Eden said. 'What about me?'

'What about you?'

Roxy grabbed a cushion and hid her face behind it. She needn't have bothered, thought Eden. It was hardly her face that was causing offence.

'If you're closing the shop, where does that leave me? Are you sacking me? If so, how much notice are you giving me? I need to find another job. I haven't even got anywhere to live. Well, I suppose I could go back to Mum and Dad's, but it's a bit embarrassing. I mean, I'm twenty-six now, for God's sake. Mind you, they're away for the summer. They're staying with my Auntie Amanda and Uncle Robin in Tenerife. They've got an apartment out there, and often invite my parents over, now Dad's retired. There's no room for me, 'cos they only have two bedrooms and there's no room to swing a cat. Not that you'd want to swing a cat, of course. Will I get severance pay? Redundancy, or whatever? How much would it be? I know I've only worked for you for three years, but I'll need a deposit for another flat, or something, and I don't know how long I'll have to wait before I find another job. I suppose I could ask Gavin if he's got any shifts. I mean, it's a bit cheeky. I haven't been near The Red Lion for three years, but at least I know the work and how he runs the place, and he never could keep staff. Oh, crap. This is awful.'

Roxy lowered the cushion and peered at her. Cain's mouth dropped open. It wasn't an attractive sight, Eden thought.

After a moment's hesitation, he gave a huge sigh and shifted himself off Roxy. Turning round to zip up his leather trousers, while she frantically made herself respectable, he muttered about *bleeding women*, and how they'd be the death of him, and he should have had a vasectomy after the first four kids and saved himself a lot of trouble.

She supposed Honey was a bit more difficult than his other children, to be fair. Actually, there was no suppose about it. Scarlet and Jed were the eldest and had gone back to America after the divorce, with their Texan ex-model mother, Lowri, who was Cain's first wife. Scarlet had become an actress and Jed played in a band, though neither had made it big. They rarely saw their father, though they did send cards and gifts to Honey at Christmas and on her birthday, which Eden thought was rather nice of them, given that—unbelievably—they'd never actually met her face to face. Her other sister, Emerald, was the daughter of Cain's second wife, Cassandra, and she was a hippy who was off somewhere in Europe, discovering herself. She'd met Honey a few times but made it clear she disapproved of her and never bothered with her. Then there was Marcus, the illegitimate son of Cain's mistress, Sandy, who had got herself pregnant while he was still married to Cassandra, and just before he met Freya. Marcus was only five years older than Honey but completely different. He worked for a bank, had a wife called Janette who worked for a dentist, and had a little boy called Justin who was doing well at nursery and was already learning to play the recorder. Honey despised Marcus, though he was always perfectly pleasant to her and sent her a birthday and Christmas card every year, complete with a twenty pound gift token for Debenhams, much to her disgust.

'Right.' Cain turned round to face Eden and put his

hands on his hips.

She bit her lip, trying not to laugh. A bit of his shirt was poking through his zip, his heavily lacquered blond hair stuck up on end as if he'd been electrocuted, and his mascara had smudged—the mascara he absolutely on no account ever wore, of course. He looked a complete fright. Even more than usual.

'So you want me to keep the shop open just to suit you?' he asked.

'Well, no, but if the shop's closed, what will I do?'

'Maybe you should've thought about that when you were keeping secrets from me. Enough's enough. Taking the piss, she is, and she don't need you helping her. I'm proper miffed with you about this, Eden, I won't lie. You should have told me and I could have stopped it before it got this far.' He sighed. 'Look, you're a good girl. You've never caused me any bother, until now, and you've kept your mouth shut about the comings and goings in this house, so I tell you what. While Honey's serving her time in the wilds of Yorkshire, you can have a holiday on full pay. Then, when she gets back, I'll see how the land lies. There may be something you can do, there may not. It's a question of trust, see? Can't make promises I can't keep, now can I?'

'I suppose not.' Eden knew she should push him for a firm answer. This was her future they were talking about, after all. But, after three years, she knew all too well that when Cain was in a bad mood, there was no reasoning with him. He was more likely to get even more annoyed and sack her just to make his point.

'Well, then, are we done? Can you push off now? I'm a bit busy, if you get my drift.'

Roxy put the cushion to her face again, and Eden nodded and left. As she closed the door, she heard Cain say, 'Now then, sweet cheeks. Open up and let the dog see the rabbit.'

Eden tutted. Just the sort of line you'd expect from a prospective knight of the realm.

****

'This is the worst thing that could ever have happened to me!' Honey was lying on her bed, staring in horror at her iPad. 'Have you seen this? It's a nightmare. My life is over. I don't care what you say. Shoot me now.'

'As tempting as that offer is, Honey,' Eden said, 'I seriously doubt things are that bad. By the way, your dad can't guarantee I'll still have a job in two months' time. Thanks for asking.'

Honey didn't even pretend to be interested. Instead, she pushed the iPad towards Eden and rolled over onto her back, staring up at the ceiling and muttering, 'Fuck, fuck, fuck,' over and over again.

Eden picked up the iPad and peered at the screen. Evidently, Honey had been Googling information about the area of Yorkshire she was being banished to.

'Skimmerdale? Never heard of it.'

'No one's heard of it. It's the end of the earth,' Honey wailed dramatically. 'They may as well be sending me to Tibet, or the Antarctic, or somewhere. There's nothing there but sheep.'

Eden flicked through some images. 'Oh, Honey, it's pretty,' she said. 'Look at the fields and the hills, and the lovely old stone buildings. And it says there are wildflower meadows in Skimmerdale between May and early July. What a shame you've just missed them. Look at the colours!'

Honey gaped at her, and Eden wondered what on earth she'd been thinking. As if Honey would give a fig about wildflowers.

'It's definitely wilder than the Cotswolds,' Eden admitted, 'but that's not necessarily a bad thing, is it? It says *Skimmerdale is one of the most northerly dales. The*

River Skimmer runs from the Pennines through the valley, to the town of Kirkby Skimmer, which is famed for its ruined Benedictine abbey, which stands high up on Mikkel Rigg, an escarpment that shelters the town. Skimmerdale is dotted with tiny riverside hamlets and villages, but sheep far outnumber the human inhabitants, though it attracts many tourists, mainly walkers, especially in the summer months.'

'Have you quite finished?' Honey sat up and snatched the iPad off her.

'I was only trying to cheer you up.'

'Cheer me up? Did you see any mention of a Whistles? A Jo Malone? A Jigsaw, for God's sake?'

They lived in the pretty village of Upper Bourbury, in a house made of golden Cotswolds stone, with a view to die for, a tennis court, a sunroom, a hot tub, an outdoor swimming pool, and an expanse of lawn that Snarler took great delight in racing up and down on in his sit-on lawnmower—yet the only positive thing Honey would ever say about living in such a place was that she was more or less midway between Cheltenham and Oxford, and could whizz to either town in less than forty minutes to make full use of her credit cards.

At least once a month, she would catch the train to London and return loaded down with goods she swore she couldn't live without and which simply weren't available in the provinces. Her favourite day out was a trip to Bicester Village, and the only time she ever agreed to visit her mother in Brighton was if she was promised free rein in the shops. Eden had only ever heard her tell her father she loved him once, and that had been when he'd paid for her and her friends to go to New York for a shopping weekend, for her twenty-first.

If the beauty of the gentle Cotswolds didn't delight her, the wild Yorkshire Dales weren't going to appeal, either. For the first time, Eden realised how badly the situation was going to affect Honey. Then again, it might do her some good. Make her realise there was more to life than maxing out credit cards.

'You have to think about that poor man and his three children,' she reminded Honey. 'They've lost a wife and mother. Can you imagine how that feels?'

'That was two years ago. I'm sure they're over it by now,' she said.

'Over it? How can they be over it? I cried just saying goodbye to Mum and Dad for the summer,' Eden said. 'If anything happened to your mother, how would you feel?'

'Depends what she left me, I suppose,' said Honey, flicking her hair thoughtfully. 'I've been promised the Brighton house, but she keeps threatening to leave the Chelsea place to my crawling cousin. If she does, there'll be hell to pay. I'll contest the will, that's for sure.'

'Honey!' Even after three years of living with her, she still managed to shock Eden. 'That's your mother you're talking about.'

'Oh, for God's sake, Eden. She's hardly been the most maternal of women, has she? Couldn't wait to palm me off on Dad as soon as she could. And she spent most of my childhood dragging me abroad, to various lovers' yachts, or to their Spanish villas or New York penthouses. I was stuck with their dreary relatives, or a nanny, while she had a great time with her latest shag. Don't expect me to feel any great pull of love for her, because I don't. And, anyway, don't change the subject.'

'I wasn't aware I had.'

'The subject was, how do I get out of this bloody torture? Because, I'll tell you here and now, I'm not going. Hell will freeze over before I spend my precious summer in Withering Heights with some miserable git and his three sobbing kids. Crispin and I had it all planned. Almost two months of bliss together during his summer recess, while Lavinia is in a villa in Portugal.'

'You'd never have got away with it,' Eden said. 'You couldn't sneak off with him for that length of time without someone seeing you. Where would you have gone?'

'That's the point,' she wailed. 'We were going to be completely safe. Crispin's sister has a lovely holiday home in Dorset. It has its own private beach. We'd have been alone for the whole summer.'

'Crispin's sister was going to let you use her home to cheat on his wife? Charming.'

'She adores Crispin and says Lavinia's a bitch. Her husband's an old grump and wouldn't allow it, of course, but they're going to Italy for the summer, so he'll never know. Sybil's let the cleaner go for the summer, too, so there's no problem there. It would have been perfect, but now my stupid parents have gone and ruined everything. What am I going to do?'

She gave a strangled sob, and Eden almost felt sorry for her, except that she was planning to do the dirty with a married man, and Eden could hardly condone that. Plus, she knew Honey too well. This wasn't because she was in love, or anything so romantic. She viewed the whole thing as a joke, a way of getting something over on someone else. It would be the thrill of fooling his wife and her parents that excited her, not the idiotic Crispin.

'Well, there's nothing you can do about it, so you may as well get used to the fact that you're spending your summer in Skimmerdale,' Eden said.

Honey glared at her and opened her mouth as if to speak, but Eden didn't find out what she'd been about to say because, at that moment, a sound rumbled through the house like Thor himself was throwing a temper tantrum.

She and Honey stared at each other in dread. 'What now?' Eden said.

Honey jumped up and ran to the window, then turned back and shook her head. 'You're for it, Eden. He's seen the Rolls.'

'What? Oh, shit!'

With the mood Cain was in already, the damage to the car would be the last straw. He wouldn't even consider keeping her on. She'd be fired, and it was her own fault. She should never have let Joshua in the car, never mind allowed him to start it. It was her responsibility, so no doubt she'd be landed with the bill. How could she ever pay back the money it would cost to repair two such expensive cars?

Shaking, she stared at Honey with terrified eyes.

Honey flopped back on the bed and grabbed Eden's hand. 'Right. Here's the deal. I'll take the rap for you. I'll say it was down to me. I'll keep you and the eunuch out of it.'

'Why would you do that?'

'Simple. You have to go to Skimmerdale in my place.'

'What? Don't be ridiculous. It would never work.'

'Why not? I've never met Old MacDonald. He doesn't sound the sort to read the newspapers, and he probably doesn't own a mobile phone. There's not even a decent internet connection. He won't know, or care, who I am, or what I look like. As long as someone turns up to look after his brats, and is roughly my age and answers to the name of Honey Carmichael, he won't ask questions. Then I can go off to stay with Crispin, and the evil parents will be satisfied, thinking I'm safely out of the way under lock and key in Yorkshire. It's the perfect plan. Say yes.'

'No! I can't! Honey, this is ridiculous.'

'Oh? Had plans for the summer, did you?'

'I—I was going to stay at Mum and Dad's.'

'They're in Tenerife. You told me so! They won't miss you. And Dad's given you the summer off. No one will know where you are. It's the only solution, unless you want to get landed with a huge repair bill, go to court, and definitely get the sack. Up to you, of course.'

Eden could barely think straight. She was all too aware

of the sound of Cain's footsteps thundering up the stairs. Having seen him in a temper and knowing it was not a pretty sight, she shook from head to foot. Add his beloved vintage Rolls Royce to the equation, and she dreaded to think what might happen.

'Go along with it,' Honey said, as the door flew open and there he stood.

'Well?'

His voice rumbled around the room. His face was mauve. His watery blue eyes bulging. His nostrils were quivering.

Eden watched in dumb silence, hardly daring to breathe.

Honey shrugged. 'Well, what?'

'Well, what? Well, what? Who pranged me Roller?' He turned his gaze on Eden, and she saw the tiny red veins spidering across the whites of his eyes. If he'd suddenly sprouted fangs, it wouldn't have surprised her. 'Was this your fella? The dopey looking git I saw sitting in the Beetle earlier on?'

'I—I—'

'No, it wasn't.' Honey flicked back her hair and faced him with an admirable lack of concern. 'It was me.'

'You? How was it you? You weren't even driving.'

'Actually, I was. When I got back from my friend's, Eden and, er, whatshisname, were standing on the drive. Eden warned me you were on the warpath, and I panicked. I decided to clear off, so I jumped in the Beetle and tried to make a getaway. Unfortunately, my mind was so preoccupied, worrying about you and how you'd react, that I made a basic mistake and managed to smash straight into your car instead. In a way, it was a good thing.'

'A good thing? How the bleeding hell was it a good thing?'

'Well, if I'd got away, I may not have come back, knowing your dreadful temper. As it was, I had no escape and had to face the music, and you got your own way in the end, didn't you? It all worked out beautifully for you.'

Eden had to hand it to her. She made it sound reasonable that having his Rolls Royce pranged had led to a positive outcome for Cain.

He gaped at her, not making a sound, but only for a moment. 'You useless brat. You're gonna have to pay for the damage.'

'But, Daddy darling, you're cutting off my allowance,' she pointed out. 'So, as it stands, I have no money to pay for anything.' She gave a dramatic sigh. 'I should think it would be worth every penny, knowing I'm banished to the wilds of Yorkshire and there's nothing I can do about it. A whole summer without Crispin, the love of my life. Don't you think that's punishment enough?' Her bottom lip wobbled and her eyes filled with tears.

God, thought Eden admiringly, she was good.

Cain deflated like a popped balloon. 'So, you're going, then?'

'I have no choice, do I? And by the time I get back, Lavinia will be home, and no doubt Crispin will have forgotten all about me.' A tear rolled down her cheek, bang on cue.

He sighed. 'Look, darls, it's for the best, trust me on this. Yorkshire won't be so bad, and it's only for two months. By the time you get home, you'll be over him. This is just a crush. There'll be someone else out there for you, someone who deserves you. Not some married bloke looking for a quick fumble. I'm doing this for your own good. You know that, deep down, don't you?'

She whimpered and gave a slight nod before burying her head in her pillow.

Cain took a step towards her, but seemed to think better of it, and shrugged helplessly. 'I'll ring the garage. Get the cars sorted ASAP. You'll need the Beetle for your journey. And I won't stop your allowance, babe. Promise.

Not now you're being a good girl.' He looked at Eden anxiously. 'See to her, will you?'

She nodded, and he left the room, closing the door gently behind him.

Honey rolled over, wiped away her tear and sat up. 'Right, that's sorted. Now, we have to make sure you'll pass for me.'

'You deserve an Oscar,' Eden said, with grudging admiration. 'Seriously, you can't expect me to go to Yorkshire in your place? You're joking, right?'

'Oh, no, dear Eden, I'm perfectly serious. Think about it. You're trying to get back into his good books, aren't you? Do you really want him to know you're responsible for damaging his precious car?'

No, Eden didn't. Working for the Carmichaels wasn't the best job in the world, but it was a job, and she needed the money. If Cain fired her, she'd also be looking for somewhere to live. It would be so embarrassing to move back in with her parents. Then there was the small matter of having to find the finances to pay for the damage to both the Rolls Royce and the Beetle. She would never be able to afford it, especially if she was unemployed. Cain loved that dratted car of his and he wouldn't turn a blind eye.

She slumped, defeated. She had no choice, really. Honey was right.

'Now, I know you're an awful lot older than me—'

'Four years!' Eden protested.

'Hmm, and you're fatter, of course.'

'By about twelve pounds.' She was rapidly going off Honey.

'I think some of my looser clothes will fit you.'

'What's wrong with my own clothes?'

'They're not designer.'

'Why would I need designer clothes in the Yorkshire Dales?'

'I would only ever wear designer clothes. You're me for the summer. You have to do what I'd do, remember?'

'He won't know the difference.'

'He was married to Mother's cousin. I'm sure he learnt a lot. And do you seriously think my parents will go the whole summer without checking up on me? They'll get in touch with him. They'll want to know if I'm behaving myself. You have to be me in every way possible. You have to behave like me. You have to do what I'd do, otherwise they'll be tipped off something's wrong. If they ask how I'm getting on, and he tells them I'm being very kind, making cakes and reading stories to the children, they'll be highly suspicious. You have to give him plenty of ammunition to hurl at them. When they ring, I want him complaining about my behaviour. Okay?'

'Don't you think he's got enough to worry about?' Eden said, horrified.

'Serves him right for agreeing to be my prison officer,' Honey said.

Eden realised that it would be to the Harlands' advantage if she, rather than Honey, moved in with them. Honey would make their lives miserable. If she wasn't happy, she always made sure everyone else suffered with her. That little family had been through enough. At least Eden could go easier on them. Maybe it was for the best that she was to take Honey's place, after all.

Honey looked at her thoughtfully. 'You'll have to bleach your hair, of course.'

'I will not,' Eden said. 'I'm already blonde. Sort of.'

'More of a dull mouse. Fair, at best.'

'Charming. Well, that's as light as I need to be, thank you very much.'

'It's a well-known fact that Honey Carmichael is blonde,' she snapped. 'Dad and I are natural blondes, everyone knows that.'

'Natural blondes?' Eden giggled. 'So, your hair is

naturally Number Nineteen, Spun Gold, and Cain's hair is naturally Number Sixteen, Golden Glory, with Number Twenty-Nine Burnt Caramel highlights?'

Honey looked put out. 'I'm not saying we don't give it a bit of help,' she admitted.

'A bit of help? Honey, you've got brown hair. I've seen those photos of you on your seventeenth birthday, remember?'

'That was winter time. The sun always bleaches it in the summer.'

'Crikey. Where do you go for your holidays? Mercury?'

'I'm not arguing with you. You're going blonde, and that's that. I'll book you in with Marco tomorrow. He'll do it as a favour for me.'

'Forget it. I'm not going blonde.'

'We'll see,' she said and lay down on her bed again, her golden hair fanned out around her face, every inch of her resembling a Disney princess. Pity she had the heart of a troll.

Watching her, Eden had an awful feeling that, by the same time tomorrow, she'd be blonde.

CHAPTER FIVE

The girl with the long, blonde hair stepped out of her bright yellow Beetle Cabriolet and stared at herself in the window of the nearest shop. Eden peered closer. Crikey, was that really her? She didn't recognise herself. She'd refused to bleach all of her hair, but she had agreed to some highlights, and it had made an amazing difference. She had to admit, she rather liked the effect. Perhaps she wouldn't have been so convincing looking in a mirror, but staring at her reflection in the smoky glass of the vintage clothing store opposite the car, she could certainly pass for Honey. Especially if one had never met her, and, luckily, Eliot Harland hadn't.

She shut the car door and locked it carefully. She had about half an hour to spare before she was due to meet Eliot. It had taken her most of the day to get there—well, six and a half hours, actually. She'd stopped at a motorway service station after about three hours, dashing into the toilets and morphing into Honey, like Clark Kent morphing into Superman in a phone box. She was glad of the break, needing to stretch her legs and get a drink and a sandwich. She'd almost walked straight out of the café again when she saw the prices, until she remembered Honey had given her one of her credit cards and told her to feel free to buy whatever she liked. Her father would be paying the bill, and the more evidence he had of her spending in Yorkshire, the better, as far as she was concerned.

Cain had spoken to Eliot and arranged that he would meet her in Kirkby Skimmer, the only town in Skimmerdale. He was too worried that "Honey" would get lost trying to find a remote sheep farm, so Eliot had promised he'd meet up with her in the market square for her to follow his Land Rover back to Fleetsthorpe, his home.

'How much does Eliot know?' Eden had asked Cain. 'Have you told him the reason Honey's staying with him?'

'You must be joking. The fewer people who know she's been shagging a Tory toff, the better. I said she'd gone a little off the rails and needed a firm hand. With any luck, he'll think she's been taking drugs, or sumfink.'

Well, yes, obviously that was infinitely preferable, thought Eden. She wondered what Eliot would be expecting. He must be absolutely desperate, to take on such an attractive prospect.

That morning, Honey had made a great show of saying goodbye. She'd cried and raged and begged for one last chance, while Cain had tried his best to fight back tears and assured her he was doing this for her own good, and the summer would be over before she knew it.

'Right, well, I'd better ring a taxi,' Eden had said, as rehearsed. 'Time to get off to Mum and Dad's.'

'Yeah, that's the spirit,' said Cain. 'I've paid you two months' wages into your bank account, so you've no worries there. Reckon I've bin a bit mean to you, Eden. Not your fault this one don't know how to behave herself. When you come back, I'll find sumfink for you to do, okay? Don't spend the summer worrying about it.'

Eden hoped she wasn't blushing. Since Cain had calmed down, he'd been altogether more reasonable, and there she was, helping his daughter to thoroughly deceive him. She wasn't proud of herself.

Honey sighed, rather theatrically. 'I suppose I may as well drop you off on the way. I'm passing through your village, and it will at least give me some company for the first half an hour. After that, it's the lonely open road for me.'

Cain had approved and congratulated her on being so thoughtful. 'Now, Eliot's going to meet you at four o'clock in the Market Square at Kirkby Skimmer. I've programmed your SatNav for you, so you should be okay getting there. I'll be ringing the farm around six to make sure you've got there safely, and I'll telephone every couple of days to make sure you're behaving yourself, so be good.'

Honey stamped her foot. 'Isn't it bad enough that you're exiling me? Do you have to embarrass me and check up on me, too?'

'Be fair, Honey. You ain't the best-behaved girl in the world. I've got to make sure you ain't up to no mischief.'

'You're a tyrant, and I'm glad to be getting away from you.' She jumped in the car and slammed the door.

'I don't mean to be horrible to her,' Cain whimpered, his eyes even more watery.

Eden shook her head. 'Don't worry about her. She'll be fine. She's just trying to make you feel guilty. Don't let her win, whatever you do. Remember, it's for the best.'

'Yeah, yeah.'

Eden's heart went out to him. How had things got so out of hand? She wished she could rewind and get out of this awful situation, but it was far too late. All she could do was hope and pray that she was doing the right thing for everyone. She knew that it was definitely better for the Harlands that it was her and not Honey that would be heading to Skimmerdale, but it had also occurred to her recently that it might work out better for Cain, too. The more Honey was told she couldn't have something, the more she wanted it. Being parted from Crispin would only make her cling to him more. On the other hand, being free to spend an entire summer in his company, she might well discover that he wasn't as exciting as she thought. If giving Honey what she wanted resulted in her growing tired of Crispin and ending the affair herself, it would be the best possible outcome. She really hoped so because she couldn't take much more guilt. 'Think of the knighthood,' she suggested, and he brightened immediately.

'You ain't wrong there,' he said. 'Take care, Eden. See you in September. Honey,' he called, 'love you, darls.'

Honey had winked at her as they set off, not seeming to mind at all that she was deceiving her father and leaving him wracked with guilt. She was far too excited about meeting up with Crispin, whom she hadn't seen for over a week—something she informed Eden of every five minutes, as they left Upper Bourbury behind and headed for the village of Carpington, just outside Oxford, where Crispin would be waiting for her.

Eden really didn't know what Honey saw in the guy. In his mid-thirties, he was the pretty boy of the Tory party, according to the tabloids, but he was far too well-groomed for Eden's liking. She suspected he must spend hours in front of the mirror, tweezing, cleansing, moisturising, and faffing with his immaculate fair hair.

When they arrived at the lay-by, the romantic destination they'd chosen to meet, he was slumped in his car with a miserable expression on his face. Two other cars were parked up. Inside one, a couple were snogging the faces off each other, while in the other—a bright red Mini—a man was hunched over a newspaper, seemingly absorbed in a crossword puzzle, or something.

Honey leapt out of the car and raced over to Crispin's borrowed Volvo. Apparently, he'd wisely decided his Jaguar would be too conspicuous. She banged none-too-discreetly on the window, and he reached over and unlocked the passenger door.

'Help me with my things,' she said, but he shook his head.

'I can't be seen. Hurry up and put your stuff in the back seat, then get in. I can't hang around. Lavinia has friends everywhere. I'm a nervous wreck.'

She gave him a scornful look and called across to Eden. 'Bring my bags!'

'Yes, m'lady.' Grumbling, Eden lifted her suitcases and vanity case out of the boot and struggled across to the Volvo with them.

'Right, here's my mobile, so you can answer any texts Dad or Mother send me. Don't speak to them if they telephone, whatever you do. They probably won't be able to get through, anyway, but just in case.'

'What about when they call Eliot on the house phone? They're bound to want to speak to you.'

'Well, don't speak to them, for God's sake. You'll think of something, I'm sure. I've got a new phone, and I've put my number in the contacts for you, but don't get in touch with me unless it's an absolute emergency, okay? I don't want to be interrupted. Okay, I think that's everything. All you need now is my attitude. Don't be a wimp. Make sure Eliot and the brats know who's boss. I wouldn't take any crap from them, so you'd better not, either. Remember, when in doubt, think Honey!'

'Hurry up!' whined Crispin. 'I don't feel safe here. I feel as if I'm being watched.'

'Don't be pathetic,' said Honey. She patted Eden's arm in some kind of attempt at affection. 'Right then. Off you go. Give those northerners hell. See you in September.'

Eden had given her a weak smile and headed back to the Beetle. She'd barely had time to put on her seatbelt, before Crispin was roaring out of the lay-by and back onto the main road. She started the engine of the Beetle and began to pull away, stopping suddenly as the crossword geek in the red Mini pulled out in front of her. Eden blasted him with the horn. She may as well get into character from the off. This was it. From that moment on, she was Honey Carmichael.

Having arrived in Kirkby Skimmer, though, and standing there in the pretty, cobbled market square, she felt a twinge of nerves. She hitched up her bag—or rather, Honey's bag, bought from LK Bennett not six months ago and now deemed out-of-date, in spite of the fact that she'd paid over two hundred pounds for it. In the handbag—the most expensive she'd ever carried, by a mile—she had Honey's iPhone, the keys to a nearly-new car, a purse containing her credit card, and Eden's own bank debit card giving access to her account, which contained the most money she'd ever had in her life, since Cain had paid her two months' wages in advance.

If she got mugged, the perpetrator would think it was Christmas.

Her eyes darted from side to side as she strolled around the market square, on the lookout for any potential pickpockets or violent robbers. She had to admit, it hardly seemed the location for such people. In spite of the heavy, grey skies, which cast a gloom over the place, it was obviously a pretty, Georgian town. The shops were all small, and many seemed to be independent businesses. Some of them were even rather quirky. There were some vintage clothes shops, a plentiful supply of tearooms, a bookshop and an old-fashioned sweet shop, among others. There wasn't a Costa or a McDonald's in sight, though she spotted a Laura Ashley outlet and a Lakeland store.

The tourist information centre looked pretty busy as she passed. Several people in kagoules and hiking boots were clustered in the doorway, studying maps, as if the threat of rain was no obstacle to their intended walks. They were obviously made of sterner stuff than Eden, who was eyeing the dark skies with increasing anxiety. People here seemed oblivious to the weather, milling around outside the gift shop, peering through the windows at the displays of plates and mugs, fridge magnets and keyrings, or examining the rack outside, which was stacked with postcards of local views.

She glanced at her watch, wondering if she had time to pop into the little teashop she'd spotted. Some people were sitting at tables outside and were tucking into the most delicious looking scones covered in jam and clotted cream. You couldn't beat a cream tea, in Eden's opinion, and she realised suddenly she was hungry. The sandwich of tasteless white bread and an anaemic processed cheese slice, which she'd bought at the service station, hadn't filled her up at all.

Could she risk it? She had ten minutes to go, after all.

She thought about Eliot Harland. She could picture him clearly in her mind's eye. He'd be stocky and red-cheeked, with a weather-beaten face that came from working outside a lot of the time, tending sheep. He'd probably be dour. It seemed to be the general opinion that all farmers were dour, and northern farmers doubly so. She realised she had no idea how old he was. He'd been married to Freya's cousin, and Freya was around forty-eight, although a great many of her body parts were considerably younger, it had to be said. Eden guessed he must be around fiftyish. So, how old would that make the children? He'd probably married late, being so isolated up here, and had met his wife later in life. The kids were possibly teenagers. No wonder he couldn't cope with them alone. She shuddered at the thought of dealing with all those hormonal surges. This wasn't going to be much fun at all.

She decided against going into the teashop. She didn't want to incur his wrath from the first day. He was going to despise her pretty quickly, anyway, the minute she slipped into Honey mode. Besides, she was sure she'd felt the first drop of rain. Maybe she'd be wiser to get back to the car.

Reluctantly, she turned away from the inviting smell of the scones and saw someone standing by the Beetle, peering in through the window. Her heart began to thud as she tried to remember if she'd left anything on the backseat. She was sure it was all in the boot, but what if she'd forgotten something? Or what if Honey had put something there, and it hadn't occurred to her to remove it when she got out? Just her luck to attract a thief on her first day.

She hurried as fast as she could manage in her high wedges towards the car. 'Can I help you?'

As the man straightened and turned to face her, her heart did the quickstep, and she had to physically stop herself from murmuring, "Wow".

Dark gypsy curls, flashing brown eyes, a tall, toned frame, highly kissable lips...

Staring at him in awe, she could only think, *Welcome to Yorkshire, Eden Robinson.*

'Honey Carmichael?'

Eden gasped. It couldn't be. Old MacDonald had never looked like this in her picture books. This vision couldn't be more than thirty-five, for a start. 'Eliot Harland?'

'Aye. That's me. Wondered where you'd cleared off to.'

'I thought I'd have a look around,' she said weakly. 'Take in the sights.' Though she needn't have bothered. Standing before her was the prettiest sight of the day by a mile. And even tastier than a freshly baked scone with clotted cream and jam. Eden couldn't think of a higher accolade than that.

'Right. So, you didn't think to stay in the car 'til I got here?'

'What for? I was only across there.' She waved her arm in the general direction of the teashop and felt several drops of rain land on the back of her hand as she did so.

'And how would I know that? I didn't have a clue what you looked like, remember? Your dad told me to make sure you got here safely, and you buggered off the minute you got here. You should have stayed put and waited for me.' He glowered at her.

Really, Eden had never known what a glower looked like until that moment, but there was no mistaking it. He was glowering more than the sky, and goodness knows, that was glowering pretty badly itself. He stood there, all dark and brooding, seemingly not noticing the rain that had begun to fall pretty steadily. His dark eyes narrowed at her, and she swallowed.

So this was her fate. She was to spend eight weeks in a remote farmhouse in the wilderness of Yorkshire, in the company of Heathcliff. Eden would have felt intimidated, but she wasn't Eden. Not anymore.

She was Honey Carmichael. And Honey Carmichael was more than a match for the dourest of men.

Let the game commence.

CHAPTER SIX

Following Eliot's Land Rover in the Beetle, Eden barely had the opportunity to register the landscape around her. She was too busy trying to stay calm, as the car climbed to ever greater heights. She hoped the roads would be smooth and wouldn't damage the suspension. Honey would kill her if she knackered the car, especially since it had only just come out of the garage, newly-repaired after Joshua's unfortunate accident.

In front of her eyes, the windscreen wipers worked hard, trying to clear the glass of the rain that was falling hard and fast. This wasn't what she'd imagined, at all.

When Eden did dare to take her eyes off the Land Rover for a moment, she wished she hadn't. They were high in the hills, and she could see the river way below her in the valley. From up there, the landscape seemed to be punctuated with Lego brick-sized stone huts, and what looked like tiny toy sheep in the distance. She couldn't believe there were actual sheep up so high. They balanced on the hillside, looking down at her, or wandered at the side of the road. Fleetingly, she wondered why their fleeces didn't shrink when they got wet. The woollen jumper her mother had given her for Christmas certainly had. There was one of life's mysteries, she thought, while clutching the steering wheel and praying she'd make it safely to the farm where the Harland family lived.

Eliot drove slowly ahead of her, for which Eden was thoroughly grateful, particularly as the cars began a steep descent into the valley. They passed a village, or rather a hamlet, called Upper Kell, then headed out again, following the line of the river for what felt like forever, though it was actually only ten minutes. They drove through a much larger village called Ravensbridge, which seemed to be far more civilised, but unfortunately, Eliot didn't show any signs of stopping. He carried on, out through the village and back into the wilderness. As they continued along, Eden caught the odd glimpse of the river, which had narrowed considerably by that point, as well as a church steeple in the distance. Next, the village of Camacker was upon them, a charming little place with a riverside car park that seemed full even in the dismal weather, a pub, teashops, and even an art gallery.

She wondered if they were anywhere near the farm yet. Living near this village wouldn't be so bad, she thought, but even as it crossed her mind, they left the cottages and shops behind and moved out into open countryside again. She barely registered the next cluster of buildings, in a village called Beckthwaite, having given up hope of ever reaching Fleetsthorpe and growing increasingly tired. They had been driving for almost three quarters of an hour, although the milometer showed that they'd driven less than twenty-one miles. The tarmac road in and out of Beckthwaite had long since been left behind, and as the road got rougher the farther out they went, the Land Rover's wheels began throwing water and mud in the direction of the Beetle. Eden dreaded to think what state Honey's precious car was in.

Eventually, they came to a fork in the track, and Eden saw an old wooden signpost pointing left, with the word Fleetsthorpe roughly carved into it. The road wasn't the only thing that branched off at that point. The river seemed to split itself in two, also, and a stream appeared to be following the road.

Noticing they'd begun climbing slightly again, Eden realised the stream was actually running down from the hills to meet the river. She hoped they wouldn't be driving all the way back up those dratted hills again. They were more like mountains, and she felt she'd punished Honey's car enough.

To her relief, they made a sudden right, and ahead of

her, through her rain-lashed windscreen, she saw what could only be Fleetsthorpe. It had to be. There was nothing else around.

Eden followed Eliot's Land Rover along the track, over a stone bridge that carried them across the stream, past a jumble of old barns and sheds, and on into a farmyard.

They bumped into a roughly half-tarmacked yard, and she thought he could at least have tried to avoid the small potholes he seemed intent on driving over. It was as if he was deliberately trying to soak her car.

To the left of them stood a stone farmhouse. A narrow flagstone path led from the door and along the front of the house, to a garden that was closed off by a stone wall. Eden could see a line of—it had to be said—rather dingy washing, which didn't fill her with confidence. Pointless waste of time that had been, hanging out washing in such weather.

Opposite the garden loomed a huge barn, made of the same grey stone as the house. Between the garden and the barn was a rough earth track, all boggy and full of puddles. Evidently the money for the tarmac hadn't stretched that far. Where the garden ended, she saw more stone outbuildings, and in the distance, behind them, loomed the hills—dark, menacing, threatening.

It couldn't have been more different to the pretty Cotswolds farms she'd left behind, and her heart began to thud as she stared into the charcoal and purple distance, feeling almost claustrophobic. She looked at the drab net curtains hanging at the windows and took a deep breath, wondering what she was letting herself in for. If the outside of the farmhouse was this bad, what would it look like inside?

Eliot climbed out of the Land Rover and slammed the door shut, and a black and white dog appeared at his side, as if it had been waiting for him, which it probably had.

Eden stepped tentatively out of the Beetle, avoiding

the small sink cover she'd inadvertently parked right beside.

She didn't even have time to close the car door, before the farmhouse door opened and two little girls, no more than nine or ten, raced outside and threw themselves at Eliot. Though Eliot wore a green waxed jacket, the girls were in summer clothes, and Eden wondered if they possessed coats, or if they'd developed waterproof skin living out in the wilderness.

'All right, all right.' Eliot laughed, hugging them to him. 'Watch what you're doing. Nearly had me over then.'

He put his arms around them, and they all turned to look at Eden. She felt like a fool, standing there all shivering and wet in Ben de Lisi wedges and a thin cotton jacket over a short Ted Baker dress. Honey had insisted it was what she would have chosen. In contrast, Eliot's girls were far from dressed up. In fact, it was fair to say the girls' T-shirts could do with a good wash. So could their hair, by the look of it. Even brushing it would be a start, and she found herself wishing she'd ignored Honey and gone for the jeans and trainers she'd wanted to wear.

'Go on in, girls,' said Eliot, nudging them gently towards the house. 'You'll get soaked. Ask Daisy to put 'kettle on while I get this lass sorted.'

The girls obeyed him, sidling past Eden with wide eyes. She suspected they'd seen nothing like her before. She self-consciously twisted a strand of her newly-highlighted hair and watched their father with wide eyes.

'Well?' he said.

Eden started as he suddenly took a step towards her. 'What?'

'Are you going to stand there, all gormless, like, or are you going to get your bags out o' the car?'

She almost apologised but remembered, just in time, that she was Honey. She straightened and gave him her best icy stare. 'Really, what sort of gentleman expects a lady to carry her own luggage? It's all right for you, in your farmer's coat. I'm getting wet through here.'

He closed his eyes for a moment, rubbing his forehead wearily with one hand. 'Aye, and so it begins. Me own bloody fault, I suppose.'

He strode past her and opened the boot. She heard him muttering something under his breath, as he began to pull out Honey's Luis Vuitton suitcases. Eden couldn't blame him. Anyone would think she was going to be staying at a place with no washing machine, as Honey appeared to have packed at least two outfits for every single day she would be away. Although, thinking about the row of washing on the line and the state of the girls' T-shirts, maybe they didn't even possess a washing machine. That thought didn't fill Eden with joy. Would she be expected to do all the washing by hand in the sink? Or the bath? Would there be a bath? God, what if he kept the coal in it? She was almost sure she'd heard of such things before. She felt distinctly Honey-like as her lip curled in horror at the thought of what lay behind the rather shabby door of the farmhouse.

Eliot slammed the suitcases onto the ground, one by one, and Eden felt it only right she reminded him that they were pretty expensive pieces and not meant to be dumped on soggy ground, so could he be more careful with them? She managed to stop short of adding a please. Honey certainly wouldn't have.

He gave her a look that made her wither inside and reminded her of Honey's assertion that she wouldn't spend a single day at Withering Heights. Maybe she hadn't been so wrong, after all. Those brown eyes were flashing in contempt. Eden had made a terrible start, which, in its own way, was perfect. Eliot already despised her. She was playing her part to perfection.

'Get yersen in, then. Don't mind me. I've nowt better to do than run around after some jumped up rich girl, who's way too big for her boots.'

Inadvertently, Eden looked down at her wedges. When she looked up, Eliot was looking at them, too. His gaze took in her bare legs, but he quickly looked away. 'Don't suppose you've even brought any wellies?'

'Wellies? I don't possess any wellies,' she admitted.

'Nah. Didn't think you would,' he said. 'You'd best see if there's a pair of Daisy's in there that fits you. If not, you'll have to go into Ravensbridge and buy some. You'll be worse than useless around here in them things.'

Eden took a deep breath. 'Given that I'm here to look after your children, I shouldn't think I will be needing wellington boots. I don't intend to be tramping through muddy puddles, or wading through sheep muck with them. I shall be mostly indoors, surely?'

He stared at her for a moment, then gave a hearty laugh. 'By heck, you've got a shock coming to you. It's the summer holidays in a couple of days. If you think them bairns will be content to sit in front of the telly all day you've got another thing coming. You'll need them wellies, 'cos you'll be outside, rounding up the lasses like my dogs round up sheep. They've been confined to a classroom for weeks. They need the fresh air. And judging by your pasty look, they're not the only ones.'

'Well!' Eden's indignation was genuine. After all, it was her complexion he was criticising there, not Honey's.

'Come on. By the time we get inside, bloody tea'll be stone cold.'

He hoisted a suitcase under each arm, picked up another one with each hand, and nodded towards the Mulberry holdall he'd dumped unceremoniously on the ground. Eden wondered if he had any idea how much it had cost. Would he care, even if he did?

She picked it up and shut the boot, then followed him, stomach churning, as he strode towards the open farmhouse door.

What fresh hell awaited her within those cold, stone walls?

****

The minute they stepped into the hallway, the smell of polish hit Eliot. Daisy had obviously gone all out to make the house look and smell good. The question was, who was it she was trying to impress, him or Honey?

He tried not to show his astonishment at how tidy and neat the hallway was. The grey flagstone floor had been neatly swept. The white walls of the hallway had obviously had a good scrubbing, as there wasn't a trace of the mud or the dirty handprints that had been there when he'd left earlier that afternoon. The girls must have remembered to take their shoes off when they came back inside. He supposed he should do the same, but he was too weighed down with luggage to mess about. He'd just have to mop the floor later.

He raised an eyebrow on seeing that even the stair carpet had been vacuumed, then frowned when he noticed that she'd hung a couple of pictures on the walls. He supposed it made it look friendlier, more welcoming, but where the hell had she dug them out from? He vaguely recognised them, but couldn't for the life of him remember where he'd packed them away. She must have had a really good look around while he'd been out.

The white sideboard, which stood against the right hand wall, near to the front door, looked new. No one would've known it had been piled high with junk that morning. Now, the only things on display were the house telephone, a vase, and a couple of candlesticks, complete with candles. He'd forgotten they had those.

He glanced at Honey. She was wiping her feet on the doormat, staring around and looking surprised, and he felt a stab of satisfaction. No doubt she'd been expecting the worst. He'd seen her face when she caught sight of the farmhouse and the yard for the first time. It hadn't impressed her. He was glad Daisy had got to work, even if it did mean he now owed her an even greater debt of gratitude.

He led Honey down the long hallway, past the stairs, where he turned right, glancing at the large pine bookcase, whose books had been neatly stacked according to size. Turning left again, he led her through the open door at the end of the corridor and into a room he knew for a fact would be the last thing she'd be expecting.

Honey said nothing, but her expression revealed her surprise.

Eliot knew it wasn't a typical Skimmerdale farmhouse kitchen. Jemima had made sure of that. The first thing she'd done when she moved in was hire an architect to make plans, to improve the small, dark room that had once been there. It had taken a while to get everything as she wanted it, and it had been stressful. Their first baby had been on the way, and the last thing they'd needed was a horde of builders, plasterers, electricians and plumbers in the house. He'd had to admit, though, it had been worth it. Three small rooms had been knocked into one, to create a large kitchen with the same flagstone flooring throughout, thick wooden beams, and an expensive oak kitchen.

'You can't deny, it looks miles better,' Jemima had said, and he couldn't. What annoyed him was that, three years later, she'd announced she was bored with the oak kitchen and it was time for an update. So, the units had gone and been replaced with the ones that had stood in there since.

White, wooden units with oak worktops, a huge electric range with ceramic hob, as Jemima had never taken to the old range that had been in there since his grandmother's day, and a Belfast sink—the kind his father had ripped out and replaced with a stainless steel sink unit to make things easier for his mother. It all seemed crazy to him, but it made Jemima happy. He'd put his foot down after that, though. No more work on the house. It was fine as it was, and no, they didn't need a bloody loft conversion. She'd sulked for a few days, then she'd found a pine dresser at an auction and nagged him to buy it for her. He had, and peace was restored. She'd stripped it, painted it and filled it with the kind of junk his mother would have put in a skip. She said it was on trend, whatever the hell that meant. He'd never fathomed her out, but it had been worth it to see the light in her eyes and the smile on her face.

He didn't want to think about Jemima, though. It still hurt too much.

His heart lifted as his two daughters ran down the stairs and rushed to his side. He ruffled their hair. Both of them had the same mop of dark curls he had himself.

'Do you like it?' Libby, his eldest child, smiled at Honey rather shyly. 'Daisy's been working right hard all day, to make it nice and clean.'

Ophelia giggled. She'd never been as shy as her sister, a fact she demonstrated as she leaned towards Honey and confided, 'She said it were filthy and we'd better get it sorted before you got here, 'cos you're proper posh. Are you proper posh?'

Seeing Honey's stunned expression, Eliot interrupted. 'Never mind asking daft questions. Has that kettle boiled? Where's Daisy and George?'

'She had to rush upstairs,' said Libby. The two of them exchanged glances, and there was amusement in their eyes.

Eliot's heart sank. What had happened?

'George did a runny pooh. Daisy had to put his trousers in soak.'

They glanced at the Belfast sink, which evidently contained the evidence of George's wrongdoings. Eliot shook his head then looked at Honey, expecting some comment.

She cleared her throat. 'Well, that's charming, I must say. I sincerely hope George is a child and not an adult. Still, at least this place isn't the hovel I was expecting, so that's something.'

Eliot's eyes narrowed as he surveyed her. Who the hell did she think she was, anyway? 'You were expecting a hovel?'

'What's a hovel?' asked Ophelia, clearly puzzled.

'You know,' said Libby. 'Like Granny Allen's.'

Ophelia, not surprisingly, screwed up her nose in disgust. 'Yuk. Why would you think we lived somewhere like Granny Allen's?'

'I can't really say,' said Honey, airily, 'since I haven't the faintest idea who Granny Allen is, or what her home looks like. However, I will admit I wasn't expecting a farmhouse in the back of beyond to be so charming. I was expecting something a lot more primitive, so at least that's a positive.'

'You haven't seen it all, yet,' said Eliot evenly. 'Wait 'til you see the tin bath and the outside toilet, and the gas lamps upstairs.'

'Very amusing. I'm glad to see you have a sense of humour. Your manner earlier on led me to believe you were a typical northern farmer.'

'And what's a typical northern farmer?' He glared at her, a challenge in his eyes.

'Er, you know. Gruff, sullen, dog glued to your ankles ...' Her voice trailed off as her gaze found the sheepdog sitting beside him.

Eliot spread his hands and looked around the kitchen. 'As you can see, I fit the picture of the typical northern farmer. I'm gruff, I'm sullen, I rarely go anywhere without Lug beside me, and—'

'Lug? Your dog's called Lug? What on earth sort of a

name is that?'

'A short one. Easy to call. What's it to you?'

'It's short for Buggerlugs,' said Ophelia, with her usual helpfulness. "cos Dad says he's a proper one.'

'Aye, all right, love, that'll do.'

'Lug's Dad's best dog. We've got four others. Having dogs is in our blood,' said Ophelia solemnly. 'And we've got sheep and chickens and a cat and a pony. What animals have you got?'

Honey looked a bit rattled. 'I don't do animals.'

'Really? Thought you were one of the horsy set?'

He remembered for a moment, being curled up on the sofa in front of the stove with Jemima, just weeks before Libby was born.

'I heard from Freya today,' she'd said.

He'd tensed, knowing it hurt her to hear from the family who wanted little to do with her since she'd lowered herself to marrying a sheep farmer. 'Everything all right?'

'Oh, yes. Wanted to brag about her perfect life, as usual. Honey was blooded today at the hunt.'

'And that's a good thing?'

'A twelve-year-old child being blooded at the Boxing Day hunt? Oh, yes, that's a good thing.'

'Sounds disgusting.'

She'd laughed. 'Not in that world, darling, I assure you. Wait 'til summer comes. It will be nonstop phone calls to update me on Honey's latest show jumping cup, or how many rosettes she's won at the gymkhana. Hardly surprising, given that Freya spent a fortune buying her two ponies and paying for her expensive lessons.' She'd sighed. 'Our child will miss out on all that, I suppose.'

'When he or she is old enough, we'll get them a pony—though I draw the line at that hunting malarkey.'

'Really? You wouldn't mind?'

'Of course not.' He could hear the delight in her voice.

She'd put her arms around him and kissed him, and he'd known at that moment he'd do anything—even buy their child a hundred ponies—if it made Jemima happy.

He blinked, dismissing the memory. 'I heard you were one o' them kids who followed the hunt and got blooded by the master? And you had a whole wall full o' rosettes from them gymkhanas, and what not.'

She looked blank. 'Who told you that?'

'Who do you think?' He struggled to keep the anger out of his voice. Had she forgotten who he was married to?

'Oh, right. Yes, well, that was ponies.'

Eliot tutted. 'And ponies aren't animals?'

'They're transport,' she informed him.

He looked at the girls, who were staring up at her in astonishment. They were obviously as stunned at her comment as he was. What a spoilt brat she was, really. He didn't know what he could say to that when there were children present. Fortunately, he heard footsteps on the stairs, and a few moments later, Daisy entered the kitchen, carrying George in her arms.

'Daddy!'

'Georgie! Come on, then. Cuddles.' He felt a surge of joy as he lifted the little boy from Daisy's arms and held him closely. 'Thanks for minding them, Daisy. I really appreciate it. And for all you've done in the house. You've made quite an impression on our guest.'

'It were no bother, Eliot.' She smiled at him. 'You know I love having the bairns. Wish I could help out more often, but you know what it's like.'

''Course I do, and don't you be worrying about it. I don't expect you to put yersen out for me and mine.' God, no, he really didn't. She'd done more than enough. He was grateful to her, of course he was, but he knew the reason she'd done it. He just couldn't bring himself to face up to it.

'Evidently,' Honey said, 'that task is now mine.'

Daisy glanced at her, her disapproval apparent. 'Aren't you going to introduce me, Eliot?' she said, looking at Honey with flinty eyes.

'I doubt it,' Honey assured her, 'seeing as he hasn't even bothered to introduce me to his own children.' She gave Daisy a sweet smile. 'Are you his sister? His older sister, perhaps?'

Eliot rushed in at the look of horror on Daisy's face. 'Daisy Jackson, this is my wife's second cousin, Honey Carmichael,' he said coldly. 'Honey, this is Daisy, a neighbour and a good friend. She lives on a farm up yonder.'

'Up yonder? Please, don't let's get bogged down in the details,' Honey drawled. 'And what about your children? Do they have names? I understand the one with the lack of bowel control is George. What about the girls?'

That comment sent a spark of fury through Eliot, so much so that he seemed unable to speak.

Daisy's voice was as hard as the expression in her eyes. 'That's Liberty,' she said, nodding at the eldest child. 'And that's Ophelia.'

'Heavens.'

'What do you mean, heavens?' Eliot said, immediately on the defensive.

'I mean, what interesting names. I was expecting a farmer's children to be called Jack and Jill and Jane, or something. You're full of surprises.'

'Evidently, you've formed the wrong image of us. I reckon it's gonna take some shifting.'

'I expect you've formed an image of me, too,' she said.

'Aye. And happen it were the right one.' He handed George back to Daisy and picked up his guest's bags. 'I'll take these upstairs. Honey, follow me, if you want to see where you'll be sleeping. Daisy, love, if you could make us all a brew I'd be grateful, but if you need to get off, say the word. I won't be long.'

'I'm in no great hurry,' said Daisy immediately. 'I'll bring the washing in, in a minute. Sorry about leaving it on the line. I got distracted. I'll stick it in the dryer. Libby, take George into the living room, while I sort this out,' she said, gesturing towards the sink.

'Don't forget to wash your hands,' Honey reminded her. 'Basic hygiene, please. I don't want to be invaded by bacteria leftover from the child's dirty clothes.'

Daisy gaped at her, rather unattractively.

Eliot took a deep breath then left the kitchen, followed up the stairs by Honey. At the top, he showed her into the spare room.

It was a pretty room. Jemima had made it as appealing as she could, in the hope that, one day, a member of her family would deign to spend some time with them at Fleetsthorpe. It had never been used. Painted white, as were most of the rooms, it had thick, rose pink curtains at the window, a deep pile pink carpet, white bedding with pink cushions at the end of the bed, and a large white wooden wardrobe and matching chest of drawers.

Honey stood silently taking it in. No doubt, she was distinctly unimpressed and profoundly lacking in gratitude. It was going to be a really long eight weeks.

Eliot wished with all his heart that he'd any other option than to accept help from Honey Carmichael, even though he knew deep down he'd had one—and he hadn't been able to bring himself to take it.

CHAPTER SEVEN

'You're not serious?' Honey's voice was incredulous. 'We've just arrived, and the first thing you want to do is call your wife?'

Crispin paled. She hadn't thought it was possible for him to look any whiter, but somehow he managed it. 'It's not that I want to call her, darling. It's simply that I think I ought to. After all, we don't want her getting suspicious, do we?'

'Why on earth would she get suspicious? She's sunning herself in Portugal, for God's sake. I doubt very much she's given you a second thought since she arrived.'

Lavinia, it seemed to her, had a pretty good deal. Eight weeks in the Algarve, lying in the sun, drinking cocktails, and maxing out Crispin's credit cards. It seemed a much better prospect than being holed up in some Dorset house, which wasn't nearly as grand as she'd been expecting.

When they'd arrived, Crispin had unlocked the front door and thrown it open with a flourish, obviously very proud of the place. His sister, who was over a decade older than him and married to a wealthy businessman, had bought it as a holiday home when he was a teenager, and he'd spent many happy summers there, apparently. 'Isn't it lovely?' he kept saying. 'You must see the view from our room. The window looks out on the cove. It's wonderful to wake up in the morning, open the curtains, and look out over the sea.'

Honey, who'd assumed the house would have at least six bedrooms and a swimming pool, wasn't impressed. 'What do you mean, our room? Who chose it?'

'Well, it's my room. I mean, I always stay in that one when I stay here.'

'So, you've slept in that bed with Lavinia?'

He looked panic stricken. 'Well, yes. Obviously.'

'Then, I think we'd better find another room,' said Honey firmly. 'There's no way I'm sleeping in the bed you've shared with your wife.'

'But, Honey!'

'No buts about it, Crispin,' she said. 'I'm sure there are other rooms.'

'Only two, but one of them's little more than a box room.'

She looked appalled. 'What sort of a holiday home is this? Three bedrooms! Well, there's nothing for it. We'll have to take your sister's room.'

'Don't be ridiculous!'

'I beg your pardon? It must surely be the best room in the house, so we'll take it. Can you direct me?'

He opened his mouth in protest.

'Oh, don't stand there gawping at me like that. It's most unattractive.'

'We can't take that room. It's Sybil's and Rupert's room.'

'They'll never know.' She pouted. 'Can't you understand how I'm feeling? This has all been on your terms. I had to work everything around your holiday dates, keep out of the way, not tell anyone about us, be discreet. Now, I'm to be holed up here for weeks without another soul to talk to, all to protect your reputation and career, and you expect me to sleep in the bed where you've been having sex with your wife. It's too much.'

'Who says I've been having sex with my wife?' Crispin said, looking guilty. 'You're making huge assumptions there.'

Honey stroked his face. 'It's all right. I know you and Lavinia must have a very active love life.'

'Well, no, I mean—'

'How could she keep her hands off you? I can't keep my hands off you. She'd have to be superhuman to resist.'

Crispin looked deeply smug. 'Well, I suppose —'

'So, you take my point? Don't you realise how hard for me all this is? Having to share you with her! It breaks my heart. Can't I at least have this one precious summer, when I've got you all to myself, with no memories of Lavinia to intrude upon us?' She kissed him gently.

He took hold of her hands. 'I suppose you're right. I am being selfish. I'll show you to Sybil's room, and while you unpack, I'll ring Lavinia. Get it all out of the way.'

'I can't believe she makes you ring her every day. Anyone would think she didn't trust you.'

'I know. It is a bit much,' he agreed.

'I loathe clingy women,' said Honey. 'Come on, let's find our room.'

In the event, Honey wasn't too impressed with the master bedroom, either. It wasn't much bigger than the room Crispin had earmarked for them, and it didn't have a sea view. Its only saving grace, as far as she could see, was that it had an en suite, but given that there were only the two of them, it hardly mattered. She gazed out of the window at the boring front garden and wished she'd kept her big mouth shut. She wasn't going to tell Crispin that, of course. Let him think it mattered to her that he'd slept with his wife in this house. No doubt he was flattered by the thought, and that would work in her favour. In actual fact, she'd simply wanted the grandest room in the house. Though, this one hardly seemed worth the effort.

She finished unpacking and wondered, as she put the last of her clothes in the old-fashioned pine wardrobe, how Eden was getting on. She really hoped she wouldn't let her emotions get the better of her. Eden was far too sentimental, and the thought of a widowed father, trying valiantly to cope with three young children, had really tugged at her heartstrings. Eden liked to romanticise things. She saw the whole episode as a tragic love story. Honey thought differently. If Eliot Harland had really loved Jemima, he would surely have told her to find someone more suitable, and not have condemned her to a life of hell in a Skimmerdale farmhouse. What sort of love was that, for heaven's sake? You could stick it.

She headed onto the landing. Hearing Crispin's voice, she sneaked quietly downstairs, desperate to eavesdrop on his conversation with his wife.

'No, of course I won't forget. The second Saturday in August. I'll be there. No, of course I won't miss it. What do you take me for? Anyway, how can I forget, when you're going to be ringing me every day to remind me? I do wish you'd have a little faith in me, darling. It's dreadfully belittling.'

Honey edged closer to the living room. What was he on about? What was happening on the second Saturday in August? They were supposed to be having an uninterrupted break, for God's sake. Surely, Lavinia wasn't coming back?

'No, it's just the same here. Nothing ever changes, does it? Oh, pottering around. I'm looking forward to some rest and relaxation. How about you? Really? Well, remember to put your sun cream on. I hope you're using a high factor. You don't want to burn. Yes, all right. Have a lovely day. I'll speak to you tomorrow. Love you. Miss you. Bye.'

'Love you? Miss you?' Honey put her hands on her hips and glared at him, as he replaced the receiver. 'What was that all about?'

'Just words, my darling. Have to keep her sweet. You know I only love you.'

'And what's happening on the second Saturday in August?'

'I have to get back to my constituency for a surgery.'

'A what?'

'Surgery. You know, I meet any of my constituents who need help with things.'

'What sort of things?'

'Oh, gosh, all sorts of things. Litter, traffic problems, schooling. I once had a chap turn up to complain that his benefits had been wrongly stopped. It was extraordinary.'

'What was extraordinary about that? Lots of people get their benefits stopped.'

'No, I mean that one of my constituents was on benefits. I think he's the only one I've ever met. It's not the norm in Windleby-on-the-Weir, you know.'

'No wonder you've got one of the safest seats in the country, then,' muttered Honey, who was only aware of that fact because her father had banged on about it so often.

'You ought to be jolly glad I have,' said Crispin. 'If I had a marginal seat, I'd probably have to hold surgeries every week to drum up support. Can you imagine how tedious that would be? Having to tootle back up to the place every seven days?'

'But you're on holiday!'

'Darling, an MP is never really on holiday. At least, he can't be seen to be on holiday. Really, if any journos find out someone's had more than a fortnight away, they seem to take a gleeful delight in labelling us spongers, and printing sneaky photographs of us in their ghastly rags. It's bad enough that Lavinia's taken herself off to Portugal for eight weeks.'

'I don't see what she's got to do with anything,' said Honey, sulkily.

'Well, to be fair, I do pay her thirty-five grand a year to be my office manager,' he admitted. 'The tax payers can get pretty miffed about things like that. One can't be too careful.'

'So, you're going home in three weeks and leaving me alone?'

'Oh, darling, I'll be back before you know it. Just need to show my face, make some sympathetic noises, promise to look into things, then I'll head back. It will hardly impact on our holiday, I promise.'

'Hmm. Well, now you've phoned Lavinia and shown me around this tiny excuse for a house, what do we do next?'

Crispin's eyes glinted with delight as he put his arms around her and pressed himself tightly against her. 'Ah, now. I'm awfully glad you asked me that question.'

CHAPTER EIGHT

Eden knew, without a shadow of a doubt, that the minute she got home she would throttle Honey. It wasn't going at all as she'd imagined. It had seemed simple when it was all theoretical. Just be horrible to a grumpy, middle-aged farmer who had, after all, agreed to keep Honey a prisoner, and use her as an unpaid babysitter. At least, that was Honey's take on it, and in spite of her compassion for his predicament, Eden had tried hard to see it from that point of view. And, given that scenario, how difficult could it be? There was no way she could have predicted that he'd be gorgeous; she could never have known he'd have raven curls that were crying out to have her fingers run through them, or brown eyes as dark and shining as tempered chocolate. He was far tastier than *any* chocolate, which wasn't something she'd thought she'd say about any man. He did things to her that poor Joshua couldn't have imagined, even in his wildest dreams. One look at that face and body, and she had been overcome with a strange desire to sweep clean the kitchen table, drag him onto it, and do her level best to heal the north-south divide. It was all most unexpected.

Having no desire to hurry downstairs to face a bunch of people who already despised her, she set about unpacking the cases, taking her time to unfold and hang up the clothes Honey had packed for her. She knew she should have insisted on doing her own packing. This stuff was useless. Half the clothes Honey had selected were hopelessly impractical for life on a farm, and the rest of it was probably far too tight for her. Eden was fairly slim, but Honey was a stick insect. She rarely ate anything substantial, preferring instead to pick at fruit, the odd prawn and bits of salad, all washed down with copious amounts of expensive mineral water. Eden, who shared

Cain's love of steak and ale pie, and treacle pudding and custard, couldn't see it was worth it, considering there was only around a stone between them. She'd far rather squeeze into a bigger size and eat.

Once she'd hung the clothes up in the wardrobe and stuffed the last of her underwear—thankfully, her own—into the drawers, she sank onto the bed and wondered what to do next. She checked her phone. As predicted, there was no signal, although it didn't really matter. She had no one to call. Her mum and dad were, no doubt, out and about in Tenerife, and Honey would kill her if she interrupted her. She wondered how she and Crispin were getting on, then pushed the thought away. She really didn't want to think about that, and, anyway, she was still feeling guilty that, by taking Honey's place, she was allowing the two of them to cheat on his unsuspecting wife.

Muffled voices drifted up from outside, and standing, she edged close to the window. The rain had finally stopped, and, peering round the net curtain, which was nowhere near as dingy as the ones downstairs, she spotted Daisy collecting the washing from the line in the garden. The girls were helping, and there was a lot of giggling going on. As she watched them, her heart melted. The girls were the spitting image of their father, and had therefore won her over already. Eliot obviously adored them, too, although she suspected George was the apple of his eye. The way his face had lit up when Daisy brought him into the room and how he'd immediately took hold of him revealed how precious the little boy was to him.

George was nothing like Eliot, having blue eyes and fair hair, but his chubby cheeks and dimpled smile were adorable. Eliot had been careful not to reveal too much of what he was thinking in front of her, but when she'd insulted his son, he'd really reacted. She realised George couldn't have been very old when his mother died. She'd been killed roughly two years ago, and George was about two now. How tough it must have been for Eliot to have been left with two little girls and a baby to care for. How had he coped? Was he looking for a replacement mother for them?

Was it Daisy he had in mind?

There was no doubt she had a crush on him. It was obvious from the way she gazed adoringly at him, and how she'd worked so hard to take care of the house and children that day. How did Daisy feel about Eliot having a new guest, Eden wondered. She was quite pretty, with a round face, dimples, large brown eyes and a shiny brown bob, and she looked a similar age to Eden. There was quite a lot there to attract Eliot, and the children seemed fond of her, anyway.

Realising she may as well face the music and go downstairs, Eden moved away from the window. A glance at her watch revealed that Cain would be telephoning the farm pretty soon, to check up on her. She still had to think of an excuse not to talk to him.

In the kitchen, she found Eliot at the table, his hands cupping a chipped mug. George sat in a highchair next to him, while Eliot encouraged him to drink his juice from the plastic cup he clutched in his chubby little hands.

Eden sat opposite her new employer, so she could get a good view of that gorgeous face. He was irresistible, and the way he interacted with the little boy was lovely. Watching them, she felt another pang for their loss. They'd all been through so much. It was so unfair.

'Your tea went cold, so I threw it away. Make yersen another one, if you like.'

That snapped her out of her daydreaming. She had to remember who she was supposed to be, and stop mooning around after him like a lovesick teenager. 'Charming,' she said. 'Do you always treat your guests so well?'

'Never had a guest before,' he said. 'And after this, I doubt I'll have another.'

'Well, I certainly won't be recommending you to anyone, that's for sure,' she said.

'You're not exactly a guest, any road. You're here to work. I'm not putting you up for nowt, remember. And them little lasses will keep you on your toes when school breaks up. Not to mention miladdo here.'

He nodded towards George, who seemed to be enjoying himself tremendously, taking mouthfuls of juice and then spitting it back into his cup.

'He has his father's manners, I see,' said Eden.

Eliot's eyes narrowed. 'He's a good lad. Reckon you're not used to kiddies. Probably don't know owt about them. Well, you'd better learn and fast. I'm not happy about you taking care of them, and if I had any other choice, I would take it.'

'I feel so special.'

'You know as well as I do, you're here on sufferance.' He looked at her, obviously curious. 'What did you do, any road?'

'What do you mean, what did I do?'

'Oh, come on. Strikes me that with the kind of life Cain Carmichael's led, it would take a lot to shock him. Your mother says he was desperate to get you out of the way, and if you've done something to make him send you all the way up here so I can keep an eye on you, it must be something big. You must have been a very bad lass.' His lips twitched in amusement.

Eden watched them, fascinated. He had a beautiful mouth. She wondered what those lips would feel like, pressing against her own. And the way he said, "You must have been a very bad lass," in that broad Yorkshire accent, was making her feel very peculiar. She was glad she'd sat down. Her legs felt suddenly rather shaky.

'Well?'

'Well, what?'

'What did you do?'

'I—nothing. I didn't—'

Luckily for Eden, the back door flew open and the two girls ran into the room, followed closely by Daisy carrying the basket of wet washing.

She looked at Eliot, then at Eden, who sensed that the sight of the two of them sitting together wasn't exactly a welcome one to her. 'Right, that's that brought in,' she said, far too brightly. 'Reckon the rain won't hold off for long, so I'll put this lot in the dryer. Shame. I was hoping I'd have time to iron it all before I left.'

So, she'd done the washing? It was too good an opportunity to miss. Eden studied her nails carefully, mainly because she couldn't bear to see Daisy's face when she said what she was going to say.

'You did the washing, did you? I take it the washing machine's broken? Or did you stick the dirty laundry on the line and hope the rain would wash it clean?'

'What are you on about?' Daisy's chin tilted defiantly.

'Well, are the clothes always that shade of grey, or did you have an accident with a black sock?'

Ophelia looked puzzled. 'They always look like that,' she said.

Eden hoped her face wasn't as red as Daisy's. So, Eliot had turned the clothes grey? Well, that was embarrassing. She wanted to crawl under the table and hide, but Honey would never have done that. Instead, she laughed and said, 'Goodness. Maybe it's time you got a new washing machine.'

Eliot stared at her. 'Have you finished?' He stood up. 'Come on, Daisy, I'll run you home. You've done enough for today, and I can never repay you.'

'Oh, I bet you could,' said Eden.

'You don't have to take me home,' said Daisy. 'Honestly, I can walk.'

'I won't hear of it. Honey can look after the kids. It will be good practice for her, and she's got to start somewhere.'

'Well, if you're sure ...'

'Of course he's sure. Don't be such a fool,' said Eden. 'If I were you, I'd stop playing hard to get. It's not very convincing, and it's terribly unattractive in a woman of your age.'

She wondered what on earth had happened to her. It was becoming frighteningly easy to act like Honey. That's what you got for hanging around with someone who didn't give a fig for other people's feelings for so long.

Daisy hung her head, but Eliot looked livid. 'Drop the attitude,' he told her. 'Remember your manners, or I might just forget mine.'

Eden flushed as the two of them stared at each other. It was a few moments before she became aware that Ophelia was tugging on her father's arm.

'Dad, Dad, the phone's ringing.' She was wide-eyed, as if they didn't get many calls.

'You can get it,' said Eliot, nodding coldly at Eden. 'It will be your father, any road. He said he'd check you got here all right.'

Eden felt sick with panic. She couldn't possibly talk to Cain. One word from her, and he'd know immediately she wasn't his daughter.

'Well?'

'I'm not answering your phone,' she said haughtily. 'That call could easily be for you. What am I, now, your receptionist?'

Daisy gasped.

Eliot shook his head. 'Unbelievable.' He stormed into the hallway, leaving her sitting in the chair, trying not to tremble.

'Here's a shock,' he called after a moment. 'It's for you. It's your dad.'

Eden swallowed.

Ophelia looked at her with interest. 'Don't you want to talk to your dad?'

'Not particularly.'

Libby's eyes were full of sympathy. 'Has he been mean to you?'

Eden smiled suddenly. 'Yes, yes, he has. He's been terribly mean. I don't want to speak to him, so I won't.'

Ophelia ran into the hallway. 'Honey doesn't want to talk to her dad. He's been mean to her.'

There was some muttering, then Eliot reappeared in the kitchen. 'What are you waiting for? Your dad wants you.'

'Well, I don't want him,' said Eden firmly.

'Have you gone mad?'

'Certainly not, though I think it's only a matter of time. I mean, look at this place. My father has the cheek to send me to this wilderness, and then expects me to talk to him on the phone as if he's done nothing wrong. This is all his fault. I have nothing to say to him, and you can tell him that from me, thank you very much.'

Eliot glanced round at his daughters, who were watching Eden in awe. George took the opportunity to tip his cup of juice all over the table, which seemed to snap Daisy out of her trance. She rushed to get a cloth, and Eliot leaned towards Eden.

She suppressed a shiver as his lips brushed against her ear. 'Don't for a minute think this is how it's going to be,' he murmured. 'It's day one, my kids are here, and I'm trying hard to be a gentleman, but be warned ... my patience is wearing thin already. Don't push me.'

It was terribly wrong of her, but Eden couldn't help thinking how attractive he looked when he was angry. She sat still, as he strode back into the hallway. She heard him telling Honey's father that his daughter had arrived safely, and that she was behaving like a spoilt madam and throwing her weight around already. He assured Cain he would keep a close eye on her, and he'd keep her busy. That should reassure Cain, at any rate. Honey was behaving exactly as he'd expect.

Realising she'd been holding her breath, she slowly released the air. That was one bullet dodged, anyway.

Daisy pushed past her, carrying the basket of washing under her arm as she headed towards the boot room, where the dryer was kept. There was definite curiosity in her eyes. She would have to watch that one. If Daisy got the slightest inkling that all was not as it should be, Eden had no doubt she would do everything in her power to make sure Eliot got the truth.

Daisy already saw her as a threat. Eden would have to up her game.

****

Lavinia moaned softly as Gregorio's expert hands smoothed the suntan lotion into her shoulders.

'You like that?' he asked.

'Divine. You know just how to do it.'

'Turn over, and I will rub some onto your chest.'

She laughed. 'Oh, no, you don't. We both know where that will lead.'

'That would be a bad thing?' He leaned forward and kissed her neck.

She closed her eyes for a moment, sorely tempted to take him up on his offer. The trouble was, it was so lovely out here, lying by the pool, soaking up the rays of glorious Portuguese sunshine. She wasn't sure she could be bothered to go indoors and start all that messiness again. The man was insatiable, and as flattering as it was to be wanted so badly, by a rather attractive hunk at least ten years her junior, the fact was that her main priorities this summer were to sunbathe, swim, drink plenty of delicious cocktails, and get a deep, golden tan. Sex was all very well and good, but she'd never been short of it. Crispin kept her well satisfied, and she could have Gregorio any time she liked. Sunshine and leisure time, on the other hand, were in short supply back in Windleby-on-the-Weir. Gregorio could wait until after dinner. She didn't want him to start taking her for granted, after all.

'Be a darling and fetch me another Margarita.'

He tutted, clearly annoyed. 'You cannot have one afterwards?'

'Afterwards? Don't make assumptions. I'm not here to spend my entire time in bed with you. Now, let's both have a drink. Or maybe you'd like a dip in the pool? Might cool you down a bit.'

'Be careful I do not freeze on you.'

'I sincerely doubt that will happen, but if you're not enjoying yourself, feel free to leave. After all, I've only paid for this fabulous villa, your flights, and a whole new wardrobe of clothes. Still, if you want to go back to your bedsit in England, feel free.'

He stared down at her with panic in his eyes.

She smiled at him. 'On the other hand, you can stop moaning and enjoy the break from your sad little gardening job. Why don't you make us two Margaritas? We can have a lazy afternoon in the sun, enjoy a cosy dinner, and then head to the bedroom, where you can do what you do best. What do you say?'

He hesitated but nodded. 'You know it is only because you are so beautiful. It is hard to keep my hands off you.'

'Yes, I know. You're awfully sweet. I shall let you put your hands anywhere you want tonight, I promise.'

His eyes lit up, and as he headed into the villa to fix their drinks, she sighed. It was like training a puppy, really. A system of withholding attention and rewarding good behaviour. He'd get the hang of it, eventually.

She tutted when her mobile phone started to ring and made the enormous effort to reach over into her bag, which was lying beside her sun lounger.

'Hello?'

'Darling, is that you?'

'Well, of course it's me, Daddy. Who else would it be? Anything to report?'

'They arrived yesterday. Just as we thought, she's there with him. It's disgusting, really. She looks about eighteen. What on earth is he playing at?'

'Oh, I think we both know what he's playing at.'

'I don't know how you can be so calm. You're letting him get away with it. I felt like banging on that door last night, and kicking the pair of them out of that bed and down the stairs and all the way back to Windleby-on-the-Weir. They're laughing at you.'

'Daddy, I can assure you, I am not letting Crispin get away with it. When this is over—and it will be over, as soon as he's got over this silly infatuation with the girl—I shall make him pay. I can promise you that. In the meantime, why rock the boat? He has a promising career ahead of him. I'm not going to let some stupid fling jeopardise that. As long as they're discreet, I'll leave them to it.'

'Why go all the way to Portugal to leave them alone? Why make it easy for them? I don't understand.'

'Daddy, I explained all this. If I'd been at home all summer with him, he'd have had to sneak around so he could see her. The chances of him being spotted by the press would increase beyond measure. With me out here, he was free to take the little scrubber away to that hovel in Dorset, where no one can get near, and no one will even think to look. It was damage limitation.'

'Maybe so. It doesn't seem fair to me, though.'

Lavinia gave a martyred sigh. 'I know. I knew when I married him I would probably have to make sacrifices. Being a politician's wife is never easy. I'll be all right here, Daddy. I'm catching up on my reading, and I'm doing a lot of swimming.'

'Are you sure you don't want me to come out there? I

can keep you company. I hate to think of you all alone in a foreign country.'

Lavinia sat up in alarm. 'No, Daddy! Certainly not. It's vital you keep an eye on Crispin and the slapper. We must make absolutely sure he doesn't mess this up. Any sign he's in danger of being discovered, and you must tip him off, do you understand? There are bigger things at stake here than some silly little fling with a girl who looks as if she's barely left school.'

'Well, I suppose you're right. As long as you're sure.'

'I'm sure, Daddy.' Lavinia put her finger to her lips as Gregorio wandered over, carrying the cocktails. 'Speak soon. Love to Francesca.' She replaced the phone in her bag and leaned back in her sun lounger, heaving a sigh of relief.

'Your father? Everything is all right?'

She took a sip from the glass. 'Everything's perfect, darling.'

She thought about Crispin, tucked away in his sister's Dorset cottage, with the blonde bimbo. Honey Carmichael, spoilt little rich girl, with not two brain cells to rub together. Not that Crispin would care about that. It wasn't her brain he was interested in. Oh, no.

She closed her eyes, trying to shut out the images of her husband and his tart writhing around in that bed, or maybe on the beach. It was secluded and completely private. Maybe they'd risk it. Crispin was usually up for anything, and Honey was so young. She'd have boundless energy and very few inhibitions.

She sighed.

'You are sure you are okay?' Gregorio's voice was loaded with concern. His attentiveness and obvious desire for her were like balm to her wounded soul.

She reached over, depositing her drink on the ground, then held out her hand to him. He took it uncertainly.

'You know, darling, you really are divine. I can't think

why I wanted to wait 'til tonight. Put down your glass—that's right. Now, where did you say you'd like to rub that suntan lotion?'

CHAPTER NINE

There were noises coming from downstairs. Eden opened her eyes reluctantly. The room was still dark and she felt as if she'd only slept for a couple of hours. What the hell time was it? She turned over and reached for her phone, pressing the button to see the screen. Six thirty! She only woke up at six thirty if Honey or Cain staggered into the house after a night on the town. No one at the Carmichael home surfaced before ten. Eden herself had got into a pattern of staying up 'til past one and then sleeping in 'til around nine. She was amazed she'd fallen asleep last night so early, but then, it had been a long journey. She could still use another couple of hours' sleep, though. She just hoped whoever it was down there would quieten down sharpish.

At a sudden tapping at her door, she rubbed her eyes and called uncertainly, 'Who is it?'

The door was pushed open. Libby stood there, smiling shyly. 'Dad said to tell you your cup of tea's ready and your breakfast won't be a minute.'

'You're joking, right?'

Libby looked at her in confusion. 'No. Why would I be joking? Aren't you hungry?'

'It's six thirty!'

'I know. You've slept for ages. Come on, it's a full English. I'm starving!'

She ran downstairs, and Eden sat up in bed, pushing her hair out of her eyes and yawning. Was this what it would be like every day?

She reached for her slippers and pulled them on, then stood up and went over to the window. Pulling the curtains apart, she blinked as daylight flooded the room. So it was true, it really was morning. It wasn't the brightest start to the day, though. Surely, it wouldn't rain again today? There must have been a full month's quota tipped on Yorkshire yesterday.

'Bacon and eggs coming right up,' said Eliot, as she shuffled into the kitchen. He paused, spatula in hand, as he took in the sight of her, standing there in her pyjamas. 'I'm guessing you're not a morning person?'

'This isn't morning,' she informed him. 'It's still the middle of the night.'

He laughed. 'Don't be daft. Here, sit down and get that cup of tea down you.'

'At least there's waiter service in this hotel,' she said, falling into a chair and cupping the mug with one hand while stifling a yawn with another.

'Hmm, you can get them ideas out of your head,' he told her, dishing sausages onto the plates. 'Now you're here, you can take over the breakfasts. Reckon it's my turn to be waited on, for a change.'

She thought he had a point. If he was up this early he deserved to have his breakfast cooked for him, at the very least. She doubted Honey would agree, though. 'Certainly. If you don't mind waiting until around ten o'clock, I'll be happy to help.'

'Ten o'clock! Day's almost over by then. You should be up at six. Set your alarm. You'll soon get used to it.'

'I sincerely doubt that. I'm sure it won't hurt you to do your own breakfast and let the rest of us sleep in. Throw a few Coco Pops in a bowl, or something.'

The look he gave her told her exactly what he thought of that idea, and Ophelia and Libby stared at her, obviously sharing his opinion.

She took a sip of tea to stop herself from laughing at their faces. Honey would be proud of her. 'Where's George?' she asked, seeing as he wasn't in the kitchen.

'Still asleep,' said Eliot. 'Doesn't usually wake up 'til gone seven.'

'So, let me get this straight,' she said. 'A two-year-old

has more sense than the rest of you put together? Says it all, really.'

'There are things to be done around the farm,' said Eliot, obviously struggling to be patient. 'It's not a nine-to-five job. I can't put on a suit and head out to work at ten-to nine, you know. I have to get on with it.'

'And why do the girls have to be up so early? I mean, if you have to be out at this ungodly hour, fair enough, but why make them suffer? Can't they have a lie in, or do you want them to be as downtrodden as you?'

He poured some tomato gravy onto the plate and slammed it onto the table in front of her. 'They had to get up when I got up. There was no one else to see to them, so they had to have their breakfast when I did, and that gave them plenty of time to get themselves ready for school. Daisy used to come over, if she could, for around seven thirty. She'd see to George and take him home with her for a few hours before work, while I got the girls to school and got on with the jobs round the farm.'

Eden thought what a palaver it all sounded. He must have really struggled to keep things going without Jemima, and of course they'd developed a routine. They'd have had to. She thought he probably wouldn't have managed at all without Daisy. She'd obviously been a massive help to him. What was in it for her, though? As if she couldn't guess.

'So, now I'm here and school finishes in a couple of days, I suppose we can develop a new routine,' she said to the girls. 'As in, let's all stay in bed, except for Daddy. At least until George wakes up.'

Ophelia frowned. 'We always have our breakfast with Dad. And, besides, we collect the eggs and let the hens out, and feed them and water them.'

'And I've got Flora to see to,' said Libby. 'She's our pony. Got to give her fresh water, and sometimes she needs brushing, and in the winter, there's feed to sort and mucking out to do, and fresh hay and clean straw.'

'The child is joking, of course?' said Eden in her best Honey voice.

Eliot said nothing, but put a plate of bread in the middle of the table.

'And the dogs and Mummy's cat need feeding,' continued Ophelia.

'And Ophelia's usually got homework to finish,' said Libby.

'No I don't!' said Ophelia, glaring at her.

Libby gave her a knowing look and reached for some bread.

'Dry bread?' said Eden. 'So, this is your idea of a full English breakfast? Sausages, fried eggs, mushrooms, bacon, all smothered in this tomato gravy stuff, and with dry bread to dip in. Well, you don't get this kind of thing at The Fat Duck.'

'What's a fat duck got to do with it?' asked Ophelia.

'Of course, I've eaten bacon ice cream. That was very good.'

Ophelia's and Libby's eyes widened. 'Bacon ice cream? You can't get bacon ice cream.'

'Yes, you can. If you go to the right places, of course. Heston Blumenthal is a creative genius.' She was mimicking Honey perfectly and rather impressing herself. 'I drew the line at the snail porridge, I admit, but it beats dry bread and tinned tomatoes.'

She lowered her head quickly to hide her face. Eliot was glowering again. Gosh, he looked devastatingly handsome when he glowered. Not that he didn't look handsome all the time, but the glower really added a certain something. She was sure she had lust in her eyes, and she mustn't let him see that. It was worth annoying him to see that smouldering expression. He was sex on a stick. How inconvenient.

Handing the girls their plates and telling them to close

their mouths and stop looking so gormless, he finally sat down and began to eat. God, he even looked sexy when he ate. Sort of all manly and hunky.

She thought of Joshua, picking up everything and inspecting it before nibbling at it as if it would bite back, and Cain wolfing everything down as if he was under a four-minute warning. She'd often thought he didn't taste a single thing. Food didn't stay in his mouth long enough for his taste buds to start working.

Noticing her looking at him, Eliot paused, returning her gaze with a challenge. 'Aye? Summat up?'

He had a sausage on his fork, which he held in the air while he waited for her answer. Eden gulped. 'No, nothing. I like to see a man enjoying his food.'

He looked suspicious, as if trying to decide if she was insulting him or not. After a moment's hesitation, he carried on eating. 'Tuck in,' he told her. 'Not got all day.'

She did as she was told, surprised to find how tasty it all was. She wondered what bacon ice cream actually tasted like. Honey had raved about it, but she was just showing off because her friend had managed to bag a table after being on a waiting list since she was about four. Personally, three rashers of back bacon and a couple of Cumberland sausages was like manna from Heaven for Eden. She ate it much slower than she would have liked to and hoped Eliot wouldn't tell Cain how she'd finished the lot, even mopping up the last of the gravy with a slice of bread. Cain would be instantly on his guard if he knew, because Honey would have run a mile from that little lot.

'Right.' Eliot pushed back his chair and stood, collecting his plate. 'Time to get on. Oh, looks like it's raining again,' he added, glancing at the window, where the first drops hit the glass. 'You all right to do the pots?' he asked her.

She'd expected to be doing them, anyway, but she rolled her eyes, and tutted. 'I suppose so. If I must.'

'Aye, you must, at least for this morning. I've got enough on. Lorry's coming today.'

'What lorry?'

Libby looked sad. 'For the lambs.'

'What do you mean?'

Ophelia mimed slitting her own throat. 'End of the road for the fattest lambs today.'

'You're joking!' Eden wondered how an eight-year-old could be so blasé about the whole thing. 'But lambs are so sweet.'

Eliot looked at her in obvious despair. 'Well, yes, but they're also where I make my living. Enjoy the bacon did you?'

'Yes, but—'

'So you're not a vegetarian, then. Pigs have as much going for them as sheep, but you didn't say owt about tucking into your full English, did you?'

'But lambs are babies!'

'Aye, and their meat fetches a much better price than mutton, sad to say. Not that it's a fortune. Don't know how we keep going, half the time.'

'Can't you sell the wool and live off that?' she asked.

Eliot glanced at his daughters, and they all laughed.

Eden frowned. 'What's so funny?'

'You don't know the price of wool, then,' said Libby.

'Costs me more to shear the bloody sheep than I get back for the fleece,' said Eliot.

'But, I thought—' Eden shrugged. 'I know that in the Cotswolds, fortunes were made in wool. Half the place exists because of the fleeces.'

'That were a long time ago. Things have changed. My sheep are Swaledales—good, strong, hardy sheep. Their wool's only really used for carpets and rugs, and the like. There's no money in that side of things. Not anymore.' He sighed. 'Not much in the meat, either, truth to tell. Hard times. Hard times.' He shook his head and put Ophelia's empty plate in the sink with his own. 'I've put some breakfast in the microwave for George. Can you listen out for him? And can you make sure the girls are dressed and ready for school by eight? I'll pop back around then, to give you directions to the school. It's about nine miles away. I'll put George's car seat in your car, too.'

'Where are you going?' she asked, flummoxed to realise she would be alone with the children.

'Like I said, busy day. Lorry's coming for some of my lambs and some of me barren ewes, and I've got drenching to do, too.'

'Drenching?'

'Worming. My ewes, and the lambs I want to keep, need dosing.'

'Oh, lovely,' she said.

'Do you want to help me collect the eggs?' asked Ophelia. 'You can meet the hens.'

'Or you could help me with Flora,' suggested Libby.

Eden shuddered. Horses scared her to death. 'Er, no thanks. It's raining, in case you hadn't noticed. Again. I think I'll stay inside this morning, get my bearings. Maybe tomorrow?'

'Can you feed the cat?' asked Eliot. 'I'll sort the dogs out, no worries. They eat in the boot room, but they all sleep in the barn, apart from Tuppence. Bella, though, is definitely a house pet.' He motioned to a cupboard. 'You'll find her food in there. Very particular, she is, so follow Libby's instructions. I'll be back to see the girls off to school.'

'Hang on!' said Eden, starting to panic. 'What about George?'

'What about him? Like I said, his breakfast's in the microwave. Make him a cup of tea, he likes that. His cup's in the cupboard. Make sure his tea's cool enough. No sugar. He had a bath last night, so just clean his teeth, brush his hair, and stick a clean nappy and fresh clothes on him.'

'Nappy! I don't know how to change a nappy.' She really didn't, either, and wasn't looking forward to learning.

Eliot sighed. 'Libby will show you. She's a dab hand.'

'Is she?' Eden looked at the little girl with respect.

'Can I go now?' he asked her impatiently.

She nodded reluctantly. Talk about being thrown in at the deep end.

CHAPTER TEN

She managed to find the school. Eliot had hunted around and found an old letter from the headmaster and punched the postcode into her SatNav.

'Should be all right. Libby and Ophelia know the way, any road.' He'd planted a kiss on George's cheek. 'Don't you look smart with your hair all brushed to the side.' He'd grinned. 'You managed to change his nappy, then?'

'Hmm.' Eden glanced at Libby. 'She helped. A lot. God, what the hell have you been feeding him?'

'There's nothing wrong with him. He's a growing lad. I reckon we'll have to start potty training him in a couple of months. The lasses were out of nappies by the time they were two and a half.'

Eden screwed up her nose. 'What's with the *we*? I won't be here in a couple of months, so you can deal with that little task all on your lonesome, thank you very much.'

Eliot had rubbed his forehead. 'Aye, happen you're right.'

He'd looked so weary for a moment that Eden had longed to give him a comforting hug and tell him she'd happily stay and help out a bit longer, but Honey wouldn't have, so she couldn't. Besides, he'd think she'd gone mad. She was practically a stranger, and, quite honestly, she had the feeling that Eliot wasn't one to encourage random hugs.

Ravensbridge was almost ten miles from the farm—a large village on the banks of the Skimmer. Square, stone cottages with slate roofs gathered round a village green, where several old men in waterproof jackets and flat caps sat on wooden benches, watching their world go by and not seeming to notice the fine rain that still persisted. As far as Skimmerdale went, it appeared Ravensbridge was practically cosmopolitan, containing a small police station, the primary school, a tiny doctor's surgery, a museum of farming life, and a cluster of shops that sold crafts, home-baked goods, general provisions and newspapers, and outdoor clothing. There were three pubs, and even a post office, which seemed to be the only post office between Fleetsthorpe and Kirkby Skimmer. There was also a children's playground, which Libby and Ophelia assured Eden they had visited on several occasions with their friends after school. Eden wasn't sure if they were hinting that she could take them, like they'd been taken before, but she wasn't about to make any promises until she'd cleared it with their father first.

The primary school itself seemed to consist of three stone buildings, with large casement windows and big double wooden doors, that circled a concrete playground. It was about half the size of Eden's own primary school, and seemed rather old-fashioned and quaint in comparison.

'You've got everything?' she asked, as the girls pulled up the hoods of their coats and climbed out of the car. Not that it mattered. She could hardly go all the way back to Fleetsthorpe, if they'd forgotten anything, could she?

'Yeah. We're fine.' Libby tugged on her skirt, which was a little too short in Eden's opinion, and glanced nervously at her sister.

Eden frowned. The little girl looked pensive. 'Are you okay, Libby?'

'Yes, 'course I am. I'll see you at three. You *will* be here?'

'Of course. Right where I am now.'

Libby nodded, and Ophelia hooked her arm through her sister's. 'Come on, Libby. Only two more days, and then we're free.'

They walked through the school gates, and Eden watched them thoughtfully. Libby's reluctance was apparent. Was there a problem, she wondered?

George let out a wail of boredom, and she blinked, turning round to face him. 'You can shut that up, for a start, young fella,' she told him. He grinned back at her, and she found herself smiling. He was a real cutie, even though he was capable of producing nappies that could be used as chemical weapons. 'Come on, then. Back to the fray,' she said.

Keeping George occupied while tackling the housework wasn't easy. He got bored very easily, and Eden soon found that sticking him in front of the television and hoping for the best wasn't an option. Instead, she sat him in his highchair and gave him a cup of milk and a banana, while she mopped the kitchen floor and washed the unit doors and worktops. There was all that ironing to do, too. Daisy had washed and dried it, but it was still sitting in the laundry basket in the boot room. She brought it into the kitchen and put it all on the table. George clapped his hands and reached out towards the piles of clothes.

'You want to help me sort it?' She smiled at him and began to pull out various socks, holding them up one at a time. 'Shall we count them? One, two, three ...'

George laughed and made noises that could well have been him counting along with her, or, at least, trying to say the words.

After an hour of ironing, during which time she'd pulled faces, sang songs, and generally talked herself hoarse to George, Eden finally unplugged the iron and folded up the ironing board. 'Right. Now what?'

She looked up as a pitiful mewling came to her and Bella strolled into the kitchen looking annoyed.

'Crap! I forgot to feed you, didn't I?' She hunted in the cupboard, found the cat food and then realised she didn't know what she was supposed to feed her, and Libby wasn't around to ask. 'Oh, well, pot luck for you,' she said, squinting at the label and not understanding a word of the directions. She unbuckled George and carried him with her to the boot room, where Bella's bowl was. Eventually, after a lot of faffing about, putting George back in his chair, and trying to decide how much biscuit to add to the meat, she plonked Bella's bowl back on the kitchen floor and told her she could eat in there for once, as a special treat. 'Don't tell anyone,' she added, wondering if she was going a little bit crazy.

Hunting around, she found some polish and a duster and carried them, and George, into the living room. Plonking George on the sofa, she began to dust. George got bored after about ten minutes, though, and started to whine.

'Won't be a minute,' she told him.

After polishing, she picked him up to cuddle him and realised he felt damp. Drat, she would have to change his nappy again. After finding the baby wipes and nappies, she laid him carefully on the carpet and took off his nappy, praying she would be able to put a fresh one on him with no problems.

Luckily, he hadn't done anything vile, and it was a quick and easy job to change him. After pulling up his trousers, she left him on the carpet, while she rushed into the kitchen, deposited the nappy in the bin and washed her hands. Then she rushed back into the room, picked him up, and sat him on her knee. It was only half past ten and she was knackered already.

'Shall we put the telly on for a bit? Bound to be something there to occupy you.'

Maybe, if she could distract him for half an hour, she could change the litter tray. It definitely needed doing. Once he fell asleep, she might risk vacuuming the bedrooms and checking all the beds were made. Then she'd have to think about dinner. Or tea, as the Harlands called it. She picked up the remote and flicked the television on, putting her arm around George and letting him snuggle into her. She'd let him settle and then she'd tackle the litter tray.

'Having a nice, easy morning, are you?'

George whooped in delight. 'Daddy!'

Eliot smiled and ruffled the little boy's hair. 'All right, Georgie? So, not finding things too difficult, then, Honey?'

Eden glared at him. The injustice of it! After all her hard work, too. 'I was trying to settle George, then I was going to change the litter tray.'

'Right.' He obviously didn't believe her.

She stared at him crossly. 'What are you doing back, anyway? Aren't you supposed to be getting your baby lambs ready to be murdered?'

He didn't rise to the bait. 'Cup of tea time. I'm parched. Stick 'kettle on, will you?'

'What did your last slave die of?' she snapped, but got up anyway. The least she could do was make him a drink, even if his attitude was infuriating.

'Did you find the school all right?' he asked, when she returned with the drinks.

'Yes, no problem.' She hesitated. 'Is Libby okay at school?'

'What do you mean?' He peered at her over the mug. 'Okay in what way?'

'I don't know. Just, she seemed a bit reluctant to go inside.'

'Oh.' He shook his head. 'Probably wants to hang around here. Can't blame her, can you? And she's besotted with that pony of theirs, so I reckon she'd far rather be riding round the place than stuck in some classroom. I were the same at her age.'

'I don't doubt it.'

George seemed enthralled by some colourful television programme he was watching and kept pointing at the screen and insisting Eliot look, so Eden didn't pursue the subject.

After ten minutes, Eliot stood up. 'Right, well, thanks for the drink. I'll be in around half twelve, if you wouldn't mind having some dinner ready.'

'What am I? Your personal servant?'

'Thought that was why you were here,' he pointed out. 'To help. After all, I'm not charging you anything to stay here.'

'I should hope not!'

'You'd be amazed how much folks pay to stay in the Dales. You're lucky to get it all for free.' He scowled at her, planted a kiss on George's head, and left the house.

Eden folded her arms. Typical that he'd come in just as she had sat down. Now he'd never believe all the work she'd done that morning. Although, she supposed, that could be a good thing. If Cain rang that night, it would set alarm bells ringing if Eliot praised her for the quality of her ironing. Honey didn't even know where the iron was kept.

George finally fell asleep at twenty-past eleven, and Eden whizzed round the place with a vacuum cleaner and tidied the girls' beds. She hesitated outside Eliot's room, wondering if she should clean in there, but decided against it. It felt like too much, too soon. She would ask him if he wanted anything doing at the weekend. She supposed she ought to think about his lunch, or rather, dinner. That was confusing enough. Dinner at lunchtime and tea at dinnertime. Crazy. Oh, and there was another problem. How could she prepare him good, hearty meals, when Honey couldn't cook?

She searched the cupboards and fridge, wondering what she could rustle up that would fill his belly while not demanding too many skills. In the end, she made him a pile of cheese sandwiches and hoped for the best.

When he entered the kitchen at twenty-past twelve, she

was dismayed to see he wasn't alone. Two men were with him—one so old, Eden wondered how he still stood unaided. The other was young and pleasant enough. They both nodded at her, where she stood at the sink, almost up to her elbows in suds as she washed the cups and knives.

'This is Mickey,' Eliot said, indicating the old man. 'He used to work for my father, and he's forgotten more about sheep than I'll ever know. This other fella's Adey. He's hoping to become a farmer, and he helps me out now and then.'

'Thought we'd come and see the new member of staff.' Mickey cackled.

Eden drew herself up indignantly. 'Do you mind? I'm hardly staff. I'm a guest.'

Mickey glanced at the other two. 'Eliot, fancy making tha guest wash pots,' he said, nodding at her in amusement.

She remembered the suds and scowled, ignoring Eliot's laugh. 'I think you'll find you're the staff,' she said coolly, thinking Honey would make mincemeat of these two, but she daren't push it that far.

'No, they're not,' said Eliot. 'They're friends, and I couldn't have managed without them. Mickey retired years ago, but he's always ready to lend a hand when I need it, and Adey's at agricultural college. Comes up here when he can, to get hands-on experience.'

'Oh. Well, where are your real staff?' she asked.

'What staff? Just me and these two, as and when.'

'But you must have hundreds of sheep!' she said, astonished.

'Over a thousand. Like I told you this morning, there's hardly any money in it these days. Can't afford full-time help anymore. Usually, it's just me. Except for busy times, of course, like lambing. Mickey does most of the shearing, and someone comes to do the dipping now. Too many rules and regulations, see. Other than that—well, now you know why I'm needing a bit of help. Speaking of which, did you do me some dinner?'

'Yes.' She felt embarrassed as she handed him the plate of cheese sandwiches.

'By heck,' said Mickey, shaking his head. 'What a feast. Did tha go to catering college to learn that, love?'

If he only knew, she thought. She could wipe the smirks off their faces and rustle them up a meal to marvel over, if only she wasn't being Honey. Instead, she tried to look affronted and informed them of her expensive private education, and her unique little shop in Upper Bourbury, failing to mention that it hadn't made a penny and was now closed permanently.

'Blimey,' said Adey. 'Should I curtsey?'

'Daft bugger,' said Eliot. He sat down and picked up a sandwich. 'You couldn't make these two one, could you? Hungry, lads?'

Lads! Mickey looked about a hundred and two. Still, she didn't mind making them a sandwich and a cup of tea.

'So, tha's Jemima's cousin, eh?' said Mickey, chewing on his sandwich ten minutes later, with what remained of his teeth.

'I am.' Eden tried to calculate the exact relationship, but it was too complicated for her. 'Well, second cousin, or something.'

'Hmm.' With one word, Mickey managed to convey exactly what he thought of her. Whether that was because he didn't think much to Jemima, or because she was part of the family that had snubbed Eliot's wife after their marriage, she couldn't be sure.

They looked round, as George called from the living room. 'I'll go,' said Eliot, standing up and leaving the kitchen.

'Good lad, that,' said Mickey, sucking loudly on his sandwich. 'Gave him a proper hard time.'

'Who did? Oh, you mean the family.' Well, she

couldn't argue with that. They'd been horrible, but knowing Freya, she was hardly surprised.

'He's been through hell,' said Mickey, leaning towards her and watching her with eyes that seemed to bore into her soul. 'Not that I'm saying owt about it. None of my business, like. Took us ages to bring him through it, didn't it, lad?'

Adey swallowed his crust and nodded. 'Oh, aye. Terrible times.'

'Yes, well, at least he's all right now,' said Eden.

'Does tha think? Well, think again,' said Mickey. 'Not that I'm saying owt, mind. Wouldn't betray a confidence, would I?'

'I'm sure you wouldn't,' said Eden.

'He's still not right. Not proper right. Mind, this is between me and thee, and I wouldn't say owt normally, but tha's going to be here with him for the next few weeks, and tha should know how it is.'

'Right.' Eden frowned. 'So, how is it?'

'He's delicate, like.' He must have seen her face because he shook his head impatiently. 'Not physically. Strong as an 'oss. I mean up here,' he said, tapping his temple, 'and in 'ere,' he added, putting a rather grubby hand over his heart. 'Bruised and battered, like. We don't talk about it,' he said with a sigh. 'But I know.'

'Oh,' said Eden. She didn't see what else there was to say.

'Tha'd best be good to him,' said Mickey sharply. 'No messing him about. Lovely lad, that. Salt o' t' earth.'

Eden nodded. Well, she could agree with him on that, even if she didn't have the first idea what Mickey was talking about.

CHAPTER ELEVEN

'So that's it. You're free now!'

Eden suppressed a smile, as Eliot swept his daughters into his arms and gave them a huge hug. It was hard not to show her delight at the little girls' excitement that the school term was finally finished and the holidays had officially begun. More than six weeks to run around, exploring the countryside, playing with the dogs, riding the pony, and generally having fun. Honey, however, wouldn't be thrilled at that prospect, so she turned away and busied herself making drinks and hunting around for some biscuits. They always seemed to be starving when they got home from school, and, as Eliot didn't really stop working 'til gone six, the evening meal was late. They needed something to fill the gap until then. She had queried why they couldn't have their meal earlier, but Eliot had been adamant they all ate together.

'With me out all day, and them stuck in school, it's our chance to sit at the table and catch up wi' what's been going on. Precious time. I'll not have you coming in and changing that to suit yersen.'

Eden had held up her hands in defence. 'Okay, it was just a suggestion. If you're happy to let your children starve for two hours, that's up to you.'

He'd given her a poisonous look and stamped outside. She hadn't suggested any more changes. Now, as she poured cups of juice, she realised this was where things really got tricky. The girls had been out most of the day up 'til that point—miles away at the school in Ravensbridge. She'd certainly attracted some attention when she turned up at the school gate in her bright yellow Beetle, and tottered into the playground in Honey's Jimmy Choos—bought over two years ago, and, though worn only twice, deemed fit for only Eden to wear now—and her leather biker jacket, which had cost over three hundred pounds from Whistles last winter, over an almost-new Stella McCartney day dress. That one outfit alone had cost more than Eden had earned in a month working at The Red Lion. No wonder the mothers of the other children had looked astonished. She felt ridiculously out of place and overdressed, and, although Honey owned some lovely clothes and Eden was thrilled to have been given them, they really weren't suitable for looking after children and tidying the house.

That was another problem. Eliot didn't seem to expect her to do anything, except look after George all day, take the girls to school and pick them up afterwards, feed them all and make sure they were safe. She'd assumed he'd demand she clean the house, but he hadn't. To her amazement, he'd washed up after both the evening meals she'd cooked, and she'd longed to tell him to sit down and let her do the dishes, but Honey wouldn't have dreamed of doing that, and she was desperately afraid he would give a glowing report to Cain, so she had to let Eliot get on with it. It made her feel heartless, particularly when she could see how tired he was after a day's work.

It was a good job men rarely noticed when housework had been done. She was vacuuming, dusting, ironing and washing, and he didn't even seemed to have realised. No wonder her mum complained so much about her dad's lack of appreciation, she thought.

'You'll have your work cut out now.' She hadn't realised he was standing beside her, and her hands shook as she tried to open the packet of biscuits. 'Do you think you're up to this?'

'I'm sure that, after a two-year-old, an eight and ten-year-old will be easy.'

He grinned. 'You've a lot to learn.' He had the most beautiful smile. She wished he'd smile more often, although, with having to put up with "Honey's" dreadful behaviour on top of the workload he had, expecting him to smile was probably too much.

'Are you in for the day?' she asked. He wasn't usually around when she brought the girls home from school, but he'd obviously made a special effort to be there to greet them on their last day of term.

He shook his head. 'Not finished yet. I'll probably be done in a couple of hours.'

'I'll have tea ready for six.'

'Aye. Grand.' He dropped kisses on the heads of all three children, and whistled to Lug, who was lying patiently under the table. Once he'd left, the kitchen felt empty.

Ophelia sidled up to her. 'What are we having for tea?'

That was another problem. Eden had racked her brains to think what sort of things Honey could cook. She was having to tread so carefully. With Cain in constant touch with Eliot, demanding to know in minute detail what she'd been up to, she could hardly start whipping up hearty casseroles and stews for Eliot, much as she'd like to. She'd remembered, with immense difficulty, that Honey had once cooked a stir-fry, and she'd managed to do a curry once, although that was using a jar of sauce and microwave rice. A quick search of Eliot's cupboards and fridge had revealed no jars of sauces or packets of noodles. or even any rice—microwave, or otherwise. She'd contented herself with sticking to basics like egg and chips, jacket potatoes and beans, and sausages and mash. It was a bit boring. She loved to cook—often putting her skills to use feeding the Carmichaels—and she thought the Harlands deserved something a bit better than they were getting. She would have to put her thinking cap on.

If only Cain would stop pestering Eliot for details, but he didn't seem about to give up. He had tried, in vain, to speak to her and seemed to have accepted that she wasn't going to give in and talk to him, but he wanted Eliot to tell him everything she was up to. There was no mobile phone signal at the farmhouse, but she'd managed to get one in Ravensbridge. She'd had a message from her mother on her own phone, telling her Tenerife was fabulous, and she and her father were having a lovely time, missed her, and they hoped she was all right and enjoying the summer. On Honey's iPhone, there were six missed calls from Cain and four texts, begging her to talk to him. Then there was a final message that said, "Well, bugger you then. Don't think I'll stop calling because I won't, and Eliot tells me EVERYTHING so be warned!"

Eliot, meanwhile, seemed to have reconciled himself with the fact that he'd have to update Cain on her behaviour at frequent intervals. He'd been perplexed about the whole thing and had asked her several times what on earth she'd done to warrant such close observation. Cain had even asked him to put a child lock on the phone, which only Eliot would know the pin number for. Eliot had more or less agreed to do it, but informed Eden he had no intention of carrying out Cain's wishes.

'What if there's an emergency and you need to call an ambulance for one o' the bairns? Think I'm jeopardising their safety 'cos you can't be trusted? Think on.'

It was fine by Eden, too, though she knew that if Cain had an inkling that "Honey" had free access to the phone and could have called Crispin at any time she chose, he would have a fit.

'Fish fingers and chips okay for tonight?'

The girls seemed to have no problem with that. She would give Eliot extra portions and bulk it up with bread and butter. Maybe she could buy a cookbook and pretend to learn from that? Something would have to be done.

George seemed delighted at the news, too. He had a passion for chips. He also seemed to have developed an extraordinary fondness for Eden. He ran to her frequently to show her things, and asked her endless questions and wanted cuddles. Eliot was baffled, as Eden rarely spoke to George when in his presence. He wasn't to know that, when it was just the two of them, she read him stories, sang songs to him, and played endless games with him. George, who had probably been lonely until her arrival, lapped it all up and had evidently decided "Honey" was his new best friend.

'Honey, would you like to meet Flora now?'

Flora was the girls' pony. Libby had tried to take Eden to meet her several times. She had resisted so far, not least because she had no suitable footwear or clothing, but also because she had a fear of horses she could hardly confess to, given Honey's apparent prowess in the equestrian field. With three eager faces looking up at her, though, she couldn't bring herself to say no.

Instead, she gave an exaggerated sigh and said, 'I suppose so, though don't expect me to touch the dirty thing.'

Ophelia giggled and grabbed her hand. 'Come on, then.'

'Hang on! Let me put George's shoes on. And put your coats on, please. It's raining, in case you'd forgotten. Just for a change.'

They set off from the house ten minutes later, Ophelia pulling excitedly on her arm while Libby led the way, clearly bursting with excitement to be able to show her precious pony off to her. Tuppence, the elderly Border collie, emerged from the garden and followed them. She was Lug's grandmother, and much loved by the family. Two little Jack Russells raced round excitedly, yapping loudly. They were called Fagin and Dodger, and lived in one of the outbuildings, being excellent ratters, apparently.

Ophelia ran ahead, splashing ungraciously through puddles, past the barn and the garden, on past the row of stone outhouses and stables, to the gate at the end of the track.

'She's here,' she called excitedly. 'Come and say hello.'

Eden gripped George's hand tighter—partly to stop him running ahead and getting into the paddock, where he could be mowed down by a vicious beast with four hooves and some very big teeth, and partly to steady her own nerves. She hadn't had much to do with horses. They seemed very big and very scary to her. She wasn't sure she could bluff her way out of this one.

As they approached the gate, Libby beamed up at her. 'There she is. Isn't she beautiful?'

The pony stood to the left of the gate, hidden by the outhouses and stables, so it wasn't until Eden caught up with Ophelia that she got her first glimpse of her.

'Oh!'

'Do you like her?' Libby clambered onto the bottom bar of the gate beside Ophelia.

'She's, er—'

'Pretty,' shrieked George. 'Flora! Flora! Come here!'

Even the two-year-old wasn't scared of her. The pony was extremely beautiful, even allowing for the mud on her legs. She was a dapple grey, with a black mane and tail, and she stood grazing contentedly in the paddock, occasionally swishing her tail to keep the flies at bay. When George yelled for her, she raised her head and, after hesitating a moment, sauntered over to the gate.

Libby reached into her pocket and pulled out half a packet of Polos. She held one in the flat of her hand and offered it to the pony.

'Mind your fingers,' Eden warned, hardly daring to watch, but the pony took the mint gently from her hand, looking blissful as it munched on it.

'Polos are her favourite,' confided Ophelia. 'She likes apples and carrots, but mints are best.'

The pony had large dark eyes and thick eyelashes.

Eden hadn't known that horses had eyelashes. As ponies went, she was certainly a looker, and she wasn't very big, either. In fact, looking at her, she wasn't sure she was big enough for Libby.

'Is she all right, standing out here in the rain?'

'Don't be silly. She's got a shelter if she wants it, and besides, her breed is used to being outdoors in all weathers. They're ever so hardy.'

'What type is she?' Eden asked, hoping she sounded knowledgeable.

'She's a Welsh Mountain pony,' said Libby, which, in all honesty, meant nothing to Eden. 'Section A?' she added, as if that would make things clearer.

'Oh, right.' Eden nodded and tried to look as if she knew what Libby was talking about.

'What pony did you have?' asked Ophelia.

Eden could feel her face burning. 'Er, it was brown.'

The girls looked baffled. 'Brown?'

'Yes, and it was a boy.'

'Oh.' Libby thought for a moment. 'What was his name?'

Eden's mind went blank. 'Bacon.'

'Bacon?' They exchanged glances and then burst into helpless giggles. 'Why did you call your pony Bacon?'

Eden had no idea. Who in their right minds would call a pony Bacon? Where the hell had that come from, and why hadn't she censored it in her mind before she opened her mouth?

'Me stroke Flora,' demanded George.

'Oh, I don't know about that,' said Eden nervously.

'Why not?' asked Libby.

'Well, he's so small. She might bite him.'

'Don't be daft.' Ophelia looked scornful. 'Flora doesn't bite. Besides, George has ridden her before.'

'Ridden her?' Eden squeaked in disbelief.

'With Dad holding him,' said Libby. 'And only round

the paddock.'

'Good grief.' Eden was glad she hadn't witnessed such reckless behaviour. She'd have been a nervous wreck. Cautiously, she lifted George up and let him stroke the pony, who bore his enthusiastic patting with great fortitude.

When he tried to grab her forelock, however, Eden decided enough was enough. She moved him away, much to George's dismay. He lunged forwards, trying to reach Flora again, but Eden was firm.

'That's enough now. Time to get back and start thinking about tea.'

'Fish fingers?' George stopped struggling and looked at her eagerly.

She smiled at the delighted expression in his big blue eyes, and impulsively dropped a kiss on his chubby cheek. He was so adorable. He threw his arms around her neck and cuddled her, and she had an overwhelming desire to hug him tightly to her. It was amazing how quickly she was growing attached to the three children. It was scary, really.

Turning to go back indoors, she stopped dead as she saw, on the other side of the beck, a whole bunch of people strolling by. A few of them raised their hands and waved, and the girls waved back cheerfully.

'Who are they?' said Eden. It was a bit weird to be in such a remote location and see so many people all at once passing the farm.

'Walkers,' said Libby. 'We get them all the time up here. Sometimes they stop and ask for a drink of water. Sometimes they sit on the grass and rest for a bit. It can get really busy in summer, but we even get them in the winter.'

She supposed she should have guessed. Who else would be walking past this place, through squelchy grass and endless mud, wearing hiking boots, thick socks, khaki shorts and anoraks? 'They must be barmy.'

'Why? It's proper grand walking country round here,' said Ophelia, sounding about sixty.

'I'm sure it is if the sun ever comes out,' said Eden, not entirely convinced such an event ever occurred. 'Still, you'd need your head examined to come up here in the winter.'

She walked towards the beck, wondering how many walkers there actually were. As she arrived at the edge of the water, she looked out across the dale spread before her. The wet grass seeped round her ankles, mocking her pointless shoes. A fine, damp mist hung over Skimmerdale, but she could still make out in the distance the network of stone walls criss-crossing their way across the valley and up the hills, and a dark shape that was one of the many stone huts that dotted the dale. To her left, the line of walkers were striding out, hoods up against the rain, chatting among themselves as if they were actually enjoying being out in the murky weather.

From somewhere in the distance, she heard the faint bleat of a sheep, and something inside her fluttered in response. Eliot was out there in the mist, up on the hills, taking care of his flock.

'You can ride Flora, if you like.' Ophelia appeared beside her, tugging at her arm.

Eden laughed. 'I think she's a bit small for me, don't you?'

'Not really. I mean, your feet will probably dangle. Libby's feet are starting to dangle a bit, already, but Flora's very strong, and you're not fat. Wouldn't you like to ride? Don't you miss your pony?'

'Is your pony in heaven?' asked Libby, joining them.

Eden had no idea. She hadn't even known Honey rode. It wasn't something she seemed interested in these days, at any rate. Her head was far too full of fashion, sex, and illicit affairs with married men. What a shame.

She looked at the two little girls and wondered, would they one day put their passion for ponies behind them and dream only of expensive cars, shopping for designer clothes, and finding the perfect man? They had genes in them from Honey's family, after all. Jemima was obviously a different kettle of fish to her second cousin, though. Honey could never have settled in a place like this in a million years, whereas Jemima had turned it into a home and had adored her children and loved Eliot with a passion. Eden thought she would have liked Jemima. It seemed terribly sad that she'd been taken away so brutally—not least for these sweet kids, and for the grieving farmer, who had done his best to raise them on his own, and was still obviously desperately cut up by his wife's death.

'No, my pony lives on a farm with lots of other old ponies,' she said, figuring the children had dealt with enough sadness in their lives. She turned back to the farmhouse and hitched George higher on her hip. 'Now, peas or beans with your fish fingers?'

CHAPTER TWELVE

Honey risked moving the curtain, ever so slightly, and stared out over the front garden of the cottage. She thought she'd never been in a more depressing holiday home in her life.

God knows, she'd stayed in many in her time. Most of her friends' parents had second homes in the country, by the sea, or abroad. Her mother, who had her own homes in Brighton and Chelsea, had managed to wangle many free holidays from her own friends, who had homes in Cornwall, Somerset, Hampshire, Kent and Dorset, as well as villas in Ibiza, Spain, and Greece, rustic farmhouses in France, or swish apartments in Italy. Honey had been to them all and had grown used to making herself at home wherever she happened to be, but this place wasn't making her feel welcome. Not at all.

She supposed it didn't help that they were sleeping in Sybil's and Rupert's room. There was a large, framed photograph of the couple on the wall above the bed which was distinctly off-putting. It was her own fault, she acknowledged. She should have been content with the guest room, but it was too late now.

She sighed, looking out over the dullest front garden she'd ever had the misfortune to view. Crispin said the lawn had been dug up because Sybil and Rupert weren't frequent visitors and didn't want to pay for a gardener, so in its place they'd stuck a heap of gravel and a concrete drive. It was completely soulless. It was a good job it was hidden behind a high hedge, because anyone passing by would have been disgusted at the state of it. It was hardly conducive to a holiday mood.

Then there was the fact that she was a virtual prisoner in the place. Crispin was terrified she would be spotted. The cottage was two miles from a popular tourist town, so he refused point blank to let her leave the confines of the grounds. She supposed she should be grateful there was, at least, a large back garden with access to a private beach. It wasn't a huge stretch of sand, but it could only be reached through the garden or by sea, so it afforded almost total privacy. She could sunbathe and swim without worrying about bumping into holidaymakers, although, even there, Crispin was nervous. He pointed out that, although the beach was private, there was nothing to stop people turning up in a boat, or sailing past with long lens cameras. Honey could think of no reason on earth why anyone would do that, but Crispin insisted one could never be too careful. He risked the occasional paddle in the sea, but spent most of his time scanning the horizon for passing ships loaded with inquisitive journalists. Honey was reluctantly coming to the conclusion that he was a total wimp who was scared of his own shadow and was rapidly losing patience with him.

She longed to go into town and shop, but he was adamant that she mustn't be seen. Although not strictly a celebrity in her own right, she had, nevertheless, appeared in the papers and in various magazines on occasion, usually to persuade the public that Freya was a model mother in every sense of the word, or to demonstrate the softer side to Cain Carmichael and convince everyone that he'd become a respectable citizen and doting father, rather than a wild, irresponsible rock star, and was therefore more than worthy of a knighthood. Crispin was terrified that someone would recognise her and follow her back to the house, putting two and two together and tipping off the press.

'Why are you so scared?' she demanded, tired of being told she mustn't venture out of the grounds. 'So what if they find out you're having an affair? You won't be the first politician to play away. I'm sure your political career would survive.'

'Bugger my political career.' Crispin shuddered. 'Lavinia is determined that one day she'll be the wife of the Prime Minister. If I screw that up for her, she'll castrate me. I have to protect my assets.'

She could see why he was desperate to preserve his genitals. It was becoming increasingly clear to Honey that they were not only Crispin's biggest assets, they were his only assets. Confined in this cottage with him, she was finding him incredibly dull. He insisted on scouring the internet every day, reading the papers online, keeping up with the news. He regaled her for hours with tales from Parliament; he bored her to tears as he mumbled on about some protest meeting that he simply must attend at Windleby-on-the-Weir at the beginning of September; he made her want to stick her fingers in her ears when he furiously defended some bill or other that had been passed a few months ago, which the press were now insisting was damaging and indefensible. She felt like packing her bags and heading home, and only the thought that she would be doing something that would please and relieve her parents stopped her. She was beginning to think Eden had a better deal, after all. At least she could go shopping.

She watched, suddenly curious, as a red Mini drove up the lane and slowed almost to a halt outside the cottage. From the bedroom window, she could just see the driver over the hedge, as he turned to stare at the garden gate. She leaned forward, and the movement of the curtain must have caught his attention, because he gazed up at the window. Squinting, she tried desperately to make out his features, wondering who he was, but the car moved before she could, and she watched it drive away, leaving her rather puzzled. She didn't know anyone with a red Mini, and, anyway, no one she knew would be anywhere near this Godforsaken place.

Behind her, Crispin stirred in the bed. She dropped the curtain and turned back to face him. He blinked sleepily at her for a moment, then she saw the passion stirring in his eyes as he took in her naked form.

'Good morning, gorgeous,' he murmured, pulling back the duvet and patting the space beside him.

'I'm bored,' Honey announced, climbing back into bed. 'If I have to spend another day listening to you banging on about politics, I'll go mad.'

Crispin pouted. 'I'm sorry, darling. I didn't realise. I thought you were having a good time.'

'A good time? In Colditz?'

'Colditz?' He looked offended. 'This has been in our family for years. We've always loved holidaying here.'

'I'm sure when you came here previously, you weren't confined to barracks. Can't I go shopping? It's so tedious here.'

'You know it's better to be safe than sorry.'

'It makes no sense. And how come you can go into town? You're much more recognisable than I am.'

'People know I holiday here regularly. They won't be surprised to see me. It's you that mustn't be spotted. You know all this, darling. Please don't spoil it. We've been having such a lovely time.'

'You have,' she said sulkily. 'I'm thoroughly fed up.'

He cupped her breast and began to caress it, kissing her neck and nibbling her ear. Honey squirmed, feeling herself melting against him, in spite of herself. How did he do that, she wondered? He was so dull and not particularly handsome, once she'd spent a bit of time with him, but he knew exactly what to do to make her forget all that and just long to be with him.

'I'm not joking,' she muttered, as he softly stroked her inner thigh, her breathless voice betraying her increasing lust.

Crispin began to kiss her, his tongue finding its way into her mouth, and Honey had to concede, as Crispin's hand snaked its way between her legs, that there *were* worse ways to spend the day.

CHAPTER THIRTEEN

Eliot knew there was something different about the house as he approached it. He just couldn't think what it was. Beside him, Lug and Jake, his two faithful sheepdogs, paused the moment he did. They sat patiently, looking up at him as he stood still, gazing thoughtfully at his home. He scanned the door, the windows, even the roof. What was it that was making him think something had changed?

Then he realised. The net curtains were gleaming. Instead of dingy yellowing nets shaming the windows, they were now adorned with crisp, white ones that uplifted the look of the entire house. Honey had clearly been at work.

He couldn't believe it. Surely, she wouldn't have lowered herself to do some washing?

He hesitated. Had Daisy been round? She had a long shift today at The King's Head. He couldn't imagine she'd had time to pop round and do the laundry, especially with that miserable old bugger to see to, on top of everything else. Besides, it had been pouring with rain all day. He couldn't see her heading up here in that kind of weather.

He pushed open the door and took off his muddy boots, picking them up and carrying them to the boot room off the hallway. Until Jemima moved in, boots had been left scattered all over the place, but she'd taken a dim view of that. When the architect began to draw up plans for the kitchen, she'd insisted he find room for a small space with access to the garden, where boots and dog bowls could be placed without messing up the rest of her house. When she'd been alive, he hadn't dared use the front door, instead heading round to the garden to enter the boot room through the side door that had been created for such a purpose. For the last eighteen months or so, though, he'd reverted to using the front door. He tried not to dwell on the reason for the change.

Inside the boot room, he dropped the boots on the ground, shaking his head when he caught sight of Honey's ridiculous wedges and high heels stacked up near the back door. Surprised to see that two of the three dog bowls had already been filled with food, and the water bowls topped up with fresh water, he paused. The third bowl was empty, but as Tuppence wasn't around he guessed she'd already had her tea and was snoozing in the kitchen. She was the only one of the dogs who lived in the house, being elderly. Well, that saved him a job, at any rate. Maybe the girls had done it. They must have been bored stiff, stuck indoors while the rain pelted down. Hopefully, the poor weather would hold off for at least some of their school holidays.

He wondered how Honey had coped, having them under her feet. He hoped she'd attempted conversation with them and not stuck them in front of the television all day. With a light pat on each of the dogs' heads, he left them to eat their well-deserved tea. Later, he would take Lug and Jake to their beds in the barn, where they slept alongside Fagin and Dodger.

When he entered the kitchen, he was greeted with the astonishing sight of his daughters rushing towards him, carrying a plate with the most peculiarly-shaped buns he'd ever seen. They were decorated with splodges of runny pink icing, most of which had run off the buns and pooled on the plate, but he'd not seen his children looking so proud of anything for a long time. Bella had a suspicious splodge of pink stuck to her fur, and Tuppence looked smugly satisfied as she eyed him from under the table.

'Well, what have we here, then?'

'We made you some cupcakes. Do you like them?' Ophelia's eyes shone.

Eliot ruffled her hair. 'You made these? All by

yourselves?'

'Well ...' Libby glanced at Honey. 'Honey helped us a bit. She doesn't know much about baking, though. They don't look as good as Mummy's cupcakes, do they?'

'Oh, I don't know about that.' Eliot shook his head, wondering if she'd ever believe him if he told her that all of her Mummy's *homemade* buns and cakes had come from the supermarket on the outskirts of Kirkby Skimmer. 'The important thing is how they taste. Have you tried one?'

They all shook their heads. Honey was looking a bit pensive, leaning against the sink as she waited for the kettle to boil. George had cake mixture in his hair. Evidently, even he had got in on the act.

'You have to have the first one, Dad,' Ophelia informed him.

He'd had an awful feeling she was going to say that. He smiled. 'Just wash me hands, then.'

He headed over to the sink and began to scrub his hands and arms with soap and hot water.

Honey murmured, 'They spent ages doing these. Even George stirred the mixture. They really enjoyed themselves.'

He looked at her in surprise. Was that a tone of affection he heard in her voice? Surely not.

He dried his hands and reached for a bun. He bit into it and chewed tentatively.

'Well?' Libby stood there, hands on hips, demanding a verdict.

'They're really good.' Astonishingly, they did taste delicious. 'I'm not kidding. Where did you find the recipe?'

'The internet,' said Ophelia.

Eliot glanced at Honey. 'You found the laptop?'

'Libby brought it to me from your office upstairs. She said she was allowed to use it. I hope you don't mind.

There was no password on it, so I thought ...'

He shrugged. 'I don't mind. Sometimes you can get a good connection, sometimes you can't. Point is, I promised your dad I wouldn't let on I had a computer. What with that and the phone, I'm not doing a very good job of guarding you, am I?'

She grinned, and he found he was smiling back.

'Why isn't Honey allowed to use the internet?' asked Libby.

It was a good question. Eliot's smile dropped. What had she done so wrong that someone as badly behaved as Cain Carmichael felt she needed watching twenty-four seven? Evidently, there was more to the story than he knew.

He squeezed Libby's cheek. 'She gets carried away, buying too many things,' he said.

'Oh. It's sausages and chips for tea,' she said.

'Ooh, chips again, eh? Lovely.'

If he hadn't known better, he would swear Honey looked apologetic. 'I was thinking of going into Kirkby Skimmer in a day or two. There's a supermarket there, isn't there? I thought I'd look up some recipes online and start trying out something different.'

'Really?' He raised an eyebrow. 'I wouldn't have thought cooking was your thing. And, by the way, I see you've washed the nets. They look miles better. Don't know how you managed to get them so white, but thanks.'

She looked embarrassed for a moment, but shrugged. 'Well, I had to do something to keep myself occupied. It's hardly the best place to be marooned, is it? I mean, there's simply nothing to do. A girl could go mad unless she found something to pass the time.'

'Oh, aye. Terrible place. Surprised you can stand it. Oh, I forgot. You've no choice, have you? Cain rung yet to check up on you?'

Even to his own ears his voice sounded churlish. She

brought out the worst in him, no doubt about it. Just when he thought she might have a softer side, she had to go and spoil it.

'Not yet.' She turned away from him and busied herself with the chip pan. 'You know, if you must have fried chips, you should really get a deep fat fryer. Chip pans are dangerous.'

'They were good enough for my mam and gran. A big chip pan, a third full of lard, and—'

'Lard?' She spun round, looking horrified. 'That's disgusting.'

He tutted. 'Seems everything about this place is disgusting.'

'Not everything.'

He looked at her, surprised.

She grinned at him. 'The nets look absolutely lovely.'

In spite of himself, his mouth twitched. 'I'm going to get a shower while you do tea, if that's okay?'

'Fine. It should be ready when you are.'

He pushed away from the counter. 'Could you feed Fagin and Dodger, Libby? And put Jake and Lug in the barn for the night, please. I'm off to scrub this muck off me. Reckon I'll be bathing you straight after tea, an' all,' he said, nodding at George with a smile. 'Happen you've got half the cake mixture in your hair, young lad.'

'I'll bath him, if you like.' Honey looked as surprised at herself for the offer as Eliot was. 'I mean, it will give you time to sit with the girls for a bit. They haven't seen you all day.'

'Thanks. If you're sure?'

'Oh, yes. It's fine.'

She turned back to the cooker, and he frowned, wondering what to make of her. She seemed like a really decent human being one minute, then she'd open her mouth and reveal herself to be a total bitch in the next. He couldn't fathom it, but right then he was too tired to think about it. All he wanted was to stand under a hot shower, wash away the dirt and mud, and soothe his aching bones. Everything else could wait.

****

The sausages and chips were a success. Eden had added practically a full tin of beans to Eliot's plate and three slices of bread and butter to try to bulk it up, but, as she watched the hungry farmer clearing his plate, she was more determined than ever to brave the drive back to Kirkby Skimmer and find the supermarket. She wouldn't need to buy meat, at any rate. The chest freezer in the boot room was packed full with chicken, lamb and pork. There didn't appear to be any fruit or vegetables, though, which surprised her. Probably, when Jemima was alive, things were more organised.

She had taken the children to the nearest village, Beckthwaite, that morning, a place that had thoroughly enchanted her, in spite of its tiny size. Beckthwaite perched on the edge of the River Skimmer, and was reached by driving over a quaint stone bridge that crossed the water, which was fairly narrow at that particular point and looked little more than a stream. As Eden drove over the bridge, she saw that the road forked a few yards ahead. Turning left would take her out of the village, past an old chapel, which she later discovered had become a holiday cottage, and on through the dale, climbing the hills towards the upland village of Felltoft. Turning right, she drove slowly down what appeared to be the only street in the entire village. Consisting of little more than a dozen or so cottages, the ancient and thoroughly charming pub, The King's Head, some crumbling stone barns, a tiny shop and a red phone box, Beckthwaite nevertheless was busy with tourists. Several people in kagoules and sturdy boots sat at tables outside The King's Head, while more of them stood outside the shop, clutching bottles of water and studying a map.

She'd only just parked up and got the children out of the car when she was swooped on by a resident of the village, eager to find out how she was coping at Fleetsthorpe, how Eliot was doing, and to pass on their condolences for the loss of her second cousin. Eden had been astonished the woman even knew who she was, but she hadn't been the only local who knew that she was staying at the farm. Several people approached her as she walked towards the shop, and as none of them mentioned Cain, she suspected they hadn't the faintest idea who Honey was, other than that she was Jemima's relation, come to help out at Fleetsthorpe.

Pushing open the door of the little shop, she'd been pleasantly surprised to find an extremely attractive interior, with goods laid out in wicker baskets and on carved pine shelves. There was a fairly basic supply of essentials that the villagers would need, but a lot of space was given over to things that would appeal to tourists, which seemed a bit of a shame. Obviously, Beckthwaite was firmly on the map as far as ramblers, hikers and even, as she later discovered, mountain bikers were concerned.

As she'd searched the shelves for flour and icing sugar, she'd been approached by an elderly lady, who studied her carefully for some moments with gimlet eyes before finally announcing, 'Tha's Honey Carmichael, no doubt.' When Eden had gulped and nodded, she'd folded her arms in satisfaction. 'Aye, I knew it. Shame tha couldn't come earlier.' She sniffed. 'Reckon Eliot could have used thee most a couple of years ago.'

'Yes, I suppose ...'

The woman scowled at her. 'A bad time, it were. Never seen a man so in bits. And trying to do his job and cope with the kiddies, like, all while dealing with a broken heart. Lucky he's got a lot of friends round here, and we look after our own.'

'Well, that's good to hear,' said Eden, trying to move off. She had all she needed, and the girls were looking bored. Worse still, she was acutely aware of a rather unpleasant odour wafting towards her from the woman's direction.

'He couldn't have managed without Daisy,' added the old lady. She gave Eden a pointed stare. 'Good girl, that. Been there for him and these bairns since it happened. Mind you, it cuts both ways.'

'Does it?'

'Oh, aye. Eliot's helped her dad out many a time. It's like that round here, tha knows. Folks look out for each other. Happen tha thinks living out on't Fleetsthorpe no one knows what's going on up there. Tha'd be wrong.'

'Right.'

'We probably know more about each other's lives than any folks in the city.'

'Okay.'

'We make it our business to know. Got to work together up here, see? Who else is gonna do it for us, if not our own?'

'Hmm.'

The woman nodded at the children. 'Does tha like having this lady to look after thee, eh?'

Libby and Ophelia stopped examining the jars of toffees on the shelves and nodded. 'Yes, Granny Allen. We're going to do some baking this afternoon.'

'Oh, aye? That's nice, I'm sure.' The woman turned back to Eden. 'He's a good man, Eliot. Been through a lot.'

'I know,' said Eden, thinking, so this was Granny Allen. She wasn't surprised the woman lived in a hovel, having met her. 'It's a tragedy. I feel for them all.'

The woman stared at her for a moment, as if trying to read her thoughts. Then she bent down and gently stroked George's hair. He was fast asleep in his buggy, and looked cherubic. Seeing the old woman's dirt-encrusted fingernails, Eden winced.

'Bless him,' said Granny Allen. 'I don't know. Sometimes the best things come out of the worst times, don't they?'

Eden had no idea what she was talking about. She merely smiled and nodded. Granny Allen seemed satisfied that she'd managed to get her point across and left them to it. She wasn't the only one who seemed intent on informing her that the situation at the farm was being monitored, that Eliot was a good man, and he'd been through enough. She guessed they were all warning her that she'd better behave herself and not let him down, because there were plenty of people who wouldn't be very happy with her if she did.

As she'd bundled the children and the shopping back into the car, and left Beckthwaite behind, she'd mused on his popularity. Now, watching him interact with his children, she could understand it. When he eventually stood and began to collect the plates, Eden couldn't help herself.

'Let me,' she said. 'You've had a long day. I'll wash up.'

He looked astonished, but sat down again. She collected all the dishes and announced she'd make them all a lovely cup of tea and they could all have buns to go with it. The suggestion was greeted with much delight, and she filled the kettle, feeling strangely contented.

Libby jumped up when a knock on the door interrupted their happy moment. 'I'll go.'

'If it's not raining tomorrow,' said Ophelia, 'can we go goosegog picking?'

'Firstly, if it's not raining tomorrow, it will be a miracle,' said Eden, as Eliot said he didn't see why not, 'and secondly, what on earth are goosegogs?'

'Gooseberries,' he said. 'I take it you've eaten those in your time?'

Eden couldn't say that she had. She knew what they

were, obviously, but didn't think one had ever passed her lips.

'Really?' Eliot and Ophelia exchanged incredulous glances. 'Nothing better than a goosegog crumble,' he informed her.

'Did Jemima have a recipe? Maybe I could try to make one.'

She saw it clearly in that moment. The light in his eyes switched off instantly. It was palpable, and she felt a weird clutching at her heart. His grief was still raw, that much was apparent. How much he must have loved his wife. It gave her a strange fullness in her throat, thinking about it, and she turned away from him, unable to deal with his pain.

'It's Daisy!' Libby skipped into the kitchen, and Eden gave an inward groan.

That was all she needed. She wondered, suddenly, why she felt such a rush of resentment towards the poor woman, who had done nothing but help Eliot in his time of need. They'd been having a lovely evening, but she'd already spoilt it by mentioning Jemima. Besides, if anyone was the intruder here, it was Eden herself, not Daisy, who had been a good neighbour and friend to the family.

Guilt forced her into being pleasant to their guest. 'Cup of tea, Daisy?'

Daisy looked as dumbfounded by the offer as Eliot did, and Eden realised she had become far too Eden-like lately. She'd been so contented at the farmhouse, being with the children and in the company of this hardworking man, that she'd slipped back to her old ways, forgetting to be Honey. The farm was such a contrast to the Carmichael home, where everything had been loud and dramatic.

Despite there being three young children in the house, they didn't tire her out like watching over Honey did, and she was never bored here. She remembered the long hours, sitting in the shop, staring at the walls while she waited for a customer. There was no waiting for something to happen at Fleetsthorpe. The house was a hive of activity, and she was thoroughly enjoying herself. It was hard to think she had to hide how much she was loving life in Skimmerdale, but she knew she had to.

'Er, thanks.' Daisy reached into her bag and pulled out a cake tin. 'I made you all this, for after your tea. Chocolate cake, girls—your favourite.'

She beamed at them as she placed it on the table.

Eden took a deep breath and turned away, reaching for another mug. 'Oh, you needn't have bothered. We made cupcakes this afternoon, didn't we, children? We had a super time. Even George helped. Perhaps you can take the cake home and have it yourself?'

'Don't be daft.' Eliot rose from the table and collected the milk from the fridge. Handing it to her, he shot Eden a look that was a clear warning. 'Sit yersen down, Daisy. You came all the way up here in this weather to bring us this? Chocolate cake, and a cupcake each! Not had a feast like this in a while, have we, kids?'

The children all agreed they hadn't. Eden bit her lip, pouring milk into mugs and wondering what to do next. She hated getting on the wrong side of Eliot, or disappointing the children, but Honey would have no such qualms. She had to remember why she was here, and who she was supposed to be.

She handed out the drinks then placed the plate of buns on the table. Beside Daisy's rather lovely chocolate cake, they looked very amateurish. 'Do help yourself, Daisy. Or are you on a diet?'

Daisy, who was built a little more solidly than Eden, paused a moment as she unbuttoned her coat, her face colouring. 'No, I'm not.'

'That's so brave of you. I do admire a woman who knows her own mind and refuses to conform to society's expectations. Good for you.'

It was basically code for "You're fat", and Daisy knew it. She glared at Eden, who felt wretched already. Daisy was annoying, in as much as she hung around the Harland family and made it obvious she had a huge crush on Eliot, but she hadn't done anything wrong. Not really. And certainly nothing to offend Eden or warrant such a personal attack.

She rather admired Daisy when she threw off her coat, reached over, and picked up a bun, biting into it determinedly.

'Do you like it, Daisy?' asked Ophelia.

'Lovely. Really tasty. Did you make it?'

'We all did. Honey told us what to do, and even George stirred the mixture.'

'Did he? Oh, bless him. What a clever boy.'

'Of course, they're not as good as Mummy's cupcakes, are they?' Libby was watching Daisy, her eyes suddenly anxious. Eden noticed Daisy and Eliot glance at each other in a very strange way.

'They're better,' said Daisy eventually.

Libby shook her head. 'No, no, they're not better. Mummy made the best cupcakes in the world. She couldn't even enter the Skimmerdale Show because she would have won everything, in spite of Mrs Edwards, and it would have upset the other ladies.'

Crikey, thought Eden, Jemima was nothing if not modest.

Daisy smiled. 'Yes, well, maybe not quite as good as your mummy's, but not far off.'

Libby seemed to find the answer acceptable, and happily munched on some chocolate cake, which she pronounced to be "not bad", much to everyone's amusement.

'I was thinking, tomorrow I'll make one of my stews and bring it round,' said Daisy.

Eden raised an eyebrow. The offer bordered on pushy. 'No need.'

'Really? It's no trouble, and I think it would make a nice change from chips.' Daisy looked meaningfully at the draining board, where the pile of dirty plates sat, complete with leftovers.

'There's no need because I intend to start cooking some meals. Proper meals.'

'You do?' Daisy didn't bother to hide a smile. 'Done much cooking, have you?'

Eden was tempted to tell her how much cooking she actually had done, but had to restrain herself. 'Not really. I've found some recipes, and I'm going to do some shopping for ingredients. How hard can it be? You manage it.'

'I've had years of practice. I've had to take care of my father.'

'Is he still alive?'

She looked startled by the question. 'Yes, of course.'

'Then I presume you're still taking care of him?'

Daisy glanced at Eliot, her face nervous. 'Yes.'

'In that case, why don't you concentrate on looking after your father and leave this family to me.' She smiled sweetly, but Daisy wasn't to be fobbed off.

'I can do both, and I don't mind at all. I enjoy looking after them. I've known Eliot all my life, and he knows I'd do anything for him, don't you, Eliot?'

Eliot shifted in his seat, looking uncomfortable. 'You've been a good friend.'

'And that's very sweet of you, I'm sure,' Eden said. 'Although, at your age, shouldn't you have other things to fill your time? Friends, family, a boyfriend even?'

As Daisy turned scarlet, Eliot pushed his chair back. 'I think I'll bath George,' he announced, collecting the little boy from his highchair.

'You don't have to. I said I would,' said Eden.

'It's all right. I'll do it. You stay and make our guest welcome,' he said, nodding at Daisy. 'Thanks again for the cake. You really shouldn't have. You've got more than enough on your plate.'

'More than enough,' Eden agreed, looking meaningfully at the plate in front of the poor woman, which contained a fat slice of chocolate cake and another bun.

As soon as Eliot had carried George out of the room, Daisy stood. 'I think I'll be going now,' she said, shrugging on her damp coat.

'Really? Are you sure? Would you like a doggy bag to take that home with you?'

'No, thank you.' Daisy glared at Eden, who was left in no doubt that she could cheerfully have strangled her. 'Enough's as good as a feast.'

She smiled at the girls. 'I'll see you soon.' As Eden showed her to the door, she murmured, 'I know what you're trying to do. It won't work.'

'I'm sorry?'

Daisy's eyes were cold. 'I can see it all over your face. You've fallen for him. Well, you can forget it. He's been down that road once before. He's not daft enough to go there again. You're not what he needs. He needs someone who understands this way of life, someone who will look after him, look after his kids.'

'You mean, someone like you?'

'I never said that.'

'You didn't have to. Look, I have no idea what you're talking about. Eliot is my second cousin's widower, that's all. I have no designs on him, whatsoever. Good heavens, why would I? Who in their right mind would want to be tied down to a sheep farmer in a wilderness like this?'

The colour drained from her face, as Eliot's voice came from behind her. 'I can't find George's special towel. Do you know where it is?'

She spun round, to find him standing there, George in his arms, his face expressionless. 'In the dryer. I washed it this afternoon,' she croaked. Feeling suddenly sick, she turned back to see Daisy smirking at her. 'Goodbye,' she said, and, opening the door, she practically pushed the other woman out into the yard.

After one last, satisfied look, Daisy walked away.

Eden closed the door and leaned against it, her heart hammering in her chest. What was she so upset about? She had done what she was supposed to do. She had shown Eliot that Honey Carmichael was a spoilt brat, with no interest whatsoever in him or his family. The heart-breaking thing was, she would never be able to show him the truth about Eden Robinson.

CHAPTER FOURTEEN

Cain would never have believed he could feel so lonely in his own home. He'd been looking forward to the peace and quiet; a few weeks without Honey giving him grief about something, or other, had sounded like paradise to him. In reality, it was boring. He missed her. Wild horses wouldn't make him admit it to her, of course, even if he could speak to her, and there seemed to be no chance of that. Spoilt brat still wouldn't take his calls. How long did she intend to punish him for, for God's sake? She didn't even reply to his texts.

He got frequent updates from Old MacDonald, but, truth to tell, he couldn't make out half of what the bloke was saying. He'd thought he'd be able to understand him, no problem. After all, he sometimes watched *Emmerdale* with no trouble. That fella was on a different scale, though. Cain had to concentrate so hard on what he was saying that when he ended the calls he invariably had a headache.

He wondered how Honey was managing without a translator. Eliot had been pretty scathing about her at first, and Cain had bristled with indignation on her behalf, even though he knew that, in all fairness, Eliot was probably underplaying her bad behaviour. He knew what Honey was like when she was forced to do something she didn't want to do. He'd bet his last quid that she was giving the poor sod hell.

Why did she have to go and shag a Tory MP, for God's sake? And not any old Tory MP, but Golden Boy himself. Crispin Cavendish was destined for great things, and his pals in the ranks of blue would never forgive him if it was down to Cain's daughter that his career was flushed down the toilet. Why couldn't the stupid git keep it in his pants, anyway? It was all his fault. Cain had quite gone off him.

He just had to hold on 'til the beginning of September, then Parliament would reconvene, Lavinia would come home from Portugal, and Crispin would be so buried in work and keeping the wife happy, he'd forget all about Honey. Please, God.

He paced up and down his den. Snarler was having a couple of days off. No doubt he'd got pissed the night before and was sleeping it off in his hovel of a house in the village. He briefly contemplated going round there to wake him up, just for the hell of it, but he couldn't really be bothered.

He glanced at his phone, ever hopeful, although he knew, in his heart of hearts, she wouldn't have rung him. He'd spoken to his other kids the previous day, out of sheer desperation. Scarlet and Jed were busy, busy, busy, or so they said. Scarlet was planning her wedding. She gushed about how much it was costing, and how her stepfather, Clint, (bleeding Clint!) was paying for it all and had insisted she go all out and get the best of everything. She'd met her fiancé on the set of some two-bit soap opera she was appearing in, and, apparently, he was the perfect man. Cain had managed to stop himself making a sarcastic comment. Perfect man? If Clint was her role model, she'd set herself a pretty low benchmark.

His smirk dropped when he realised he'd hardly been a shining example to her himself. He rarely saw her after Lowri took the kids back to the States. He should have made more of an effort, but things had been pretty bitter with his first wife, and it had all seemed like such a drag. Now he wished he'd risen above the petty arguing and kept in touch with Scarlet, and also with Jed, who was at least into music and played in a band. Mind you, it was a pretty shit band, from what he'd heard. Kind of embarrassing that Cain Carmichael's son couldn't even get a proper recording contract.

Scarlet had invited him to the wedding, more as an

afterthought than anything. He'd told her he'd have loved to attend, but he was busy that day. She hadn't believed him, he could tell, but she hadn't pushed it.

Jed had barely managed five minutes on the phone with him. After confirming he still hadn't got a deal and was still working part-time in a bar and playing gigs whenever he could get them, there had been a deathly silence that seemed to stretch on forever. Cain had started sweating. His mind went blank. Luckily, Jed had told him he had to go, as his girlfriend had turned up. Relieved, Cain had told him to get stuck in and ended the call.

Emerald had only answered the phone because she hadn't realised it was him calling. When she recognised his voice, she said, 'For fuck's sake, Dad, I'm busy right now. You pick your fucking moments, don't you?'

'I'm sorry, darls. Didn't realise. Where are you?'

'I'm in Provence at the moment. As you'd know, if you ever took the slightest bit of interest in my life, but that would be too much to ask, wouldn't it? How's the blonde bitch?'

'Don't be 'orrible. Roxy's all right.'

'Who the fuck's Roxy? I meant that spoilt little cow of a daughter. Is Roxy your latest shag? Jesus, you never give up, do you? You're a fucking embarrassment.'

'Well, thanks for that. What are you doing in Provence, anyway?'

'Finding myself. I had my chakras aligned this morning, and I'm getting myself centred. I'm focusing on positivity, love and light, so I don't need you getting in my pissing way, okay?'

'Message received.' He'd hung up, wondering how much it was costing Cassandra to help their daughter find herself. If she'd had any sense, she'd have left her well and truly lost.

Marcus was out, so he'd had to content himself with a brief conversation with Janette, who bored him to tears telling him all about Justin's recent recorder recital at nursery school, and how they were about to go to the Isle of Wight for a fortnight's holiday, where they were looking forward to visiting Osborne House and taking James to a donkey sanctuary.

After that little lot, he was missing Honey even more. He gave a big sigh and switched on the television. There must be something that would take his mind off this miserable situation.

The news was on. Great. Just what he needed to cheer himself up. He grabbed the remote again and was about to flick channels, when something on the screen made him sit up.

'What the—' He pushed the volume button and leaned forward in his chair, his face creasing into a scowl as he stared at the image of his nemesis, Rex Scotman.

'The Scotman Foundation is very proud of its achievements to date, but there's no doubt we have more to do,' he was saying. 'We've brought a lot of joy to the children of the region, who would otherwise never have had the opportunity to learn to play instruments. Currently, we employ four local staff, who teach the children traditional African music.'

'You sound very passionate about this project, Rex,' said the gullible reporter. 'You've been involved in this mission to bring music to the poor little children of East Africa for a few years now. What keeps you interested?'

'Oh, believe me, it's a privilege,' said Rex. 'If you could only see their little faces, and, of course, we're also providing a living for some local adults. My staff live and breathe music. They're only happy when they're blowing and banging away.'

Cain almost choked. Was Rex taking the piss, or what?

'My son, Theodore, has been working over there for three years now. He has devoted all that time to helping build our new school and overseeing the development of the project. We're now keen to expand and introduce drama classes and art classes.'

'Really? How wonderful.'

Well, you can't underestimate the importance of the arts to a child's development. It's become my focus in life. Music saved me, and I want to make sure as many children as possible get the chance to develop their skills in the creative arts. Who knows what talent we may uncover?'

'Is your son still over there?'

'No, no. He came back a month ago. He's working with me now, developing the project from home.'

'Yeah, from the comfort of your armchair, while a load of mugs do the work for you,' muttered Cain.

'We intend to start a fund to aid in the expansion of the school, and hopefully, one day, open schools in other areas of Africa. To that end, we are currently planning a charity festival, which will be held in my own back garden.'

The reporter laughed. 'That's a sizeable garden!'

'Oh, yeah. Lark Court is plenty big enough, and we've secured permission from the powers that be, who recognise the importance of this occasion and the cause it's supporting.'

'And who will be taking part in this festival?'

'I'll be contacting all my old mates in the music industry. I'm sure they'll all be eager to help out.'

'You can stick it where the monkey sticks its nuts, mate,' muttered Cain.

'Well, I think it's wonderful,' said the reporter, who was clearly star-struck and a bit dim.

Cain turned the television off in disgust. As if an OBE wasn't enough, that prat was obviously wangling for a knighthood. And after that little performance, he was bound to get one. Worse still, when Rex contacted him to ask him to take part, he would hardly be able to say no, would he? There was no doubt that if he did, Rex would make damn sure the press got to hear about Cain Carmichael's lack of compassion for the little African children. Bugger it. The old git had got him over a barrel. As if things weren't bad enough already.

He leaned back in his chair and thought for a moment, then he picked up his phone. Roxy was away with her best friend, having a girlie weekend, whatever the hell that entailed. Luckily, her sister Suki would be at home, and she was a very obliging girl. All it took was a takeaway, a bunch of flowers, and an assurance that she was far prettier than Roxy, and she was up for anything. It wasn't the greatest way to spend an evening, but it was better than sitting here, waiting for a phone call from Honey, which probably wouldn't come. Or a phone call from Rex, which probably would and would be as welcome as a fart in church. He couldn't imagine what he'd done to deserve it all.

CHAPTER FIFTEEN

'I'm not happy about you going.' Eliot's face was pinched with worry. 'You don't know these roads. And I don't see why you have to go all the way into town, any road.'

Eden wondered what his problem was. She was only going to Kirkby Skimmer for a couple of hours. She'd thought it would be a treat for the children, getting them off the farm for a short while. Eliot, Adey and Mickey were going to be busy harvesting all day. The farm was on high ground and unsuitable for growing crops, but there was plenty of hay in the lower meadows to cut for the sheep's winter feed, and, having had a week of dry weather, they wanted to get on with it while it held.

She'd intended to put the girls in some decent clothes, for a change. Usually, they seemed to live in shorts and T-shirts. It all hinged on whether she could dig out some stuff that Eliot hadn't ruined in the washing machine. The girls' hair had been neatly washed, brushed and tied back, and they could be made to look quite presentable. It would do them good to have a wander round the shops, and a drink at one of the many teashops in the town—and possibly a small gift to bring home with them. She'd had it all planned, and she wasn't going to let Eliot spoil it.

'People travel these roads all the time,' she said. 'I don't see what the big deal is. I have a SatNav and it's a fine, dry day. I'll be careful. Besides, I need to get to the supermarket. I want to start trying out some recipes. You, of all people, should be glad of that. Aren't you sick of chips?'

She smiled at him, hoping he'd smile back, but he looked pretty grim. 'You go slowly, you understand? You make sure the kids have their seatbelts on at all times, and you bloody well crawl to Kirkby Skimmer.'

'Heavens, you do fuss.' She was trying to be as flippant as she knew Honey would be, but she could see his face was lined with anxiety. 'I'll be careful, cross my heart. What a shame you're harvesting today, or I could have rung you later to check in.'

She was being sarcastic, but he seized on her comment. 'There's usually a signal at Kirkby Skimmer. If you ring me, say at one o'clock, I'll be in the house, waiting. Will you?'

Was he for real? 'Well, I suppose so.' She couldn't help feeling sorry for him, although she thought he was being a bit dramatic. 'Tell you what, I'll make you all a big lun—dinner—and leave it in the fridge. If you're coming back for the phone call, you may as well eat something while you're here. One o'clock. I promise.'

He'd eventually hugged the children and headed out, leaving Eden to tidy up and get them ready for their journey as she mused over his odd behaviour.

'Right, kids, who's up for a trip into town?'

To her surprise, Libby and Ophelia looked less than enthusiastic. 'Do we have to?'

'Don't you want to? I thought you'd love a trip out. What's wrong?'

Libby said nothing, but Ophelia was more forthcoming. 'Will we have to go round the dress shops while you try stuff on?'

Eden shook her head. 'Of course not. I don't want any clothes.'

'Don't you?' They exchanged surprised glances. 'Oh.'

'What about looking at vases and pictures, and stuff like that?' said Libby, suspiciously. 'Will you be spending hours choosing things for the house?'

'No, promise.' Eden laughed, but then it occurred to her that was what trips into town with Jemima must have been like. 'I want to get some stuff to make your dad a nice tea, and I thought we could have a look in the shops and you could all choose a present to take home. Maybe we could have something to eat in the teashop. What do you say?'

They cheered up then, so Eden took them upstairs, and they began to rummage around in their wardrobes and drawers, trying to find something suitable to wear.

'I really don't think your father understands the concept of separating colours and whites for the washing machine,' she said, holding up what had once been a white blouse. 'I think most of your clothes are only fit to be thrown away.'

Libby quietly nibbled at her thumbnail as she sat on the bed, watching.

'What's the matter, Libby?'

Libby shook her head. 'Nothing.'

'She's upset,' said Ophelia.

'Upset about what?' Eden dropped the blouse and sat next to the little girl on the bed. 'What's wrong?'

'She's upset about what Florence Taylor says.'

'Who's Florence Taylor?'

'She's in Libby's class.'

'Shut up, Ophelia,' said her sister. 'I'm not upset.'

'Yes, you are. You were crying in the playground. I saw you.'

'Okay, okay. What's this about? What did this Florence Taylor say that upset you?'

Libby shrugged, obviously unwilling to discuss the subject. Luckily, Ophelia was determined to finish what she'd started.

'Florence says we get our clothes from the charity shop, and she says we're dirty little orphans.'

'What!' Eden's hackles rose. 'Have you told the teacher this?'

Libby shook her head.

'Why not? She's bullying you. She shouldn't be allowed to get away with saying such horrible things.'

'We're not orphans, are we?' said Libby suddenly. 'If

we've still got a dad, we're not orphans. That's right, isn't it?'

'Yes, that's right. And you're very lucky, because you've got the best dad in the world, who works so hard for you and loves you so much.'

Libby nodded. 'I know. That's what I think, too. I don't mind about the clothes. Not really. Dad gets very tired, and sometimes there's nobody to help at all, because everyone else is busy. Like when it were lambing time. It were full on, and there were no time to do things in the house or worry about clothes, but Florence doesn't believe me because she lives in Ravensbridge, just in an ordinary house, and she doesn't understand about lambing and stuff like that.'

'She's probably jealous,' Eden said.

'Jealous? What about?'

'What do you think! You live in this lovely farmhouse, and you have a cat, and dogs, and a beautiful pony, and chickens. I'll bet Florence wishes she could have all those things, too, so she says nasty things to you to make herself feel better. I think it's much nicer to have the things you have than the things Florence has, don't you?'

Libby considered. 'So, you think Florence wishes she could have a pony and dogs more than posh clothes?'

'Of course! Okay, if you had the choice, which would you pick?'

'I'd rather live here, any day,' said Ophelia firmly.

'Me, too,' admitted Libby. 'Poor Florence. She must be right bored in the holidays.'

'Exactly,' said Eden. 'Fat lot of good having nice clothes does you, when you're stuck indoors all day, or you're wandering the streets. Much more fun to ride Flora, and collect the eggs from the chickens and pick goosegogs!'

They all grinned, remembering the previous day when they'd rambled round the farm, collecting as many wild gooseberries as they could find. It had been a lovely day, and the girls had thoroughly enjoyed showing her their favourite places on the farm. Now the rain had stopped and there was even some mild sunshine, it looked like a different place. The cold stone of the barns and the house had seemed warmer and mellow, somehow. The stream, or beck as the girls called it, no longer seemed like some cruel boundary, dividing Fleetsthorpe from the rest of the civilised world, but more like a sparkling celebration of life and nature, as it threaded its way through the land, heading downhill to join the River Skimmer. Everything around them had seemed lush and green, and the hills that loomed up on either side of the dale seemed more like kindly guardians than the prison walls they'd appeared to be upon her arrival. The sense of space was awe-inspiring.

Fleetsthorpe land stretched as far as the eye could see, a patchwork of green in shades of laurel, apple, moss, fern, olive and teal, all stitched together with the golden thread of York stone walls. The only sound to be heard was the faint rushing of water from the streams that raced down the hills to meet the Skimmer, and the occasional bleat of one of the many Swaledale sheep that grazed on the hills—sturdy, thick-fleeced creatures with curled horns and black faces. Old stone field barns dotted the landscape, along with wind-bent trees, which provided much needed shelter for the sheep in bad weather. Everything smelled fresh and clean, and Eden's soul soared with the joy of recognising what a privilege it was to be standing there, part of something so huge, so ancient, so heartrendingly beautiful.

She had allowed herself to daydream for a moment, picturing herself tearing along the moors, clad in a Victorian dress and shawl, while somewhere ahead of her, Heathcliff waited, his eyes desperately scanning the horizon for his secret love. She'd adored *Wuthering Heights* since she was a young and impressionable teenager, and had also watched the film version so many times, her mother had threatened to snap the disc in half and make her watch *Bridget Jones* and *Love, Actually* on a loop, like normal girls. It was very odd, though, that, in her daydreams, Heathcliff no longer looked like Laurence Olivier or even Tom Hardy, but now bore a startling resemblance to Eliot. How had that happened?

Having collected her own body weight in gooseberries, she'd announced she had no idea what on earth she was going to do with them all, and Eliot had suggested she make jam—which she'd never attempted before—and crumbles, which were his favourite pudding and could be frozen. She'd taken him up on the challenge, and that was another reason she needed to visit the supermarket, for ingredients. Now, she decided she would be buying something else while she was there.

'You know, supermarkets sell some nice children's clothes,' she said. 'We could have a look, if you like? Get you some new outfits that aren't various shades of grey?'

'Can we?' Ophelia looked delighted. 'Oh, but Dad might get narked.'

'Why would he get, er, narked?'

'I don't know. But he used to get narked a lot when Mummy came home with new clothes.'

'Right. Well, I think even your dad would have to admit that you need new stuff. And you're growing so fast, the things you have won't fit you much longer. Clothes are essentials, and no one can tell you off when you buy essentials.'

Libby considered. 'Okay, then. If you don't mind.'

'I'd love it,' Eden assured her. 'Now, let's try to find you some socks that match.'

As she dug around in Libby's drawer, her hand closed on a velvet box. She pulled it out, puzzled. 'What's this?'

Libby and Ophelia glanced at each other.

Eden looked at them both. 'What is it?'

Ophelia said, 'Open it and see.'

'It's Mummy,' whispered Libby.

'Would you like to see her?' asked Ophelia.

Eden hesitated. 'What do you mean, it's Mummy?'

Libby stood up and took the box from Eden's hands. Gently, she opened the lid and fumbled with something. Then she handed it to Eden. 'That's Mummy,' she said quietly.

Eden looked inside, surprised to see a pretty silver locket, open to reveal a picture of a very attractive young woman. She had fair hair and blue eyes, and Eden took a sharp breath as she realised how strongly George resembled her. No wonder Eliot treasured his son so much. He was a constant reminder of the woman he'd loved and lost.

'She was very pretty,' she said softly, her heart aching for these children who had so cruelly lost her, and for Eliot who clearly hadn't got over her death. 'Whose locket is this?'

'We've both got one,' said Libby. 'The other one's in the drawer, too. They're the same. Dad gave them to us last Christmas.'

'We've got their photograph albums, too,' said Ophelia. 'And their wedding album. Dad said we could have them. And there's a photograph in a silver frame on the top of the wardrobe. That will be George's when he's old enough.'

'And there's Mummy's wedding and engagement rings,' added Libby. 'We're taking care of them for Dad.'

'Why have you got them all in here?' asked Eden. 'Why are they hidden away in your bedroom?'

The two girls fell silent for a moment, then Ophelia, ever helpful, said, 'Dad cried. When Mummy went, he cried lots. He took all her pictures down, and he gave all her stuff away to the shop in Ravensbridge. He doesn't like seeing her photo, and he doesn't like talking about her.'

'He really loved her,' explained Libby. 'She were right beautiful. It hurts him to see her, but he doesn't want us to feel we can't look at her picture whenever we like. That's why he bought us the lockets, so we can keep her close to us. We don't wear them much, though, 'cos we don't want to lose them round the farm.'

'I suppose when you're older, you can wear them more. It's a lovely thought. He's a very thoughtful man ...' Eden's voice trailed off, swamped with sadness for them all. Life was so cruel.

'She died on the way to Kirkby Skimmer,' said Libby flatly.

'What?'

'Her car went off the road. Dad said it wasn't her fault, but I heard Daisy talking to Adey and Mickey, one day, and I heard them saying she was driving far too fast, and it wasn't surprising she crashed. I didn't tell Dad that, though.'

Eden swallowed. These little girls were carrying a heavy burden, and they were doing it to protect their father, but she imagined that, if Daisy, Adey and Mickey were aware of the true circumstances of the crash, Eliot was all too aware of it, too. He was obviously protecting his daughters. There was so much love in this house. How awful there'd also been so much tragedy. And it made sense now—the reason Eliot was so worried about her driving to Kirkby Skimmer with his children in the car.

She carefully replaced the box in the drawer. 'This is obviously still raw for you all. I'm so sorry.'

'George won't remember her, will he?' said Ophelia. 'I feel sad about that.'

'I suppose not. Eden sighed.

'He were only four weeks old when Mummy died.'

'Four weeks!' Eden hadn't realised. Good God, things got worse and worse. It must have been hell at

Fleetsthorpe. She imagined the news filtering through to the farm, Eliot's shock and heartbreak, having to tell the children, coping with a tiny baby as well as his job, organising a funeral—all the time, dealing with his overwhelming grief and loss. She wished she could do something to make his pain go away, but she knew it was hopeless. Time alone would heal him, and she wouldn't be around to see him finally emerging from his mourning. She would be back in Upper Bourbury, listening to the histrionics of the Carmichaels and wondering what on earth she was going to do with the rest of her life. She knew that, after this experience, life with Cain and Honey would seem even emptier than it had before.

****

Shopping with three children in tow turned out to be harder work than Eden had imagined. Trundling round the supermarket, pushing George in the trolley, while the girls held onto the sides and pulled her to a halt every five minutes to examine something on the shelves that looked interesting, was exhausting and not a little frustrating. She was used to whizzing round and getting everything she wanted as quickly as possible. Shopping wasn't her favourite thing.

'What are you doing?' Ophelia whined, as Eden chose spices and herbs for the lamb casserole she was planning on making that evening.

'Buying food for tonight, and you'll be glad of it when you discover how nice it tastes later on.'

Ophelia didn't seem convinced, and even Libby looked fed up.

Eden quickly finished collecting the ingredients for the meal and threw in some store cupboard essentials then gave them a big smile. 'Okay, so, shall we have a look at the clothes?'

That cheered them up, to her relief. She wheeled the

trolley, struggling a little, as George seemed intent on hurling himself from side to side in his seat, making the load even heavier. Libby and Ophelia were soon excitedly looking through racks of clothes, and Eden leaned against the trolley, talking to George so he didn't decide it was all too boring and throw a tantrum.

The girls selected leggings, jeans, T-shirts, new underwear, pyjamas, and a couple of sweatshirts each. Eden added some respectable-looking skirts and sweaters that would be appropriate for school. Ophelia looked longingly at a Disney Princess costume, and unable to resist, Eden threw it into the trolley, receiving a delighted hug in return. Libby selected a backpack bearing the image of a young pop idol, which she said would be brilliant to take to school and would make all the other girls jealous. They helped Eden choose some new clothes for George, too, who seemed thoroughly unimpressed with their selection, scowling at the little trousers, shirts and pyjamas Eden showed him. The only thing that caught his interest was a pair of slippers with Spiderman on them, so Eden bought them, even though Libby assured her George had never seen Spiderman and would have no idea who he was.

With the goods bought and paid for and loaded into the car, they headed to the bookshop, where Libby selected a Michael Morpurgo novel, and Ophelia chose a David Walliams story. After making the shocking discovery that none of the children had ever heard of *The Very Hungry Caterpillar*, Eden bought it for George, and having put smiles on all their faces, she decided it was time to end the shopping excursion with lunch in a nearby teashop.

'Can't believe how hungry I am.' She peered at the menu in the window of The Teapot Café, noting that they served milkshakes, which Libby and Ophelia had insisted was the only thing they would consider drinking after all their exertions.

'Bet I'm hungrier than you,' Libby said, pushing open the door and ushering her younger sister in. 'I could eat a scabby 'oss.'

'Oh, really!' Eden grimaced. 'What a delightful expression. Come on, let's find a table and look at the menu.'

A huge array of mouth-watering looking cakes sat displayed at the counter. Eden planned on making a gooseberry crumble later and wanted to make sure they all had room for it, but, after all, they tended to eat late in the evenings. She was pretty sure she could fit some cake in after her lunch, and she was equally certain the children would manage it, too.

They made short work of their meals—quiche with salad for Eden, pizza for the girls, and a lasagne for George, as Ophelia had informed Eden that it was by far his favourite meal.

'Sure about that, are you?' Eden muttered, fishing in her bag for baby wipes and mopping George's tomato smeared face with one hand, while simultaneously scooping up dollops of mince and pasta that he had cheerfully hurled out of his high chair, with the other.

'Oh, yes. He loves chucking it all over the place,' said Ophelia, swallowing her last bit of pizza and sitting back in her chair with a contented expression on her face.

'I was thinking more along the lines of, "What's his favourite thing *to eat*",' said Eden, exasperated.

'Oh.' Ophelia shrugged. 'You never said.'

'Are we having cake?' Libby was already scouring the menu. 'They have triple chocolate cake in here, Ophelia, and red vel—'

When she didn't finish the sentence, Eden stopped wiping George's highchair down and turned to her. 'What's the matter?'

Libby stared ahead of her, and Eden followed her gaze, seeing only a couple, perhaps in their thirties, hovering round the counter. As she watched, the man turned his head their way. She noted the look of surprise on his face, but then he smiled and nudged the woman beside him, who turned and looked equally astonished to see them all sitting there.

'Who are they?' Eden whispered.

Ophelia turned her head away. 'Mr and Mrs Fuller. They're our friends, aren't they, Libby?'

Libby folded her arms, saying nothing.

Eden frowned. 'You don't look too sure. Is there something—'

'Do you mind if we join you?'

Mr Fuller appeared at their table, patting George's head as if he was a pet spaniel. 'My, you've grown. What a handsome chap you are.'

George scowled and banged his fists on the tray of his highchair.

Ophelia shuffled up on the bench, and Mr Fuller sat beside her. 'Thank you, sweetie. And how are you? Haven't seen you for a while.'

'You don't come up to the house anymore,' said Ophelia accusingly. 'You both used to visit all the time.'

He looked most apologetic. 'You're right. I'm terribly sorry about that. We've both been so busy, and with everything that's been going on ...' He looked at Eden, his eyes full of curiosity. 'I don't believe we've met.'

'Your coffee.' The woman handed him a cup and waited as Ophelia and Mr Fuller shuffled farther along the bench to give her some room.

'Thank you, darling.' The man smiled at her before turning back to Eden. 'I'm James Fuller, and this is my wife, Beth. We're long-standing friends of Eliot and Jemima. And you are?'

Eden swallowed. 'Er, Honey Carmichael. Pleased to meet you.'

'Honey Carmichael?' Beth frowned. 'Rings a bell. Oh,

aren't you Jemima's cousin, or something?'

'My mother was her cousin,' said Eden uncomfortably. Actually saying those things out loud brought it home to her what a web of deception she'd been weaving. She felt like a criminal, and as Beth's eyes bored into hers, she almost threw up her hands and yelled, "You've got me banged to rights, guv'nor. It's a fair cop!"

'Goodness. You're a long way from the Cotswolds,' said Mr Fuller. As Eden raised an eyebrow, he explained, 'I'm a fan of your father. Back in my younger days, I played his records nonstop. It was the most effective way I knew to wind my father up. No offence.'

'None taken,' Eden assured him. She'd grown up with Cain's records blaring out of the stereo. She could well imagine they'd been the bane of Mr Fuller Senior's life.

'Your dad was a popstar?' Ophelia's eyes widened, and even Libby looked impressed, in spite of the fact that she hadn't spoken two words since the Fullers arrived.

Eden wondered what was troubling her. It wasn't like Libby to be so unsociable.

'Not a popstar, exactly,' said Mr Fuller with a grin. 'He was a rock star. One of the old school. Not the sort of music you'd enjoy, Ophelia.'

'Can I listen to some of it and make up my own mind, please?' She looked indignant that he'd decided for himself that she wouldn't be a Cain Carmichael fan, and even though Eden was pretty certain that Mr Fuller was correct, she was rather admiring of Ophelia's determination to make her own decisions.

'I don't have any of his stuff with me,' she said.

Ophelia tutted. 'That's what the internet's for. I'll download some when I get home.'

Eden and Mr Fuller exchanged nervous glances. Cain's music was definitely not something an eight-year-old girl should be listening to. It was highly doubtful Eliot would approve, that was for sure.

'What brings you to the Dales?' Beth sipped her coffee, eyeing Eden with suspicion over the rim of her cup. 'I shouldn't have thought it would be the sort of place you'd want to visit.'

There was an edge to her voice. Eden wondered why for a moment, then remembered Jemima's family had never bothered to visit the farm when she was alive, so it was no wonder Beth was a bit hostile to one of them suddenly turning up when it was too late.

'I—er—I was at a bit of a loose end, and Eliot needed help with the children during the summer holidays, so I thought, why not?'

'And your Dad made you come here,' said Ophelia, slurping the last of her milkshake. 'That's why you won't talk to him when he telephones.'

There was an awkward silence for a moment. Trust Ophelia to say it like it was, thought Eden.

'How are you, Libby? You're very quiet,' said Beth, providing a welcome change of subject.

Libby shrugged. 'I'm fine, thank you.'

'What have you been doing in Kirkby Skimmer?'

Libby looked meaningfully at the bags of shopping, which were piled on the floor and hanging over the handles of George's buggy, but said nothing.

Beth flushed a little. 'Shopping, then. Did you buy anything nice?'

'Honey bought us some clothes,' Libby mumbled.

'And books,' added Ophelia.

'Splendid,' said Mr Fuller. 'And how's that beautiful pony of yours getting on, eh?'

'Oh, Flora's lovely,' said Ophelia eagerly.

'Excellent. Grand little mare, that. Now, will you be coming to our open day, do you think?'

'What open day?' Even Libby sat up straight and looked at him with interest.

'It's a little something we're doing for local charities,'

said Beth gently. 'Nothing grand. People can look round the house and gardens, and there are some stalls and fairground rides for the children. You'd be most welcome.'

Libby shrugged, and Eden realised it was Beth she seemed to have a problem with. She wondered why. The woman seemed rather affable. She had a warm expression in her dark eyes, and a gentle voice. She looked rather hurt by the little girl's attitude, and it seemed to Eden she didn't understand what the problem was, either.

'You must have a very big house,' Eden said. 'Whereabouts do you live?'

'Thwaite Park, just outside Beckthwaite. Not too far for you to get to, at all. House has been in our family for about a hundred and fifty years.' Mr Fuller leaned forward and tapped the side of his nose. 'My ancestor won it in a game of cards, can you believe? Those were the days. Regency house. Rather lovely, if I say so myself. Come and have a look. See what you think.'

'I'm sure that would be a lot of fun,' Eden said. 'Thank you for inviting us, Mr Fuller.'

'Oh, please, call me James,' he said with a smile. 'Now, how about you girls go to the counter and treat yourselves to cake?'

He rummaged in his coat pocket and handed them a ten pound note. 'Honey, would you like some cake?'

Eden nodded. 'Thank you. I'll have the red velvet cake, please, girls.'

She stood up, allowing Libby to leave the table, and watched as she and her sister headed off to the front of the café.

'Is Libby all right?' asked Beth, a little anxiously. 'She doesn't seem her usual self.'

'I know. I'm not entirely sure what's wrong with her,' admitted Eden. 'She was fine earlier.'

'Probably a shock, seeing us,' said James with a sigh. 'Let's be honest, darling, we've rarely been to the house since Jemima died, and we've lost touch with them. I expect seeing us brought it all back.' He looked at Eden. 'We've rather failed them, I'm afraid. It was a tremendous shock, you see, and Eliot was in such a state and was rather—er—unwelcoming for a time. He shunned everyone. Grief, I suppose. Anyway, he pushed us away, and we let him. I expect, if we're really honest, it was too much to deal with. We took the coward's way out. Easier to stay away, you see. No wonder Libby's cross with us.'

It could have been that, but Eden had a feeling there was more to it.

Beth pushed her empty cup away. 'We must go, James. Your dental appointment's in ten minutes.' There was a sudden curtness to her voice, but if her husband noticed he gave no sign.

He glanced at his watch. 'Good heavens, so it is.'

The two of them edged their way out and stood up. George reached over and smacked Beth's arm. She gave him a nervous look, but James laughed and squeezed the little boy's cheek. 'That's no way to treat a lady, young man. Be a good chap, now. No playing up your lovely young nanny!'

Nanny! Bloody cheek. Although, to be fair, she supposed she was, though she couldn't imagine what the real Honey would have said to that. Actually, she could imagine all too well, and the thought made her smile.

The Fullers called goodbye to the girls, who waved and turned back to the counter. Eden waved, too, as they left the café. As the girls returned to the table, she watched Libby. She seemed to be her usual self again, nudging and giggling with Ophelia, and arguing about which cake they'd chosen. Considering the Fullers were long-standing family friends, her behaviour had been odd. It seemed Beth had offended her in some way. Eden wondered what it was she could possibly have done.

CHAPTER SIXTEEN

Eliot closed his eyes and took a deep breath. The bright yellow Beetle was sitting outside the barn with not a mark on it, telling him they were home safe. He'd tried to put it out of his mind after Honey had telephoned at one to reassure him they'd arrived in Kirkby Skimmer. He didn't have time to hang around the house all day, worrying about it, when he had so much to be getting on with, and he knew he was being stupid. She was right—loads of people made that journey every day. There was no reason to expect catastrophe. She wouldn't be in the tearing hurry Jemima had been in, after all.

He parked the Land Rover and locked it up safely behind him. The dogs followed him into the house, sniffing the air curiously as they entered the hall, and Eliot's stomach rumbled in appreciation. Something was baking, and it smelt fantastic. He hadn't felt hungry all day—in fact, he hadn't even been able to face his dinner, which had meant double portions for Mickey—but now he realised he was starving.

The dogs fell upon their bowls, which had been filled in readiness. He must find out who was doing that. He'd meant to ask, but kept forgetting. He shut the door of the boot room and went into the kitchen.

Libby and Ophelia were sitting at the table, spoons in their hands, apparently eager to start the meal. George was in his highchair, happily banging a spoon on the tray. Honey was busy dishing out some sort of stew. Just the sight of it made his mouth water.

'Dad!'

'You had a good time in town? Looking very smart,' he acknowledged, noting they were wearing their best dresses and their hair was neatly tied back. He hadn't seen them look that smart for—well, a long time. Even George was clean and tidy, wearing a spotless pair of jeans and a shirt, of all things. Eliot didn't remember him even possessing a shirt. His hair was combed, and his face didn't have a single speck of dirt on it. He looked even more angelic than usual, and Eliot's heart swelled looking at him.

'We had a brilliant time,' said Ophelia. 'Do you like my new book?' She passed him the *Gangsta Granny* paperback, her eyes shining.

He nodded. 'Aye, right grand.'

'Honey bought it for me. George got *The Hungry Caterpillar*, and Libby got *War Horse*.'

'Can't believe they've never heard of *The Hungry Caterpillar*. I had to put that right,' said Honey, smiling.

She looked a different person when she smiled. Funny, he hadn't imagined she'd be the type to read, even when she was a kid. He'd assumed the most she would ever manage was a quick flick through some glossy magazine. Jemima hadn't read. She'd said it was boring. He realised, with some shame, that his children didn't have many books at all, and he hadn't really read to them much over the years. Something else to feel guilty about. It was becoming a long list.

'That's good of you. Thank you.'

'Oh, it was no bother. I hope you like this,' she said, passing him a plate that was piled high with stew, mashed potatoes, and a mountain of vegetables. 'I defrosted the lamb last night, ready.'

She passed the children their dishes then sat next to George, taking the occasional mouthful from her own plate in between coaxing him to eat and wiping his face.

Eliot's eyes widened as his taste buds registered the sheer perfection of tender lamb cooked in a sauce that sent his senses into overdrive. 'This is delicious,' he said. 'How did you make this? Thought egg and chips was your signature dish?'

Honey shrugged. 'I saw the recipe online, and really, it's not that difficult. Anyone can follow simple instructions, can't they?'

'Aye, I suppose. If they bother to read them,' he added, thinking ruefully of the washing machine. She was full of surprises. How had she managed to pick it up so quickly? He still struggled with beans on toast. 'So, how was town?'

'Surprisingly busy,' said Honey. 'There were an awful lot of tourists. The teashops and gift shops were packed. We had a lovely afternoon, didn't we, girls?'

'Yes, and we got loads of new clothes,' said Ophelia, scooping mashed potato onto her spoon.

'New clothes? What's this?' Eliot looked at Honey sharply. 'You've been buying them new clothes?'

'Well, they did need some, and I thought—'

'I don't expect you to buy my kids clothes. If they need any, I'll buy them myself. Let me know how much they cost, and I'll reimburse you.' He could provide for his own children, and no one was going to say he couldn't.

'Don't be silly,' said Honey. 'I enjoyed myself, and it was only a few things. Do you like George's outfit? Doesn't he look smart?'

'You bought him this?' Eliot looked at his son. He knew he hadn't recognised that shirt. 'Not much use out here, is it? What does he need smart clothes for?'

'Well, I—I thought he'd look cute in them. And he does, doesn't he? You can't deny he's a beautiful child,' she added with a laugh.

Eliot's hand tightened on the spoon. 'Waste of money,' he muttered, taking another mouthful of stew.

There was an awkward silence, until Ophelia announced, 'We saw Mummy's friends today.'

Libby dug her in the ribs, and Eliot's scalp prickled. 'What friends?'

'You know, Mr and Mrs Fuller.'

Eliot paused in his eating. He was quiet for a moment, then he turned to Honey. 'What did they want?'

'Just being friendly, I think. They were in The Teapot Café and they recognised the children, so, of course, they wanted to know who I was, and why I was looking after them.'

Eliot put down his spoon. 'None of their damned business.'

Honey looked surprised. 'I thought it would be all right. They seemed perfectly pleasant. Mind you, I could be biased since they bought us all cake.'

She smiled at him, and Eliot pushed his plate away. 'What did you tell them?'

'Well, that I was Jemima's second cousin and was taking care of the children for the summer, as you were so busy.'

'We've been invited to their open day,' said Ophelia, grinning widely at him. 'I'm not bothered about going round the boring old house, but they said there will be fairground rides. I want to go on the big wheel. There'll be a big wheel, won't there?'

Eliot didn't look at her. 'No.'

'You don't think there will be? Pooh! I like that best. Well, there's bound to be some dodgem cars. I can go on those. Ooh, and I'll bet there's a—'

'I mean, *no*, you're not going to the open day.'

Honey stared at him. 'Why on earth not?'

'I don't need to give a reason.'

'But it's just a bit of fun for the local children. I'm sure it will be perfectly safe.'

'Oh, and you know that, do you? Got a crystal ball, too, eh?'

'Well, no, but surely—'

'I said *no*, and that's the end of it. No more talk of the damn open day, all right?'

Libby eyes had gone wide. 'Are you mad at us, Dad?'

He swallowed hard then shook his head. 'No, not at all.'

'Ophelia said they were family friends,' said Honey, obviously puzzled. 'I'm sorry. Is everything all right?'

'It's fine. Why the hell wouldn't it be?'

She looked at him steadily for a moment, then he saw her whole demeanour change. 'Well, in that case, there's no need to be so rude, is there? It's hardly my fault, if you can't make up your mind who your friends are. Who needs friends like you, anyway? You can't even be bothered to attend a simple open day in aid of local charities, or let your children attend. God forbid they have any fun. Much better for them to be stuck out here in the wilderness, while their friends mingle and have a good time.'

'They're not really Dad's friends,' said Libby defensively. 'Don't be nasty, Honey.'

'Well, honestly, I like that,' said Honey. 'You were the ones who said they were friends, and all I did was try to defend you. I shan't bother in the future.'

Eliot cleared his throat. 'All right, that's enough. They weren't really friends of mine. Jemima was keen on them. Her sort of people. You know.'

She nodded. She'd obviously realised that already. Probably taken to them immediately. They were her sort of people, too, after all.

He felt suddenly exhausted. 'Think I'll go up and get a shower,' he said, standing.

Honey tutted. 'But you haven't finished your meal. And I've done gooseberry crumble for afters.'

'Leave mine in the oven. I might have it later. I'm not that hungry, truth to tell.'

Funny that. His appetite had completely vanished. He left the kitchen and headed upstairs as fast as he could. Throwing open his bedroom door, he stared round at the room that Jemima wouldn't have recognised. It was as plain and stark now as it had once been pretty and feminine. He'd got rid of everything she'd bought for the room, removed every trace of her and stripped it bare of its softness.

He sank onto the bed that she'd never slept in and put his head in his hands, wondering if the nightmare would ever be over, and if the guilt would ever leave him. Somehow, he doubted it, and the realisation that this was as good as it would ever be made him sick to his stomach—not so much for himself, but for the three children downstairs who would grow up in the shadow of his despair.

****

Eden covered the gooseberry crumble and put it in the fridge, wondering what on earth she'd said that merited such a change. He'd been fine until she mentioned buying the children clothes, and then it had gone completely pear-shaped when she'd mentioned the Fullers. She wondered why. They'd seemed perfectly pleasant. Beth was a little strained, but then, she'd been Jemima's friend. She was probably still missing her, and maybe wary of Eden and wondering what she was doing with her friend's children.

As for the clothes—was it wrong of Eden to buy them? She'd enjoyed it. They weren't expensive, and she'd paid for them herself out of her wages, rather than using Honey's credit card. She'd wanted to cheer them up, and she wanted Libby to go back to school with her head held high, looking smart and wearing decent clothes that fitted her properly. She must drum it into Eliot's head that he had to separate coloured clothing from whites, otherwise the new things would end up as grey and dreary as their old stuff.

She felt a sudden pang as she realised she wouldn't be around to see how they'd get on when in school again. She'd be back in the Cotswolds once the summer holidays were over. Whoever would have thought she'd be so reluctant to leave Skimmerdale? Honey would be baffled.

She really would have hated it here, Eden thought, as she began washing the pile of dishes. She wasn't the type to go gooseberry picking, or trail three children around a supermarket, or cook meals for them all. She wouldn't have gone with the children to collect eggs, or stood in a muddy field watching Libby and Ophelia taking it in turns to ride the pony. Although, to be fair, Eden wouldn't have thought she'd be the type to do those things, either.

She'd never had much to do with animals before, and was amazed how much she'd taken to life at Fleetsthorpe. She loved being around the children, too, taking care of them. And of their father. She tried not to dwell on that, though. She was in his bad books yet again. What she had to keep reminding herself was that she was *supposed* to be in his bad books. That had been the whole mission. She was letting her feelings get in the way of the plan.

She stacked the last plate, emptied the bowl of water, and reached for a tea towel, deep in thought. She loved the children already. Libby, so earnest and serious, always trying to put the feelings of others before her own; Ophelia, who was far more outgoing and likely to say what she thought, but who, even at eight years old, had already developed a protective streak towards her father and sister.

Then there was George. Clearly, he was the apple of Eliot's eye, and having seen Jemima's photograph, she could understand why. He was so like his mother, and having him around must have been like seeing his wife every day to Eliot.

As for Eliot himself? Eden felt a strange fizzing sensation in her stomach at the thought of him. There was something deeply sexy about a man who was a good father. Of course, it helped a lot that he had those amazing chocolate ganache eyes, dark curls and beautiful smile, plus a fabulous physique, created by hard work, rather than hours pounding a treadmill in a gym somewhere. Just the thought of him made Eden come over all peculiar.

She shook her head, grinning to herself. She was supposed to be his babysitter, not drooling over his undeniable assets.

'Honey?'

She spun round, almost dropping the tea towel on the kitchen floor, and found him standing in the doorway, looking sheepish. 'What is it?'

'I want to apologise. I've just had a right rollicking from the lasses. They reckon I were proper mean to you, and they're very annoyed with me. I'm sorry.'

'Oh.' She wasn't sure what to say to that. *Come here, kiss me as if your life depends on it, and I may forgive you*, perhaps? No, she didn't think that was appropriate, somehow. 'It's okay.'

'No, it's not.' He sighed, sinking down into a chair and running strong, capable hands through that shock of dark hair.

Eden turned away hastily. She could use a cold shower.

'Thing is, Ophelia's just told me what's been going on. At school, I mean. I had no idea.'

'Oh.' She'd already said that once. It seemed her grasp of the English language had deserted her. She sat down in the chair next to his, fighting the temptation to take hold of one of his hands. Or both. Or launch herself at him and fix her lips on his. That mouth of his was sheer perfection. It was crying out to be kissed. 'Are you ready for your gooseberry crumble?'

Are you ready for your gooseberry crumble! Had she really said that? She felt her face start to burn with embarrassment. For God's sake, Eden.

He looked a bit puzzled, not surprisingly. 'No, thanks. Maybe later. I gather the girls told you about what that little madam in Libby's class has been saying.'

'Yes.' She gulped. At least it was a step up from "oh". 'You know what some kids are like. She's probably horrible to plenty of other children, not just Libby. Not that that makes it better, of course.'

She didn't think he was even really listening. His hands were entwined, and he rested his chin on them, obviously deep in thought. 'I hadn't realised how badly I've been doing,' he said eventually. 'I thought I were managing. It didn't really occur to me, about clothes and hair and all that stuff. To be honest, just getting them bathed every night was a job in itself. I were so knackered every time I got in, and half the time I had tea to cook, and then I had to clear up afterwards. By the time I got them all to bed, I didn't have the energy to get the clothes ready for the next morning, then it would be a mad rush to get them ready for school the next day. I left them to brush their own hair, and do their teeth and that. I never noticed the clothes—how drab they were getting, or how small. Poor Libby. Why didn't she say something?'

Hesitantly, Eden laid a hand on his arm. 'Because she thinks the world of you, and she didn't want to add to your problems. You've done a brilliant job with them. They really love you.'

He made a funny sort of noise, and she peered at him closely. Were those tears in his eyes? She had the oddest reaction to the sight. Her throat seemed to swell, and she had to fight to keep her arms from going around him and drawing him into a hug.

'Thanks for buying their clothes today,' he said eventually, his voice gruff.

'It's okay,' she said, with some difficulty. 'Eliot, how have you been managing? I mean, you can't have done all this for two years on your own?'

He shook his head. 'Everyone rallied round. It's like that, round here. As soon as—as soon as everyone knew, they were up here, doing all they could. Daisy was amazing. I couldn't have managed without her.'

'Is Daisy ...?' Her voice trailed off. She didn't think she wanted to know who Daisy was to him.

'Her brother were my best pal. Known each other most of our lives. She's eight years younger than us, and used to trail round after us, getting on our nerves.' He gave a short laugh and shook his head. 'Poor Daisy. Tom cleared off years back. Found work in Leeds and left Daisy to it. She lives at Crowscar Farm, a few miles from here. Her mam died four years ago, and she's been looking after her dad ever since. He's a cantankerous old bugger, and she doesn't have it easy with him. She works at The King's Head, an' all, in Beckthwaite. Think she took the job on to get out of the house every day. When—when it happened, she took loads of time off to be here for me. They were very understanding—Dave and Jill, I mean. They own the pub, and they let her come here to help and kept her job open. Everyone chipped in. Even Granny Allen cooked us a few meals, not that we'd risk eating them, of course. Bugger that.'

'Who is Granny Allen?' Eden asked, curiously. 'I met her in the village, and she seems terribly protective of you. Is she your grandmother?'

'God forbid.' He laughed. 'Bless her, she's an old lady who lives on the outskirts of the village. Never married or had any kids of her own, but she kind of adopted all the local children. Used to get us all doing odd jobs for her when we were little. Cornered us whenever we went to the shop, or if she saw us out and about in the lane near her cottage. She's harmless enough, but let's just say, she doesn't rate hygiene very highly.'

'Ugh.' Having stood downwind of her, Eden could well believe it.

'Aye, but she tried to help me, in her way. Everyone did. But it were a tough time. People round here live very busy lives. There was a lot to do on the farms, and it was all hands on deck. The local women did their best to pop up here every day and do what they could, while getting on with their own jobs. And Mickey and Adey—well, I wouldn't be here now, if it hadn't been for them. They took on extra work. Did almost everything, while I looked after the kids, for the first few months.'

'You stayed with the children?'

'Aye.' He quieted for a moment. 'They'd lost their mother. They needed me. George needed me, too. He was a tiny baby. I had to prove I could do it—take care of them, I mean. I didn't want social services on my doorstep, accusing me of failing them.'

'Why on earth would they do that?'

He shrugged and began picking at the table. 'You know. Dad on his own. No mum around. Tiny baby. Two impressionable young girls. No family to call on. I was scared they'd think I couldn't cope.'

'Oh, Eliot.' Eden almost sighed his name and jumped up in embarrassment. 'Well, that's all behind you now. You've proved you can cope beautifully and no one can accuse you of failing them. I'll put the kettle on. Are they all asleep?'

'George and Libby are out for the count. Ophelia's looking at her book for a bit. I said she can read for half an hour. Thanks again for buying them the books. I forget things like that, an' all. God, I'm really not cutting it, am I?'

'Don't say that! Look, you've had a tough time. You've had to deal with all the pressures of the farm, take care of three young children, and all the while you've been grieving for Jemima. It must be so hard. I know how much you loved her.'

He rubbed his forehead then stood up. 'Think I'll watch the television for a bit. That okay with you?'

'Of course,' Eden said, startled by his sudden change of subject. Obviously, mentioning Jemima was still out of bounds. How was he ever going to work through his grief, if he didn't start talking about it? Still, she didn't think then was the time. He'd opened up to her more than she'd ever imagined he would. Best to take it slowly. 'You go on in, and I'll bring you a cup of tea. And,' she added, grinning, 'I'll bring you that gooseberry crumble. You will taste it, Mister, and you will give me a verdict.'

He smiled, and Eden's heart turned to crumble, too. 'Right you are. But I warn you, you'll have a long way to go to match my mother's gooseberry crumble. Still, we'll give it a try, eh?'

He headed into the living room, and she stood there for a moment, trying to calm down. He was just being nice, which was pretty amazing of him, given the way she'd acted for the last couple of weeks. Evidently, he was a forgiving man. But that was all it was, she reminded herself. He was kind and decent, and was willing to give the second cousin of his late wife a chance. It was nothing more than that, and Eden had to remember she was there under false pretences and would be leaving soon, anyway.

As if she needed reminding. The summer was flying by. Soon it would be September, and she couldn't imagine anything more depressing than leaving the farm and its inhabitants behind to head back to a life of endless drama with the Carmichaels.

CHAPTER SEVENTEEN

Honey couldn't believe it. She watched, open-mouthed, as Crispin headed through the living room carrying his overnight bag. 'You're actually going? After everything I said last night?'

He stopped, giving a big sigh, and turned to face her. 'Whatever you said, you obviously didn't listen to my replies. I have to go. I explained this.'

'But you already went back once to do that stupid surgery. You said that would be it.'

'I'd forgotten about the village fete. What am I supposed to do? Pretend they didn't invite me to open it?'

'Why not? It's hardly switching on the Oxford Street Christmas lights, is it? Just some poxy village fete. Who cares if you miss it?'

'I'd care, and so would my constituents. And so,' he added with a shudder, 'would Lavinia.'

'Oh, Lavinia!' Honey threw herself on the armchair and pouted. 'That's what this is really about. Your bloody wife, and how you're too scared of her to do anything she wouldn't approve of. Why don't you grow a pair and man up?'

'Honey, I'm getting rather tired of this attitude.' Crispin put down his bag and folded his arms. 'When you behave like this, you remind me how young you really are, and how little you understand about my career.'

'How dare you! I've sacrificed my entire summer for this relationship. I've risked being branded a marriage-wrecker, and I've lied to my own parents.' Honey tried to sound genuinely upset, but she was too angry. 'You, on the other hand, have done nothing but lounge about here in this Godforsaken dump, heading out into the town whenever you fancied, and going back to Windleby-on-the-Weir at the drop of a hat. Not to mention phoning your dragon of a wife every bloody five minutes. I'm a prisoner here. I feel like sodding Rapunzel, stuck in a tower with no means of escape.'

'Except a handsome prince,' said Crispin, beaming at her with what he probably imagined was a killer smile.

It had no effect on Honey any longer. She glared at him. 'Yes, well, who knows? While you're away, pretending to be someone who matters, I may head out and actually find a handsome prince to take me away from this crap.'

She'd barely finished the sentence before his arms were around her and his tongue was shoved so far in her mouth, it was practically down her throat. Honey wondered how she'd ever thought his kisses a turn-on. She summoned all her strength and pushed him away from her.

'Honey, darling, please. What's wrong?'

'I've told you what's wrong. Are you deaf or stupid? I've had enough. I'm bored here, and it's not going to get better while you're away, is it? I might as well have booked myself a holiday in Alcatraz.'

'I'll make it up to you, as soon as I get back, I promise. And, look, it's just one night. That's all. I swear, tomorrow, we'll do something. Go somewhere. Have some fun.'

She peered at him, unconvinced. 'You mean it?'

'Hope to die.'

'Be careful what you wish for,' she told him darkly. 'You'd better not let me down. This is your last chance. If you don't change your ways, I'm leaving, and I don't care who sees—or hears—me go. Understand?'

She saw by the look of fear in his eyes that he indeed understood, and felt some satisfaction. As she waved him off, she stood by the door for a moment, wondering what she could do while he was away. Watch yet another DVD? Read yet another trashy magazine? Paddle in the sea yet again?

She closed the door and leaned against it, sighing heavily. Closing her eyes, she tried to push away the thought that she really couldn't stand another day all on her own. She had no choice, so there was no point worrying about it. Or did she?

She opened her eyes, feeling a sudden rebellious urge to disobey Crispin's commands and brave the outside world. Why shouldn't she? Who would notice her, or care? He was paranoid, and she'd been a fool, playing into his hands by going along with it. Well, that stopped right now. She was a grown woman and she could do as she liked. After all, when all was said and done, what did she have to lose? Crispin was the married one, not her. And he was the one with the precarious public image that could be damaged beyond repair, not her. She had no political career to protect, no husband to anger, no image to sully. If anything, discovery would boost her career.

Sod Crispin. She was going out.

****

The town centre, such as it was, was busy, and Honey had high hopes of an exciting day out at first. It didn't take long for her to discover, however, that most of the shops sold nothing more interesting than sticks of rock and tacky little ornaments made of shells. *A Present From Worthingby* seemed to be painted, stamped, or etched on every item, and she couldn't believe the amount of tat that was for sale. It made her cross, thinking of her own little shop, which had stocked beautiful and elegant things that had barely shifted. Why would people rather spend money on stupid little trinkets, and boxes of confectionary with seaside postcards stuck on the front and the message *Thanks for Looking After Our Dog* written below, than on classy and expensive items that would enhance any home? People were idiots with no taste. Sad but true.

She mooched around the streets for a while, thinking she would never go anywhere with Crispin again. He had been a huge disappointment, and that was a fact. She finally found a café that offered a wider choice than egg and chips, fish and chips, or sausage and chips, and sat down at a table, having had to queue for ten minutes at the counter, just to order a toasted panini and a latte. She was annoyed and thoroughly fed up.

Maybe, she thought, it wouldn't have mattered so much if she was still besotted with Crispin, but it pained her to admit to herself that her feelings had distinctly cooled towards him. It was odd, but she'd never thought that the actual nuts and bolts of a relationship would affect things between a man and a woman in bed. She'd never understood it before. People could argue and bicker, but if you fancied someone, well, that didn't change, did it? And making love after an argument would surely be the best way to resolve your differences? Having put up with Crispin's dull and obstinate behaviour for the last couple of weeks, however, she had finally come to realise that feelings couldn't be switched on and off as easily as that. Her annoyance with Crispin could no longer be wiped away by a gentle caress, the pressure of his lips on hers, or the exquisite touch of his fingers on her skin.

Not so long ago, she'd forgive him anything, put up with any inconvenience, for the sheer pleasure of seeing him naked. He was a wonderful lover, and could almost bring her to climax simply by getting in bed beside her. Lately, though, he'd been having to work a lot harder to get her to forget her grievances. Last night, she'd only managed one orgasm, for goodness sake, and that had taken huge effort and a massive amount of concentration on her part. Since his prowess in the bedroom had been the one and only reason for her interest in him, she couldn't help but come to the conclusion that his days were numbered. It was all very tedious, and incredibly disappointing. She'd been so enjoying driving her parents to distraction, and the thought she was getting one over on that bossy bitch Lavinia had never ceased to make her smile. She couldn't dismiss the thought that, really, she ought to have more sympathy for Lavinia. The poor cow was stuck with her dreary husband for life. She deserved a medal.

The waitress, a dowdy young woman who could barely crack a smile, handed her a paper cup containing her latte, which only made Honey even more cross. They couldn't even serve her drink in a glass with a handle? Or even a ceramic cup? She supposed it was because they couldn't be arsed to do the washing up. She tutted as the waitress returned with her panini. It was supposed to be served with a side salad, but she hardly considered two lettuce leaves, a couple of cherry tomatoes, and two slices of rather withered cucumber a salad. So much for her lovely day out.

She sipped her latte and eyed the panini with suspicion. It stated on the menu that it contained bacon and brie, but she wasn't feeling confident that they even knew what brie was. Just her luck to take a bite and get a mouthful of melted cheddar, or even a plastic cheese triangle. She sighed and leaned back in her chair, gazing at the other customers. They looked as fed up as she did. So much for the *bustling, seaside resort of Worthingby* that Crispin had assured her repeatedly was a gem on the Dorset coast, and would enchant her as much as it had his family. They must be easily pleased, that was all she could think.

'Do you mind if I sit here?'

Honey sat up straight, looking around her in confusion. There were plenty of spare seats. Why did anyone need to share her table?

He didn't wait for an answer, but pulled out a chair and sat opposite her. What a cheek! 'It's a bit sad, isn't it?

Sitting in a café on your own, I mean.' He gave her a sympathetic smile.

'Excuse me! I'm not sad, at all, and if you think that's some sort of chat up line, I can tell you it's the worst one ever.' She flicked back her hair and gave the stranger one of her best icy stares. She was exceptionally good at them. She'd practiced loads on her father and Eden, after all.

He grinned at her, which wasn't the effect she'd been expecting. He was quite young—possibly around her own age—and had thick, brown hair and greenish-brown eyes with flecks of gold in them. He was attractive, in a youthful, gauche sort of way.

'Teddy,' he said, holding out his hand.

Honey stared at it before taking it tentatively. 'Er, Eden.'

'Eden?' He looked at her, seeming surprised for a moment. 'You don't look like an Eden. Still, lovely name.'

'Isn't it. Better than Teddy, at any rate.' She dropped her hand and took a sip of her coffee, watching him suspiciously over the rim of her paper cup. He looked tanned and fit. She'd bet a pound to a penny he hadn't got that healthy glow from lying on the beach at Worthingby.

The waitress arrived, carrying a cappuccino. He took it, flashing her a smile. To Honey's disgust, the waitress blushed a deep red and giggled, before turning back to the counter. How pathetic. Who did he think he was, anyway? He was hardly Brad Pitt. Come to think of it, he reminded Honey of someone.

She watched him thoughtfully. There was definitely something familiar about him. Where had she seen him before?

'So, er, Eden. Do you live here in Worthingby, or are you on holiday?'

She shrugged, shuffling uncomfortably on the cheap, plastic chair. 'On holiday. What about you?'

'On holiday.' He looked around, then leaned towards

her, lowering his voice. 'It's a bit of a dump, isn't it?'

Honey's eyes widened. He may be odd, but at least he had taste. She smiled. 'You're not wrong there. I would never have come here, if I'd known what a wretched dive the place was.'

'Are you here with family?'

She shook her head. 'A friend.'

'Ah.'

'What about you?'

'I'm here all alone,' he said, placing his hand on his heart, as if the fact greatly saddened him and he needed her sympathy.

She rolled her eyes. 'Now, that really is sad,' she said. 'Why would anyone come here alone?'

'I had some business to take care of and thought I'd combine it with a short break away from home.'

Honey's mouth twitched in amusement. 'What business? You look as if you've just left the sixth form.'

He looked rather wounded. 'For your information, I'm twenty-four, and I work damn hard for a charitable organisation.'

'Hmm, if you say so.' She tried not to laugh. He probably volunteered in an Oxfam shop, bless him.

'So, this friend,' he said, obviously trying to sound casual, and failing dismally. 'Male or female?'

'As if that's any of your business!' Honey couldn't believe the nerve of him. She didn't know him from Adam, and he wanted her life story. He could whistle.

'Oh, come on. What's the harm in telling me that, at least? You must know why I chose this table to sit at. You're a very beautiful young lady.'

'I know. Doesn't give you the right to pry into my private life, though.' She stabbed at a tomato, frowning when she noticed it was already beginning to wrinkle. Lovely. She didn't think she'd bother with the salad, such as it was. Dare she risk the panini?

'Is that the bacon and brie?' He shook his head. 'I had one yesterday. I wouldn't bother.'

'Thanks. I'd come to that conclusion myself.' She pushed the plate away and leaned towards him, resting her chin on her hands. 'Look, who are you? What exactly do you want?'

'I just saw you and thought how lovely you were,' he said, all wide-eyed and innocent. 'I thought I'd like to get to know you a little. Is that a crime?'

'No. Suppose not.' At least he was talking to her, which was more than Crispin ever did. And he was rather nice to look at, she had to admit that. Spending the afternoon with him would help to pass the time, and if it annoyed Crispin when he found out, well, it served him right. He should never have abandoned her to go to some pathetic village fete. 'So, how do you propose to get to know me?'

His face flushed a little. 'We could go for a walk on the beach?'

She screwed up her nose in disgust. 'Boring. I've been on that damn beach every day, and I hardly think it's going to change and become interesting just because you're there, too.'

'Ouch. You really know how to boost a man's confidence.' He put down his cup. 'Even the coffee's rubbish.'

'Hmm.' Honey thought for a moment, then picked up her bag. 'I know somewhere that makes better coffee, and we could, er, *talk* in private.'

'Really?' He looked thrilled. 'Where?'

She stood up. 'Well, come with me and you'll find out.'

As they left the café, she thought that, really, it was all Crispin's fault, so she couldn't be blamed for the way things had turned out. Anyway, she wouldn't tell him, so he needn't fret about it.

As Teddy took her hand, she felt a frisson of excitement that she hadn't felt for days. She had a feeling she was about to catch up on her orgasm quota, and maybe she'd encourage Crispin to go back to Windleby-on-the-Weir again, quite soon.

CHAPTER EIGHTEEN

Eden had had a busy morning, preparing chicken chasseur for the evening meal, cleaning the house, and working her way through three large piles of washing. George had finally fallen asleep after lunch, and Ophelia and Libby were—after a morning spent cleaning out the henhouse and riding Flora—settled on the sofa, reading their books. Taking the opportunity, she headed out of the back door into the garden, to hang out some washing. It was a bit cold, but it was dry and there was a good strong breeze, so it shouldn't take long to get the washing dried. She put down the basket and took a couple of pegs from the bag that was hooked on the line. A group of walkers passed by the bridge and called a greeting to her. She waved cheerfully before lifting a towel from the basket.

Five minutes later, as she pegged one of Eliot's shirts on the line, she heard someone cough behind her and spun around in fright, expecting to see one of the hikers. Her face relaxed into a smile for a moment, when she registered James Fuller's face, then she remembered Eliot's reaction to their meeting and felt anxious again.

'Sorry. Did I make you jump?' He pushed open the garden gate and came to stand beside her. 'Here, let me help you.'

'Thanks,' she muttered, as he handed her another shirt. It seemed all wrong, having him there on Eliot's land, handling his clothes. She felt distinctly uncomfortable.

'I thought I'd bring this leaflet over for the children,' he said. 'Just a few pages about what's going to be on offer during the open day. We're so delighted they're coming. It will do them good to mix with other children. They are rather marooned out here at Fleetsthorpe. All right during term time, of course, but during the holidays they must feel so isolated. I do know Jemima worried about it.'

'Hmm.' Eden knew she would have to tell him. 'I'm afraid they won't be going, after all.'

'Oh?' James raised an eyebrow. 'Why is that?'

'I—Eliot felt that perhaps ...' Her voice trailed off. She couldn't think of a reason that wouldn't offend him, and, after all, the Fullers had done nothing wrong. They'd been perfectly pleasant and obviously cared about the children's welfare. This was all very awkward.

'Let me guess. Eliot doesn't want them at our house.'

'I'm sorry. I don't know what's going on, but that's the gist of it, yes.'

'Sure.' James fumbled in his pocket and brought out a glossy little pamphlet. 'Here's the information, anyway. Perhaps you should show it to the girls and let them make up their own minds?'

Eden shook her head. 'Of course I can't. I'm sorry, Mr Fuller—'

'James,' he interrupted, smoothly.

'James. Yes. I'm sorry, James, but there's no way I can encourage them to disobey their father.'

'Would he have to know?'

'Of course he'd have to know! I couldn't possibly ask them to deceive him.'

He laughed suddenly and stuck the schedule back in his pocket, considering her with a very odd expression on his face. 'Funny that.'

'What is?'

'Your distaste for deception. Very funny.'

Eden swallowed nervously. 'What do you mean?'

'What do I mean? Well. Let me see. After our delightful meeting the other day, I thought I'd do a little research on Miss Honey Carmichael. Just taking a neighbourly interest, you understand. After all, Jemima was our friend, and we wanted to be sure that whoever looked after her children was fit for the job.'

Eden's stomach churned.

'You know, it's a very odd thing.'

'Wh-what is?'

'Well, either you take an appalling photograph, or—' He leaned towards her and hissed into her ear. '—you're not Honey Carmichael, at all.' He stepped back, watching her, and she felt the colour drain from her face.

'It's not what you think.'

'I haven't told you what I think,' he pointed out.

'Please, let me explain.'

'Oh, I insist on it.'

'I do know Honey. In fact, it was all her idea. I'm not some random stranger who turned up on the off chance. It was all planned. I didn't have a choice.'

'You didn't have a choice?' His tone was disbelieving.

'Honestly, I didn't. I work for Honey, you see. Well, strictly speaking, I work for Cain, and he insisted Honey come here to look after the kids, but she didn't want to. She hates being away from the shops, and she's not exactly maternal. I owed her a favour, and she kind of called it in.'

'What sort of favour?'

'It doesn't matter. The point is, she had me over a barrel, and the deal was that I come here and take her place, while she goes off and does … something else.'

'What do you mean? Where is she?'

'I'm sorry, I can't tell you that. It's not relevant, anyway, is it? The point is, she knows I'm here, pretending to be her, and if you think about it, it's probably a good thing I am. Believe me, there's no way Honey would be standing in a garden hanging out washing. The children are better off with me, trust me.'

'Trust you? Odd choice of words, in the circumstances. There's really no reason why I should trust you. I know nothing about you. Perhaps I should contact Cain Carmichael. Ask him for a character reference.'

'Oh, please don't!'

'Or maybe I should tell Eliot the truth about you, and let him find out more about you for himself. I'm sure he'd want to know. After all, we don't want to deceive Eliot, do we?'

He'd used her own words against her. Eden slumped, rubbing her forehead with her hand. She couldn't think of a way out of the situation. Cain would find out the truth and he'd sack her, no question about it. Honey would be livid, and Eliot ... She put her hand over her mouth. Why was it that Eliot finding out was the thing she dreaded the most? Even losing her job and facing the wrath of the Carmichaels paled into insignificance.

'On the other hand ...' He came to stand beside her, leaning casually on the wall, considering her carefully. 'Perhaps we could help each other out, in the circumstances. After all, you seem to be good with the children. I don't think they're suffering. And looking at this,' he added, sweeping his hand towards the line of washing that blew in the breeze, 'it seems you're taking care of all the jobs Eliot fails so dismally at. Perhaps I should keep my mouth shut. For now, at least.'

'Thank you,' Eden murmured, aware there was more to come. What did he mean, *help each other out*?

'In return,' he continued, 'you could help me keep an eye on the children. I'm not a bad person, Honey, or whatever your real name is. What is it, by the way?'

She hesitated, then swallowed. 'Eden,' she managed eventually.

He raised an eyebrow. 'Eden? How charming. Well, Eden, I care about those children, and so does Beth. We've been more or less pushed out of their lives since Jemima passed, and it's not fair. Beth, in particular, has suffered. I think it only fair that, given my discretion, you return the favour and make sure we have regular contact with them.'

'What? I can't!'

'I'm not asking for weekend access, for goodness sake. Just now and then. It's not much to ask. And I think the open day would be a good starting point. Bring them all. Make an afternoon of it. Let the poor little things have some fun, for a change. Why shouldn't they? Beth would adore to see them, and they'd meet up with their friends and have fun on the fairground rides. It's not going to hurt them, and what Eliot doesn't know won't harm him.'

'I'm not sure.'

'Well, Eden, think about it.' He pushed the schedule into her hand. 'After all, what's a little deception between friends?'

'I'll—I'll try,' she muttered.

He nodded, giving her a wide smile. 'Thank you. That's all I ask, Eden. We owe it to Jemima to be part of her children's lives. Eliot has been most unfair to us, but you can help us now, and in return, I'll help you. Fair's fair. Your secret's safe with me.'

'Thanks. I'd better go in, check on the kids.'

'I must go, anyway. Do show them the brochure. I look forward to seeing you all.'

He winked and walked away, making sure the garden gate clicked shut after him.

Eden watched him, her mind whirling. How was she going to get away with this? And how could she bring herself to deceive Eliot, and—even worse—get his own children to deceive him, too?

****

Eden had to pick her moment, of course. It came quite quickly, the next afternoon, which happened to be Sunday. Thankfully, Eliot was in a good mood, having eaten the huge roast dinner she had prepared.

'I can't believe how quickly you've cottoned on to cooking,' he announced, pushing his plate away. 'Like a duck to water. Your dad'll never believe it.'

You're not wrong there, thought Eden. Cain was still calling every couple of days, but Eliot had stopped asking her to speak to him. He still pulled a face and tutted at her when they heard the phone ringing and she made no move to answer it, but he no longer said anything, simply heading into the hallway to reassure Cain that all was well, and Honey was fine and more or less behaving herself.

'Don't tell him,' she said quickly.

He raised an eyebrow. 'Why not? I should think he'd be right pleased you've found something you enjoy that you're really good at.'

'Because—' Eden racked her brains desperately. 'Because if you tell him, he'll have me slaving over the oven every night for him, when I get back.'

'But would that hurt? You like cooking. You said yourself you're really enjoying it.'

Eden cringed inwardly, but she couldn't think of another reason. 'Yeah, but that's to keep me occupied while I'm here. I mean, there's nothing else to do here, is there? At least cooking keeps me from going mad with boredom. Back home, I'll have far better things to do.'

'Oh. Right.'

At the disappointment in his voice, she turned away, unable to bear it.

Libby trudged into the kitchen, her boots covered in mud. 'Honey, would you help me groom Flora, please?'

It had been raining all night, and Libby had evidently forgotten the rule about boots in the boot room. Eden looked pointedly at the little girl's feet. There were muddy footprints all over the kitchen floor.

'Look at the state of that now,' she said. 'I'll have to mop that up. Can't Ophelia help you groom her?'

'Ophelia's cleaning tack,' said Libby. 'Come on. It will be fun.'

Fun? Eden shivered. She couldn't imagine anything

scarier than being so close to a horse. All those hooves and teeth. Besides, she wouldn't have a clue what to do, and given Honey's equestrian background, she could hardly confess she wouldn't know where to start.

Eliot watched her, a question in his eyes. She knew another black mark was heading her way, but she didn't know how she could avoid it. Damn.

'Certainly not. I don't groom ponies, thank you very much.'

Libby looked hurt. 'Why not? It won't take us long.'

'You must have groomed your own ponies?' Eliot's voice was challenging. She'd annoyed him, she could tell.

She drew herself up and put on her haughtiest tone. 'Never. That's what grooms are for. Ponies were brought to me clean and saddled. I just rode the things.'

'Oh.' Libby shrugged. 'Okay. I'll do it myself.'

She left the kitchen, and Eden turned away, busying herself at the sink so she didn't have to see the look in Eliot's eyes. 'I'd better get the floor mopped. You really must tell the girls that dirty boots go in the boot room.'

'They don't usually forget.' She heard the scraping of his chair, and then he was beside her, putting his plate on the draining board. 'Reckon I'll head upstairs and do some paperwork.'

'Fine,' she said, her voice brittle. 'Give me a shout if George wakes up from his nap, and I'll come and fetch him.'

'If you're sure it's not too much trouble,' he muttered and left the kitchen.

Eden leaned on the sink and closed her eyes for a moment. They'd been making such good progress, and now she'd had to be a total bitch again. Well, what did it matter? She was supposed to be a bitch. She was supposed to be Honey. What would it achieve to be nice to him? Nothing would come of it. She would never see him again once she left Skimmerdale.

She cleaned the dishes and mopped the floor, then she sat for a moment, wondering how to make it up to Libby. There was no sound from George, and Eliot was still tucked away upstairs in his tiny office, doing some of the seemingly enormous pile of paperwork he had to cope with. It was the perfect opportunity to talk to the girls about the open day.

She took the brochure from her bag, shoved it in her jeans pocket, and headed outside. As she passed the jumble of empty barns and outbuildings, she stopped for a moment, distracted from her task. All these buildings, standing empty. Obviously, not all of them. Some were used for lambing, or for keeping the sheep clean before market or shows, for storing hay and winter feed, the machinery and tools. But there were a couple of large barns being allowed to crumble away. It was a shame. More than that, it was a huge waste of potential. She thought about the walkers that passed by the farm so regularly. Wouldn't they like somewhere to sit down, perhaps have a cup of tea and a cake, or a sandwich? Wouldn't they perhaps like somewhere they could bed down for the night? How many beds could one barn hold? If they were offered breakfast, too, how much would they be willing to pay? It could be the answer to Eliot's financial worries. It was certainly worth looking into. She would mention it to him, although not today. She wasn't exactly in his good books at the moment.

Remembering what she'd come to do, she sighed. Better get on with it.

The girls, as she'd expected, were in the stables. Libby was brushing a rather smart looking Flora, and Ophelia was sitting on an upturned bucket, polishing a saddle. They looked up as she entered then glanced at each other. Evidently, Libby had informed her sister of "Honey's" condescending attitude earlier.

Eden took a deep breath. 'Sorry about the grooming

thing,' she said, leaning against the wall and reaching out to stroke Flora's face with some trepidation.

"S'all right.'

Quite clearly, it wasn't.

Eden tried again. 'Thing is—well—it's all a bit embarrassing, really.'

They stopped what they were doing and looked at her with sudden interest.

'What is?' Libby asked.

'I was never shown how to groom the ponies, or clean the tack,' she said. Well, that was the truth, anyway. She just had to embellish it a little. 'Other people did it for me, and so I have no idea how to do it.'

'Really?'

'Yes. And—' Oh, sod it, in for a penny, in for a pound, '—the truth is, I've lost my nerve around ponies.'

Libby and Ophelia looked deeply sympathetic. 'Did you have a fall?' asked Ophelia.

Eden nodded. 'Yes. Yes, I did.'

'Didn't you get straight back on?' asked Libby.

Eden shook her head.

'Oh, Honey! You should always get straight back on. So, how long is it since you last rode?'

'Gosh.' She tried to remember. There'd been a trip to the seaside when she was about eight, and she'd been persuaded to sit on a donkey. She supposed that counted. 'Years ago.'

'You poor thing. No wonder you didn't want to help.'

Their animosity was obviously forgotten, and Eden tried to push down the guilt she felt for lying to them. She had a worse task to do, after all. 'I'd rather you didn't mention it to your dad,' she said. 'He'd think I was being stupid.'

'No, he wouldn't,' Ophelia assured her. 'You should tell him. Maybe he could help you get over your nerves.'

Eden seriously doubted that, but she smiled at the girls

and took out the brochure. 'I was thinking. About the open day ...' Her voice trailed off. How could she do this? What sort of person had she become?

'Dad won't let us go,' said Libby with finality. 'So, that's that, really.'

Ophelia took the brochure from Eden's hand. 'There *is* a big wheel. I knew it. Now I'm proper fed up.'

'Well … Eden took a deep breath. 'Maybe you could still go? I mean, I know your dad said no, but that's only because he can't take you. You have me now, and I'll look after you.'

Libby put down the brush and turned to face her. 'But if he says no, what can we do?'

Ophelia's eyes brightened. 'Are you going to let us go, Honey? Without telling him?'

'Of course not!' Libby glared at her sister. 'We can't do that.'

'I don't see why not,' said Ophelia.

Eden had suspected she'd be up for it. She'd been whining about how unfair it all was for days, and had made it quite clear that she considered the ban to be a massive injustice. Now she needed her to help persuade her sister. Dear God, how low had she sunk?

'What the eye doesn't see, the heart doesn't grieve over,' Ophelia said.

'Where on earth did you hear that?'

'I heard Granny Allen say it once. I think it means, what Dad doesn't know can't hurt him.'

Eden shook her head. The child was a one-off, which was probably a good thing.

Libby chewed her thumbnail. 'But if he found out—'

'We'll have to make sure he doesn't find out, then, won't we?' said Ophelia cheerfully. 'Besides, it will be too late by then. We'll have a right good time on the rides, and we'll bring him something nice home to eat, and he'll be that pleased, he'll forget to be cross.'

'Dream on,' muttered Libby.

Eden decided it was time to step in. 'Look, I'm not usually one to encourage disobeying your father. I just think, well, it's a little open day. No big deal. It's in the garden of your friend, Mr Fuller. We'd be home before your father finished work. There's no need to worry him about it. I think he's just afraid you'd get lost, or hurt yourselves, but that won't happen. I'll keep an eye on you. After all, you haven't seen your friends since school term ended, and it would be good for you to meet up with them and have some fun. Of course, it's entirely up to you. I'm not trying to influence you, one way or the other.'

Libby looked deeply sceptical, and Eden hoped the children couldn't see her blushes in the gloom of the stables.

'It's a no-brainer, isn't it, Libby?' squealed Ophelia. 'I can't wait!'

'I don't know.' Libby looked thoroughly confused, and Eden wanted to give her a hug and tell her to forget the entire thing. 'Dad won't be happy.'

'Oh, come on, Libby. You heard what Honey said. Why should we miss out? Besides, don't you want to see our friends? I'm sick of riding round the farm, aren't you? And think of the fairground rides! How often do we get to go to a fair? It will be fun! Say yes.'

'There's no pressure, Libby,' said Eden gently. She meant it. She wished she'd never brought the subject up. Damn James Fuller.

'Libby, stop being so wimpish,' said Ophelia. 'I think you're scared!'

'I'm not scared,' protested her sister. 'I don't want to upset Dad.'

'How can we upset him? He won't even know. And if he does find out, he won't be able to say we could have been hurt, because we won't have been, so that will be a pointless argument.'

Eden could well imagine that Ophelia would be the image of Honey in ten years' time. That was just the sort of logic she applied to arguments with Cain.

Libby sighed. 'All right, then.'

'Yay! I'm going on the big wheel. Do you think there'll be dodgems, too?'

'I don't know. I haven't seen the brochure.'

'I'll leave it here with you,' said Eden. 'I'd better go back to the house, in case George wakes up. Remember, not a word.'

Ophelia giggled. 'Our secret.'

Libby nodded hesitantly. 'Okay.'

Eden left them poring over the brochure and headed back to the farmhouse, thinking she was a horrible person, and if Eliot did find out, she wouldn't blame him in the slightest if he sent her packing immediately. James Fuller was as bad as Honey, using information against her to make her do things she should never have done, both of which involved lying to the man she wouldn't want to deceive in a million years if she had any choice in the matter. That was the problem, though. She didn't have a choice.

****

Lavinia threw down the Jackie Collins novel and rolled over onto her back. The late morning sunshine was already getting too hot, and the sun lounger was uncomfortable. She was sick of having to shade her eyes, and she'd missed a bit on the back of her leg when she'd smothered herself in lotion yesterday, with the result that she had a very red, sore patch on her calf. Gregorio was getting on her nerves with his constant demands, too, and she was completely cocktailed out. Between the two of them, they'd practically drunk the well-stocked bar in the villa dry.

She adjusted her sunglasses, checked her watch, and

gave a big sigh. Gregorio was still asleep. He would no doubt wake up at around lunchtime, feeling horny.

She shifted uneasily and reached for her bag. Time to add more lotion. Her gaze fell on the novel, and she sighed. The trouble was, Gregorio didn't do it for her. He may have been young and gorgeous, but he didn't have the effect on her that Crispin had. She missed him. How terribly inconvenient it was to actually fancy your own husband. She was the only one in her circle of friends with that problem. They often told her how much they envied her. If they only knew the truth.

When the phone rang, her heart leapt momentarily, hoping to hear his voice, telling her he loved her, even if it was a lie. She tried not to feel disappointed to see her father's name displayed on the screen. Then she felt a twinge of nerves. What was he ringing to tell her?

'Sweetheart.'

'Hello, Daddy. How are you?'

'Well, since you ask, I've been suffering all bloody week.'

'Suffering?'

'My hip. It's no use pretending any longer. I reckon I'll be booking myself in for a hip replacement soon. I can't carry on like this.'

Lavinia thought of the amount of time her father spent on the golf course. His hip didn't bother him when he was striding towards the nineteenth hole, laughing and clapping his cronies on the back because he'd beaten them yet again. Now wasn't the time, however. 'Sorry to hear that, Daddy. What's the news?'

'Ah, well, that's what I'm ringing to tell you. There *is* news. Big news. We've got the little bitch this time.'

Lavinia sat up straight—not easy on the wretched sun lounger. 'What do you mean?'

'She went into town yesterday, and I followed her. She ended up in this tatty little café on the seafront, and I sat at a table not far from hers.'

'I hope she didn't spot you.'

'Well, she did, but so what? She had no idea who I was, and besides, she had more important things going on.'

'Oh? Meaning what?'

'Meaning, she met up with some fella.'

Lavinia felt a frisson of excitement. 'A man? Are you sure?'

'Jesus Christ, Lavinia, I may be getting on and ready for a hip replacement, but I'm pretty sure I know what a man looks like.'

Lavinia pushed down her impatience. 'I meant, are you sure he was that sort of man? You know, someone she was involved with romantically? He could have been a friend, a relative. Who knows?'

'*I* know. They were flirting like mad, and then, the best bit of all, she took him back to the cottage.'

'What? You're not serious!'

'Oh, yes. While Crispin's away, the demonic little tart will play.'

Lavinia lay back and closed her eyes. So, Crispin's bit on the side had a bit on the side of her own. How ironic.

'He stayed a few hours. Saw him move in front of the bedroom window a couple of times. No doubt what's going on there. I reckon they've been involved for a while.'

'What makes you say that?'

'I'm almost sure I've seen him before. There's this red Mini, you see, that's been parked round the corner from the cottage on a few occasions. I'm almost certain he's the driver. I think he's been hanging round, waiting for Crispin to leave. I must have missed him the other times. I mean, I may be wrong, but ... Anyway, point is, she's cheated on Crispin, and all you have to do is ring him up and tell him, and that will be that.'

'Ring him and tell him? Are you insane?'

'Well, what are you going to do, then? Let her get away with it?'

'Of course not! But this can't be blurted out over the phone. I need to think about this. Plan a strategy. I don't want him to shoot the messenger, after all.'

There was a silence for a moment, then her father's voice replied, 'I suppose you're right. I mean, if he's in love with her, he's not going to want to hear it, especially from you.'

Lavinia felt a knife through her heart. In love with her? He couldn't possibly be. An infatuation, perhaps. That was bearable, even understandable, given her youth and beauty, but love? No, she was far too young, too selfish, too stupid. Crispin couldn't possibly love her. Could he?

'I need to think things through,' she said. 'I'll be in touch. Keep watching, Daddy. And thank you.'

'Well, think things through pretty damn quickly,' he said. 'I'm bored stiff in this dive, and the sea air is very harsh on the joints. Don't be too long, or I may just confront the pair of them myself.'

CHAPTER NINETEEN

It was the morning of the open day at Thwaite Park, and Eden felt sick with nerves. She'd tried to tell herself it was all perfectly harmless to take the children, at first. After all, it was just a local get-together with some rides and stalls. She understood that Eliot was protective of his children, but there was such a thing as being overprotective. They were precious to him, and she totally got that, but they had to have a life outside of the farm. Why shouldn't they join in with the other children and have some fun with their friends? When school resumed, why should they be the only ones who hadn't been to the fair? It would single them out again. It seemed very unjust to Eden.

Anyway, Beth and James were friends of Jemima's, and she was sure that if Jemima had been around, she'd have taken her children herself. She was only doing what their mother would want her to do, surely?

No matter how much she tried to justify it to herself, however, she knew that what she was doing was wrong. She wished she hadn't agreed to take the children to the open day without Eliot's knowledge. It seemed a horrible betrayal of his wishes.

Libby was barely controlling her nerves, as they waited for Eliot to finish his dinner and head out for the afternoon. He'd spent the morning drystone-walling and seemed in no hurry to finish his meal and resume work, even asking for an extra cup of tea, before pushing his plate and mug away and announcing it was time for him to get off.

'Right,' Eden said, as he finally rode out of the yard on the quad bike, with Lug running behind him, 'let's get you ready. Are you absolutely certain you want to do this?'

It wasn't like Libby to go behind her father's back.

Eden wanted her to be certain that she knew what she was doing. If the children decided they didn't want to do it, she would drop the whole idea. James Fuller would have to do his worst.

'Your dad won't like it, you know,' she continued. 'If he finds out, there'll be hell to pay. Are you sure you want to go ahead?'

Libby looked nervously at Ophelia. 'What do you think?'

Ophelia stared at her, dumbfounded. 'Are you changing your mind?'

'No, but ... Dad won't like it.'

'Dad won't know, so it doesn't matter,' said Ophelia. 'Or are you scared?'

'Scared? Of what?'

'Of going on the rides and chucking up in front of all those people.' Ophelia giggled.

'Of course I'm not. I just don't want to upset Dad.'

'Who's going to tell him? And anyway, I'll bet he won't be mad when you come home with a candy floss, or something, for him. I bet he'll be chuffed to bits. You know he gets scared that we'll hurt ourselves, but we won't. Don't be a wimp, Libby.'

'I'm not a wimp!' Libby glared at her then shrugged. 'Fine, we'll do it.'

As she put George's shoes on him and combed his hair, Eden wished with all her heart she hadn't agreed to the event. It felt sneaky and sly. As if she hadn't fooled Eliot enough by pretending to be someone she wasn't, she was now helping his children lie to him, too. It was all wrong. But she could hardly back out now, could she? They'd be so disappointed. And, besides, she wouldn't put it past James Fuller to open his mouth. He'd left her in no doubt that, as nicely as he put it, he wouldn't hesitate to drop her in it if she didn't give him what he wanted. She tried to tell herself it was only because he cared about his wife's feelings, but she couldn't help feeling uneasy. What if he decided there was something else he wanted her to do? How far would she have to go to keep his silence?

By the time she'd washed the dishes, tidied the kitchen, and brushed and tied back the girls' hair, it was time for them to set off. She fastened George into his car seat, and loaded the buggy and a bag containing a comb, purse, phones, keys, drinks, tissues, spare clothes for George, nappies and baby wipes, into the boot.

Music came from the grounds of Thwaite Park as they approached. Eden's stomach churned with nerves. What if Daisy was there? Someone was bound to mention to Eliot that they'd seen them at the wretched open day. Why hadn't she thought of that before? There was no way this would remain a secret. Sooner or later, she was going to have to come clean and admit she'd gone behind his back. She wondered if it would be better if she told him tonight, before anyone else got in there first.

The entrance gates had been strung with bunting, and there were signs advertising free parking. Inside a wooden kiosk that had been set up inside the driveway, an elderly man was selling tickets to the event. They were five pounds each for adults and two pounds for children, with under-threes free. Eden reached out of the car window, paid the money, and took the tickets, before heading slowly up the drive while admiring the large Regency house ahead of them. She followed the signs for the car park, where she unloaded the buggy and strapped George in, hooking the bag over the handles. Then they all headed off in the direction of the music.

'Well, hello. You came!'

Eden tried not to smirk, as, walking past the entrance to the house, they were greeted by James Fuller.

Dressed in a tweed suit, in the style of a nineteen-thirties country squire, he looked, frankly, a complete pillock. 'I'm so glad you turned up,' he said, bending down and pinching George's cheek. 'You made the right decision. Eliot needs to loosen up. He does like to keep the children closeted away up at Fleetsthorpe, doesn't he?'

'Not at all,' Eden said, lying through her teeth. 'If he knew how much it meant to them, I'm sure he'd agree.'

'Really? You got his permission, then?' James smirked, seeing Eden's obvious embarrassment. 'Thought not.' He smiled down at the children. 'So, what are your plans? Do you want a guided tour of the house?'

Ophelia pulled a face. 'I want to go on all the fairground rides until I'm at the point of hurling.'

'That's the spirit,' said James.

'Ah, the Harland children,' said Beth, rushing towards them, a fixed smile on her face. She wore a summer dress and looked incredibly elegant.

Eden had put on one of Honey's dresses, but didn't feel anywhere near as smart as Beth. Beth was one of those women who made it look effortless—a bit like Honey herself. Eden wondered how they managed it.

'I wasn't sure you'd make it,' Beth added.

'We're going on the big wheel,' Ophelia informed her. Beth smiled.

'Are you? How wonderful. Don't make yourself sick. There's a tea tent and they're selling rather lovely cream teas.' She glanced down at George. 'He's growing,' she said. 'His face changes every time I see him. He's not like his sisters, at all, is he?'

'Well, thank God for that, darling.' James laughed. 'It would be pretty awful for him, if he looked like a girl, wouldn't it?'

'Well, in a way, he does. He's got a strong look of Jemima,' she said. She bent down, tilting George's face up and staring at him intently.

Eden almost pointed out that he wasn't in a showing class and didn't need inspecting, but then she realised that George was the closest thing Beth had left to her friend, so she shut up.

'Can we go on the rides now?' demanded Ophelia.

'Of course, of course. It's a pound a ride, which is rather good value, and all for charity, of course. What about you, Honey? Are you up for a tour of the house?'

'Maybe later,' said Eden, uncomfortably. 'I want to stick close to the girls, make sure they're okay.'

'Of course they'll be okay. They'll have the time of their lives,' said James.

'Perhaps we should leave them to it, darling,' said Beth. 'Enjoy yourselves, children. Maybe we can meet up a little later and share a cream tea?'

'Who shares a cream tea?' demanded Ophelia. 'I want one to myself, thanks very much.'

'Ophelia, you're such a pig,' admonished Libby.

Her sister shrugged and pulled on Eden's hand. 'Come *on*, Honey. Let's go.'

Eden gave the Fullers an apologetic smile and headed towards the fairground, from where loud music and excited shrieks could be heard. No doubt most of the girls' classmates were there enjoying themselves, too.

At a pound a ride, the fairground was good value for money, but it still meant an expensive afternoon for Eden. By the time Ophelia declared that she needed a break from whizzing around on rides that even Eden would have thought twice about, Eden had spent a small fortune.

Having surrendered half an hour previously, Libby was sitting on the grass, recovering from her dizzy spell, when her sister bounced over and declared herself ready for a jam and cream scone.

'Are you sure you can face it?' said Eden doubtfully.

'Of course I can! What's up with you, Libby? You look green.'

'I'm all right,' said Libby, forcing herself to her feet and giving Ophelia a defiant look. 'Cream tea sounds good to me.'

More money, then, thought Eden, checking in her purse and sighing. It may have been for charity, but she didn't even know which one. She hoped it was worth it and wasn't simply lining the pockets of James Fuller.

'Hook-a-duck!' Libby seemed to have recovered her composure, and pointed the stall out to her sister as they headed towards the tea tent.

'We have to go on that,' confirmed Ophelia. 'I'm ace at hooking them. Takes me ten seconds, or less. Can we have a pound, Honey?'

'Have your scone and a drink first,' Eden advised. 'We've got all afternoon. Take it easy.'

Ophelia pulled a face but didn't argue. The lure of the scent of freshly-baked scones was probably too strong to resist. They did smell delicious. Eden's stomach rumbled in anticipation.

As she devoured the last bite of her cream tea, Eden sank back in her chair and sighed. 'That was gorgeous. Would it be too greedy to buy another, do you think?'

'You can finish mine, if you like,' said Libby, pushing her plate towards Eden. 'I think maybe I should have said no to the waltzers, after all.'

'You're such a wimp,' said Ophelia. 'Bet George would have loved them.'

'I think the merry-go-round was fast enough for George,' said Eden firmly. She eyed the little boy, who was smeared in jam and cream and had a good spattering of crumbs around his mouth. 'I'd better clean him up,' she said, reaching in her bag for the baby wipes. 'Do you want to go on the hook-a-duck now?'

Ophelia nodded eagerly, and even Libby looked a little less green at the prospect. Eden fished around for her purse and handed them a ten pound note. 'Right, there's enough there to go on a couple of games, and to get yourselves a candy floss or toffee apple to take home with you. You have to promise not to wander off, though. Just stay near the stalls. Promise?'

The girls agreed and Eden finished cleaning up George as they shot out of the tea tent, the ten pound note clutched tightly in Libby's hand. Within moments, Eden was joined by Beth, who laughingly admitted that the two of them had practically knocked her over in their rush to get to the hook-a-duck stall.

'Sorry. They're really excited. They've had a lovely afternoon.'

'I'm so glad. They deserve it, after all they've been through.' Beth sat down beside her and folded her hands in her lap. 'I must say, I'm astonished Eliot allowed them to come here.'

Eden felt her stomach flip over with nerves. Was the woman onto her? She was pretty certain she'd guessed Eliot had done no such thing. The question was, why? Why was Eliot so against his children spending time with his late wife's friends?

'He does tend to keep the children close to him since Jemima passed. Not surprising, of course. It was a terrible tragedy, wasn't it?'

'Um. Terrible.'

'She was a remarkable woman, wasn't she?' Beth stared toward the cream tea counter, where a long queue had gathered. Eden had the strongest feeling that Beth wasn't even seeing the people standing in line so patiently. 'Incredibly beautiful. No wonder Eliot fell for her.'

'To be honest,' Eden said, 'I never met her.' Then she remembered what Freya had said to Honey and tried to amend her statement. 'At least, Mother says I did, but I honestly can't remember.'

'Really? I'm surprised. Once seen, never forgotten,' she said.

After a moment of quiet, Eden put the dirty baby wipes in her bag and smoothed George's hair. He grinned up at her, and she smiled back at him.

'You're very fond of them all, aren't you?' said Beth suddenly.

Eden suppressed a sigh, wishing she'd clear off. She couldn't shake the feeling she was compounding her disloyalty to Eliot by talking to the Fullers, and Beth was getting annoying with her inane remarks. 'Yes, I suppose so. How could I not be?'

'You're right, of course. I used to be very close to them,' Beth said, a hint of sadness in her voice.

Eden peered at her. 'What do you mean, used to be?'

'Things were … strained—at the end. Jemima and I had a falling out, of sorts. We would have made it up eventually,' she added hastily. 'It's just, we never got the chance.'

'That's a shame.'

'Yes.'

Her voice was wistful. She reached out and stroked George's face.

He responded by sinking his teeth into her hand.

'Ouch!'

'Sorry,' Eden said. 'Think he needs a bone to gnaw on, or something. He's always biting something.'

Beth smiled. She looked lovely when she smiled. She was an attractive woman, when she didn't look so pinched and anxious. 'I expect he's getting some more teeth.'

'He is,' Eden confirmed. 'His top molars are coming through. He's not happy about it.'

George informed her that he was thirsty, so she asked Beth if she'd mind getting the bag that was hooked over the buggy's handlebars. She obliged, and Eden rummaged around, managing to retrieve his cup.

'Is that your phone ringing?' Beth asked suddenly.

Eden froze. Was it? Or was it Honey's? She listened intently. It was her own ring tone. She grabbed the phone from the bag and glanced at the screen. Cain! What the hell did he want with her?

'Would you mind holding George a minute?' she asked. 'I need to take this.'

Beth looked nervous. 'Me? Well … I suppose so.'

Eden handed George, who was happily supping from his cup of juice, over to her and moved away to a corner of the tent. Casting a glance over her shoulder, she watched as Beth awkwardly sat George on her knee and felt uneasy. Another betrayal of Eliot's wishes. Sighing, she answered her phone. What would Cain be ringing her for?

****

Cain closed his eyes and sighed. 'Aw, that's better. Nothing takes your aches and pains away like a hot tub.'

'I wouldn't know,' said Roxy. 'I haven't got any aches and pains.'

He frowned. Show off. Just because she was thirty-odd years younger than him, there was no need to rub it in. Unless *it* was an anti-inflammatory gel. He found that stuff increasingly valuable. 'It was a figure of speech,' he lied. There was no need to remind her of the age gap by banging on about his creaking knees, aching back, and various other ailments. The only part of him guaranteed to be stiff these days was his neck. It was a sorry state of affairs.

'Can I play Candy Crush?' She peered longingly at his iPad, which lay tantalisingly close on the edge of the hot tub, but was strictly out of bounds, as far as Cain was concerned. He liked to keep it close at all times, but she knew as well as he did that it wasn't allowed too near the water. He'd told her enough times.

'No, you can't. You'd probably drop it, and then where would we be? Besides, you're not here to play Candy Crush.'

'Ooh, so what am I here for?' she cooed. 'Are we going to play *park the purple Porsche* again?'

God forbid, thought Cain. Sitting there, with the soothing water bubbling all around him, he was pain free for the first time in ages. He wasn't going to risk losing that for a bit of how's-your-father with a woman who was irritating him more every day.

He tensed as her hand reached out and stroked his chest. 'Why don't you sit back and relax?' he asked her, trying to keep the annoyance from his voice.

'But I'm bored, Cainey baby. Are we playing *hide the sausage*, or what?'

She was doing that stupid childlike voice again. He shuddered. 'For Gawd's sake, Roxy, play your bleeding Candy Crush. But if you drop my iPad, you'll pay for a replacement. Right?'

She smirked and reached out for the iPad, but tutted when she picked it up. 'Someone's trying to get in touch.'

'Who? Is it Honey?'

He sat up straight, forgetting all about the risks of water to the device, and grabbed the iPad from her. His face dropped into a scowl when he realised who was trying to call him.

'Freya! What the bleeding hell does she want?'

'Ignore her,' Roxy began, but he'd already accepted the call, and his ex-wife's face loomed up on the screen.

'What do you want?' Cain snapped.

Freya wrinkled her nose. 'Well, aren't you all charm. Where on earth are you? Please tell me you're not in the middle of something distasteful. You appear to have forgotten your shirt.'

'I'm in the hot tub.'

'Oh, dear God. Do not lower the iPad, I beg of you. I still have nightmares about your nether regions.'

'Have you just rung me to insult me?' he demanded.

Roxy tutted. 'Are you gonna be on that thing long? I wanna play Candy Crush.'

'Oh, you're babysitting again,' purred Freya. 'How

sweet of you. Give the child some Smarties and send her off to play while the grown-ups talk.'

'Don't be a bitch.' Cain noticed Roxy was wearing a most unattractive pout and had folded her arms. She looked scarily like a stroppy teenager. He nodded at the back door. 'Rox, go and pour us a drink. I'll be there in a minute.'

Roxy glared at him, but she climbed out of the hot tub and padded up the path towards the kitchen. Cain watched her for a moment, wondering how many bikinis one woman could possess. He didn't think he'd ever seen her wearing the same one twice. No doubt, he'd paid for them all, too. He was beginning to think she wasn't worth it.

'Earth to Cain Carmichael. Hello?' Freya's voice caught his attention, and he blinked.

'Sorry. I was—'

'I know what you were doing, thank you very much. I recognise that leer. Ugh. Anyway, enough of all that. I wondered how you were feeling?'

'Eh?' Cain peered at the screen suspiciously. 'What are you on about? I'm fine. Why shouldn't I be?' *And why the hell would she care, anyway*?

'Oh, that's good. I was so worried about you, after I saw it on the news. I thought you'd have taken it badly, but I forget you're made of sterner stuff, being working class. I should have known.'

'What the hell are you babbling on about, woman?' He was growing increasingly annoyed. Bleeding women. They did your head in, no doubt about it.

She smiled, which thoroughly unnerved him. Freya smiling was always a bad sign. 'Well, the line-up, of course. You know. Rex Scotman's mega-gig.'

'Mega-gig!' He almost spat in disgust, but her words suddenly hit him. 'What line-up? What are you on about?'

'Didn't you see the news? Rex was on again. I must say, he's quite the flavour of the month, isn't he? I'll be astonished if he's not made a knight of the realm before too long. The concert's all organised. Everyone who's anyone is playing. I must say, I was surprised you weren't taking part. I suppose you're too busy? Are you helping Roxy with her homework that evening?'

'Piss off, Freya.'

'Well, that's lovely. I can see you're not in the mood for socialising, so I'll bid you farewell. Do give my love to little Roxy, won't you? Such a shame she won't be able to watch the concert herself, what with the teenybopper bands playing, but I expect she'll have to be in bed by the time it's shown on television.'

'Freya!'

She giggled. 'Bye, Cain. We must do lunch sometime. Maybe in twenty years or so?'

She vanished, leaving him glaring at the blank screen. He fought the urge to throw the iPad as far from him as he could manage, though given his dodgy shoulder that wouldn't be very far. Instead, he put it down gloomily and sank back, feeling the water churning around him. He hadn't felt this gloomy since his twenty-second album, *Fucking at Hell's Door*, had failed to make the top one hundred. Even having the title track banned on Radio One, the offending word on the album cover replaced with a row of asterisks, and a fake demo organised outside the record label's offices, in protest at the lewd and blasphemous content, hadn't shifted it. It had been the end of his recording career, to all intents and purposes. In recent years, he'd gathered some new fans and a certain nostalgia value. He'd guested on modern artists' tracks and had hoped his career would be revived. And now that twat Rex Scotman had scuppered his chance to headline in the biggest gig of the decade. How had it come to this?

'Cainey!' Roxy's whiney voice drifted out from the kitchen.

Cain sighed. She'd be standing there, drink in hand, all

lip gloss and quivering bosom. He really couldn't be arsed. And that was worrying in itself, come to think of it. He'd really lost his sex drive lately. Even her sister had failed to raise more than a polite interest. Was this what old age did to a man? He needed taking out of himself. He needed someone to argue with, someone who didn't simper and sulk and want sex every five minutes. He didn't want Roxy's company. He wanted Honey's. She'd always been his favourite kid, although that wasn't saying much, truth to tell. She was a git and gave him a headache, with her arguments and demands, but she made him laugh, and she was a match for his quick wit. Not many were, least of all Roxy.

He picked up the iPad and stared at the screen, unsure. What if she wouldn't talk to him again? He didn't think he could stand much more. As if it wasn't bad enough that the rest of his kids thought he was a waste of space, to lose his baby would be too much. He should never have sent her away. It was his own fault.

A minute later, he put the iPad down and rubbed his forehead wearily. She hadn't answered. What did he expect? There hadn't been any answer from either the farm, or her mobile. He'd sent her dozens of texts in the last few weeks and she'd ignored them all. Anyone would think he was the one who'd been shagging the Tory MP, the way she was acting. On impulse, he picked up the iPad again and tried another tack.

After several rings, she answered. 'Hello?'

'Eden! Thank Gawd! At least you're talking to me. Have you heard from her?'

'No. Haven't you?'

'Jesus. I thought she'd at least have spoken to you. What the hell's going on?'

'She's sulking. You should know what she's like. Don't let her rattle you.'

'I feel bleeding mean. What if she's really miserable up

there? Was I wrong?'

'Look, Cain, that's Honey's problem—you always give in to her. Stop feeling guilty. You didn't have much choice, did you? You know what Honey's like, once she makes her mind up about something. She would never have stopped seeing Crispin, if you didn't make her.'

'True. True.'

There was a long silence before Eden, sounding agitated, said, 'Was there something else?'

'Not really. I wanted to talk to her. Little git's all I got, really. You won't believe what's happened. That bleeding Rex Scotman's bin on the news again, announcing the line-up for his charity gig. Everyone's taking part. I mean, everyone. There'll be Sting and Bono and Macca, and all the other usual suspects.'

'Well, that's good,' she said.

'No, it ain't. Notice anyone missing?'

'Er, Elton John?'

Was she trying to wind him up? 'Me! The miserable git ain't asked me! Can you believe it? I mean, how's it gonna look, eh? Biggest charity event of the decade, and yours truly ain't gonna be part of it. How am I ever gonna get me knighthood? He's done me over, Eden. Stitched me up like a kipper. I ain't bleeding happy.'

'No, well, you wouldn't be. Why don't you call him? Ask him what's going on?'

'Are you mad? Give that lousy, stinking pig the opportunity to laugh at me? Let him know he's got one over on me? Hell will freeze over first.' He gave a big sigh. 'I wanted to talk it over with Honey. Me other kids wouldn't listen, or care. Honey would snap me out of it. She'd tell me to stop being so pathetic and get a grip.' He sighed again, fondly. 'Maybe I should go up there to Yorkshire. Talk to her.'

'Are you mad?' Eden sounded horrified. 'You can't give in to her like that.'

'But I miss the little git, Eden,' he said wistfully. 'I wanna hear her voice, and if she won't talk to me. ..'

'Look, I'll call her. See if she answers me.'

'You won't be able to get through on her mobile. No signal up there. I can give you the house number, though. Have you got a pen?'

'Yes, yes. Go on.'

Cain reeled off the number, which he knew by heart after dialling it so much.

'Okay, got it. I'll call her and persuade her to talk to you.'

'Promise? If you can do that, Eden, I'm your pal for life. If she won't—well, I reckon I'm gonna have to pay her a visit. I'll speak to you later, kid. See you.'

'Bye, Cain.'

He put the iPad down again and climbed out of the hot tub. He'd had enough. Even the bubbles weren't helping to soothe him anymore. Stupid thing had been a waste of money, anyway. Roxy's idea, of course. "Everyone's got one, Cainey. They help you relax, Cainey. All them bubbles will do you the world of good, Cainey."

Bleeding bubbles. If he wanted bubbly water, he just had a bath after eating a curry. Made plenty of bubbles then.

He pulled on his towelling robe from off the back of a nearby chair, fastened the belt, and, collecting the iPad, headed into the house, where Roxy would, no doubt, be waiting for him. He'd have to make the effort, he supposed. At least he had one thing Rex Scotman didn't have—a blonde, buxom beauty with half a brain cell, and a libido on overdrive. Lucky him.

****

Eden ended the call from Cain and immediately scrolled through the phone book, searching for Honey's new number. 'You'd better answer this,' she muttered.

The phone rang and rang, and Eden began to despair, but just as she was about to give up, Honey's voice said, 'What?'

Her usual charming self, then, thought Eden. 'Honey, your father's rung me.'

'And you answered? Are you stupid?'

'He rang me, not you!' She was calling Eden stupid? Rich. 'He's desperate to talk to you.'

'He can be as desperate as he wants,' she said sullenly. 'He shouldn't have packed me off to the wilderness, should he?'

Eden tutted impatiently. 'Are you forgetting that you didn't go? You got away with it. Stop being so horrible. He's really upset, and he needs to talk to you. He's had a bit of a blow.'

'Regular occurrence,' she said coolly. 'Have you seen Roxy's collagen mouth? I'll bet it's not a *bit* of a blow.'

'Honey! That's your father!' Honestly, thought Eden, she was impossible. Fancy thinking that about your dad. 'He's been left out of the charity gig.'

'What bloody charity gig?'

'Rex Scotman is having a massive fundraising concert for his school in Africa, and he's invited just about every pop and rock star of the last five decades to take part. Everyone, except your father.'

She actually laughed. Eden wondered if she had even an ounce of compassion in her. 'Priceless! Serves the old goat right.'

'Honey, he's really upset about it. He wants to talk to you,' she said, although she couldn't imagine why. One of Honey's little chats might finish him off. 'He says if you won't talk to him on the phone, he's going to come up to the farm and talk to you in person.'

'He wouldn't,' she said confidently. 'He thinks he needs a passport for anywhere farther north than Birmingham. He's bluffing.'

'I don't think he is,' Eden assured her. 'You didn't hear him. He means it. You have to talk to him.'

'Oh, bollocks. One way or another, he always manages to spoil things,' she said. 'All right, I'll bloody call him. But I'll make it perfectly clear that he's to stop pestering me in future. And you can stop pestering me, too, come to that.'

'Well, I'm very sorry, I'm sure,' Eden said. 'It's going well, then?'

She tutted. 'I wouldn't go that far. It's boring as hell here, and can you believe it, Crispin's left me twice now, to go to his constituency and deal with political business? He's supposed to be on holiday.'

'He still has duties to do,' Eden said. 'Just because Parliament's in recess doesn't mean he doesn't have—'

'Oh, shut up, Eden. You sound just like him. And he has to report to bloody Lavinia every day, too, as if he was some sort of naughty child. Honestly, how can I respect him, when he behaves like that? So much for a powerful man.'

'Well, I'll leave you to it,' Eden said, thinking it sounded as if the novelty was well and truly wearing off with Crispin, thank God. 'You will ring Cain?'

'I said so, didn't I? Now bugger off.'

'Spoilt little madam,' Eden muttered as she hung up.

Shoving the phone in her pocket, she turned around … and froze in her tracks.

Eliot and Beth stood near the entrance to the tent. Eliot had George in his arms, and judging by the dark expression on his face, he was about as angry as Eden had seen him yet, despite Beth's efforts to placate him.

Eden swallowed. She was in huge trouble.

CHAPTER TWENTY

Eliot was trembling and couldn't seem to stop. He held George tightly to him while glaring at Beth. 'So, where is she?'

Beth looked alarmed. 'Just over there. She got a phone call. Eliot, calm down.'

'Calm down? You can say that to me, of all people?' He held her gaze, until she looked away, biting her lip.

'It was a long time ago. We've all moved on. You have to let this go.'

He knew she had tears in her eyes, and a part of him longed to reach out and comfort her. 'Beth ...' His voice trailed off. There was nothing he could say that could possibly bring her any comfort, and she didn't need to hear it all again. 'I'm sorry, but I'll never let it go.' He kissed the top of George's head.

'Jam,' said George, pointing vaguely in the direction of the table.

Eliot glanced round. Evidently, they'd all been having a marvellous time eating scones, as if nothing he said made any difference. He would throttle Honey. How dare she go against his wishes like this? She'd lied to him, deceived him. He wondered why he was so disappointed.

'Eliot.' She was beside him suddenly, her face scarlet with embarrassment. At least she knew she was in the wrong, which was more than some people. 'What are you doing here? I thought you'd be busy all day.'

'Evidently,' he said. She held her arms out for George, but he half turned away, moving George out of her reach. 'I distinctly told you the children couldn't come to this damn open day. You knew how I felt. I couldn't have made it any plainer.'

'I know, and I'm sorry. It's just that the girls really wanted to come, and their friends were going to be here, and I thought—'

'You thought, what I didn't know wouldn't hurt me? Why doesn't that surprise me?'

'Eliot,' murmured Beth.

He turned back to her, seeing and hearing her pain and feeling helpless. 'I'm sorry, Beth. I really can't do this.'

'You can't punish the children,' she said. 'And you have to stop punishing yourself. What we did—'

'What we did was a big mistake, and look what it led to. Oh, aye, I know. You're right. What's done is done, and I can't turn the clock back, but it doesn't mean I can carry on as if nowt happened. What do you want me to do?'

He swallowed, suddenly aware that Honey was standing there, looking baffled.

'Take George home,' he said. 'I'll get the lasses.'

'But you can't,' Honey protested. 'They're trying to win some prizes, and they're having a good time. You can't show them up in front of all their friends. You take George home, if you must, and I'll wait.'

He leaned towards her, his face determined. 'I said, *take George home*. Now.'

She looked shocked for a moment, then her face hardened. 'Don't come over all Heathcliff with me, Eliot Harland. I'll take George home, but only because I actually care enough about him to avoid a scene.'

'Don't even start on that,' he said. 'Seriously.'

'Well, if you cared anything about him, you—'

'I'd what? Go on, what would I do?' He was aware he'd raised his voice. Several heads turned to look at him, and Honey took a step back. He felt Beth's hand on his arm and shrugged it off. 'Never, ever tell me that I don't care about George. Never try to tell me how I should be raising my own bloody kids, and don't contradict me when I tell you what they can and can't do. Do you understand? They're *my* kids. Do you hear me? You do anything like this again, and I swear, I don't care what your father says, I'll send you packing and look after them myself. Now, take George and *go*.'

She hesitated, but only for a moment before she reached out and took a wriggling George from his arms and headed over to the buggy, where she proceeded to strap him in. Even from where he was standing, he could see her hands trembling and felt ashamed.

Beth folded her arms. She was shivering. 'I think we need to talk.'

'We've said it all, Beth,' he said flatly. 'There's nothing left to say.'

'Isn't there?' Her eyes were wide, scared.

They could talk all day, but what good would it do? Besides, he didn't want to discuss it, to actually put it into words. Knowing it was one thing, admitting it out loud was quite another. 'I'm sorry, I really am. What happened—we have to live with it. I don't see how talking about it will help anything now.'

'But it wasn't our fault, Eliot. Not really. Please—'

'Beth, I care about you, I really do, and I'm sorry for everything. More sorry than you could ever possibly know. But I want to keep my life, and my children's lives, separate from yours now. You have your life here. It's best for everyone if we keep things distant. Please try to understand.'

He couldn't bring himself to explain further. Impulsively, he bent over and kissed her gently on the cheek, then straightened, flushing slightly as he realised Honey was staring at the two of them in astonishment.

Beth squeezed his hand, saying nothing, then nodded and walked away, and he turned to face Honey, who was leaning on the buggy, obviously shocked.

'You still here? Go home.'

She opened her mouth, as if she was going to make some sharp retort, but then seemingly thought better of it.

She began to push the buggy away, and Eliot let out his breath and sank onto the nearest chair. He would let the girls win their prizes. It wouldn't make much difference now, and Honey had been right in a way. They wanted to do what their friends did. He could hardly blame them. Let them at least have that much.

What was he going to do? He never had enough time for anything, and the fear gnawed away at him constantly—fear of losing the children, fear that one day they'd know the truth. How would that change things? Would they ever be able to forgive and forget? It was all such a mess.

Not for the first time, he wondered if it was all worth it. Fleetsthorpe had been in the Harland family for generations, and it was the only life he knew, or wanted. Yet, if he had a safe, nine-to-five job, he could be there for his children more. In a town, there would be childcare facilities, nurseries. Yet, he felt he would go mad, living in a town. Was he already mad? If not, it was a miracle. Besides, what did he know, but farming?

Of course, there was an easy option. A way out. He could take it any time he wanted and be assured his children would be looked after and cared for, the house kept neat and tidy, and no social worker or court would say the kids were being failed. It wouldn't be so difficult, would it? Couldn't he make that sacrifice?

His stomach churned in protest, and he sat up straight, shaking his head as if shrugging the whole idea off. Unbidden, the image of Honey came into his mind. Honey stirring a pot of stew and looking so proud as she tasted it; laughingly mopping up George's mess as half of his dinner inevitably landed on the tray of his highchair; coming home from town with bags full of new clothes and books for the children, bought and paid for with her own money. He tried to remember the sarcasm and the arrogance, but funnily enough, he could only remember the smiles and the kindness.

His stomach flipped again, and he was gripped with sudden panic. He was an idiot. More than an idiot. Once was idiotic, twice was sheer lunacy. He stood up, pushing his way out of the tent and making his way towards the stalls.

Several villagers nodded and smiled at him, while others raised eyebrows, evidently surprised that he'd turned up. He focused on getting to the hoopla stall, where Ophelia was being handed a coconut by the vicar, who was valiantly manning the attraction for the afternoon.

'Very well done,' he was saying, as Eliot approached. 'You're one of the very few to have won. Have you been practising? Fond of coconuts, are you?'

'Not really,' said Ophelia. 'But Libby said I couldn't do it, so I had to prove I could.'

'Ah, well, perhaps you can give it to your father. I'm sure he'd appreciate the gift, and the level of skill that went into winning it for him.'

Ophelia and Libby exchanged glances and shrugged. Eliot hated himself in that moment. 'I most certainly will,' he heard himself saying. 'Very impressive, Ophelia. And I love coconut.'

'Splendid,' said Mr Edwards. 'Nice to see you here, Eliot. Good to have a break, sometimes.'

The vicar moved round the other side of the stall, to take money from some other children, leaving the girls staring at Eliot in obvious horror.

'I'm sorry, Dad,' said Libby, but Ophelia seemed to have decided it was best to act as if this was all perfectly normal.

She waved the coconut in the air and shrieked at him, 'Look, Dad! Hardly anyone wins a coconut on these stalls, and Libby said I had no chance, but I knew I could do it.'

He raised an eyebrow and tapped his foot on the ground, waiting.

Libby hung her head.

Ophelia, on the other hand, brazened it out. 'What are you doing here, anyway? Wish I'd known, I'd have looked out for you. You could have a go, if you like. See if you can beat me. Bet you can't.'

'Shut up, Ophelia,' muttered Libby.

Ophelia scowled. 'Are we in trouble?'

'What do you think?' he said, trying to suppress a smile.

'I don't see why we should be,' she protested.

'Did I tell you not to come here today?' he asked.

'Well, yes.'

'So, I'm sure you know why you should be in trouble,' he replied.

She tutted. 'Well, it's not fair. Loads of our friends are here, and their parents don't mind. They came with them. We only had Honey. Where is Honey, anyway?'

Eliot straightened. 'I sent her home.'

'Why?' demanded Ophelia, while Libby looked worried.

'She knew you weren't to come here, and she went behind my back to bring you. Do you think that's right? Because I certainly don't. I told her to take George back, and I'll speak to her later.'

'Oh, Dad, please don't blame Honey,' begged Libby. 'It really wasn't her fault.'

'She's the adult, and she's supposed to be looking after you,' he began, but Libby moved to his side and pulled on his arm.

'It was my fault,' she said. 'I begged her.'

'No, you didn't,' said Ophelia, with an air of resignation. 'You said we should do as we were told. You know it were me who begged her. I wouldn't shut up. I right chewed her ear off, truth to tell.'

Eliot bit his lip. She was a little madam, but he loved her honesty, as much as he loved Libby's kindness. They were wonderful girls and deserved so much better.

'Nevertheless,' he said, 'she shouldn't have given in to you.'

'Oh, come on, Dad,' said Ophelia. 'You know what I'm like. She just wanted to help us.'

'She did, really,' said Libby. 'She's been that nice to us, and she tries to make things lovely at home, and she cooks our favourite things, and lets us help her bake and doesn't moan about the mess, and she let us try on as many clothes as we wanted, and she helped us choose those books and didn't mind that we took ages trying to decide, and she makes a cracking crumble, and ... Please don't be mad at her. We really like her.'

'You do?' He wondered how that had happened. How had Honey won them over so easily?

Given her appalling reputation and her initial bad behaviour, it was staggering that she'd settled in so beautifully and done so much to make the children happy. George clearly adored her, too. He remembered the first couple of days after she'd arrived at the farm. She'd been so cutting, so sarcastic, and downright cruel, at times. She hadn't seemed interested in Fleetsthorpe, or the children, and had been pretty dismissive of their entire lives. What had caused her to change so thoroughly? How had she ended up being so important to them all and so well-liked?

'It really matters that much?' he asked.

They nodded. 'We don't want you to be narked with her,' Libby said. 'We don't want her to leave. It's been so much nicer at home with her there.'

He pulled them both to him, his anger forgotten. 'All right. We'll leave it at that. But you have to promise me that when I tell you not do something in future, you'll do as you're told. It could be really important. You understand?'

'We understand,' said Libby.

'Promise,' said Ophelia.

'And you do know, don't you, that Honey will be going home in a few weeks? When you go back to school, she'll be going back to the Cotswolds. You understand that?'

They looked at each other. 'Does she have to?' asked Libby eventually.

'You could ask her to stay,' suggested Ophelia. 'I bet she would. She likes you.'

He laughed and shook his head. 'I think you're wrong there, sweetheart. She puts up with me. Liking might be stretching things a bit far.'

'Oh, but she does,' insisted Libby. 'You can tell she likes you.'

'Oh, aye? How's that, then?'

'Well, Dad, have you seen the look in her eyes when you're in the room? She goes right funny, and all dreamy, like.'

Ophelia giggled. 'Honey loves you, Dad.'

'All right, all right, that's enough of that rubbish,' he said. 'Come on, let's get you home before I change my mind and decide to punish you after all.'

They left Thwaite Park behind them, heading back in the Land Rover to the farm, and Eliot's mind replayed the conversation over and over again.

She goes right funny and all dreamy.

He couldn't say he'd noticed. Had he? Maybe he'd been too busy pushing away his own thoughts to notice hers. What was happening between them?

He clenched his fists, mentally berating himself. Nothing was happening, and nothing ever would. He'd finished with that kind of thing. In his experience, it came with a heavy price, and he was still paying it. There was no way he was walking into that trap again.

Besides, what was he thinking? Honey Carmichael was rich, glamorous and spoilt. She lived the sort of life his girls would only ever read about in magazines. The idea that she would want to spend the rest of her life in a remote farmhouse in the Yorkshire Dales was ludicrous. God knows, he had proof that it was complete madness, didn't he? Absolute, physical proof.

CHAPTER TWENTY-ONE

Eden placed the bowl of cereal in front of George and sat down heavily in the chair beside him. It was going to be a difficult day. James Fuller had been on the phone, asking—very nicely of course—if she could bring the children to meet him at Kirkby Skimmer that afternoon.

'I have to meet my accountant. It would be the perfect opportunity to have some lunch with you all before my appointment.'

'I don't know. I don't think I can get away at such short notice.'

'The Daffodil Café. One o'clock. You know it?'

'No, I don't. And, like I said—'

'It's easy to find. I'll see you then. Looking forward to it.'

He'd rung off, leaving her in no doubt that he expected her to be there with the children. What would be his next demand? How far was this going to go?

To make matters worse, Eliot had barely spoken two words to her since he'd got back from Thwaite Park. In fact, he'd avoided eye contact with her.

In a way, she supposed, it was a good thing. At least he hadn't ranted and raved at her, as she'd suspected he would. He hadn't done anything much. It was like he was trying to pretend she wasn't there. God, he must really hate her. If she'd known how badly it would affect him, she would never have taken the girls to the damn event.

Of course, it was her own fault. She should have known better. Now she'd really hacked him off, and that was upsetting her more than she cared to admit. She wondered, yet again, who had tipped him off that she'd taken the children to the open day. He'd refused to say, but she'd lay odds on it being Daisy. She must have been there and seen them. No one else would rush to cause so much trouble.

Libby eyed her warily over the Weetabix.

Seeing the anxiety in her eyes, Eden tried to smile. 'You okay, Libby?'

Libby nodded, saying nothing.

Ophelia, ever helpful, sprinkled sugar over her cereal and said, 'She's worried 'cos Dad's being right mean to you. Don't worry, I told him it was my fault. He'll calm down in time. He always does.'

Was the child really only eight? Eden reached over and ruffled her hair. 'You're very kind to take the blame, but honestly, it was my fault, not yours. I should have been responsible. I'm the adult, after all.'

'But we should have done as we were told,' said Libby, her voice heavy with guilt she should never be feeling. 'I'm ever so sorry, Honey.'

'Dad's okay now,' Ophelia assured her and grinned at Eden. 'We were talking about the Skimmerdale Show earlier. We're going to enter the gymkhana games. Dad said we could. He's going to be taking part, of course.'

Eden's eyes opened wide. 'Your dad's entered the gymkhana?'

The girls collapsed into giggles. Libby shook her head, dark curls bouncing. 'Don't be silly! He enters the sheep classes. The Skimmerdale Show is very important, you know. If his sheep do well, they sell better at auction.'

'Oh, I see.' Eden grinned. 'Thought he'd look a bit daft on Flora. So, it matters, then? The show, I mean. Getting a good price.'

Libby and Ophelia looked at her as if she was crazy. 'Of course it matters. Dad's selling our best tup, Gideon, and if he can win at the show, people will pay so much more for him.' She nudged her sister. 'Do you remember Roger?'

Ophelia screwed up her face. 'I think so. Was he the goldmine?'

Libby nodded.

'Who's Roger?' Eden asked. 'And what do you mean, goldmine?'

'Oh, Dad calls him that. He was our best tup a few years ago, but Dad says he thinks Gideon's even better. It will be wonderful if he can beat the price he got for Roger. Dad sold *him* for twenty-five thousand pounds.'

Eden nearly choked on her tea. 'Twenty-five thousand pounds! For a sheep! I think you may have got that wrong, Libby.'

Libby shook her head. 'No, I didn't. I remember it well, because Mummy and Dad, and Adey and Mickey, and Mr and Mrs Fuller had a party when we went to bed, and they thought I was asleep, but I wasn't, and I crept downstairs and peeped through the door. They were all on the beer, and there was a lot of laughing and singing going on, and ...' She stopped suddenly.

Eden looked at her, surprised. 'And?'

'It doesn't matter.'

Ophelia tutted. 'What doesn't matter? Tell us.'

Libby blushed. 'I saw Mrs Fuller kissing Dad.'

Eden's heart thudded.

Ophelia shrieked. 'You never said!'

'You were only a kid,' said Libby.

'But what about Mummy?' Ophelia whispered. 'And Mr Fuller?'

'They were both in the kitchen,' said Libby. 'Dad and Mrs Fuller were outside, in the garden.'

'But they kissed? You're sure? How could you see them, if they were outside?'

Libby bit her lip. 'Because I was going back up to bed, and I saw them from the landing window.'

'I'm sure they were just celebrating,' Eden said, trying to sound matter-of-fact.

There was something not right about it all. Eliot's behaviour at the open day had been suspicious enough.

The way he'd been talking to Beth, the things they'd said ... Had they been having an affair? Was that why he felt so guilty?

'Sometimes, grownups kiss people they shouldn't when they've been drinking. It doesn't mean anything.'

'I know.' Libby stared at her cereal for a moment. 'Dad really loved Mummy, you know. He cried and cried after she—after the accident.'

Ophelia's eyes filled with tears. 'I remember.'

Eden decided the conversation had turned gloomy enough. 'Right, well, do you know what we're going to do today?'

The girls shook their heads. 'What?'

'We're going into Kirkby Skimmer. I think it's time you two got your winter coats sorted for the new term, don't you? And I'm fairly willing to bet that you also need new shoes, and pens, pencils, rulers ... I think we'll be there a while, so we should have lunch there, too. What do you say?'

Smiles were immediately restored, and Eden heaved a sigh of relief as they began chattering excitedly about the things they needed.

When Eliot walked in, an hour later, the girls practically mobbed him, telling him all about their forthcoming adventure.

Eden held her breath, waiting for the inevitable refusal. She really should have run things by him first, she mused. She had meant to, but she'd wanted to distract the children from their sad memories. 'Is it okay?' she asked anxiously. 'I know I should have asked you, but you're always so busy, and they really do need the things for school. Time's getting on.' Wasn't it just, she thought sadly. It was midway through August already. She'd be going home before she knew it.

Eliot surveyed her for a moment, making her nervous, but then he nodded. 'It's fine. But, look, I'd rather you didn't take George, if you don't mind.'

'Oh? Why not?'

He sat down at the table and ran a hand through his curls. Watching him, Eden tried not to gulp. She hoped her pupils hadn't dilated. It was a dead giveaway, apparently.

'I've been that busy, these last few months, I've hardly spent any time with him. I reckon I've earned a few hours off. I'm going to sit in this afternoon and mind him, while you take the lasses to town.'

'Oh, right.' Eden couldn't help wishing she was staying in with him. James bloody Fuller could wait. Too late now, though. 'Fair enough.'

'I'll give you my debit card,' he added. 'It's in the kitchen drawer. Just get what they need.'

'I can pay,' she began, but he scowled at her.

'They're my kids, and I'll pay.'

'Sorry.' Eden felt her cheeks warm and turned away, opening the drawer and seeing his debit card dumped in there for anyone to pick up. How trusting.

'No. I'm sorry.' He was suddenly behind her, and she tried to suppress a shiver as she felt his breath on her neck. 'I'm being rude. No need for it. Look, do me a favour, will you? The girls are entering the Skimmerdale Show. Could you take them to Hunter and Brockett's and get them some new riding clothes? Their old stuff is a disgrace, and they need to look as good as the other kids. Reckon they've earned it, the time they've had lately.'

The girls whooped with joy, and Eden's skin scorched when he smiled at her. His eyes were so beautiful—brown and sparkling and delicious. Her gaze dropped to his mouth, which curved upwards, for once, and she thought how soft and inviting his lips looked.

It took her a moment to be aware that his mouth had changed shape. He was no longer smiling. When her eyes met his, there was a different look in them, and she caught her breath. She could no longer hear the girls shrieking in the background, but she could have sworn she heard two heartbeats pounding in perfect synchronisation.

Eliot pushed away and headed to the highchair, where George happily banged his spoon in his bowl of cereal. 'Never mind splattering it all around the kitchen, me lad,' he said, gently squeezing the little boy's cheek. 'How about you try actually eating some of it, eh?' He sat down beside him and guided the spoon into George's mouth.

Eden tried to sound normal as she said, 'Right, girls, let's get ready for our day out, eh?'

Whatever that look had meant, it had passed. She'd probably read far too much into it, anyway. Eliot had no interest in her, and between Jemima, Beth and Daisy, it seemed he'd already had more than his fair share of women. She wished she could fathom out exactly what had gone on where Beth was concerned, because it was certain there was more to the whole set-up than she'd realised.

There had to be.

****

Eden didn't think she'd ever spent so much money in one go. She felt sick thinking about it, and wondered how Eliot would feel when he learnt how much it had cost to equip the girls with everything they needed. New shoes, bags, winter coats, pencil cases, pens, pencils, as well as various other items that they insisted they needed had already ensured that his debit card had taken a battering. When they got to Hunter and Brockett's, however, the bill had been bumped up by a further two hundred pounds.

'Get them whatever they need,' he'd murmured to her through the open car window, as she fastened her seatbelt. 'I mean it. They've had nowt new for as long as I can remember. Make sure they've got everything for school, and that they can hold their heads high when they go to the show, an' all.'

'You know, Eliot, I had a thought a while ago, and I meant to talk to you about it. I know now's not really the time, but have you considered converting one or two of the barns?'

'The barns?' He frowned. 'What do you mean? Like into a house, or something?'

'No, no. I was thinking about a bed and breakfast business. You have loads of spare outbuildings. You could perhaps set up a sort of hostel, with lots of single beds for walkers, or perhaps make a few decent en suite rooms and have fewer guests but charge more. There are so many hikers passing by this place, it's a missed opportunity.'

'Right.'

'You could even do cream teas for the people who pass by and want to sit down for half an hour. I could look into it, if you like.'

'Dunno about that. I'd have to think.'

'Yes, of course. No rush. Just, well, it would certainly help with your finances,' she said.

He gave her a look that clearly said he didn't want her worrying about his finances, thank you very much.

She flushed. 'Well, anyway, I'll get off. Is there a limit you want to spend?'

He shook his head. 'I trust you not to be daft.'

'Do you?' Her eyes widened at that revelation, and he held her gaze for a moment before turning away.

'Aye. Now get off with you, before I change my mind.'

She wondered if he'd regret that when she presented him with the numerous receipts later that day. For then, though, there was no point worrying. She was laden with bags, her feet were aching, and Ophelia and Libby were demanding to be fed.

She glanced at her watch. James Fuller would be there any moment. Time to find The Daffodil Café.

'What about here?' she asked, pausing outside the pretty little teashop, which she'd found, eventually, tucked away down a little side street. She peered at the menu fastened to the inside of the window, gratified to see that they had children's specials at reasonable prices.

The girls seemed glad to finally be allowed to stop walking. They hadn't understood why they couldn't go back to The Teapot Café, and Eden couldn't justify her refusal.

They all shuffled inside, trying not to knock other customers with their bags. Eden found them a table, and they shoved the shopping on the spare chair and eagerly perused the menu. The children were in agreement, they wanted fishcakes and chips and banana milkshakes, so she left them scanning the list of desserts and headed to the counter to order. Adding a coffee to their list of requirements, she took some money from her purse, and was about to hand over a twenty pound note, when a voice behind her said smoothly, 'Let me pay for those.'

Startled, she spun round, swallowing when she saw James Fuller standing there, smiling at her. It was on the tip of her tongue to say she'd pay for the meals herself, but then she thought, why shouldn't he? He was the one who'd insisted she bring the children to meet him, after all.

'Thanks.'

'No problem.' He handed a credit card to the girl behind the counter, who watched them both with keen interest. He gave her a charming smile. 'Add two espressos to that order, please.'

She nodded. 'I'll bring it all over. Table fourteen, right?'

He glanced at Eden for confirmation. She nodded, wondering how she'd got herself into this. She felt most uncomfortable speaking to James Fuller. He may be charm itself, but he was also a blackmailer, after all. Given that she suspected Eliot had been up to no good with Beth, it should be James she felt sorry for, but she didn't. She knew she was letting Eliot down, just by talking to him, and she was pretty certain he wouldn't want his daughters sitting with the man.

'You found the place all right?' he asked, tapping his pin number into the card machine.

'Eventually. Why couldn't we have met in The Teapot Café?'

'Because Beth loves this place and always comes here for tea and cake. It would have looked suspicious if we'd *accidentally* met you in a place we don't usually go into. We only popped in last time because this place was closed that afternoon, due to a private function.'

'Beth's here?'

'Well, of course she's here. I told you, this is all for Beth. She misses those children. So be careful what you say, because I don't want her to know this is all behind Eliot's back.'

Eden turned away and spotted Beth chatting to an animated Ophelia and a suspicious looking Libby.

'Where's George?' James demanded, as they headed back to the table.

'Eliot wanted to spend time with him,' she murmured. 'He's hardly seen him lately and wanted to make it up to him.'

'I said we wanted to see all of the children,' he said. 'Couldn't you have come up with some excuse?'

'What excuse? He's perfectly entitled to spend time with his son, and it's better not to have George on a shopping trip. It would have looked very odd if I'd insisted.'

James scowled and pulled up an extra seat. Libby and Ophelia seemed delighted to see him, at any rate. She suspected that he brought back memories of happier times—times when they had their mother in their lives. He and Beth had been good friends to Eliot and Jemima, though Beth, perhaps, had been rather too good a friend to Eliot. She wondered if James knew what—if anything—had gone on between the two of them.

'They've been on a grand spending spree,' Beth informed him, smiling at the girls.

James nodded towards the shopping bags, which they'd had to squash under the table to free up the fourth chair. 'Been spending your father's money, eh?'

'We've been buying our things for school,' Ophelia told him.

'And new riding clothes for the Skimmerdale Show,' added Libby.

Beth raised an eyebrow. 'So, you're competing, then? I wasn't sure you would.'

Eden felt a compulsion to defend their father. 'Eliot was very keen for them to take part. He told me to get them whatever they needed.'

'Really?' James smirked. 'He must be feeling flush, for once. Perhaps he's expecting to do well at the auctions this year.' He looked at the girls expectantly.

Libby said nothing, but Ophelia gushed, 'Oh, yes. He thinks Gideon will do even better than Roger. Reckon, if he does, we'll be quids in.'

Eden hid a smile. She sounded just like her dad for a moment. She wondered how Jemima had felt, hearing her children developing broad Yorkshire accents. Somehow, she doubted their mother had ever adopted one. Realising James was asking her a question, she turned to him. 'Sorry. What did you say?'

'I said, are you going to the show, too? It seems like it's going to be a special event, if the girls are competing in the gymkhana and Eliot is parading his sheep for the world to see. It would be a shame if you missed it. I expect George would like to be there, too. I'm sure he'd enjoy it.'

'I don't know,' said Eden. 'Is it a big event?'

'For this part of the world, it is,' said Beth. 'All sorts going on. Not just animal shows, either. There are fairground rides and exhibitions, and classes for vegetables, baking, jams, preserves—you name it. There are sheepdog demonstrations and—'

'Yeah, okay, I get it.' Eden laughed. 'It's a big event. I should think I'll be able to go. If Eliot's busy with the sheep, I'll need to be there to help the girls.'

'Or, perhaps, Daisy will do that?' suggested James.

Something in his tone made her wary. What was he trying to say? 'I'm sure she'd be willing to help,' she said carefully. 'Eliot has lots of friends.'

'He does,' James agreed. He beamed at the waitress as she brought their drinks to them. 'Thank you,' he said, then turned back to Eden, still wearing the dazzling smile. For a moment, she felt a prickle of unease, of something nagging away at her, but she just couldn't think what it was. He handed the girls their milkshakes, and the moment was gone.

The waitress returned with the food, and for the next twenty minutes, they concentrated on eating, making occasional remarks about the forthcoming show.

'Honey, why don't you enter the cake show?' said Libby. 'Then we'd all be taking part. I bet you'd win. Your cakes are scrummy.'

'Only if Mrs Edwards is ill and can't take part,' said Ophelia.

'Mrs Edwards?'

Beth put a hand over her mouth in a feeble attempt to stem her laughter. 'You shouldn't say things like that! Although, to be fair, you're probably right. Mrs Edwards is the wife of the vicar. She wins every year. She's far too scary, and no one dares take the prize away from her.'

'I bloody would if I was judging,' said James. 'Old bat. No wonder her husband turned to God. Still, good idea about the cake. Why not enter, anyway? You never know, and it would be good to be part of it all, rather than just watching, don't you think?'

'I'll think about it,' Eden said.

As the waitress collected the empty plates and cups, James asked the girls what they'd like for pudding. As they'd been perusing the menu the whole time they were eating their main course, they had a pretty good idea. He rummaged in his pocket and handed Beth a twenty pound note.

'Darling, shall we treat them? Why don't you take them to the counter and let them choose something delicious and gooey?' he suggested.

'Would you like that?' said Beth, smiling at them.

They shot a look at Eden, who shrugged. 'It's okay. You can go if you like.'

They thanked James and, highly delighted, scrambled out of their seats and headed to the front of the café, Ophelia holding Beth's hand.

Eden waited. James, no doubt, had something he wanted to say out of the girls'—and Beth's—earshot.

'He was okay with you?' he asked. 'Eliot, I mean. When you got back from the open day, he was okay?'

She blinked. It wasn't the conversation she'd been expecting at all. 'Of course. Why wouldn't he be?'

'There was no … no unpleasantness?'

Eden frowned. 'What do you mean?'

James sighed. 'Look, Eden, this is awkward. I know you work for him, and I appreciate your loyalty, but Eliot—well, he is rather known for his temper.'

'His temper?' Eden shook her head. 'I've never seen evidence of his temper. I mean, he can be a bit abrupt at times, but that's all. What are you implying?'

He fiddled with the menu, turning it round and round in his hand, then he leaned toward her, his face serious. 'Eliot's not what you think. Jemima had a hell of a life with him. You do know they were on the verge of divorce, when she died?'

Eden's mouth fell open. 'I don't believe it! He adored her. I mean, they were devoted to each other. The girls are always telling me how much he cried when she was killed.'

He gave an abrupt laugh. 'Yeah, right. Probably guilt.'

She felt a wave of discomfort as she recalled his strange conversation with Beth at the open day. What did they have to feel guilty about? Had they been having an affair? Did James know?

'The thing is,' he continued, 'their marriage was a sham. Had been for years. Eliot was a brute to Jemima, and she was—well, she was a real lady. She wasn't used to it, and she couldn't cope. Didn't know how to handle him. Oh, there was no physical violence, don't get me wrong, but he could be extremely cruel in other ways. Cutting. Putting her down all the time. Bullying, really. He's all right with you?'

Eden didn't know how to answer. It was so utterly not what she'd expected to hear. Eliot's marriage to Jemima had been a sham? But he seemed so genuinely upset about her, and the children were adamant he'd been heartbroken when she died. Was it really all an act? Or was James right, and it had been guilt that had caused his tears, rather than grief?

James patted her hand. 'I can see this has come as a shock to you. Well, obviously, you've not seen that side of him, then. I'm glad. Maybe losing Jemima has brought him to his senses, and he's learnt to control his anger. I hope so. Beth will be relieved, too. I'm not a bad person, Eden. I know you probably think the worst of me because I made you bring the children to the open day, and then today ... But, you see, I have to keep an eye on them. I—we—owe Jemima that. I suppose he hasn't made a move on you, yet?'

'What?' Had she heard him right?

'Bit of a ladies' man, I'm afraid. I think, at one point, he had a bit of a thing for Beth. Not that she'd ever be interested in him,' he added, with a laugh. Eden swallowed, as James continued, 'Then there's Daisy, of course. She's devoted to him. Jemima was well aware of the fact. Always suspected they were having an affair.'

An affair? Daisy and Eliot? So, where did Beth fit in, then? This was all getting too much for Eden.

'She'll always stick up for him, no matter what. She hated Jemima. Well, she would, wouldn't she? Jemima lured away the man she was destined to marry. At least, that's how Daisy sees it. She made Jemima's life a misery. Between the two of them ...' He shook his head sadly. 'Jemima had a hell of a life. And she didn't deserve it. She really didn't.'

'I-I see.' Except she didn't. Not really. The man James spoke of seemed like a complete stranger to her. All right, Eliot had been a bit gruff with her sometimes, and he had glowering down to a fine art, but he wasn't cruel.

She recalled the moment when he'd turned up at the open day and shouted at her. He'd seemed quite menacing, his eyes dark with rage. He'd been a bit intimidating, she had to admit it. Everyone lost their temper occasionally, though, and God knows, she'd pushed him far enough.

As for womanising ... She realised that was possible. He was gorgeous, after all, and Daisy was obviously devoted to him. And Libby had seen him and Beth kissing ...

'Just don't be fooled by him,' said James, his voice suddenly urgent. 'You can see why it's important that you continue to allow Beth and me access to the children? You do see that?'

'Of course. Yes.' She didn't have time to think about it, as Beth returned with the girls, who shuffled back into their seats, arguing about the fact that Ophelia had taken so much time to choose a dessert after changing her mind and deciding she didn't want a banana split, after all.

'Well, you have to think about these things,' protested Ophelia. 'I didn't want to choose the wrong one, did I?'

'It's only pudding,' said Libby, rolling her eyes.

'So, what did you get?' asked James.

'I got treacle tart and custard, and Ophelia got a knickerbocker glory,' Libby informed him.

'Sounds lovely. I hope you enjoy them.'

Hovering beside the table, Beth tapped her wristwatch. 'Sorry, darling, but it's almost time for our appointment.'

'So it is. I'm afraid I'm going to have to leave you lovely ladies to it. Time flies when you're having fun.' He stood, scraping back his chair and smiling broadly at them all.

'Thank you for paying for all this.' Eden waved her arm vaguely across the table. 'It was very kind of you.'

'Not at all. We look forward to seeing you all again at the show.'

As he turned, Eden felt the same prickly unease that she'd felt before. There was something ...What was it? Something nagging away at her.

She pushed it away as he walked out of the café. She had more important things to think about. Now she was more confused than ever, and the only thing she was certain of was that she liked James Fuller even less than she had before.

CHAPTER TWENTY-TWO

Eliot had forgotten how tiring it was, entertaining a two-year-old for hours. They'd sung songs, played games, watched some God-awful programme on the television that George apparently watched with Honey and obviously adored, and had a picnic on the living room floor—which was probably a bad idea, given the amount of crumbs and splodges of butter, and trampled-in biscuit that now covered the carpet. He knew he'd better clean that little lot up before Honey got back, but George had finally fallen asleep on the sofa, and Eliot didn't want to risk waking him by switching on the vacuum cleaner. Besides, he was tired himself. He wouldn't mind a nap for ten minutes.

When he opened his eyes, he wondered where he was for a moment. He seldom slept downstairs, so it was a shock to find he wasn't in his bedroom. Then he remembered it was still the afternoon, and he'd been sitting beside George. He must have fallen asleep, after all.

He turned his head, expecting to find his son sound asleep beside him, but George wasn't there.

Frowning, Eliot glanced around the living room. He wasn't there, and the door was open.

Okay, Eliot, don't panic. He went into the kitchen, where there was still no sign of George. The back door was closed, and he hurried into the hallway. The door to the boot room was open.

He glanced inside. The place was a mess but there was no sign of his son. At least the door into the garden was closed. The front door was closed, too. Even if, by some miracle, George had managed to open the door, he would hardly have closed it behind him, would he?

He ran upstairs, calling his son's name, and checked all the bedrooms and the bathroom. There was no sign of him there, either. *Stay calm*, he thought. *Just think*!

But what if someone had taken him? He tried to think logically, but the fear persisted, and he knew why. Where else could he be?

He ran out into the garden, but there was no sign of him either in the garden or yard. Should he check the barns? Call the police? He couldn't think straight. Would Beth know?

The thought kept nagging at him and he couldn't shake the feeling that calling her was his only choice.

He was about to go back in the house when he heard a car and felt almost sick with relief on realising Honey was back. He didn't know what he expected her to do, but he was so glad she was home. Somehow, she made everything easier to deal with.

'What is it?' Her concern showed in her voice, and he realised the panic he was feeling must have been reflected in his face.

Not wanting the girls to worry, he whispered in her ear, 'I can't find George. He's gone, Honey.' He heard the anxiety in his voice and cursed his own weakness, but the fear was growing. Had the thing he dreaded most finally occurred?

'All right, calm down. Tell me what happened.'

Her voice was soothing, and he quickly explained the situation to her. 'How could I have been so stupid as to fall asleep?' He pulled at his hair in frustration, and she reached out and took hold of his hand.

'Stop that. Help the girls with the shopping. I won't be a moment.'

'What? Where are you going?'

'Just checking something out. Help the girls,' she called.

Eliot stared after her. Didn't she realise how serious this was?

'Is everything all right, Dad?' Libby stared up at him,

her eyes curious.

He patted her head and tried to smile. 'Aye, everything's fine, love. Come on, let's get the shopping, eh?'

'We got loads,' said Ophelia, struggling with three bags. Eliot took them off her and quickly got the rest from the boot. He was so worried, he didn't even notice how many there were, but he didn't miss the look of anxiety that passed between his daughters.

After slamming the door of the boot shut, he followed the girls into the house. He dumped the shopping in the hallway and called for Honey.

'In here!'

Her voice came from the boot room. He headed that way and stopped dead, his spirits soaring when he saw her standing there, holding George in her arms.

He'd checked the boot room. His son hadn't been there. 'Where the hell was he?'

She grinned. 'He was playing his favourite game. Hide and seek. Didn't you notice the mess?'

He looked around, seeing for the first time the piles of laundry spread over the floor. 'He was under that lot?'

'No.' She giggled. 'He was in the laundry basket.'

'What?'

'He emptied it, then pulled the basket over him. He was easy to see, but I expect you were panicking by then.'

He leaned against the doorframe, his legs suddenly weak. 'Aye, you could say that. Little bugger.'

'It's my fault. We play all the time, and he's very familiar with the laundry basket,' she admitted.

'Is he?'

'Yes. You see, he helps me count the socks when I do the washing, and he likes to help me fold the clothes.'

'Does he?' Eliot asked, astonished. He looked at Honey with new respect. She was amazing.

'Well, why don't you take Georgie into the living room

and let the girls show you their new things? I'll clean this mess up, and then I'll make us a strong cup of tea. I reckon you could use plenty of sugar in yours for shock.

She smiled at him, and he fought the urge to pull her into his arms and hug her tightly. Instead, he nodded and took George from her. 'Thank you,' he murmured. 'I feel proper daft now.'

'Don't,' she assured him. 'I expect every parent has one of those awful *where the hell is my child* moments.'

No doubt, he thought, *but not every parent has a real reason to worry*. 'Come on, Georgie Boy. Can't believe you did that to me. Nearly finished me off, do you know that?' George smirked at him, and he laughed. 'Aye, you know it all right, don't you? I'm going to have to watch you.'

He glanced at Honey, but she wasn't laughing any more. She was staring at George in a most peculiar way.

'You all right?' he asked.

She blinked. 'What? Oh, yes, yes. Go on, get out of here. Bet the girls are dying to show you their new stuff.'

He nodded and carried his precious load away, vowing that, before long, he would fix a lock on every dratted door in the house.

****

Eden gathered the clothes from the floor and shoved them back in the laundry basket, feeling dazed. Things were becoming increasingly confusing.

Eliot was sitting on the sofa when she went through to the living room, George on his knee while he watched the girls hold up their various purchases and tell him excitedly of their day in Kirkby Skimmer. Eden's tummy flipped as she waited for the bombshell. Sure enough, Ophelia was the one who brought it up.

'And we had lunch with Mr and Mrs Fuller. They bought us pudding. I had knickerbocker glory, and Libby had treacle tart. There was loads. I was really full up, but I finished it all, even though I felt sick, but Libby left some of hers.'

'I ate all the custard, though,' said Libby.

Eden put the cups of tea on the coffee table and sat down, waiting for the inevitable outpouring of anger. Eliot kissed the top of George's head and said calmly, 'You met the Fullers again? Quite a coincidence.'

'I know! I think they must like cafés as much as we do,' said Ophelia. 'They didn't stay long, though. They had an appointment.'

'Right,' said Eliot. He glanced at Eden.

She gave him an apologetic look. 'They were just there. What could I do?'

He shook his head. 'It's all right. How is Beth, anyway?'

'She's fine.'

'Mrs Fuller thinks Honey should enter in the cake show, Dad. What do you think?'

He peered up at her. 'I think that's a grand idea. Mind, you won't win. Not with the vicar's wife taking part.'

'So I've heard,' she said.

'You should win, though, if there's any justice. You make the best cakes I've ever tasted. Any road, I think it would be good for you to enter. Be part of the community, like.'

'You do?'

His gaze held hers, and she held her breath as she saw the expression in his eyes. What was he trying to say? He swallowed and looked down at George. 'What do you think, Georgie? We love Honey's cakes, don't we?' He waved his hand apologetically at the floor. 'Looks like we've walked a full cake into the carpet. Sorry.'

Eden registered the mess for the first time. 'Good grief, look at the state of that! What's been going on in here?'

It was Eliot's turn to look apologetic. 'We had a picnic.

Sorry. I meant to clean it all up, but then I lost Georgie here, and I forgot all about it.'

'I'd better get that vacuum cleaner out,' she said.

'No. Let's drink our tea, then I'll clean it up.'

She looked at him, surprised. 'Are you sure?'

He nodded and smiled at her. Relieved, she smiled back. Evidently, finding George had put her in his good books. He even seemed willing to overlook the lunch with the Fullers.

They all had a pleasant evening together. Eden helped the girls carry their new things upstairs, while Eliot vacuumed the living room, keeping a close eye on George, who sat on the sofa, beaming at him and clapping his hands. He obviously found the sight of his father cleaning up most amusing. While Eliot bathed his son, Eden, Libby and Ophelia hung the girls' new clothes in the wardrobes, before Eden started work on the evening meal. As Eden did the dishes, Eliot and Ophelia fed the dogs and went for one last wander round the farm. Later, Eden and Libby shut the hens up for the night and made hot chocolate, and they all settled down to watch the television for an hour or so.

Finally, when all the children were in bed, Eden and Eliot sank onto the sofa and reflected on a long and eventful day.

'Have you recovered from the trauma, yet?' she teased him.

He shook his head and placed his hand on his heart. 'It's still jumping about all over the place,' he said. 'What a bloody fright I got. Thank God you knew where to look. What would I have done without you?'

She bit her lip and turned away, feeling an ominous tingling of desire. When he looked at her like that, when he spoke to her so kindly, she melted.

After a moment of quiet, he said, 'So, the Fullers again, eh?'

That broke the spell. She shrugged. 'They were just there. I didn't know what to do. I know you don't like them, and I can understand why.'

'Can you?' He seemed doubtful. 'Beth's all right. I've nowt against her. It's him. He's—'

'I know.' She drew her knees up to her chin and wrapped her arms around them. 'He's dodgy. I don't like him.'

'You don't?' He sounded surprised, relieved even.

'No.' She gave him a slight smile. 'Oh, he's very charming. He knows exactly what to say. But I wouldn't trust him as far as I could throw him.'

His eyes twinkled. 'You're a bloody good judge of character, then.'

'Were he and Jemima very close?' She knew she was pushing it, talking about Jemima, but she wanted to know. She needed to know. And, she thought, maybe it was time he started to open up, for all their sakes.

The twinkle disappeared. 'He was her sort of person, I suppose. Him and Beth. They chummed up with her pretty quickly. Like finds like, I guess. It became obvious, soon after she moved here, that she wasn't going to fit in with the other villagers. I suppose, finding the Fullers came as a big relief to her.'

So, Jemima hadn't fitted in with the other locals? Well, that was news to her. None of them had said a bad word about her to Eden, but she supposed they were loyal to Eliot. She decided to try again. 'What did she look like? It's just—well—I noticed you don't have any photos of her around the house.' She decided not to mention the lockets.

'No. I don't.'

'So, what did she look like?'

'Fair hair, blue eyes. Look at Georgie if you want to know. He's the spitting image of her. Well, mostly.' He began to fidget, pulling at a thread on a cushion.

'So, why don't you have any photographs of her? I get

that you must miss her, and it must be painful for you to see her, but don't you think you should face up to that after two years? And I'm sure the girls would love to have photos of their mum around the house.'

'It's none of your bloody business!' He stood up, throwing the cushion onto the sofa and stormed out of the room.

Moments later, she heard the front door slam and realised she'd pushed him too far. She cursed her impatience. She should have been gentler, more careful. Served her right. They were back at square one.

She sat there, wondering what to do. There was no point going after him, she knew him that well, at least. Should she go up to her room, get out of his way? He would probably take the quad bike and go round the farm. Unless he went into the village. Maybe he'd go to the pub, meet up with Daisy? The thought was unexpectedly painful. She imagined them sitting together, discussing the nosy childminder. She pictured Daisy pouring sympathy over Eliot, and even worse, Eliot lapping it up, responding.

The door opened, and Eliot stood there, looking embarrassed. 'I'm sorry. I've done it again, haven't I? I had no right to talk to you like that.'

She looked up at him, feeling awkward. 'You had every right. I shouldn't have pushed you.'

'No, no, it were a simple enough question.' With a sigh, he sat back beside her on the sofa and examined his hands, as if they were the most fascinating things he'd ever seen. Eventually, he broke the silence. 'It's not what you think, you know.'

'Oh? And what do I think?' Eden herself wasn't even sure any longer, so she failed to see how he could know.

'You think Jemima and me were some great love story come to life. The farmer and the posh girl. Love against the odds.'

'Well, weren't you?'

'At first, maybe. I couldn't believe a girl like her was interested in someone like me.' He half smiled. 'She was beautiful, no doubt about it. Mind, she knew it. Took me a while to realise it weren't real—what she felt for me, I mean.'

'In what way? She loved you enough to marry you,' said Eden.

'Nah. She married me for two reasons. One was lust. Oh, aye. She fancied me all right, and that side of things was real enough. At least, at first. But the main reason she got with me was to spite her family. They wanted her to marry someone more suitable, you see, and Jemima wasn't one for doing what her family wanted. She liked to do things her way. They had someone in mind. I didn't know that at the time, but I soon found out. I thought they'd come round, and to be fair, I think she thought they would, too. But they didn't. Never came near the place. Cut her off completely. She paid a heavy price for trying to get one over on them.'

Eden thought of Honey. It seemed she and Jemima had a lot in common, after all. 'You're saying she never really loved you?'

He shrugged. 'I don't think so. Not real love. Like I say, there was a lot of lust — on both sides, to be fair. Sometimes, that can get confused with love, don't you think?'

She supposed it could. She wondered how one could tell the difference. How did a person know if they really loved someone? She knew it was lust that she'd felt since the moment she'd seen Eliot standing beside the Beetle in the centre of Kirkby Skimmer. Love was something else, something hard to define.

What was it she was feeling now? It wasn't just Eliot's looks anymore that set her heart fluttering and made her yearn to spend every moment she could in his company.

There was so much more to it than that. She loved his voice, she loved the way he cared for his children, the way he worked so hard around the farm, the way he couldn't manage a simple load of laundry without turning everything grey. She loved his smile. Hearing his laughter could make everything seem right with the world. She even loved him when he glowered at her. My God. Her heart seemed to fly up into her throat, and she took a sharp breath. She loved him!

He was watching her, and she realised he was waiting for an answer. 'I suppose it can, yes,' she managed, then cleared her throat, sending her heart back to its rightful place in her chest. 'But, what about you? You loved her, didn't you?'

'I did,' he admitted. 'At first, any road. I'd have done anything to make her happy, and I thought I were succeeding. Took me a while to realise it weren't me that were making her happy.'

Eden gulped. 'What do you mean?'

'Money,' he replied. 'She had her own money, and when we were first married, she loved spending it. Completely altered this house,' he said, looking round the room. 'Just about changed every room. Nothing was too much for her. And the clothes—my God! How anyone could need that many pairs of shoes, I'll never understand.'

'I know what you mean,' she said, thinking of Honey and her huge walk-in wardrobe. Then she remembered the vast amount of luggage she'd brought with her and blushed.

Luckily, he didn't seem to notice. 'Thing is, the money ran out. She'd been expecting her dad to give in by then. She was counting on him welcoming her back, and showering money and gifts on her. He didn't. Soon there was just the income from the farm to live on, and that was never going to be enough for her. Not by a long chalk.' He sighed. 'I suppose that's when it all really turned sour. She got bitter and nasty. Blamed me for everything. Said I'd ruined her life. Happen she were right.'

'Of course she wasn't right!'

He smiled at her. 'Nice of you to say so, but look at me. I'm hardly catch of the century, am I?'

Was he being sarcastic? He couldn't possibly be that blind, could he? 'I think you're amazing,' she heard herself say. 'Any woman would be lucky to have you.'

'Oh, aye. Any woman would be thrilled to live in the back of beyond with a grumpy farmer and a thousand sheep for company. It's not many would be happy with this life, especially since I've barely got two pennies to rub together.'

He sighed, and Eden couldn't help herself. She reached out and took hold of his hand. 'I think you're wonderful, and if Jemima couldn't be happy living in this beautiful place with a man like you beside her, there was something wrong with her.' She hadn't meant to say it, and she held her breath, wondering how he would react.

He looked down at her hand holding his then up at her face. His eyes bright with emotion, he gave the slightest squeeze of her fingers with his own, and without thinking, she leaned towards him until her lips lightly touched his.

He stilled for a moment, but as she was about to move away, she felt the slightest pressure on her mouth. She opened her eyes to see him staring at her in amazement. In the next breath, his eyes closed, the pressure increased as his arms wrapped around her, and she was pulled towards him.

Her lips parted, and as his tongue gently probed, she responded eagerly. She fell backwards on the sofa, bringing him with her. His body was heavy against hers, and she felt as if they were merging and knew she didn't want it to stop. It was what she'd been waiting for, and she wanted him to kiss her deeper and deeper, until there was no turning back for either of them.

Suddenly, brutally, he pulled away from her and sat up, his face ashen. 'Sorry,' he muttered. 'God knows what came over me.'

'I-I—it must have been the emotion of the day,' she said. 'A lot's happened.' She wanted to pull him back to her, tell him she didn't care what had come over him, but could he please let it come over him again? Instead, she also sat up, smoothed her hair, and glanced at her watch. She didn't even notice what time it was, but she tutted and said, 'Crikey, I should be going up. I'll see you in the morning.'

'Aye. You will. Goodnight, Honey.'

She scrambled off the sofa and headed towards the door without looking back, her face burning. ''Night, Eliot.'

It was only when she reached the safety of her bedroom that she realised she was holding her breath. She let it out and flopped onto the bed, wondering what the hell had happened, and, more importantly, how she would face him the following morning without begging for a repeat performance.

CHAPTER TWENTY-THREE

Honey threw down the remote and slumped back on the sofa, her arms crossed and her bottom lip thrust forward in a pout. 'I'm bored. How much longer are you going to be?'

Crispin barely glanced at her. He was sitting on the armchair, glasses perched on the end of his nose, reading through some papers he'd brought back with him from his last trip to Windleby-On-the-Weir. 'Hmm?'

'I said, I'm bored.' Honey glared at him. Why was he ignoring her? She was sitting there, barely dressed, for God's sake. She was only wearing one of his shirts, some fake tan and a squirt of Jo Malone, and he wasn't even looking at her. He was far too engrossed in his dull political papers. Things were getting pretty dire, if she couldn't even lure him away from work when she was practically naked. She scowled. 'I think I'll go out.'

That caught his attention, and he looked up, suddenly concerned. 'Go out? Go out, where?'

'Into town. Do some shopping.'

'But you can't!' Crispin removed his glasses. 'What if you're followed?'

'Why would anyone follow me?' she demanded, thinking she might bump into Teddy again, and it would bloody well serve Crispin right if she did. She decided to wind him up a little. 'Although,' she drawled, 'there was that car ...'

That caught his attention. Crispin dropped the papers and looked at her in horror. 'What car? What are you talking about?'

'It crawled by the house a few weeks ago. Almost stopped, actually, 'til the driver saw me looking.'

'He saw you?' His face paled.

Honey examined his features, aware that he looked older than she'd first imagined, and his lips were too thin.

Not particularly kissable, at all. She couldn't imagine why he was seen as the Tory party's new poster boy. She supposed it was down to lack of competition. 'What do you want me to do? Stay away from all windows now? I was looking out, big deal. I was bored.'

'You're always bored,' he muttered.

'Pardon?' Her voice was sharp, and he swallowed nervously.

'You say a car crawled by? What sort of car? Did you recognise the driver?'

Honey considered. 'I didn't get a good look at him,' she admitted. 'Anyway, it was a red Mini.'

'A red Mini?' Crispin frowned. 'That rings a bell.'

'You know someone who drives a red Mini?'

'Not personally but ... I know! That day when I was waiting for you in the lay-by at Carpington. A red Mini pulled up just after I did, and the bloke turned off his engine and waited. I was nervous, but then he took out a paper and seemed to be doing a crossword puzzle or something, so I thought no more of it. And, of course, I had other things to think about that day.'

'I don't remember it,' said Honey. 'Gosh, do you think we were followed? How thrilling!'

'It's not bloody thrilling, at all. If this man's a journalist, I've had it! Lavinia will kill me, then she'll divorce me. I'll be ruined. The Party will disown me. I'll be a pariah. Oh, my God!'

He really was a pathetic drip, thought Honey. If it wasn't for the thrill of being the other woman, and of causing her parents such angst and inconvenience, she would happily dump him and go home. The only thing that kept her going was the thought of Freya's and Cain's faces when she announced, in September, that she was still seeing Crispin and their little plan had spectacularly failed. She couldn't really think what would happen beyond that. She was undecided. She could either string them along for a few weeks, torturing them with her imaginary passionate affair before dumping him, or she could blow the lid on the whole thing. She would be in all the newspapers. She'd probably get a full-colour spread in *All the Goss*, and take part in *Big Brother*. Or *Strictly Come Dancing*. That would be fun. She might get partnered with a real hunk and end up having an affair with him, too. Imagine how many column inches that would get her!

She'd not intended for the affair to become public but, really, Crispin was asking for it. He'd been distracted, dull, and an utter wimp. He deserved a shaking up. She'd thought he loved her, but she had a sneaking suspicion it was more about getting one over on his dragon of a wife. The truth was, she'd had a more exciting time that afternoon with Teddy than she'd had all summer with Crispin. Teddy had been totally sweet, and rather lovely in bed. He wasn't as experienced as Crispin—she'd realised that pretty quickly—but he was willing to learn, and so obviously smitten with her that it was a terrific turn-on. Afterwards, he hadn't reached for the papers or checked his mobile phone, either. He'd lain beside her, talked to her, asked her about herself, her hopes, her dreams. He'd been so lovely, she'd had to be extremely careful not to trip up and let him know who she really was. As he was leaving, he'd asked to see her again, but she'd told him it was far too complicated. Crestfallen, he'd insisted she take his number, in case she changed her mind. The way things were going, she was jolly tempted to call him, but things were messy enough already.

Crispin chewed his fingernails, which wasn't an attractive look. 'Maybe we ought to call it a day. Both of us head home, just in case, and hope to God nothing comes of this.'

'Are you joking?' Honey glared at him. 'You're seriously saying you want me to go home, after everything I've been through?'

'You haven't been through anything,' he said. 'It's me who's been the nervous wreck for the last few weeks. It's a wonder I haven't had a coronary, I'm under so much stress.'

'So, you're finishing with me?'

He looked appalled. 'Of course not. I still want to see you, darling. It's just ...'

'Just that it's too risky, and you're too scared.'

He looked wounded by her scornful tone. 'Be fair. I have such a lot to lose, and if we *have* been followed by that chap in the Mini, God help us.'

Honey fumed. After all the effort she'd put in, he was going to throw in the towel? She was about to tell him to stick their affair where the sun didn't shine, when it came to her that she would have to go back to Upper Bourbury. Cain would discover the truth, and she would look a fool. She would have to admit he'd been right, and she'd be in huge bother for lying to him. She didn't even have a job to go back to, and if Cain stopped her allowance ... No, she couldn't risk it. She needed to keep Crispin sweet 'til the end of the summer holidays, then she could dump him and head back home, with Cain believing she'd been a good girl and served her time in Yorkshire, and ...

She sat up straight suddenly. 'Yorkshire.'

'What?' Crispin frowned. 'What has Yorkshire got to do with any of this?'

'Everything! Do you know how remote the Yorkshire Dales are? There's a place where sheep outnumber humans by a million to one.'

'Really?' He looked a bit worried, obviously thinking she'd lost the plot. Either that or he had a phobia of sheep. That wouldn't surprise her, either.

'Well, something like that anyway,' she said. 'The point is, I can't go anywhere round here, in case someone sees me. In Skimmerdale, no one would see me if I walked for miles. Well, maybe a few sheep. And even in the villages, no one has the internet, and no one would know or care who I was.'

'I'm sure they'd know who I was!' Crispin sounded indignant.

'Well, then, it can be your turn to stay shut up like bloody Rapunzel,' she snapped. 'Pass me your laptop.'

'What are you doing?'

'Booking us a holiday getaway in Skimmerdale,' said Honey, laughing. 'Oh, the irony. The very place I was supposed to be, and here I am going there of my own free will. My father would be furious. It's priceless.'

'Are you sure about this?'

'Absolutely.' She switched on the laptop and settled down comfortably. 'I'll be well and truly getting the better of my vile parents. This, my dear Crispin, is the icing on the cake.'

****

Teddy was waiting at the end of the lane, as Honey had known he would be, even though it was barely seven o'clock in the morning. He was obviously smitten, which was rather sweet and totally understandable.

'I'm so glad you called,' he murmured, slipping an arm round her waist and pulling her close. His lips eagerly sought hers and she shivered, suddenly wishing she had more time and not a mere ten minutes or so before Crispin woke up. 'Shall I come back to yours?'

Reluctantly, Honey moved away. 'Sorry, sweetie. I'm afraid I called you to say goodbye.'

'Goodbye?' His eyes widened. 'You're leaving? Why?'

'Something came up.' She glanced down at his trousers and giggled. 'Something *else* came up. Gosh, I do have a startling effect on you, don't I?'

'You know you do.' He took hold of one of her hands and squeezed it gently. 'We have a real connection, don't we? Don't you feel it, too? You must do or you wouldn't have called me to say goodbye. You could have left without saying anything. I know we haven't known each other long, but there's something between us, isn't there?'

'Yes, a huge erection,' she said, unable to keep the admiration from her voice. 'Look, Teddy, you're a darling, and we had an amazing time, but I have to leave.'

'Where are you going?'

She hesitated, but she didn't suppose it mattered that much. She would never see him again, after all. The thought gave her a sudden pang of regret, but she pushed it away. He was just a young man she'd met in a café when she'd been feeling low. All right, he'd been wonderful in bed, and he was kind and interesting and sweet, but after all, it couldn't go anywhere, could it? He worked in a charity shop, for God's sake, and, besides, she'd be going back to the Cotswolds soon. There was no point in continuing anything. 'Yorkshire,' she said.

'Yorkshire? But that's miles away. Why on earth would you go there?'

He sounded incredulous and she could hardly blame him. She hadn't been able to imagine why anyone would go all the way up there, either, after all.

'It's—business.'

'Well, whereabouts in Yorkshire?'

'Skimmerdale.'

'Never heard of it.'

'Me neither until very recently,' she admitted. 'Some ghastly little place called Beckthwaite, with no coffee shops, no chain stores. Primitive, really.'

'Then why go?' His voice was pleading and he stroked her face gently. 'Tell him to go on his own. Stay with me. Please, Eden.'

She frowned. 'Tell who to go on his own?' she said. 'Who told you I was with a man?'

He shrugged. 'It was obvious. You'd clearly sneaked me into the cottage while someone was away, and if it was another woman, why would it be a secret? Unless you swing both ways, of course.'

'Well, no, I don't. And you're right. Sorry.'

'It's all right. I knew what I was getting into and I didn't care. I wanted to be with you.'

'You're awfully intense considering you hardly know me.'

'Love at first sight,' he told her. 'I fell for you the moment I set eyes on you. I've sworn to myself that one day, you and I will be together.'

'Really?' She studied his face for signs that he was teasing her, but he looked deadly serious. 'Hmm, well, that's a teensy bit creepy, if I'm honest.'

'Don't be scared of me,' he said. 'I'd never hurt you. I'm not some weird stalker. I love you, that's all.'

Honey looked around, rather nervously. 'Look, Teddy, that's lovely of you, but I don't know you and, quite honestly, you don't know me. I have to go. He'll be awake any time now and we're setting off as soon as he's up. It's an awfully long drive. Take care of yourself.'

She gave him a quick peck on the cheek but he grabbed her and pressed his lips to hers. Honey tensed for a moment, not sure what to make of this intensity, but within seconds she found she was responding to him. There was something about him, something familiar, and something comforting. Not to mention something incredibly sexy. He wasn't her usual type but, really, he had a most peculiar effect on her. She clung to him and their kiss become more urgent, their bodies pressing hard against each other. Eventually, she pulled away, breathless.

'That was—gosh.'

'Well. Crikey.'

They stared at each other, seemingly in awe, and then Honey shook her head. 'I have to go.' She sounded regretful, even to her own ears.

Teddy smiled at her and kissed her hand. 'I know. Take care of yourself, Eden.'

She swallowed hard. 'I will. You, too, Teddy.'

He nodded and walked away. She watched him go and wondered why she was feeling a sudden desperate urge to follow him. The sea air must have been sending her mad. She tutted, impatient with herself, and headed back to the cottage.

****

'It's not raining!' Ophelia bounced into the kitchen, wearing her new jodhpurs, clean shirt, tie and jacket.

Eden, Eliot and Mickey exchanged amused glances. 'Don't you think you've got ready a bit early?' said Eliot, buttering his toast. 'It's not seven yet.'

'But I wanted to see how good I looked in my new clothes, and I do look good, don't I?'

'You do,' he confirmed. 'Not so sure how good you'll look when you've dripped butter down your jacket, mind. Not to mention the little matter of having to groom Flora yet. Or were you planning on leaving all that to Libby?'

'Oh, pooh.' She screwed up her nose and sighed. 'I suppose I'll have to get changed again.' She leaned forward and grabbed a piece of her father's toast. 'Cheers, Dad.'

'Oy! Cheeky madam.' He shook his head and looked up at Eden, his eyes wide. 'See what I have to put up with? Any more toast on the go?'

'Coming right up.' She smiled at him and handed him another plate of toast. Beneath the plate, his fingers touched hers, and her smile was obliterated at the sudden physical contact and the fleeting expression in his eyes as he obviously registered the same shock.

Thankfully, Ophelia didn't seem to notice. 'Shouldn't you be cleaning the sheep's bums?' she said, chewing her toast thoughtfully.

Eliot bit his lip, shaking his head. 'You're a little charmer, aren't you? Me and Mickey have been in the barn for ages, I'll have you know. Gideon and the others are looking superb. I reckon we've got a good chance with a couple of the ewes and lambs, too.'

'I'm thinking that young ram lamb has the makings of a champion,' said Mickey, nodding his appreciation at Eden when she handed him a plate of toast. 'Reckon we should hang onto him.'

'I hope Gideon pulls this off,' said Eliot. 'If we can get a good price for him, we can get a couple of decent new rams at the market and put aside a nice little nest egg for investment.'

'You're confident, though?' Eden collected two further slices of toast from the toaster and sat down at the table opposite him.

'You can never be sure,' said Ophelia. 'Judges can be very fickle.'

'Tha's been ear-wigging again.' Mickey gave her a stern look. 'Funnily enough, I said that to Adey just last night—word for word. Tha's got reet flappy lugs.'

Ophelia tutted. 'Does it matter? I have to learn, somehow, don't I? And it's hardly a secret, is it?'

'She's got a good point,' said Eden laughing. 'Though, I sometimes think she's got the mind of a forty-year-old.'

'Don't I know it,' said Eliot. 'Anyway, Gideon's a bloody good tup. Comes from champion stock, and he's big and solid, got good teeth, good legs. Just how the judges like them. I think he's been fattened up and groomed to perfection. It's in the lap of the gods now.'

'I didn't realise there was so much to it,' Eden admitted.

'Oh, aye. That's why the ones we're taking with us have been kept indoors for the last couple of weeks. They have to look their absolute best.'

'Dad looks very smart on show day, too,' said Ophelia. 'Wait 'til you see him in his tie and his white coat.'

'White coat?' Eden raised an eyebrow. 'And just why would you be wearing one of those?'

'Rules are rules,' he said. 'Have to wear a coat while I'm showing the stock. What did you think I'd be doing in it? Playing doctors and nurses?'

Eden's stomach decided to practice a gymnastics display. 'Maybe,' she croaked.

She took a huge gulp of tea as Eliot surveyed her, a hint of amusement in his eyes. She would have thought she'd be an expert at deceiving him by now, but she was finding it increasingly impossible to hide her attraction to him. She wondered if he was aware of the effect he had on her. Did he find it funny? Inconvenient? Or was there a remote possibility that he was equally attracted to her? If only he'd said something about their kiss, but he hadn't referred to it again, acting as if it had never happened, and she hadn't dared mention it to him, in case he dismissed it. She wasn't sure she could pretend for much longer that it didn't matter.

'Right.' He pushed away his plate and stood up. 'This won't buy the baby his bonnet. Got to get on. Ophelia, go upstairs and change, and then you'd better wake Libby up. You need to get Flora groomed and clean the tack. Me, Mickey and Adey will be taking the sheep to the showground in a few minutes, and Mickey's going to come back and take you lot and Flora at around dinnertime. Judging starts at half-past nine, so I've got to get a shifty on. Honey, have you got your cakes all ready?'

Eden pointed to the cake tins on the top of the dresser. 'One carrot cake and one Victoria sponge sandwich. I doubt I can compete with the local W.I., but it's fun to take part. My first agricultural show!'

'Dunno 'bout the W.I., but I've tasted your cakes, and I reckon you'll walk it,' said Eliot. 'Mrs Edwards, or no Mrs Edwards.'

'Me, an' all,' said Mickey.

'Why, thank you kindly.' Eden laughed. 'I should think an outsider won't get a look in, though.'

'I hope you're not suggesting these things are fixed,' said Eliot, his eyes twinkling. 'Honey, can you make sure the girls get a good breakfast inside them? Especially Libby. I know how nervous she gets, but they need to eat.'

'Of course. You get on with the sheep,' she said, 'and leave the kids to me. Teamwork.'

He smiled down at her. 'Aye, teamwork. Thank you.'

He and Mickey left the house, which was a good thing, as Eden had a feeling she'd begun melting into a giant puddle and would soon be dripping off the chair onto the floor.

Noticing Ophelia grinning at her, she coughed nervously and examined her toast. 'Well, go on, then. You heard your dad. Chop-chop.'

****

Gregorio was almost purple with effort. Not surprising, really, thought Lavinia. He'd been pounding away at her for simply ages and it was a total waste of time. He was having no effect on her, whatsoever, except to make her feel vaguely nauseous. She thought how odd it was that someone who looked so divine when lounging by a pool in skimpy trunks, tanned and toned body oiled up and gleaming, could look so repugnant when on top of her, squinting with the physical toll of trying desperately to bring her to orgasm. He didn't like failure, and it would be a source of great shame to him that he was failing pretty regularly lately. She wasn't happy about it, either. Sex was the ultimate distraction, and the one thing she'd pinned her hopes on for taking her mind off her husband's betrayal. Robbed of even that pleasure, she was in danger of wallowing, and that would never do.

She tried to concentrate, making a few encouraging noises to give Gregorio some hope.

'You come now, yes?'

Dear God, if she'd been in any danger of reaching orgasm, he'd just made sure that threat was headed off. She sighed and closed her eyes. Gregorio obviously mistook that as a signal that she was at the point of no return, and finally succumbed—his theatrical groans and squeaks being the final nail in that particular coffin. Lavinia knew there would be no repeat performance. She was done with Gregorio.

'That was perfect, no?'

'No.'

His beaming face turned into a frown. 'You mean yes, yes?'

'No. I mean *no*.' She summoned all her strength and physically pushed him off her, struggling to sit up and swatting away his outstretched hand in disgust. 'Never again. You've quite lost your charm. Sorry.'

'But you enjoy?' He obviously hadn't a clue.

'No, I didn't bloody enjoy,' she snapped. 'I haven't enjoyed for ages. I think it's time you went home.'

Gregorio looked astonished. 'I do not understand. You and me, we make the sweet music together.'

'A set of bagpipes with a puncture and an asthmatic piper could make sweeter music, chum,' she informed him, climbing out of bed and throwing on her robe. 'I'm sorry, but that's the way it is.'

He threw himself back on the bed, his mouth set in a sulky pout. 'Maybe I need a better instrument to play with,' he told her.

'I'll buy you a fucking mouth organ. Now piss off and leave me alone.'

She headed into the en suite, keen to get out of his sight before the tears came, and wondered what the hell was wrong with her. Crispin had played away before, and she'd never let it get to her like this. She'd always played him at his own game, and it had worked. Her string of lovers were always discreet, and a pleasant way of taking her mind off what would otherwise be an intolerable situation. Now she wondered if she'd gone about everything all wrong. Maybe she should have been firm with her husband from the start, instead of trying to give him his freedom. Maybe she should have told him that, if he had any more affairs, she would end the marriage. She wondered if he was aware that she knew about his dalliances, or was he blissfully ignorant? She wasn't sure which hurt her the most—Crispin thinking her that stupid, that gullible, or Crispin knowing she was aware of his behaviour and not caring that he was hurting her.

She splashed her face with cold water and stared at her reflection in the mirror. Was that another wrinkle? She peered closely and recoiled. Too close. She was thirty-four now and it showed. How could she possibly compete with a twenty-two-year-old who looked as stunning as Honey Carmichael?

Maybe the time had come to confront them, after all. Maybe she should head to Dorset and tell Crispin that, not only did she know about their affair, but she knew something he didn't—that he wasn't the only one bouncing around in Honey's bed. Would he finish with Honey then? Or would they work things out, leaving her well and truly in the cold? Would his career survive the affair? Would he care, even if it didn't?

She gripped the edge of the sink, wondering what to do. It wasn't like her to feel so unsure of everything. It was an unnerving experience.

Her phone rang in the other room, and she wrapped her arms around her body, trying to suppress the trembling. Let it ring. She didn't care anymore. Then she remembered Gregorio was in the bedroom and wasn't exactly happy with her. He could easily answer it, just for spite, and that would blow everything apart.

She threw open the bathroom door and lunged

forward, grabbing the mobile from Gregorio's hand, just as he was about to answer the call. 'Daddy?'

'You all right, sweetheart? You sound a bit breathless.'

'I was in the shower.' She scowled at Gregorio, who glared at her, and retreated back into the en suite, locking the door behind her. 'What's up?'

'Ah, well, that's the thing.' He sounded nervous suddenly.

Lavinia perched on the edge of the bath, frowning. 'What's the thing? What's happened?'

'You mustn't blame me, sweetheart.' His voice was wheedling. She knew that tone of old. It was his *I've totally fucked up but it's not really my fault so you can't get angry* voice. She remembered it all too well from her childhood. It was used a lot on her mother before she'd had the sense to leave him.

'For God's sake!' She gripped the phone. 'What is it?'

'I've lost them.'

'Lost them? What do you mean, lost them! How can you lose two people?'

'They've gone. Left the cottage, I mean. I thought, maybe, they'd gone out, but it's been a whole day now, and there's definitely no sign—'

'What have you been doing?'

'Now, Lavinia, you can't expect me to camp outside the bloody place. I went to a spa, if you must know. A soothing Jacuzzi and a decent massage. Bear in mind, my back's been giving me hell ever since I arrived here, and the hotel does have lovely facilities, and—'

'I thought it was your hip?' She was almost in tears. 'How could you let this happen? They could be anywhere. If they're seen, if this gets out—'

'I know. His career will be over.'

Sod his career, thought Lavinia. He'd be forced to choose, and who would he pick? A thirty-four-year-old with her first grey hair and fine lines around her eyes, or a glamorous blonde with bouncy boobs, endless legs, and a cool, rock star, multi-millionaire father, who was happy to donate huge sums to the Party? She wouldn't have a prayer.

'I'm coming home,' she said.

'Well, about time,' said her father. 'Enough's enough. He's gone too far, now. Go to the papers. Get your side of the story out there first. We'll destroy him, Lavinia. He'll be damn sorry he crossed us.'

'Oh, shut up, Daddy.' Lavinia nibbled her thumbnail, her mind whirling. 'We have to find him. Don't breathe a word of this 'til I get home, understand? You leave it to me now.'

'Well, I must say, you could show some gratitude. I've been stuck out here ...'

But Lavinia wasn't listening. She was already mentally confronting her husband, seeing him put a protective arm around that bimbo, watching Honey's smug smile turn to horror when she informed Crispin about the man in the café. He would have to believe her, wouldn't he? And he surely wouldn't want Honey after that?

There was only one way to find out, she supposed. Now, she just had to find them.

CHAPTER TWENTY-FOUR

Arriving at the showground, three miles outside Kirkby Skimmer, Eden could see immediately that this was no small, local event. The place was huge, and was packed with people.

While Mickey carefully parked his old, battered Land Rover, mindful of the trailer behind which carried Flora, Eden's stomach churned. How had Eliot got on? Had Gideon lived up to expectations?

'Tha looks more nervous than the lad did, lass,' Mickey observed shrewdly. 'Anyone would think it was important to thee. Not your problem, is it?' His eyes twinkled, and Eden flushed.

'Well, I know there's not much money in sheep farming, and this could make all the difference to Fleetsthorpe.'

'Tha's not wrong there. Glad tha's taking an interest. Wasn't sure it would matter to thee. Happen I was wrong. Reckon it all matters. Reckon it matters a lot.'

Eden didn't know how to answer that one.

Mickey cackled and patted her arm. 'Tha's not a bad 'un. Happen he could do worse.'

She stared at him in amazement, but he was already unbuckling his seatbelt, ordering the girls to stay by the car and wait for their father.

As Mickey waited for Eliot and Adey to appear, Eden, at his suggestion, left the children with him while she rushed over to the competition tent and placed her cakes on the table, ready to be judged.

'They look lovely,' said the woman who was filling out the entry cards. 'Have you entered before?'

'First time ever,' said Eden brightly. 'I'm a competition virgin.'

The woman looked a bit startled. 'Oh, er, I see. Jolly

good.'

Well, if she's judging, thought Eden, *I've just blown my chances there*. She headed back to the trailer, thinking how embarrassing it would be to come last. She hoped they didn't mark every entry and merely revealed the top three. She'd no idea what went on in these shows, but she'd seen *The Great British Bake-Off* enough times, and didn't want her cake pointed at in front of everyone and revealed to be a culinary catastrophe. It looked good, but would it taste okay?

Her heart skipped when she saw Eliot standing by the trailer, as Adey unloaded Flora.

'All done?' Eliot winked at her, which made her forget all about her baking worries immediately.

She nodded. 'How did it go?'

'Bloody marvellous,' he said, grinning at her. 'Gideon won his classes, and the shearling ram came second in his. My ram lamb came first, and my gimmer came third. I'm in the best of show classes this afternoon. I'm that relieved, I can't tell you.'

'That's wonderful,' she said. 'I'm so pleased for you.'

'It's been years in the making,' he said. 'Couldn't have done any of it without Mickey, here.'

'Bugger off,' said Mickey. 'Tha'll have me crying, daft lad.'

'Can we have a look around?' asked Libby. 'There are rabbits. I'd love to see those.'

'Oh, aye,' said Mickey. 'Not like we've got hundreds of flaming rabbits all over t' dale, is it?'

'Those are wild rabbits,' said Libby. 'It's different.'

'What about Flora?' said Eden.

'I'll stay with Flora,' said Mickey. 'Gonna sit meself down here and have me sandwiches and me shandy. Get tha selves off and enjoy tha selves. As long as tha's all back in time for your events, 'cos I can't walk them bloody sheep and ride that little pony at the same time.'

Ophelia and Libby obviously found the idea of Mickey sitting on Flora's back highly amusing. Eliot shook his head as they giggled and gently guided them away.

'Where do we start?' said Eden. 'I had no idea there'd be so much here.'

'Oh, aye, the Skimmerdale Show is the highlight of the area,' said Adey. 'Just about everyone who lives here is competing, or demonstrating, or visiting here. Mickey did his shearing demonstration this morning, and very popular it was, too. There's a drystone walling demo going on, sheepdog displays, cattle, poultry and horse classes—'

'Rabbit and guinea pig shows,' added Libby.

'There's some right lame things, too,' said Ophelia. 'Like handwriting classes for us kids. As if.'

'Some kids like to do things like that,' said Eliot. 'Not everyone's as animal mad as you.'

'I don't know why,' said Libby. 'There's cake shows, too, of course. I'll bet you win, Honey.'

'Mrs Edwards always wins the cake shows,' said Ophelia firmly. 'Everyone knows that.'

'Only 'cos she's so loud and bossy, and everyone's scared of her,' said Libby.

'There's some truth in that, an' all,' admitted Eliot. 'Still, you never know.' He looked around thoughtfully. 'I must remember to buy some damson jam for Granny Allen.'

Eden's eyes widened. 'Really? Why?'

'She loves her damson jam, but she doesn't make it any more. Arthritis. I did offer to bring her today, but she didn't feel up to walking round, so I promised I'd bring her a couple of jars back, instead.'

Eden felt her insides turn to mush. Honestly, he was good with children, kind to pensioners, loved animals ... Who could resist him?

Not her, that was for sure. It was becoming increasingly difficult not to touch him. In fact, it was an embarrassing fact that she had to keep her hands firmly on the handles of George's buggy to prevent herself from stroking him. She couldn't possibly stroke Eliot without giving herself away—well, unless she stroked other farmers as well, to disguise her motives, but she would get locked up if she went around stroking random sheep farmers, so it was probably better to keep her hands to herself, as difficult as that was proving to be.

Ophelia decided she was starving, so Eliot bought them all roast pork sandwiches from a stall that was emitting a smell so delicious it proved impossible to pass by without stopping to sample its wares. Even Libby managed a little of hers, despite her nerves.

After that, Libby dragged them off to look at the rabbits and tried to persuade Eliot that a little black Lionhead was an essential for a farm. Ophelia was disgusted when they stopped to watch the *Dog with the Waggiest Tail* competition. She was adamant that Dodger could easily beat the spaniel who took the title. Having seen the little Jack Russell's tail moving so fast that she was surprised it hadn't lifted the dog off the ground like a helicopter propeller, Eden wasn't going to argue with her. Ophelia decided she was definitely going to enter Dodger for the competition next year, and Eden tried to suppress the wave of sadness that overwhelmed her as she realised she wouldn't be around to see it.

They got two jars of damson jam for Granny Allen, then the girls decided they wanted to win some prizes on the stalls. Ophelia was delighted that there was a hook-a-duck stall, as she was guaranteed to win something. Sure enough, she had quickly snared a plastic duck on the end of the pole, and chose a cheap, plastic yoyo as her reward.

'I could have bought her three of those for the price of that ticket,' moaned Eliot.

'But it wouldn't have been nearly as much fun,' said Eden. 'Aren't you going to have a go?'

He pulled a face. 'I don't think so.'

'That's more like you, Dad!' Libby tugged on his arm, her face eager. 'Look, a rifle range! Show Honey how good you are at shooting!'

'Are you?' Eden wasn't sure what to think about that.

He shrugged. 'I'm not bad, I suppose.'

Adey laughed. 'Yeah, Mr Modesty. Go on, show the lovely lady what you can do.'

Eden didn't miss the look they exchanged, but she was uncertain what it meant. She had to admit, in spite of her dislike of guns, she felt a thrill of anticipation at the idea of Eliot handling a rifle.

With the girls and Adey urging him on, and George whooping with excitement, Eliot headed over to the rifle range and paid his money. He looked almost embarrassed as he took aim, but Eden couldn't take her eyes off him as he proceeded to fire at the target. His aim was straight and true, and the stall-holder shook his head as he offered Eliot the pick of the prizes on offer. Since most of the prizes were soft toys, there wasn't a great deal of choice. Eventually, he selected a Shaun the Sheep, which seemed appropriate.

'And what are you going to do with that?' asked Adey. 'Put it on the end of your bed? Cuddle up to it at night?'

'I want it,' said Ophelia.

'Why should you have it? I want it,' said Libby.

'Give it to George,' said Adey. 'Reckon he'll love it.'

Eliot hesitated, then shook his head. 'Georgie's got plenty of soft toys. Here.' Eden gasped when he handed it to her. 'For you.'

'Me?' It was hardly an engagement ring, but it felt as if she'd won the biggest prize of her life.

'Aye. To remind you of us when you've gone.' He turned away, thrusting his hands in his pockets, and Eden's heart sank. It meant nothing, after all.

She caught Adey's eye and saw a trace of sympathy in

it. She put the sheep in the tray under the buggy and mustered some enthusiasm in her voice. 'Right. What's next?'

Adey glanced at his watch. 'Happen it's time to get back to the sheep, Eliot. And you young 'uns need to get that pony ready.'

'Is it that time already? Right, well ...' Eliot's voice trailed off, as Daisy appeared at his side. 'Now, then. How's it going?'

'Fine, thanks. Long time, no see.' Daisy's voice was strained as she took in the scene. Evidently, she wasn't pleased to see "Honey" acting as if she was part of the family.

'It's been a busy time,' said Eliot, obviously uncomfortable. 'I expect you've been busy, too. You haven't been near the farm for a while.'

'Yes, well, things took a turn for the worse with Dad,' she said.

Eliot's face softened. 'I'm sorry to hear that, Daisy. Is he all right?'

She shook her head. 'Not really. He's going into a home. I can't manage him anymore, and he's been having a lot of falls. It's for the best.'

'Oh, Daisy.' His voice was sad, but she shrugged.

'It's life, isn't it?'

'I'm really sorry, Daisy,' said Eden. She was, too. She could imagine how she'd feel if her own dad was ever so ill he had to be put in a home. It would break her heart. 'It must be awful for you.'

'What would you know?' demanded Daisy. 'As if you'd care.'

'No need for that, Daisy,' said Eliot gently. 'She was just being sympathetic.'

'I don't need her sympathy,' snapped Daisy. 'What's it worth, anyway? She can't even be bothered to speak to her own father, so I'm sure she doesn't give a rat's arse about mine.'

Since there was no disputing the fact, as unjust as it was, Eden couldn't exactly defend herself. Instead, she said to the girls, 'Come on, we'd better get back to Flora. Time's getting away from us.'

'Isn't it just,' muttered Daisy. She folded her arms and nodded at Eliot. 'You in the final classes this afternoon?'

He nodded, obviously worried about her. 'Yes. Are you sure you're okay?'

'I said so, didn't I? I'm off to get something to eat. Might see you later.'

She turned and headed off without waiting for an answer. Eden felt wretched. Daisy was obviously suffering, and no doubt she would normally have turned to Eliot for comfort, but "Honey's" presence was making that impossible for her. If she wasn't on the scene, would things have progressed between the two of them? But then, she hadn't exactly done anything to stop them getting together, had she? Surely, if it was going to happen, it would have happened already? She knew Daisy was keen for a relationship, but how did Eliot feel?

Once Daisy had walked away, Eliot turned to Eden. 'I'll be over there,' he said, pointing in the direction of the sheep shed. 'I have to finish them off and get myself ready. Will you be okay with the bairns and Flora? Do you want Adey or Mickey to help you?'

'No, it's fine. We'll manage. What do we have to do first?'

'They need to get their numbers,' he said. 'The tent's not far from the trailer. The girls know the ropes—they've done this before. If you get stuck, or there are any problems at all, come and find me, okay?'

'What, and interrupt your sheep showing?' She smiled faintly at him, still feeling unsettled. 'I wouldn't dare.'

He put a hand on her shoulder, his eyes serious. 'I mean it. Don't be scared to come and ask for help.

Promise?'

What was he trying to do? Kill her off? 'Promise,' she squeaked.

He seemed to study her face for a moment, before he nodded and turned to his daughters. 'Now, behave yourselves and don't be silly. Take it easy, okay? Good luck. I'll come and watch as soon as I can.'

He crouched down in front of the buggy and kissed his son. 'See you soon, Georgie.' Glancing up at Eden, he said, 'Look after them, won't you?'

'Of course.' Crikey, she was only going across a field, not taking the kids trekking in Nepal. He needed to stop worrying and start concentrating on his own job. Time to take charge. 'We'll go and get the numbers,' she said, pushing the buggy forward. 'Come on, girls. We'll see you later,' she added, nodding at the two men. 'Best of luck. Hope Gideon wins a prize.'

'Bugger better had,' said Adey. 'We're counting on it.'

As Eden walked away, she wondered again about the barn and the missed potential. She needed to push Eliot about it. It could be a massive help to his finances, if he could get the funds to convert the building and set the project up.

Mickey waved to them as they reached the trailer. 'Thought tha'd buggered off home. Had a good time?'

'Oh, yes,' said Ophelia. 'Do you like my yoyo? I won it.'

Mickey rolled his eyes, evidently not impressed.

'Dad won a Shaun the Sheep,' said Libby. 'He gave it to Honey.'

'Did he now?' Mickey grinned at her. 'That were right kind of him, I'm sure. Happen he's in a good mood, what with Gideon doing so grand.'

Ophelia nodded. 'I reckon if Gideon wins the next class, we could get a new pony out of it. What do you think? I mean, Libby's getting a bit tall for Flora, and it would be good to have a pony each so we could go for rides together.'

'Happen so, but money don't grow on trees. Even if Gideon fetches top whack, that money's needed. Remember that, and don't go nattering your Dad, right?'

Ophelia looked disappointed but didn't argue. She and Libby began to saddle Flora, and Eden took the opportunity to take Mickey to one side.

'Mickey, has Eliot said anything to you about the barns?'

He frowned, shaking his head. 'Nay, lass. What about them?'

'I had a thought. There are all those empty buildings sitting there. It's a waste of potential. I was thinking that stone barn overlooking the beck could be done up and used as a sort of tea shop. We could serve cream teas to passing walkers. So many people hike up there, and it would be great for them to have somewhere to rest and take some refreshment. We could charge a decent price and get some income coming in.'

Mickey smirked. 'Could we?'

Eden blushed. 'I mean, Eliot could. And then there's all those other barns opposite the house. One of them could be renovated and turned into a bed and breakfast business. We could cook the breakfasts in the house and take them across. We could fit a few bedrooms and a large dining room in one barn. There's loads of room. I think it could make a huge difference to Eliot's finances.'

Mickey looked at her curiously. 'What put all this in tha mind, lass?'

'Well, I've been online, researching the state of farming. It seems a lot of farmers are struggling to make ends meet, and many of them have turned to other sources of income to help. Diversification is the key word.'

'Is it now?' Mickey nodded knowingly. 'Well, I think it's reet kind of thee to go to all that trouble.'

'But what do you think? I mentioned it to Eliot, but he didn't seem to take it seriously. Probably because he doesn't take me seriously,' she added gloomily.

Mickey patted her arm. 'I wouldn't say that, lass. Tha'd be surprised. I'll have a word, see what he thinks. Happen tha's reet. Summat needs doing. Long term, like. Mebbe we should look into it, this diversification lark.'

'Really? Oh, thanks, Mickey.' Eden felt highly relieved. At least, with Mickey on her side, Eliot might start to look into the possibilities at last.

'Tha'll be 'reet now, does tha reckon? Only, I'd like to go and help the lad wi' tup. He gets reet nervous, and this is a big deal.'

'Of course, Mickey. We can manage. Good luck.'

They found the steward's tent easily enough. Eden's heart was in her mouth as they walked towards it, not least because there were children on ponies everywhere, and she could only pray that they were under control. She still wasn't confident around horses, and even though Flora was lovely and gentle, it didn't mean that all her kind were. She'd read enough horror stories of ponies kicking out, and George was so vulnerable in his buggy.

'Number fourteen,' said Libby, coming out of the tent and fastening her number over her shirt. 'Go and get yours, Ophelia.'

Ophelia handed her the reins and rushed inside.

'What have you entered for, anyway?' Eden asked.

'I'm doing the bending and the sack race, Ophelia's doing the egg and spoon, and we're doing the Gretna Green together, obviously,' she said.

'Oh, obviously.' She had no idea what Libby was talking about, but she nodded encouragingly and added, 'Well done,' and hoped the little girl wouldn't ask any questions about any gymkhana games Honey had taken part in.

George, seeing all the ponies around, practically hurled

himself out of his buggy, hands outstretched.

'You wouldn't be so keen if you knew what they were capable of, mate,' Eden muttered, swerving the buggy out of the path of a fat piebald, who didn't look as if he stood a cat in hell's chance of winning a thing, unless there was a competition for the most sugar lumps eaten in ten minutes.

Ophelia returned with number twenty-seven and quite cross about it. 'It's my unluckiest number,' she wailed.

'How on earth can twenty-seven be your unluckiest number?' Eden said.

'I got twenty-nine out of thirty questions right in my spelling test,' she replied, 'and number twenty-seven was the only one I got wrong.'

'Oh, well,' Eden said, 'in that case, you must be right.'

'Don't be silly,' said Libby. 'You got twelve out of twenty in your maths test. Are you saying those eight numbers you got wrong are all unlucky, too?'

Ophelia considered the matter. 'Oh, yeah,' she said eventually, and looked a lot more cheerful after that, for which Eden was truly grateful. She had enough to worry about, sorting out her own nerves, without worrying about Ophelia's.

'We're going over there,' said Libby, pointing to a group of children and ponies, who were standing in the shade of some trees. 'Do you want to sit on the benches?'

The benches around the ring were already pretty full, but there were a few spaces left, and she nodded. 'Best of luck, girls. We'll be just over there if you need us. Be careful.'

Ophelia rolled her eyes, but Libby gave her a tense smile. 'Thanks, Honey.'

Eden pushed the buggy over the grass, threading her way gingerly between crowds of nervous-looking children and parents barking instructions. She made the people on the front bench budge up, pointing out that she had a buggy and needed to be at the end. They took a dismal view of that, and there was a great deal of muttering, but they shuffled up, and Eden plonked herself down, keeping hold of the buggy with one hand.

Within a few minutes, the first class started. It was a showing class for tiny tots, who were led into the ring by their proud parents. Their little legs were halfway up the ponies' bellies, and Eden's heart was in her mouth, watching them being paraded round the ring.

The children seemed delighted. There was a lot of giggling and some enthusiastic kicking going on. The ponies looked pretty glum, not surprisingly. Eden had no idea that one could get full riding kit for such young children. They were all in riding hats and breeches and boots. A couple even had tweed jackets. It occurred to her that, in a year or two, George could be in the ring, being paraded around like that. Then she dismissed the idea. As if Eliot would wander round a field, leading him on Flora to be gawped at by everyone. Then again, maybe Daisy would do it. By the time George was old enough, who knew what the situation would be between the two of them? She could be the children's new stepmother.

George banged on the side of his buggy and hurled himself forward in frustration. It was a wonder he didn't snap the straps. Hastily, Eden unbuckled him and hoisted him onto her knee, where he clapped his hands and cooed in delight at the ponies, shrieking out "Flora" every now and then, which only went to prove that one pony looked pretty much the same as another to his eyes.

Eden sat through another couple of the showing classes, for children of varying age groups, doing her best to entertain George. Finally, the gymkhana games got going. Libby competed first, taking part in a bending competition. This seemed to consist of pony and rider threading their way between a row of poles, trying not to knock any over while going as fast as possible against a few other competitors. There were various heats of the same class, and it went on a long time. Libby did very well, as far as Eden could tell. During it all, George sat on her knee, staring wide-eyed at the race and clapping occasionally. When it had finished, Eden watched, curious, as a few riders, including Libby, were called over, and then she joined in with the clapping, delighted to realise that Libby had won something, when a yellow rosette was pinned to Flora's bridle.

'Oh, well done!' Eden said out loud.

'Third,' said a voice behind her.

Eden looked up, surprised, as Beth shuffled past her to sit beside her on the bench. There was more muttering as everyone had to budge up again, but Beth didn't seem too worried.

'Are you enjoying yourself?'

'Oh, yes. Very interesting,' Eden murmured, thinking, *please don't ask me anything about my gymkhana career because I haven't the foggiest idea.*

'Have you had a chance to look around? There's all sorts going on, you know. James is watching a gun dog display, and I'm judging the flowers later. Did you enter the cake show, by the way?'

'Yes, I did. And we've had a walk round. It was great fun. When the children have finished, I'll pop over and see how my cakes have done. Hopefully, Eliot will have finished by then, too. He's over at the sheep showing ring.'

'Anxious times for him,' said Beth.

'I'd love to see him in action,' Eden murmured wistfully. God, had she really said that out loud? Beth studied her rather quizzically, and she had an awful feeling she'd given herself away. 'I mean, sheep showing. It sounds really interesting. I'd love to know what happens.'

Beth smiled at her. 'Why don't you nip across and see how he's getting on? I'm sure he'd be glad of the support.'

'Oh, I couldn't. I need to watch the children, and besides, he has Mickey and Adey for support.'

Beth hesitated for a moment before leaning in. 'I think he'd appreciate your support, too.'

'You-you do?'

'Yes. And, anyway, I'm here to keep an eye on the children, aren't I?'

Eden flushed. Beth was so nice. How could she tell her that she didn't feel able to leave Eliot's kids in her care? She didn't want to hurt her feelings, and she had no idea what the problem was between her and Eliot. Unless it was guilt because they really had had an affair, although she found that increasingly difficult to believe. Nothing added up.

Beth sighed. 'You don't want to go against Eliot. I understand that. On the other hand, if you decided to stretch your legs, take George in his buggy, perhaps, and left the girls competing here, and I happened to be sitting watching them in the crowd, well, you've hardly done anything disloyal there, have you?' She winked at Eden, and suddenly it seemed like the best plan ever.

'Thank you, Beth,' Eden said, strapping George back into his buggy. 'You're very kind.'

'And very understanding,' said Beth, folding her arms. 'Don't forget that.'

You know, don't you, thought Eden. *You know exactly how Eliot makes me feel.* Was it that obvious? Did he know? Why the hell hadn't he done anything about it, then? Unless, of course, he didn't feel the same. *Oh, crikey.*

She almost changed her mind, but decided she was made of sterner stuff. Besides, she really wanted to see Eliot in his white coat.

Rushing over, she pushed the buggy through the crowds, using it as a weapon to force the more stubborn onlookers to make way for her, and finally came to rest by the rope that fenced off the showing ring.

'Wondered how long it would take thee, lass.' Mickey grinned at her, holding up a hand when she started to make her excuses. 'I'm saying nowt. None of my business. I take it the lasses are all right?'

'Fine. Still competing.' She hesitated a moment then confessed, 'Beth's watching them.'

He nodded. 'Nowt wrong with Beth. Nice lass. Things'll sort themselves aht, reet enough.'

Eden wasn't sure what he meant by that, but she had no inclination to get into the matter at that moment. After all, she'd just caught sight of Eliot standing by Gideon, and she didn't think she could breathe and speak at the same time.

The white coat contrasted sharply with his dark curls and she thought he made all the other competitors look plain and nondescript. If it had been him who was being judged, he'd have walked it, and would have been carrying off the trophy already, but, unfortunately, it wasn't. It was all about Gideon, and Eden found she was gripping Mickey's arm, as the judges walked over to examine Fleetsthorpe's prize tup.

They seemed to take ages, stepping back to look at the poor animal, prising open his mouth to check his teeth, running their hands down his legs and along his back, and even checking his testicles. *Probably a good thing it wasn't Eliot being judged, then*, thought Eden. Gideon was patient and stood calmly beside Eliot. Evidently, the endless halter training had paid off.

'What do you think?' she whispered.

Mickey sucked in his breath then let it out in a low whistle. 'Buggered if I know. If it were down to me, I'd go for ours, or that Herdwick of Pete Blake's. Good looking tup, that. It will be close, I reckon.'

George clapped his hands. 'Daddy!' he called.

Eden hoped he wouldn't distract Eliot. Not during such

a nail-biting moment. 'God, I can't stand this,' she said, as the judges moved off and examined the next ram. 'This is agony. How much longer?'

'Eeh, you're tougher than that, surely.' Mickey frowned. 'Looks like I were reet.'

'What do you mean? Right about what? Oh.'

The judges evidently agreed with the old shepherd's opinion, as they had selected both Gideon and the Herdwick for further examination. Eden didn't know whether to close her eyes or turn her back, as they made both Eliot and Pete Blake walk the sheep up and down in front of them before lining them up again for another quick check.

'Oh, hell's bells. I feel sick.'

'Best get used to this,' said Mickey comfortably.

Eden stared up at him, wondering what he meant and why she would have to get used to it, but at that moment, there was an outbreak of applause. She turned back to see the judges shaking hands with both farmers. 'What happened? What did I miss?'

'How did tha miss it? Bloody hell, lass, we won! Gideon is the Skimmerdale champion!'

'Oh, my God!' Had she screamed that out loud? She had an awful feeling she had, as everyone turned to look at her, but they were all laughing, so she decided it didn't matter, and she hadn't committed some awful sheep showing faux pas.

'Wait here,' said Mickey.

'Can't I come with you?' she pleaded on seeing Eliot moving Gideon out of the ring toward the pens.

'Best not. It will be barmy back there, and there's the whole disinfectant thing, and with that buggy ... Lad'll be out reet enough. I'll feed and watter them all and send him out to thee. Wait over there.' He nodded toward the secretary's tent. 'That's where he'll have to go for the cup and all the other stuff later on.'

'What other stuff?'

Mickey beamed at her. 'Gideon won best aged ram, as well as champion Swaledale. There'll be a trophy, a sash, and a rosette, as well as prize money. Then there's all the rosettes and prize money the lamb, the gimmer and the shearling won.'

'Crikey. How much did they win?'

Mickey stroked his chin thoughtfully. 'All told, about a hundred and sixty quid.' He obviously saw the disappointment in her face and laughed. 'It's not the prize money on the day that counts, lass, it's what comes after. With all this to advertise, they'll fetch a grand price at the sales. This has been a good day for Fleetsthorpe. A bloody grand day.'

As he hurried off, Eden turned the buggy and began the difficult job of manoeuvring the contraption, with a wildly bouncing George, through the crowds. Finally, she reached the edge of the hordes of people, who seemed intent on standing there forever, discussing the judges' decision and the merits and faults of the various sheep. She pushed the buggy, with some hardship, over the rough grass and eventually made it to the secretary's tent, where she leaned on the handles and took a deep breath.

She was wondering how Libby and Ophelia were getting on, and thinking that, really, she ought to be getting back to them, when she caught sight of Eliot walking towards the tent. He looked up, and as his gaze landed on her, his face broke into a wide smile.

Forgetting everything else, she ran towards him and threw her arms round his neck.

He wrapped his arms around her waist and lifted her off her feet, spinning her round and laughing. 'He did it!' he cried.

'He did! You did!'

She kissed him on the cheek, and he held her for a moment, until they heard George yelling for his father.

Immediately, Eliot placed her back on the ground, where she put her arms by her sides, blushing furiously. 'We did it, Georgie,' he said, rushing over to the buggy and planting a kiss on the little boy's head. 'What do you think of that, then?'

'Want biscuit,' said George.

'Well, that's brought me back down to earth,' said Eliot, laughing. 'How are the lasses doing?'

'Still competing, I think. Are you coming to watch them?'

'You bet I am.'

'Eliot!'

They both turned at the call, and Eden tried to hide her frustration on seeing Daisy approaching them. The poor woman looked tired and drained. She deserved compassion, not impatience.

'Daisy. We were just going to watch the girls,' Eliot said. 'They're in the gymkhana.'

'Can I have a word with you? In private.'

Eliot glanced at Eden. 'Well, I—'

'Please. It's important.'

Eden took the handles of the buggy. 'It's okay. Catch us up when you can.'

He nodded. 'I won't be long,' he murmured.

Eden pushed George back towards the gymkhana ring. Whatever Daisy wanted, it sounded important. She felt disgusted with herself for wishing that the woman would leave Eliot alone. Maybe she was turning into Honey, after all. Well, that would soon be at an end. It was almost September. The time she had left in Skimmerdale could suddenly be counted in days, not weeks. Her time with Eliot was almost over.

CHAPTER TWENTY-FIVE

Eliot studied Daisy's face and felt his heart go out to her. She was pale, with dark shadows under her eyes, and she'd obviously been crying. She'd been through hell, and where had he been? After everything she'd done for him, he'd left her to it. He was disgusted with himself.

'What can I do for you, Daisy?' he said gently. 'Is it the farm? Are you wondering what to do with it? Do you need help?'

'It's not the farm.' She rubbed her face, and he saw there were tears in her eyes. 'I don't give a damn about the place. I'm not staying there a moment longer. No doubt Tom will want to sell it as soon as possible, but that's between him and the old man. I don't much care, to be honest.'

'Your father's still of sound mind. Tom wouldn't force him to sell it, and no one can turf you out of there, if you've nowhere else to go.'

'I'll find somewhere. I'm working and I'm not completely incompetent, you know.'

'Of course you're not!' He ran a hand through his hair, wondering what she wanted from him. He didn't know what to say.

'I saw you,' she said suddenly. Her voice was choked with emotion, and the tears spilled onto her cheeks.

'Saw me? What do you mean?'

'You and her. Running towards each other like you were in some soppy film. Saw you pick her up, and I *knew*.'

His face burned, but he shrugged. 'Knew what? We were just happy that Gideon won the championship cup.'

'Bollocks.' She almost spat the word at him. 'You know what's happening, don't you? You're doing it again. Falling for the same old crap as last time. What the hell is wrong with you?'

'That's enough, Daisy,' he said. He didn't want to hear all this. Not today, at least. Let him have one day without worrying, without thinking.

'It's not enough! Don't you get it? Why can't you see?' She began openly sobbing, and he looked round nervously, not wanting their conversation to be overheard.

'Daisy, please don't.' Tentatively, he put his arm round her, but before he knew what was happening, she had thrown herself at him and locked her lips on his. He didn't want to hurt her, but he couldn't do this. He pulled away, shocked.

She grabbed his arm. 'I can make you happy,' she told him. 'Please, Eliot. You know it's always been you, don't you? There's never been anyone else for me.'

'I-I—' He didn't know how to respond. The awful thing was, he knew it was true. She'd never shown the slightest interest in any other man. If only he could feel the same about her, but he couldn't. He was even more certain of that fact now.

'I won't have Dad to worry about anymore. I can devote myself to you and the bairns. I can look after you, keep your house for you, make sure you're all fed and safe. I'd love to do that. It's all I've ever wanted.'

He knew that, too. He'd known it ever since Jemima died. She'd been waiting to step into her shoes, and it would have been easy to say yes, to make sure he never had to worry about his children again. Yet, he hadn't been able to do it. He didn't love Daisy. He would never love Daisy.

'I'm sorry,' he murmured. 'I'm so sorry.'

'She's just another Jemima!' There was panic in Daisy's eyes, her voice increasingly shrill. 'You're making exactly the same mistake. Falling for another rich woman, who won't be happy when the money runs out and she realises that she's stuck on a sheep farm, with no fancy shops or posh parties to go to. You'll go through the same pain again. She'll break your heart, like that bitch did. I warned you then, and I was right. Listen to me, please.'

'All right, that's enough,' he said, his voice harsh. 'I'm sorry, Daisy, but that's it. I don't want to hear any more.'

'Of course you don't, because you know I'm right, and it scares the shit out of you. You're on the road to heartbreak, yet again, and you won't admit it. You think you love her? You thought you loved Jemima, and look how that turned out!'

'I've never said I love her,' he said, trying to stay calm. 'Nothing's happened between me and Honey, I swear it.'

She wiped her tears and sniffed, looking at him with desperation in her eyes. 'But you want it to, don't you?'

He didn't answer her. He didn't know how to. What *did* he want, anyway?

She gave a bitter laugh. 'Can't deny it, can you? You're a fool, Eliot Harland. She'll make your life hell. Well, good luck with it, 'cos you're going to bloody well need it.'

She turned away.

'I'm sorry, Daisy,' he said quietly, his eyes wet with tears. 'I wish I could tell you what you want to hear.'

'But you can't.' She drew herself up, refusing to turn back to him. 'We're done, Eliot. You've made your choice. And God help you.'

****

Eden gave Eliot an anxious smile as he edged his way along the bench and sat beside her. 'Everything okay?'

He nodded. 'All sorted. How are they doing?'

'Just about to start the last race. You're just in time.'

She wasn't fooled, despite his assurance. She could see that, whatever Daisy had wanted to talk to him about, it had shaken him. He looked tense. She felt sorry for Daisy, of course she did, but she wished he could have had one day to enjoy the glory of success, without having to deal with anything negative for a change. Hadn't he been through enough?

The Gretna Green race began, and beside her, Eliot made a visible effort to relax as Libby galloped wildly down the field, while Ophelia hopped impatiently at the far end, waving her arms and shrieking at her sister to hurry up. Her heart soared when he laughed with the rest of the crowd at the chaos that ensued, as several children tried to scramble up on their ponies behind their partners. The poor animals stood patiently as the kids tried desperately to heave themselves up, while the children who were already mounted screamed at them to get a move on and stop being so pathetic. She felt a ripple of delight when she realised that Eliot couldn't wipe the proud smile off his face when Ophelia landed in the saddle behind her sister. The girls had obviously practised hard, and had figured out a system. Ophelia used Libby's foot as a stirrup and sprang up that way, keeping a tight hold on Libby's shirt. Libby just about managed to stay seated, and then the two of them were off, streaking away down the field, with another two ponies a short distance behind them and the others still stranded at the far end.

'Go on, go on,' she heard him muttering, then he jumped to his feet and cheered when they passed the finishing line in first place.

'What a day,' said Eden, laughing.

'You're not wrong there,' he said, reaching out to tickle George's chin.

'Biscuit?' asked George, hopefully.

'Time for home,' said Eliot, with some relief.

It was ages, however, before they were ready to leave. The sheep couldn't be moved until the show finished, so they had to hang around. Mickey drove Flora home and offered to take the girls with him, but they refused point blank to leave without their father, and Eden said she would stay, too, so Mickey headed back, leaving Adey to help Eliot with the sheep when the time came.

The girls were thrilled with a yellow rosette and a red rosette, which, they assured their father and Eden, was just the start of a flourishing equine career.

'What about you?' said Eliot suddenly. 'How did the cakes go?'

'Crikey, I forgot all about them!' She had, too. 'I'd better go and find out.'

'Bet Mrs Edwards won,' said Ophelia confidently. 'You can't fight the system.'

'Why is it, whenever that child speaks, I hear Mickey's voice coming out?' demanded Eliot. 'Have a little faith.'

In the event, however, Ophelia was right. The infamous Mrs Edwards had claimed first prize for her Victoria sponge, as she apparently did every year. However, Eden's own effort had come third, and her carrot cake had come second in that class, so she was delighted.

'You were robbed,' said Libby. 'No one could beat your cake.'

'Told you it was a fix,' said Ophelia.

'Someone gag that child before we're all arrested,' said Eliot, before dashing across to the secretary's tent to collect his winnings.

By the time the show was closing, they were all exhausted. Loading the boot with the trophy, the sash, the rosettes, and all the other assorted items they'd brought with them, including George's buggy, seemed to take forever. George was fast asleep in his car seat by the time Eliot and Adey had loaded the sheep into the trailer and got clearance to leave. Adey shook Eliot's hand and waved goodbye to Eden and the children. His father had come to collect him, so he wouldn't be travelling with them. The girls were yawning when the car finally pulled out of the showground, and they began the journey home.

Home, thought Eden, who'd grown increasingly melancholy as the show began to wind down. This event had been a marker in her time at Fleetsthorpe. Now it was over, time would fly by. She would be back in the Cotswolds before she knew it.

The car trundled slowly along the roads. The children were all asleep within minutes, and Eliot was obviously concentrating on the road ahead, his hands tight on the steering wheel, a frown on his face. Eden looked out of the window, watching with a lump in her throat as they passed through the countryside. She had never seen a more beautiful landscape. It filled her with wonder and joy, and she suddenly couldn't imagine ever wanting to be anywhere else.

As they began winding their way down Mikkel Rigg, she bolted up. 'Can we pull over here? Just for a moment?'

Eliot glanced at her. 'Why? Are you all right?'

'I'm fine, but—' She sighed. 'I want to take it in. This view, I mean. Just for a moment, while the children are all asleep. Please?'

She saw him glance in the rear view mirror, where three sleeping faces would be reflected back at him. She didn't see that it would matter if they stopped for a short while, and it seemed he agreed, because he parked the car as close to the hillside as he could manage, with the trailer behind them, and turned off the engine.

She unfastened her seat belt and climbed out of the car, squeezing out of the door, which she couldn't fully open without bashing it into the hill. She edged round the car and crossed the road, going to stand on the grass verge and staring in awe at the view that lay, spread out before her.

After a moment, she felt him beside her, heard the rattle of his car keys. His breath brushed her neck as he murmured, 'Eden.'

She jumped in alarm. 'Wh-what did you say?'

'Eden,' he repeated. He nodded at the dale, his voice full of pride. 'My mam always said it were paradise here, a real Garden of Eden. Don't you agree?'

'Oh. Oh, yes.' She turned to him, smiling through her tears. 'It really is beautiful here. She was right. I mean, it takes your breath away. Look at it, Eliot.'

He followed her gaze, toward the magnificent landscape before them. Sheep were dotted on the hillside, and the River Skimmer glittered below them in the early evening sunlight like a silver ribbon threaded through a blanket of green. 'That's where it gets its name from, I reckon,' he said suddenly, nodding at the water.

She frowned. 'What does?'

'The river. Skimmer means to sparkle, to shine brightly. Comes from back when land round here was Viking territory. Lots of place names in the Dales are of Scandinavian origin. Happen a band of marauding Vikings stood in this very spot one day, looked down at that water all shining like it is now, and gave it its name right there and then.'

'Oh, what an amazing thought,' said Eden, smiling at him.

He smiled back. 'It's not as cosy as the Cotswolds, is it?'

'No.' Eden had to agree with that. 'And the Cotswolds are stunning, too, in a different way. You know what I don't understand?'

'Tell me.'

'The sheep. I mean, they roam all over the hills and fields round here, but they seem to know where they belong. How do they do that?'

'Hefting.'

'Pardon?'

He smiled softly. 'It's a process of getting to know where they live. Making themselves at home, like. Bit by bit, they settle in, get used to the place. They're part of the landscape, and the landscape is part of them. Hefting.'

'I see,' she murmured. 'Sort of like, *home is where the heart is*.'

'Happen that's true enough.'

He fell quiet, and she blinked away tears, thinking how soon she would be back in Upper Bourbury, knowing she would be leaving her own heart behind in this beautiful place, with him. She tried to drink in the view, to fix it in her mind's eye, so that she would be able to recall it when she needed it, like Wordsworth with his daffodils. The pain was as powerful as the image was exquisite. Beside her, she felt Eliot's presence, as much a fixture of the landscape as the earth beneath her feet.

The sunshine caressed her back in sympathy and the evening breeze kissed her neck and ruffled her hair with affectionate fingers, as she stood, saying a silent goodbye. She turned away eventually, knowing it was time to leave.

****

The children were all in bed early that night. The show had thoroughly exhausted them. Eliot and Honey did the usual chores in silence. There was an air of sadness over her, somehow, which puzzled him. They'd had a lovely day at the show, and she'd been popular with the locals. She really seemed to fit in, and she obviously loved the place. Perhaps that was the problem.

He looked at her, as she wiped down the surfaces in the kitchen. Was she dreading going home? Was it possible that, against all odds, she'd actually fallen for Skimmerdale? Dare he begin to hope that there was even more to it than that?

He headed into the living room, carrying the mugs of hot chocolate he'd prepared while she'd done the dishes. He mustn't jump to conclusions. He remembered one of the girls saying, at the open day, that Honey liked him. He'd laughed it off, put it down to his daughter being silly and fanciful. But then the other night—that kiss. He'd tried to tell himself she'd just felt sorry for him. After all, he'd just poured all that stuff out about him and Jemima. He didn't know why. He couldn't imagine why she'd be interested. Yet, she'd seemed so understanding, so sympathetic. Maybe that was it. She had a soft heart, and she'd wanted to comfort him, and it had gone too far. Or maybe ...

He sat down on the sofa, remembering her expression as she'd looked down upon the river from high up on Mikkel Rigg. There had been something in her eyes that reminded him of the way she'd looked at him that night. A sort of yearning, of wonder. Was it possible she felt the same way he did? Or was it all wishful thinking? And what good could come of it, anyway?

As she sat beside him on the sofa, he remembered the other night when they'd kissed, and loosened his shirt collar, feeling rather hot.

'It was a lovely day, wasn't it?' she said, smiling at him.

'What? Oh, aye. Grand. And you won two prizes. Well done.'

'I know! Can't believe it!'

'Reckon your dad will be amazed, an' all.'

Her smile faded, and she nodded. 'I suppose.'

He wondered why things were the way they were between her father and herself. 'You ought to make it up with him, you know,' he said gently.

'Pardon?'

'You and your dad. This feud you've got going on.' He shook his head sadly. 'It's not worth it. Look at Jemima and her dad. He were devastated when she died. Cried like a baby at her funeral. All that time wasted. Of course, he blamed me and wasted no time telling me it were all my fault, but truth is, he could have called her any time he liked. One little phone call. Now it's too late. Don't let that happen to you and your dad, Honey. Whatever's gone on,

I reckon it can be fixed. Can't imagine how I'd feel if my girls wouldn't speak to me.'

Honey took a sip of her drink. 'I wouldn't worry about that. It will never happen.'

He wasn't so sure. When they were older, there were things he would have to tell them, things they deserved to know. How would they feel about him then, he wondered? And George. How would he react? He knew he could lose his own children if he didn't get it right. He didn't even want to think about the future.

'Does he see them?'

'Eh?' He stared at her, surprised. 'Does who see them? See who?'

'Does Jemima's dad see the children? Seeing as he was grieving for her at the funeral, does he bother with her offspring?'

He sighed. Another sore point. 'No. Never bothered.'

'Seems to me he deserves everything he gets, then,' she said.

He'd often thought the same and was gratified to hear she shared his opinion of her own relative. 'Not fair on the kids, though,' he said.

'No.' She put her mug back on the coffee table. 'I suppose it isn't. Good job they've got you, eh?'

'Oh, aye. Struck gold there,' he said, with a rueful smile.

'I know.' She wasn't smiling.

'It's hard for me to trust people,' he said suddenly. 'After—after everything that happened. I'm sorry if I came across as a bit grumpy. Takes me a while to relax around people these days.'

'It's okay.'

'No, it's not. I haven't always been nice to you.'

'I haven't always been nice to you, either.'

'Well, that's true.' He tried to smile, to ease the tension, but she merely stared down at her lap. 'Thing is ...'

'Yes?'

'I haven't told you it all. About me and Jemima, I mean.'

'Oh?'

'There was someone else.' He was surprised that it didn't hurt to say it as much as he'd thought it would.

She was staring at him, shocked. He definitely had her full attention.

'Not me,' he said hastily. 'Her. She had an affair.'

'Did you—did you know him?'

He pursed his lips for a moment, then tugged nervously at his shirt collar. 'Doesn't really matter, does it? Point is, it happened. And it's made me wary. I don't always give people the benefit of the doubt. You see?'

She simply looked at him. He didn't think she could possibly see. He had no idea what he was trying to tell her. He wondered if he was going slightly mad. Her bottom lip was trembling.

Eliot swallowed. 'Are you—are you all right, Honey? Only, you seem a bit sad.'

She stared up at him, her eyes suddenly full of tears. 'I'll be leaving soon. Summer's nearly over.'

He was all too aware of that fact. 'I know.'

'I'll miss … this,' she said.

'It's a lovely place. I'm glad you settled. Didn't think you would at first.'

God no, she'd seemed to hate it. Funny how much she'd changed. Fleetsthorpe had really weaved its magic spell on her. She was a different woman. 'It is. I may never see it again.' Her voice caught, and he felt a sudden panic as he realised it worked both ways. If she went away, would that be it? Would he never see *her* again?

He took her hand. 'You can come back whenever you want,' he said, meaning it. He fought the urge to tell her not to go. It was stupid. Of course she would go. She belonged in a different world, just as Jemima had.

'It won't be enough,' she whispered.

What did she mean? He looked down at her hand, so soft and small in his own. 'If it's any consolation, I'm dreading the day you leave.' Why the hell had he said that?

'Are you?' She looked at him.

Seeing the hope in her eyes, he realised they were dancing around each other, each afraid to put into words what they were feeling. He recognised the same longing in her face that he felt in his heart. Just for once, should he cast his fears aside? How would it feel to stop worrying about the future, stop dwelling on the past? The desire to hold her again was overwhelming him—the sudden longing to make them both happy. They deserved a chance, didn't they? No one knew what lay in store for them. Now and then someone had to be brave, take a risk. Maybe now was that time. His turn.

He reached out, softly cupping her face in his hands. 'Honey,' he murmured, his lips moving against her ear, her soft hair brushing his skin. She smelled divine, and he breathed in the scent, reminded suddenly of his hay meadows in early summer, when they were full of the most beautiful wildflowers.

She turned her face towards him, and as her lips found his, he stopped caring about the past or the future. All that mattered was now. This was their moment.

Tenderly scooping her into his arms, he stood and carried her up the stairs.

CHAPTER TWENTY-SIX

From somewhere far away, the phone was ringing. Eliot didn't want to answer it—he didn't want to move at all. He couldn't remember the last time he'd felt so contented, so relaxed.

Beside him, Honey stirred, and he reached out a hand to stroke her face. She looked peaceful. She looked beautiful. He felt a sudden fluttering of desire and had to fight the urge to kiss her. It wasn't late, but it had been a long day. Let her sleep.

Realising the phone was still ringing, he reluctantly got out of bed. If it was her father wanting an update, he would have to be extremely economical with the facts. Though, who else would ring so late? He pulled on his dressing gown, left the bedroom as quietly as he could, and headed downstairs.

'Hello?'

'Oh, er, is that Eliot?' It was a woman's voice.

Registering the cut glass tones, he felt a sudden anxiety. 'Speaking. Who is this?'

'This is Freya. Freya Carmichael. I need to speak to Honey, please.'

It wasn't a request. Unlike Cain's pleading voice, this was a command. The woman was obviously used to getting what she wanted. It was, after all, how she'd persuaded him to take Honey on, in the first place.

Honey appeared at the top of the stairs, rubbing her eyes. 'Who is it?' Her hair was messy, and she was wearing his shirt. She must have grabbed it from the end of the bed. It reached to midway down her thighs, revealing her long, slender legs, and Eliot felt the thrill of desire mixed with a lurch of fear. She was stunning, but she was dangerous.

Your mother, he mouthed.

She shook her head, looking horrified.

'Are you there?' Freya's voice was impatient. 'Can you put Honey on please? Immediately.'

'She wants to talk to you,' he said, hand over receiver.

She shook her head again, eyes wide, and he stared up at her, confused. What was it with her and her parents? Why couldn't she have a conversation with them?

'I'm sorry,' he said, lifting the receiver once more. 'She's busy at the moment. She'll probably call you back later.'

He was about to replace the phone, when her voice shrieked into his ear. 'Oh, no, you don't! Tell Honey that if she doesn't come to the phone immediately, I'll be having words with Cain about the Rolls Royce.'

Eliot looked up at a very pale looking Honey. 'She says if you don't talk to her, she'll tell your dad about the Rolls Royce.'

The effect on Honey was startling. She practically leapt down the stairs.

Eliot handed her the receiver, wondering what was going on, and what the hell he'd got himself into.

****

Eden grabbed the receiver with a shaking hand, while Eliot ran his fingers through his curls, his face concerned. 'Hello?'

'Well, it's about time,' said Honey.

Eden covered the mouthpiece and whispered to Eliot. 'It's all right, I can take it from here.'

After a moment's hesitation, he shrugged and wandered into the kitchen.

'Hello? Hello? Eden?'

'I'm here. What are you calling for? Are you crazy?'

Honey giggled. 'Maybe I am. You'll never guess where I am.'

'Don't tell me. Gretna Green. Crispin has committed

bigamy, and you're all loved up in some Scottish hotel room.' She felt a sudden chill. Hell, what if that had really happened? She wouldn't put anything past Honey.

'Don't be stupid. Better than that. I'm in Skimmerdale.'

'You're—you're where?' Eden felt faint. 'You're kidding me, right?'

'No.' Honey laughed again. 'Can you think of a better way of taking the piss out of my parents than this? They insisted I come here, so here I am.'

'But why?'

'Oh, it's a long story. Anyway, can you come and meet me?'

'Meet you? Where? When?'

'I'm at some place called Hope Cottage. It's on the outskirts of Beckthwaite. It's a holiday cottage and I was awfully lucky because I got a cancellation. Cheap as chips! Anyway, I want you to come round and bring me some mineral water. I clean forgot to get some and I'm thirsty.'

'Are you for real?' Eden wondered if she was caught in some nightmare. Maybe she'd fallen asleep and would wake up any moment, to find herself wrapped in Eliot's arms, all safe and warm in his bed.

'Still, not sparkling,' Honey continued, as if Eden hadn't spoken.

Eden gripped the receiver. 'What are you playing at? What was wrong with Dorset?'

'Oh, that didn't work out. I'll explain when you get here.'

So, it hadn't worked out with Crispin? Well, that was something at least. But Honey was playing a dangerous game, particularly with James Fuller so close. God, as if things weren't complicated enough.

'Well?'

'Well, what?'

Honey tutted. 'Are you coming round with my mineral

water?'

'Can't you drink tea for now? I'll see you tomorrow.'

'No. I want to see you now! Unless you'd like me to come to you?'

Eden could have cheerfully throttled her. 'All right, all right. I'll come. I should be there in about half an hour.'

'Lovely. See you then. Admit it, I've livened up your dreary day, haven't I?'

Eden replaced the receiver. If Honey only knew. She'd had the least dreary day of her life. In fact, it had been wonderful. Though, she had a feeling it was all going to be downhill from now on.

****

'For fuck's sake, can you be a bit more careful with my car! Is that how you've been driving all the time you've had her?'

Eden couldn't believe Honey had the nerve to criticise her. All right, she'd pulled up outside the cottage with a squeal of brakes, but who could blame her? Her life was a total mess, and now the woman who had caused most of the chaos was standing there in nothing but a T-shirt and a pair of heels, for God's sake, having a go at her bloody driving. Unbelievable!

'What the hell are you doing here?' She grabbed Honey's arm and pulled her indoors. 'You're supposed to be in Dorset, with the feckless Crispin Cavendish. What do you think you're playing at?'

'Don't mind me,' a man's voice drawled.

Eden let go of Honey's arm and straightened up. 'Tell me you're joking.' She looked round, realising she was in a small living room, so tiny there was nothing in it but a wood burning stove, a television on the wall, and a couple of squashy sofas.

On one of the sofas, Crispin was sprawled with his hands linked behind his head, surveying her with obvious annoyance.

She shook her head and stared at Honey beseechingly. 'Why? Have you got something against me?'

'Of course not. Don't be so sensitive.' Honey threw herself on the opposite sofa to Crispin and beamed up at her. 'You've got to admit, Eden, it's one in the eye for the parents. They wanted me here. Here I am. What a hoot!'

'What was wrong with your sister's house, Crispin?' demanded Eden, sitting beside Honey, and wishing the woman would cover herself up. One wrong move and she'd be well and truly revealed in all her glory.

'Honey felt a little … stifled.'

'Stifled?'

'It was the pits,' said Honey candidly. Crispin looked offended, but Honey ignored him. 'Tiny little place. No room to swing a cat.'

Eden gaped at her. 'Have you seen the size of this room? It's hardly Buck House, is it?'

'But here I can go outside. Oh, Eden, you have no idea how awful it was to be cooped up indoors all the time. Crispin was terrified I'd be spotted, and he made me stay inside the whole time and not answer the door or go near the windows.'

She made it sound as if she'd been the victim of a kidnapping, rather than the instigator of the whole fiasco.

'That's hardly true,' Crispin snapped. 'We went on the beach almost every day.'

'Big deal,' muttered Honey.

'And if you weren't allowed near the windows, how come you saw the car?'

'What car?' Eden said.

'Oh, some car that Crispin is convinced followed us. Anyway, enough of that. How are you getting on with Old MacDonald?' She giggled. 'Does he wear one of those hats with straw sticking out of it and say ooh ah a lot?'

'How old are you?' Eden sighed. 'Look, you can't stay

here. It's far too risky.'

'That's what I said,' said Crispin.

'It's no riskier than it was in Dorset,' said Honey firmly. 'Besides, I had a good look round when we got here. There's nothing for miles.'

'There's a village not ten minutes' walk from here,' Eden said.

'In one direction. But if you go in the other direction, it's just fields. And sheep. Lots of sheep. I hardly think they're going to ring the papers. No, this is perfect. I can walk around without worrying, and I can go into the village and—'

'The village? You can't possibly go into the village!'

'Why ever not?'

'Because *I* go into the village. And as far as everyone there is concerned, I'm Jemima Harland's cousin, Honey Carmichael. Remember?'

'That's all right. I'll be Eden Robinson. That's who I was in Dorset.'

'To whom?' said Crispin, clearly puzzled. 'You didn't speak to anyone there, did you?'

'Well, in my mind,' said Honey quickly. 'Anyway, no one will ask me my name. Why should they?'

'They won't have to ask mine,' said Crispin. 'Someone is bound to recognise me.'

'Well, you'll have to stay hidden indoors,' said Honey.

'What? I can't do that! I'll go mad.'

'Yeah, see how you like it,' she snapped.

'Honey, listen,' said Eden. 'There's something you don't know. Something a bit worrying.'

'Oh? What?'

'There's a man living here who knows I'm not you. He and his wife were friends of Jemima's, and they wanted to check I was suitable to look after her children. He looked me up—I mean, you up—on the internet. He knows who I am, and he would definitely recognise you. You can't be seen by him.'

'Why hasn't he told Old MacDonald, then? If he knows, I mean. What did you do to buy his silence?' She giggled again. 'I hope you've been behaving yourself, Eden.'

Eden blushed. If Honey only knew. 'He wanted me to let him see the children. Eliot had a falling out with the two of them, and his wife misses the girls and George, so in exchange for my silence, I had to make sure they got to see them.'

Honey frowned. 'Blackmail? I'll be having words with him when this is over. What a cheek! Anyway, stop fretting. Even if, by some chance, he does see me, so what? He can hardly tell Eliot, when he's been blackmailing you, can he? And it's only for a few days, anyway, and then we'll both be going home to Upper Bourbury.'

'So, you're staying?'

'Of course we're staying. It will be so good to get one over on my dear mother and father. Did you get my mineral water, by the way?'

Eden rummaged in her bag. 'Since you insist that you can go to the village, I don't see why you dragged me out. I had to pop into the pub to buy this. Cost a small fortune. The shop closes at six.'

'I don't see what's wrong with tap water,' mumbled Crispin.

Honey and Eden both stared at him, and Eden wondered if he knew Honey at all.

'I have to go,' Eden said, as Honey unscrewed the cap of the bottle and took a large gulp of water. 'Please try to be discreet, and don't keep pestering me to bring you things. I have enough to do with three children to look after, and a house to clean, and four people to cook for as well as myself, and —'

'Jesus, Eden, have you heard yourself?' Honey

shuddered. 'You sound positively homely. You've put weight on, by the way. All that cooking, no doubt.'

'Phone charger,' called Crispin.

'Pardon?'

'Oh, yes, I was just coming to that. We need you to get us a phone charger for Crispin's phone. He left his in Dorset, and his phone's dead, and he's having panic attacks in case Lavinia is trying to contact him. No *in case* about it, actually. She'll be livid she can't get in touch with him. I've never known such a demanding woman.'

Eden wondered how anyone could be so oblivious to their own shortcomings. 'Where am I supposed to get a phone charger from? You said it yourself, we're in the middle of nowhere.'

'But there's that town you were banging on about before you came here,' said Honey. 'There must be shops there and one of them must sell a charger. You can't let me down. My network doesn't seem to work here, and I can't bear another day of Crispin's whining.'

'Do you mind?' snapped her fallen idol.

'For God's sake,' said Eden, 'tell me what charger you need, and I'll do my best. You have no idea how difficult this is going to be. It's hard enough to get away from the farm, and I'm not convinced there'll be anywhere that sells them in Kirkby Skimmer, anyway.'

Crispin handed her a piece of paper with the make of his phone written on it. 'I have to have this,' he said, sounding panicky. 'It's not just about Lavinia,' he added, seeing Honey's disgusted expression. 'I need to keep up with what's going on, and there's no internet connection in this rabbit hutch, so I can't even use my laptop. I need my phone. You can't let me down. Do whatever it takes.'

'Oh, yes,' said Honey. 'God forbid you miss out on any earth-shattering news from London. Not to mention the fact that there may be a pet shop that needs opening in Windleby-on-the-Weir.'

'You know, when you're being such a sarcastic little bitch, you're terribly unattractive,' said Crispin.

'And when you're whining, you're about as appealing as scabies. Suck it up,' she snapped.

Eden left them to it, muttering to herself as she stomped back to the Beetle. As she rounded the road, heading back through the village, a flash of red caught her eye, and she saw, in her wing mirror, a red Mini moving away in the opposite direction. Something nagged at her, but she couldn't think what.

She drove back to the farm, wondering what the hell she was going to tell Eliot about her abrupt departure. He'd been in the kitchen when she left the house, having galloped upstairs to pull on her clothes as fast as she could.

'Just popping out to get a bottle of something!' she'd called, and then she'd escaped, not even giving him time to answer.

She glanced in the mirror at the bottle of wine on the back seat and hoped he would think it justified her leaving him so abruptly. Personally, she didn't think a bottle of wine cut it, but then, there was nowhere she'd rather be than in Eliot's bed.

A shiver ran through her as she remembered the last couple of hours. She'd dreamed that it would be good, but she'd never expected it to be as amazing as it had. Eliot had been sheer perfection—loving, gentle, passionate. The only jarring moment was when he'd whispered her name as he kissed her. Except it hadn't been her name, but Honey's. He wasn't really making love to her at all, was he? He didn't even know who she was.

Eden turned off the main road heading back to Fleetsthorpe. It had made her mind up, anyway. She had to tell Eliot the truth. It wasn't fair on him—on either of them. The only problem was, how was she going to muster the courage to be honest, knowing that the truth might drive him away for good?

CHAPTER TWENTY-SEVEN

'What exactly is it that you're looking for?'

Lavinia slammed the drawer shut and turned to face her father, who looked rather alarmed. 'How should I know? Anything that would give a clue as to where they'd go. There must be something, somewhere. Maybe a hotel booking, or something?'

'He's not stupid.' He shook his head and came to stand beside her, placing his hand on her shoulder. 'You need to calm down, sweetheart. I've never seen you like this before.'

Probably because she'd never felt like this before. The journey from Portugal had seemed endless, and Lavinia's growing sense of panic hadn't calmed when her father met her at the airport and confirmed he had no leads, and no clue where the two of them had gone.

'He's well-known,' she muttered. 'Wherever he goes, someone would spot him, surely? What the hell is he playing at, risking it all for Honey Carmichael?'

'Unless he's gone abroad,' suggested her father.

Lavinia paled. 'He wouldn't, would he?'

'Have you checked for his passport?'

She hadn't, and she cursed her stupidity. She should have looked for that first. In fact, she should have removed it from the house when she went to Portugal, taking it with her for safekeeping. That would have ensured that Crispin didn't leave the country. He could be lying on some beach somewhere, sunning himself beside that tart. It didn't bear thinking about, especially as he always refused to go abroad with her, pleading that his skin was far too sensitive. She'd bet that floosy would be able to persuade him, though. She'd be able to talk him into anything.

'Look, make us a drink and sit down. You're all done

in. I'll look for the passport. Where do you usually keep them?'

'In the bureau in his office, but it's usually locked.' She filled the kettle with shaking hands and sat down at the kitchen table. 'It doesn't matter. It's too late, anyway.'

'What do you mean, too late? Never say die,' he said, patting her arm. She shrugged helplessly, and he pulled out a chair and sat beside her. 'What is it, sweetheart? I've never seen you in such a state. Why don't you let me call Eddie Holmes?'

'Who?'

'Eddie. He works on *The Sunday Satellite*.'

Lavinia tutted. 'That tawdry rag. Why would you want to call him?'

'To arrange an interview, of course. You should get in there fast, before someone spots Crispin and his bit of stuff and the story is blown wide open. You need to reveal the truth in your own time and your own way. Stand up and show the world you're not some cuckolded politician's wife who will stand by her man. Tell them all you found out for yourself and you're out of there, that you've got more about you than that, for God's sake.'

Lavinia's mouth dropped open and she stared at her father in disbelief.

He shifted uncomfortably. 'Kettle's boiled,' he announced as the switch clicked. 'Two sugars, please.'

'You'd better not say a word to that little worm Eddie Holmes,' Lavinia warned him, dropping tea bags into two mugs. 'I mean it. I'm sure you wouldn't want Francesca to know about your frequent visits to The Proud Peacock.'

His face turned puce. 'How did you—?'

'I always know,' she said with a sigh. 'That's the bloody trouble. Sometimes, I think being so intelligent is a curse. Milk?'

He mopped his brow with a handkerchief and coughed. 'It's not what you think. It's business, that's all.'

'Well, I'm sure money changes hands,' she said, handing him a mug of tea. 'Frankly, Daddy, I really don't care. I can't stand Francesca, anyway. Never have, never will. As long as you're discreet and use protection, it's your business.'

He almost choked on his tea. 'Bloody hell, Lavinia! What's got into you?'

'Life,' she said bitterly. She sipped her tea and reached for her phone. 'Still no message or call. It's been four days without a word from him. He's not even pretending any longer. I'm worried, Daddy.'

'Yes, well, if you won't do what I suggest, I fail to see how I can help you,' he said, rather huffily.

She shrugged and tapped her phone. If he was going to sulk, she might as well see what else was going on in the world. Any distraction from her problems would be welcome. She tapped the Facebook icon and felt some satisfaction that she hadn't been forgotten by everyone. Over a hundred notifications, three friend requests and a private message. She tapped on the message icon, wondering if one of her friends wanted to meet up for lunch, or if it was yet another sad old man, wanting to tell her how lovely her profile picture was.

She sighed wearily. 'Romeo Lovegod. For heaven's sake, at least try to be subtle.'

'Eh? Who's Romeo Lovegod, when he's at home?'

'Some saddo, who, no doubt, has seen my photo and thinks I'm his soulmate.' She scrolled down the message and sat up straight, her eyes wide. 'Bloody hell!'

'What is it? Does he want money? See him off, sweetheart. It's all a bloody scam,' her father advised.

'They're in Yorkshire!'

'Who is?'

'Who do you think? Crispin and Honey. They're in the Yorkshire Dales.'

'Says who?'

'Romeo Lovegod.'

Her father raised an eyebrow. 'Right. Well, he'd know, I suppose.'

'No, listen. *It's my sad duty to inform you your husband is currently in Skimmerdale, in the Yorkshire Dales, in a village called Beckthwaite, with Honey Carmichael. The two of them have been having an affair for some time. If you want to save his career you should put a stop to this. I am giving you a chance, but I will be going to the papers very soon, so move quickly. Your friend, Romeo Lovegod.*'

'Well, I never did,' said her father. 'What are you going to do?'

She gave him a scornful look. 'Well, what do you think I'm going to do? Sorry, Daddy, I'll have to love you and leave you. I'm going to Skimmerdale. Wherever the hell bloody Skimmerdale is.'

****

Eliot kissed his sleepy daughters and said goodnight. They'd had a tiring day, helping him get the sheep gathered, ready to separate more lambs from the ewes. Libby was always sad at the thought of all the lambs going off to market. Ophelia was much more practical.

'They've got to go, Libby,' she informed her sister. 'We're not a charity, you know.'

He'd bitten his lip when he'd heard that, to stop himself laughing. Another expression she'd obviously got from Mickey, who'd been heard saying it many times, although usually with a few choice words added.

'Any road,' she'd added wisely, 'think of the money we're going to get from selling Gideon in a few weeks! He's a double Skimmerdale champion now. We'll make a packet, and we can buy a good quality tup, so we'll get more good lambs next year. It's part of the fun, isn't it?'

'I know.' Libby had sighed and patted a particularly

affectionate gimmer hogg. 'Just look at them, though. They're so cute, and you know what will happen to them.'

'I know. But I like Honey's lamb stew, don't you? And you can't eat lamb stew then whine about lambs going to slaughter, can you? That would make you a hippocrat.'

'You mean hypocrite,' said Libby, but at least she'd laughed.

Eliot knew there would be tears when they went to the market, but personally he felt a lot easier than he had. Owning the Swaledale Champion and Overall Champion of the Skimmerdale Show meant he'd be making a tidy profit from Gideon, and he knew he had some good fat lambs to sell, too. Next year, Gideon's daughters would make him more money from their lambs, if he could buy a good tup to put them to, and with the cheque he should get from his champion's sale, that shouldn't be as difficult as he'd feared.

He closed the girls' bedroom door, feeling that life was really on the up. Farming sheep in these hills was a tough life, but it had been a good summer. His children were happy and cared for, the house was running like clockwork, and the value of his flock had increased beyond his wildest hopes. Best of all, he had Honey. She'd brought love and laughter back into his life, and at times, he couldn't believe his luck. For the last four nights, she'd slept beside him in his bed. He'd fallen asleep with her in his arms, and woke each morning to see her beautiful face on the pillow next to his.

He half dared to dream she would stay with him. It was what she'd wanted, wasn't it? The only nagging worry was her odd behaviour the last couple of days. She'd taken George into the village a few times, while the girls helped him on the farm. She'd come up with the flimsiest of excuses, too.

'Just going to get a magazine.'

'A magazine? When do you read magazines?'

'Well, I haven't had time lately, but I fancy reading one now. Won't be long.'

Or, the following day: 'Just nipping out. I'll be back in time to make the lunch.'

'Where are you going?'

'Er, I need women's things.'

He hadn't questioned that one any further. It wasn't any of his business, but he was curious and a little anxious. She hadn't even wanted to take George, and he couldn't for the life of him work out why she seemed so tense. The only time she seemed fully relaxed was when they were alone together in bed. She relaxed then, all right. It was almost as if being with him brought her peace. In a way, he felt the same about her. Even so, he couldn't help worrying. Things had become so perfect, something was bound to spoil it.

He headed downstairs, wondering how long it would be before they could risk going to bed. They'd been very careful not to let the girls suspect anything was going on between them. He didn't want them to get their hopes up, after all, not until he was completely sure that it was for keeps. He found it hard to keep his hands off Honey, though. He'd dragged her into the hallway, while the girls were washing their hands, and kissed her hard, feeling a thrill as he realised that she was as turned on as he was.

Smiling to himself, he opened the boot room door and collected the present he'd bought for her that afternoon. It had been worth the trip into Ravensbridge. He'd known as soon as he saw them in the shop that they were perfect for her. He hoped she'd understand what he was trying to tell her when he gave them to her. He wasn't good with words, but surely she'd understand what he was hoping for?

He carried them down the hall and opened the living room door, but stopped dead when he found her zipping up her leather jacket, obviously about to go out.

Hurriedly, he dropped the present behind the armchair. 'You're going out again? I thought maybe we could spend some time together, now the kids are asleep? Where are you going, anyway?'

It was a reasonable question, he thought. After all, she didn't know anyone around here, and the village wasn't exactly a hive of activity during the evening. The pub would be open, but who'd want to go to a pub on their own?

She looked up, her face flushed. 'I thought I'd take a walk,' she said. 'I feel like I've been cooped up indoors all day. Could use some fresh air.'

She was avoiding him. There was no doubt about it. The sky was heavy with rain. It had been humid all day, and he'd told her the weather was about to break. Besides, she'd had a busy day while he was with the girls, and she'd been adamant that all she wanted to do was have a nice, long soak in the bath and get an early night. She'd said it with a twinkle in her eye. What had happened to change things? Something was on her mind. Was she afraid she'd made a terrible mistake getting involved with him? He supposed he couldn't blame her, if she was.

'Right,' he said, his voice flat with disappointment.

'I won't be long,' she said. 'Promise.'

'Take your time. I reckon it will be raining soon, mind.' He tried not to sound anxious and reached for the television remote. He didn't know what was on, and he didn't care. He needed something to drown out the chattering voice in his head that was telling him what an idiot he'd been. Of course it had meant nothing to her. She was young, rich, and attractive. She came from a different world to him. What did he expect?

He froze when her lips touched his. As they pressed harder, he found himself responding, in spite of his better judgement. Her hands cupped his face, and he pulled her closer to him. She melted against him, just for a moment, then she pulled away from him, leaving him confused and flustered.

'I promise I won't be long,' she said. Her voice was shaky, her eyes anxious. She seemed to be begging him to be patient, to understand. Except, he didn't understand. He didn't have a clue what was going on.

'Think a storm's coming,' he murmured, as she left the house, going God knows where for God knows what reason.

Eliot threw down the remote and walked over to the window. What was he doing? Daisy was right. He was an idiot who deserved everything he got. He'd been down this road before. He had to stop it before it was too late—before he'd fallen for her so completely that there was no way out. But the door was closing fast. He wasn't sure he could escape anymore, and the thought was terrifying.

CHAPTER TWENTY-EIGHT

Eden glanced at the yellow Beetle with regret as she passed it. She could hardly take the damn car, since she'd told Eliot she was going for a walk. She cursed Honey. What was the big emergency this time? And why did she have to keep ringing the farm phone? All right, it was impossible to get a mobile signal in the farmhouse, but to ring the landline, when Eliot or the girls could have answered! Honey had sounded so wired, Eden wasn't sure she would have had the foresight to pretend to be Freya. They were on dodgy ground, and Eden had a feeling time was running out.

'You have to come now,' Honey had insisted.

'Honey, I'm busy, and I've had a long and tiring day. I'm going to get into my pyjamas and watch some television,' she'd replied. *Hopefully snuggled up with Eliot on the sofa, and then, please God, a delicious repeat performance of last night*, she thought. It had, if anything, been even more wonderful than the first night they spent together. Things kept on getting better and better. They were learning about each other all the time, and it had been a voyage of delightful discoveries. She shivered when she remembered the look of wonder in his eyes as he'd explored her body last night. He'd called her, *my love.* It had made her go all gooey and tingly. Bloody Honey, dragging her out again when she could be having so much fun. 'It will have to wait.'

'It can't wait. Unless you want me and Crispin to drive up there and speak to you at the farm, you'll come here. Now.'

Eden had wanted to refuse, to call Honey's bluff. Surely, even she wasn't that stupid? But then, knowing Honey's temper and obstinacy, she wouldn't put it past her. And if she was being this demanding, something major must have happened.

It had been so hard to leave Eliot. She would rather have been with him than anywhere else on earth, and having to come up with an excuse so quickly had been difficult, to say the least. A walk? Really? She was knackered. A walk was the last thing she needed, and the sky was definitely threatening rain. Seemed she had no choice, though.

Leaving the Beetle behind, she walked as fast as she could to Hope Cottage, thinking that, at the very least, Honey or Crispin had better have some violent illness, because if it was about bloody mineral water again, she'd kill Honey.

'Thank God. Come in.' Honey almost pulled her into the cottage and slammed the door behind her.

'I'm getting really fed up with this,' said Eden. 'This is the fourth day running you've made me come here. What with bottled water, the damn phone charger, and all the other things you simply can't live without, you're running me ragged. Not to mention the trip into Kirkby Skimmer I didn't want to make. Have you any idea how difficult it is to get away from the farm without the kids? And Eliot is—'

'Oh, sod the farm. Sod everything. Crispin's had a shock.'

'It couldn't happen to a nicer bloke,' Eden muttered, glancing round. 'Where is he?'

'In the kitchen, pacing.'

She wasn't wrong. When Eden went into the kitchen, Crispin was stomping up and down the room, muttering to himself and shaking his head.

'Is he having a breakdown?'

'I shouldn't be surprised,' said Honey. Since Eden had arrived, she seemed to have calmed down. She gave Crispin a look of contempt. 'He's a real wuss,' she said. 'One little message, and he crumbles.'

'One *little* message! I wish!' Crispin stopped pacing and glared at Honey. He waved the mobile in Eden's face and moaned. 'As if Lavinia's stream of texts and missed calls weren't enough to worry about!'

'Maybe if you'd grow a pair and call her to sort it, you wouldn't still be worrying,' said Honey contemptuously.

'And what am I supposed to say to her? She's demanding to know where I am. She obviously knows I'm not in Dorset. Her spies are everywhere, and now I've got this bloody Facebook message from Romeo sodding Lovegod. Oh, Christ, I think my blood pressure is out of control. It's all too much.'

'Who?' Eden frowned. 'Where have I heard that—oh.'

'Yeah,' said Honey. 'The interfering little shit who tipped off my father about me and Crispin in the first place. The entire reason our plans for the summer were altered, and we've both ended up in this dump.'

'What does he say?'

'That he knows I'm in Skimmerdale with Honey Carmichael, and if I don't leave the place immediately, he will sell the story to the papers. He claims to have pictures.' Crispin almost whimpered as he looked at Eden, a pleading expression in his eyes. 'He can't have pictures, can he? Oh, God. Lavinia will murder me. My career means everything to her. If I'm finished, she'll leave me. I'll be ruined.'

'You know, Crispin, I'm not sure you're aware of how pathetic you look when you're snivelling like this,' Honey informed him.

'And I'm not sure you are aware of how hideous you look when you're being a cold, heartless, one hundred per cent cow,' he replied.

'At least I have guts,' she snapped. 'You're the most pathetic excuse for a man I've ever met.'

'You're the worst example of womanhood,' he said. 'You don't care about anyone but yourself. Ever since we got together, it's been all about you. I should have run a mile in the other direction the day I met you. You're not worth the trouble.'

'Well, *you're* certainly not worth the trouble,' she said, her voice edged with fury. 'I only stayed with you to piss my parents off. Your reputation is deeply misleading. You're the worst lover I've ever had the misfortune to go to bed with.'

Eden left them to it. She couldn't stand much more. Wandering into the living room, she stared out of the window, thinking what a mess it all was. All this performance for two people, who, right then, couldn't stand the sight of each other. Some big romance this was. And Honey had openly admitted it was all to infuriate her parents. Typical Honey. Eden had suspected, even hoped, that letting the two of them be together would result in the end of the affair, and her plan had worked, but at what cost? Eden had been dragged into the whole mess, just so she could annoy Cain and Freya, and Eliot had been dragged into it, too. Even worse, so had the children, who had grown so close to "Honey" and wouldn't understand what the hell was going on when it was all over. She should never have slept with Eliot. It wasn't fair. He didn't even know who she was. And what if it was Honey he'd fallen for? What if the thrill of having someone from Jemima's world again was the thing that attracted him? Would he have fallen for Eden if he knew she was the daughter of a retired bus driver and a cleaner?

At some point, she would have to tell Eliot the truth, and the more she thought about it, the more she came to the conclusion that the sooner she told him, the better. He was a good man, an uncomplicated man. The way things had become between them, he deserved to know the real Eden. If she wasn't good enough for him, well, that was a chance she would have to take, because he had a right to know who he was getting involved with before things went any further. She loved him too much to fool him for even another day. She would tell him tonight, as soon as she got home. She would sit him down, take a deep breath, and explain everything from start to finish. He would understand, surely? It wouldn't change how he felt about her—would it?

She realised how dark it had suddenly become, and jumped as thunder rumbled overhead. From out of the corner of her eye, she saw a flash of red in the glow of ensuing lightning, and all thoughts of Eliot flew out of her mind.

That car. She'd seen it before. A red Mini. Where had she seen a red Mini? And what was a car doing parked up the lane so that it could barely be seen from here? There were no other buildings around.

As the clouds gave up the struggle and tipped the first of the rain onto the waiting landscape, a sudden thought occurred to her, and she turned and flew into the kitchen. Honey and Crispin must have sensed her alarm, as they stopped bickering and stared at her.

'What is it?' asked Honey.

'Do me a favour. Put the living room light on and stand in front of the window, talking.'

'What? Are you mad?' Crispin shook his head. 'If anyone was around they'd see us.'

'Exactly. Just do as I say, please. And, whatever you do, don't look at the window. I'll explain in a minute.'

They looked at each other, but obviously realised she was serious, because they did as she said.

Eden ran upstairs and made her way to the window of the master bedroom.

Someone was walking slowly towards the cottage. A man. He stopped a little away from the gate, watching transfixed as Crispin and Honey put on their show. There was something deeply familiar about him. Eden had no doubt he'd known where Crispin was. This was no coincidence.

She hurtled downstairs and called, 'Crispin! Quickly!'

Crispin, to her surprise, was behind her in a moment, and the two of them ran outside into the rain, obviously terrifying the man who turned and began to run towards the Mini.

'Get him!' Eden yelled. 'He's got something to do with all this.'

'Leave me alone!' The man struggled when Crispin and Eden grabbed him.

'No chance, sunshine,' said Eden. 'You're coming with us. You have a lot of explaining to do.'

****

Some game show played in the background as Eliot sat on the sofa, trying not to worry. The rain was lashing against the windows. Honey would be soaked. What was she doing out there, anyway?

He told himself to stay calm. Honey would be leaving in a week or so. Going home. There'd been no suggestion from her that she wanted to stay, that her plans had changed. He wouldn't ask her, either. If this was destined to be some sort of holiday romance, so much the better.

The thought came to him, though, that life at Fleetsthorpe would be almost unbearable without her. She'd made everything seem so much brighter. The girls loved her. George loved her. He loved her.

No! He shook his head, as if to deny it to some invisible presence. He didn't love her. Of course he didn't. How could he love someone he barely knew? Someone he didn't even fully trust. He didn't even trust himself when he was around her. He didn't understand her. She could be cold, bitchy, snobbish and cruel. Yet, she could be warm, loving, kind and fun. She could be passionate. Gentle. It was as if she were two different people at times. It didn't make sense. But then, hadn't Jemima confused and baffled him, at first, too?

At a knock on the door, Eliot stood, frowning, and went to answer it. He couldn't imagine who'd be paying him a visit at that time of the evening, in the midst of a storm. Daisy used the back door, and besides, she'd be working tonight.

He opened the door and gaped at the sight of the glamorous brunette, still wearing sunglasses in defiance of a summer storm. 'Can I help you?'

'Is he here?'

Eliot blinked, confused. 'Is who here?'

'Crispin.'

'Who the heck's Crispin? Think you've got the wrong house, love.'

She curled her lip at him and removed her sunglasses. 'This is Fleetsthorpe?'

Eliot nodded. 'Aye, but I don't know any Crispin.'

'Hmm. So, is Honey here?'

He felt the colour drain from his face as a sudden sense of foreboding washed over him. 'You'd best step inside. You'll get soaked.'

The woman reluctantly stepped into the hallway, her eyes widening as if she realised the house wasn't as bad as she'd feared. 'Honey? She's here, then?'

'Not right now. No.'

'So, where is she?'

'Gone out. Why? What's it to you?'

'I'll tell you what it is to me,' the woman said, glaring at him. 'I'm Crispin's wife.'

'Well, congratulations. Still no idea what you're on about.'

She peered at him, then an amused smile crossed her face. 'You really don't have a clue, do you?'

He straightened as his anger kicked in. 'Look, I don't know what this is about, but—'

'Then, let me enlighten you. Honey Carmichael has

been having an affair with my husband, Crispin Cavendish. According to several people in that backwater of a village, this farm is where she's staying. I presumed Crispin was staying with her, but obviously not. He's somewhere in this village, though, and I want to know where. Now, what time will that deceitful little slut be home?'

Eliot's legs trembled and he felt nauseous as he tried to fight the growing sense of panic. It couldn't be true. Not Honey. And yet, why not? Hadn't he half known it, anyway?

So, this was where she kept disappearing to—visiting this Crispin bloke. 'I don't know when she'll be back,' he heard himself saying. His voice sounded flat, emotionless as numbness moved in to replace the panic. Thank God for that. He knew how to cope with numbness. He was a master at it.

The woman tutted and looked out over the farmyard, not that he thought she was even seeing it. She was obviously trying to work out what to do next. Finally, she turned back to him, replacing her sunglasses. 'I'm staying at some grotty little hotel in Kirkby Skimmer,' she said, 'and I'm not best pleased about it. The Paradise Hotel, and there's a case for the Trade Descriptions Act if ever there was one. Tell that little bitch, she'd better hand over my husband within the next twenty-four hours, or I will go to the papers and tell them everything. And please, do make it clear to her that, by the time I've told my side of the story, his career will be finished, and so will she. Clear?'

Eliot nodded, unable to speak, and she stepped outside, glancing up at the dark slate skies. As he watched, she rushed back to her car, parked beside Honey's yellow Beetle, dodging puddles and trying her best to avoid the mud. Once she'd climbed inside, he shut the door and leaned against it, suddenly finding it hard to breathe. Then slowly, he sank onto the floor and buried his head in his hands.

The storm had arrived.

CHAPTER TWENTY-NINE

Honey's legs almost buckled from underneath her, as Eden and Crispin dragged the man into the living room of the cottage.

'Teddy!'

'You know him?' Eden and Crispin asked together.

Honey wondered which of the two of them sounded more astonished, as she and Teddy stared at each other in embarrassed silence.

'Well?' Crispin glared at her. 'Explain yourself. Who is he, and how do you know him?'

'I—I don't. Not really. At least—'

'Wait a minute.' Eden peered closely at Teddy before turning to Honey in shock. 'I know him.'

'You do?' Honey wondered how on earth Eden would know a charity shop worker. Unless Teddy's shop was in the Cotswolds. Honey had never been inside one in her life, but she supposed it was quite likely that Eden had. Her clothes were pretty appalling, after all.

Teddy was shaking his head at Eden, fear in his eyes. 'Please don't.'

Eden folded her arms. 'You've got a bloody nerve. I can't believe you're here again, after all this time.'

'Eden, what the hell are you talking about?' demanded Honey.

Crispin sat down on the sofa. 'For God's sake, will someone please explain what the hell is going on around here?'

Teddy was trembling, but Eden wasn't exactly being her usual sympathetic self. 'Remember that evening I first met you, in The Red Lion?' she asked Honey.

'Of course I remember.'

'Please don't,' repeated Teddy. 'She won't understand. You've got this all wrong.'

'That man,' said Eden, giving him a poisonous look, 'was the journalist who was spying on you and Troy.'

'Who the hell is Troy?' said Crispin.

Honey stared at Teddy in horror. 'You're a journalist?'

'A journalist!' Crispin sounded faint.

'Please, Honey, I can explain.'

'So, you do know who I am! I told you I was called Eden!'

'You did what?' said Eden, horrified. 'Why?'

'Because you were Honey,' snapped Honey.

Crispin groaned. 'I've got a headache.' He leapt in fright when a sudden loud bang hit the front door of the cottage. 'Oh, Christ. Now what?'

'Don't answer it,' begged Teddy.

Crispin seemed suddenly determined to take control. 'No jumped-up journalist is going to tell me what to do,' he informed them, and he marched to the door and threw it open. 'Oh, fucking hell!'

'Nice to see you, too, darling.' Lavinia took off her sunglasses and gave him a peck on the cheek. 'I thought I'd never find you. The child does like to play hide and seek, doesn't she?' She gave Honey a look of contempt, and Honey returned the look threefold.

So, the dragon had arrived. Well, didn't that put the lid on a perfect day.

Crispin staggered to the sofa and collapsed onto it. Teddy sank down beside him, head in hands.

'Goodness, quite a party you've got going on,' said Lavinia. 'So, is this invitation only, or can anyone join in?'

'Well, you're not welcome, for a start,' said Honey. What the hell did Lavinia want? Well, her husband probably, but she could whistle for him. Honey suddenly decided that Crispin was worth fighting for, after all—even if he was a wimp, and not half as good looking as she'd imagined. At least he wasn't a bloody journalist.

She looked at Teddy, who appeared to have developed

a fascination for the carpet. She was astonished, and a little afraid, at how hurt she felt to realise he'd been using her all along.

'Lavinia, I can explain,' said Crispin.

'Go ahead. I'm listening.' She sat on the opposite sofa and folded her arms.

Eden sank down beside her, looking deeply concerned for her. She always was a soft touch, thought Honey.

'Well, I—that is …' began Crispin.

'Shall I help you? You've been shagging Miss Carmichael here for some months now. You packed me off to Portugal, allowing you and her to rush off to your sister's holiday home in Dorset, then you came here. Correct?'

'How did you know that?'

Honey tutted. Honestly, he didn't even have the wits to lie. Moron.

Lavinia gave a mirthless laugh. 'We apparently have a mutual friend who has our best interests at heart. Romeo Lovegod ring any bells?'

Honey glanced at Crispin, who turned deathly white. 'Romeo Lovegod again. He's the little shit who messaged my father on Facebook and told him about me and Crispin,' she said. 'Who the fuck is he?' She noticed Eden was staring very hard at Teddy, who gave a loud gulp. 'You!' Honey dropped onto the sofa beside him, her legs weakened. 'You're Romeo Lovegod?'

His eyes filled with shame. 'Sorry.'

She gaped at him. How much worse could things get?

'He messaged me when I got home from Portugal,' said Lavinia. 'Told me, if I wanted to know where my husband was, I should head to Skimmerdale.'

'Darling, I'm so sorry,' whined Crispin. 'This has all been a dreadful mistake.'

Honey's blood boiled. 'A mistake! You said you loved me. You said she was a dragon who didn't care about anything but your career. You said your marriage was a sham.'

'You said what?' If Honey hadn't known better, she'd have sworn the dragon sounded upset.

'Well, be fair, Lavinia. If I wasn't a politician on the up, you wouldn't want to know. You don't really care about me at all, let's face it.'

'How can you say that?'

'Because it's true. Look, I've made mistakes—'

'Yes, and don't, for one minute, think that I don't know about them.' Lavinia reached into her bag and took out a handkerchief, dabbing her eyes.

'Oh, I know you knew about them. I made damn sure you did.'

'Why on earth would you do that? That's cruelty!'

Honey had to admit, it was a pretty low trick. He really was a shit.

'What does it matter? As long as I'm discreet, it's all right, isn't it? If I stay out of the papers, I'm free to do what I want. Isn't that the rule?'

'What are you talking about? What rule?' Lavinia sounded baffled.

Crispin seemed suddenly calmer. 'After my first fling—which really was a mistake, and I bitterly regretted it—I quickly realised you knew what had happened. You never said, but there were clues, and I waited for you to confront me about it.' He sighed. 'You never did, and eventually, it dawned on me that you didn't care. You didn't care what I did as long as it didn't impact on my career. Do you know how much that hurt me?'

'But, Crispin, I was heartbroken! I didn't say anything because I was afraid, if I pushed you, you'd leave me, and I simply couldn't bear that.'

Honey was aghast. 'Oh, please! You're not buying this crap, surely?'

They didn't seem to hear her.

'What couldn't you bear, Lavinia?' Crispin went on. 'Losing me, or losing the chance to one day be the wife of the prime minister? Or was it money?'

'How could you think that? I have money of my own, and I don't care about the position. Well, not really. I love you. I always have. You've broken my heart so many times.'

'Oh, God, Lavinia. I didn't realise. My poor darling.'

'Oh, Crispin, I'm so sorry you didn't feel loved.'

'For fuck's sake, what a pile of shit.' As the two of them fell into each other's arms, Honey rolled her eyes in disgust. 'You two absolutely deserve each other. I hope you'll be very happy.'

'Do you know what?' said Eden, as they kissed. 'I think they just might be.'

'Let's leave here, darling,' said Crispin, when he eventually managed to break the suction on Lavinia's lips. 'We'll start again. Forget this ever happened.' He looked at Honey as if he'd only just remembered she was there. 'I'm terribly sorry about this. No hard feelings?'

'No feelings at all,' she assured him. 'If you're both stupid enough to fall for each other's lies, that's your look out.'

'Rather harsh of you.' Crispin sounded hurt.

Lavinia tutted. 'She's a fine one to talk about lies, darling. You do know she's been sleeping with someone behind your back?'

'What?' Eden and Crispin looked astounded, while Teddy and Honey looked guilty.

Eden's mouth dropped open, as she looked from Honey to Teddy and back again.

Honey's face burned. There would no doubt be many questions fired at her before long.

'I can't believe you cheated on me,' said Crispin.

'Oh, bugger off, Crispin,' said Honey. 'You're a fine one to talk about cheating.'

'Who was it?' he demanded.

'What does it matter? You're back in the loving arms of your wife, aren't you?'

'Was it that farmer?' asked Lavinia.

Eden gave a little squeak. 'What farmer?'

'I must say, he looked absolutely devastated when I told him what you'd been up to. Another of your conquests. It's a wonder there's any elastic left in your knickers, they must be up and down so often. That's always presuming you wear any, of course.'

'What farmer?' Eden repeated.

'The one with all those curls. Rather gorgeous, actually, if a bit surly. Took me a while to find Fleetsthorpe, I must say. I had to ask at the shop, but, luckily, everyone seemed to know where Honey Carmichael was staying and couldn't wait to give me directions. Talk about the back of beyond. He was rather rude. Insisted he didn't know when you'd be back. I was about to go back to my hotel—if you can call it that—when, luckily, Romeo Lovegod came to the rescue again. Tipped me off that he'd found you and gave me this address.' She smirked at Teddy, who looked thoroughly miserable. 'Thank you very much, Mr Lovegod. Now, darling,' she added, hooking her arm through Crispin's, 'let's leave them to it.'

Honey clapped her hand to her mouth. This was all too much to take in. Teddy was not only a journalist who had been lying about his feelings for her, and had even slept with her in order to get a story, but he was also the double-crossing rat who had messaged both her father and Lavinia to cause the most devastation he could. How had she been so stupid?

As Crispin and Lavinia left the cottage, she turned to Eden in despair. Eden would get some answers from him. Eden would know what to do.

She gave a little whimper on finding that Eden had

gone.

The door slammed shut, and Honey turned slowly to see Teddy staring at her with puppy dog eyes. She wrapped her arms around herself, appalled to find tears pricking her eyes. For the first time she could remember, Honey longed, with all her heart, to see her father.

CHAPTER THIRTY

Cain cursed as his Rolls Royce bumped and bounced along the rough track. 'What kind of bleeding road is this? You'd think we were abroad. This ain't doing my suspension no good, that's for sure.'

Freya tutted. 'Well, what do you expect? Serves you right for bringing the Rolls. You were showing off. I have no sympathy.'

'There's a surprise. How was I to know it would be like this? And this bleeding rain ain't helping. My bodywork will be filthy. Well, where the hell are we? We must be nearly there by now, surely?'

She peered at the satellite navigation system, which she'd been clutching in her hand for the last two hours, since it kept falling off the dashboard, in spite of Cain's best efforts. Freya hadn't been able to stand any more of his curses and frantic fumbling, as he'd tried to retrieve it, while keeping his eyes on the road. 'Should be straight ahead.' Unable to make anything out through the blur of the windscreen, she wound down the window and stuck her head out, looking around in obvious dismay. 'That must be it,' she said, nodding towards a distant house. 'God, what a bleak place. Poor Honey must have been going insane.'

Cain glared at her. 'Have you forgotten why we're here? Poor Honey, my arse. When I get hold of the little git, she'll wish she'd kept her hand on her ha'penny.'

'Charming,' said Freya.

She cursed, when the Rolls Royce bounced over a pothole and she almost hit her head on the ceiling. Cain looked horrified, stroking the dashboard of the car as if trying to soothe a wounded lover.

'We're here,' she announced as the car pulled up outside a large stone farmhouse.

Cain turned off the engine. 'You don't say. Thank God I brought you with me, I might never have realised.'

'Oh, shut up.' Freya fastened the top button of her coat and shivered.

'You can't be cold,' said Cain. 'It may be raining, but it's bleeding humid.'

'I'm freezing,' she said firmly, reaching under the seat for her umbrella.

He tutted. 'You always was a cold arse. Central heating on full blast in bleeding August. Used to sweat me bollocks off, and you didn't care. I reckon you're single-handedly responsible for global warming.'

'Don't be ridiculous. I took public transport the other week when I was protesting in Trafalgar Square.'

'Another pissing protest! What was it this time?'

She shrugged. 'Not sure. I think it was anti-fracking. Anyway, the point is, I didn't take the car.'

'Hmm. I'd have paid good money to see you on the tube,' he said.

Freya looked appalled. 'Are you insane? I got a taxi.'

Cain ran a weary hand through his straw-like hair. 'I give up. Come on, Lady Penelope. Let's go and give our daughter what for. And no falling for her sob stories, this time, right? We've got to be tough on her.'

'I'm not the one who gives in to her,' Freya reminded him as she stepped out of the car. 'You're the one who needs to man up. Okay, let's go and sort this bloody mess out.'

She put up her umbrella and strode purposefully to the front door, avoiding the worst of the mud and the biggest puddles along the way, and banged loudly, showing she meant business.

Cain stood behind her, hands in pockets. He wasn't looking forward to the confrontation. Honey had a way of making him feel so guilty, no matter what she'd done. Mind you, he'd have a few words to say to Old

MacDonald. So much for keeping her out of trouble. This was all his fault.

He jumped as lightning ripped the sky into two jagged halves, and seconds later thunder roared overhead.

'Poor Jemima, living out here,' said Freya, shivering again and pulling her coat tighter to her chest. 'It's all rather Cathy and Heathcliff, isn't it?'

'More like Steptoe and Son.' Cain sniffed, eyeing the jumble of barns, stables, and various other outhouses suspiciously. Chickens lurked in the doorways, watching him with beady eyes. They were far too close to the house, for his liking. If they came anywhere near him, he'd soon demonstrate that he could bend it like Beckham. He started as a rat streaked past the barn, then let out a relieved sigh once he realised it was a dog. 'Scruffy little bleeder,' he muttered, putting a hand over his pounding heart, as if to calm it.

The door opened, and Cain turned, expecting to see a middle-aged, ruddy-cheeked farmer in a smock and wellies. Instead, a little girl stared up at them, a solemn expression on her face. She had a mop of dark curls and huge brown eyes that studied him curiously.

Freya put on her kindly voice, the one she generally reserved for when television cameras were around. 'Hello, little girl. Is your daddy around?'

'Yes.'

Freya glanced at Cain, who shrugged. Well, she'd asked, after all. 'Would I be able to speak to him?'

The girl considered. 'Probably not. He's not really in the mood for visitors.'

'Oh?' Freya patted her on the head, a gesture that was met with a look of suspicion. 'Well, I'm afraid we really need to see him. We've come an awfully long way and it's terribly important. We're Honey's parents, you see, and—'

'You're Honey's mam and dad?' The girl's suspicions vanished, and she beamed at them. 'Would you like a cup of tea?'

Cain wondered if Freya was as surprised as he was to see that the girl actually seemed fond of their daughter. 'Love a cuppa,' he confirmed, pushing past his ex-wife and following the girl into the hallway.

Freya stepped inside, too, folding her umbrella and propping it against the wall. She shut the door behind her, looking around the hallway, evidently pleasantly surprised at what she saw.

'Not quite the pit I imagined,' she whispered, as they walked behind the little girl and entered a kitchen that was like something out of a glossy magazine.

'Heavens,' murmured Freya.

'Christ,' said Cain. 'Who'd have thought it?'

'Sit down here, and I'll get Dad,' said the little girl. She gestured towards the table very politely.

'Thank you. You're very sweet,' said Freya.

'You'll have to be nice to him,' the girl informed them. 'Somebody came earlier and woke Georgie up, and it's taken ages to get him back to sleep. Dad looks ever so tired.' Having imparted that knowledge, she left the room.

'She must be Liberty,' said Freya thoughtfully. 'She's nothing like Jemima, I must say.'

'No, well, she ain't dead for a start,' said Cain. Freya glared at him, and he held up his hands. 'Sorry. Bit tense. Where the bleeding hell is Honey?'

'That's what I'd like to know.'

Cain looked up, shocked to see a tall, dark-haired man standing in the doorway, holding the little girl's hand. He was nothing like Cain had imagined. If he'd known what this Eliot bloke looked like, there was no way he'd have let Honey stay with him. Why hadn't Freya warned him?

His ex-wife stood and held out her hand for the farmer to shake. He didn't take it, but stood there glaring at them. Cain felt a momentary stab of satisfaction as Freya coughed nervously and sat down again, obviously embarrassed. Well, that was one point for the bloke, anyway.

'What are you saying?' Cain asked. 'You don't know where Honey is, either?'

The man shook his head. 'I don't.'

'Goodness. She really is terribly disobedient,' said Freya. 'I don't know if you remember me, Eliot. I'm dear Jemima's cousin. I know we spoke on the phone about Honey, but it's some years since we met. It must be—'

'Never,' he said coldly. 'You never bothered to visit, and we were never invited to any family gatherings.'

'Really?' Freya looked most uncomfortable, to Cain's amusement. 'Well, I'm sure I saw you once. Your face is familiar.'

'We've *never* met. Not even at the funeral. Like most of your family, you were too busy to turn up.'

'Oh. Well, it must have been a photograph somewhere.' She glanced at Cain, scowling when he grinned at her. 'Anyway, that's all beside the point. You were supposed to be looking after Honey.'

Cain nodded. She was right there. 'You promised to keep an eye on her,' he said. 'Yet, here we are, and there's no sign. And not only that, but she's been up to all sorts. We've had a tip-off. We know what she's been doing.'

Eliot glanced down at his daughter.

Cain folded his arms. 'That's right. We know. How could you let this happen, eh?'

Eliot sat down. Noticing how weary and strained he looked, Cain felt a sudden pang of sympathy for him. After all, looking after Honey was enough to make anyone look like that. He should know.

The farmer ran a hand through his hair and turned to the little girl. 'Ophelia, go upstairs and check on George, will you?'

'George is fine. He's asleep now, and, anyway, Libby's up there with him.'

'Well, get your coat and wellies on and shut the hens up for the night. I forgot, and I need to speak to these people alone. There's a good lass.'

'Is Honey in trouble?' she asked, a worried expression on her face.

'You bet your bleeding life she is,' said Cain.

Eliot closed his eyes for a moment before shaking his head. 'No, love. She's not in any trouble. I'll sort it. Just get the hens in, and then go upstairs for now, eh?'

She nodded and reluctantly left the kitchen.

Eliot turned back to his guests. 'I'm not sure what the hell's going on here but—'

'Well, I'll tell you, shall I? Bleeding Crispin Cavendish ring any bells?'

Eliot swallowed. His face was pale and there was a sudden look of sadness in his eyes. 'I know all about Crispin Cavendish,' he said, his voice harsh. 'I've had a visit from his wife, not an hour ago.'

'What? Lavinia was here? Bleeding hell, that's torn it.'

'So much for your party's golden boy,' said Freya gleefully.

'Time and place, Freya,' snarled Cain. 'Look, mate. I asked you to keep an eye on my daughter, to keep her out of the clutches of that swine, and what happens, eh? She's only bleeding shacked up with him right under your nose. And now you're telling me his sodding wife knows? How did all this happen, eh?'

Eliot stared intently at his hands, which he'd placed flat on the table. Cain wondered suddenly if he was planning to punch him, and decided a less aggressive approach might be more suitable.

'Look, mate, I know what Honey's like. She's played us all for fools. We sent her up here thinking we could keep her out of the way of that philandering sod, but between the two of them, they've made idiots of us. All this time, we've been thinking she was safe out of his way, and he's been hiding up here with her the whole summer. I can't blame you for being hoodwinked, can I? Not when she's done it to us, an' all. And Gawd knows, we should have been suspicious that she came up here so easily.'

'So, *that* is what it was all about?' Eliot's voice sounded strange, almost choked. 'She's been having an affair with this married man, and you sent her to me to get her away from him?'

'Well, obviously. Ain't I just said that?'

'Look, whatever the rights and wrongs of this, the fact is the affair has continued, and now Lavinia's found out about it, we must try for some sort of damage limitation.' Freya reached into her bag and took out her mobile phone.

Cain frowned. 'Who are you ringing?'

'Diana Ross and the Supremes. Who the hell do you think I'm ringing? Your wretched daughter, of course. She needs to get back here now, and we need to sort this mess out.'

'I don't want her back here.' Eliot's voice was hard. Angrily, he pushed back his chair and stood. 'Meet her somewhere else. Take her things and get out of here. I never want to see her again.'

Cain and Freya gaped at him.

'For heaven's sake, don't be so dramatic, Eliot,' said Freya. 'All right, she pulled the wool over your eyes.' She gave a girlish giggle. 'How appropriate for a sheep farmer! Anyway, just because she fooled you, doesn't mean you have to be so stroppy. We'll get her here, and we can all tell her what we think of her and make some sort of plan to salvage this appalling situation. Oh, damn, no signal. How ridiculous. May I use your telephone?'

Eliot suddenly lunged forward and slammed his hands on the table, glaring at her. 'Did you not hear me? I said, I don't want her back here. Take her home. Do what you like with her, but keep her out of my way, or God help me, I'll—'

Cain never knew what Eliot would do, because at that moment, the back door flew open, and there was Eden, red-faced and breathing hard, as if she'd been running. Water dripped from her soaking hair onto the floor as they all stared at her in astonishment.

'What the—?' Cain stood up, baffled. What the hell was she doing in Skimmerdale? And why was Eliot looking at her with that peculiar expression in his eyes? It was—what was it? A mixture of fury and heartbreak. What the hell had been going on? And where, in the name of Ozzy Osbourne, was Honey?

'Eliot.' Her voice was juddering, her eyes pleaded with him for understanding.

Cain had no doubt there was something going on between them. He recognised passion when he saw it, even if it had been a long time since he'd felt it—except for his Rolls Royce, of course.

Eliot turned his back on her, leaning heavily on the sink and facing the window.

'Eden, what the hell's going on here?' Cain felt like he'd crossed over into The Twilight Zone. 'Why are you in Yorkshire? And where the bleeding hell is Honey?'

Eliot swung round, and Eden looked at him with terrified eyes. 'What are you talking about? This *is* Honey.'

Freya dropped her mobile on the table. 'This most certainly is not Honey. I presume you're the babysitter?'

'The—the what?' Eliot looked stunned.

Not surprising, really, thought Cain. Poor bugger must have been thoroughly confused. It was bad enough for Cain, and he knew who everyone was. 'This is Eden. She works for me and Honey. Are you telling me this is the girl who's been staying with you the whole time?'

Eliot couldn't seem to speak. He stared at Eden as if he'd never seen her before, but eventually, he managed a nod.

'Jesus! Right, Eden. Seems you and me have got to have a little talk.'

'Sit down,' snapped Freya. 'I want to know exactly what's been going on.'

Eden swallowed and reached out a hand to Eliot, but he pulled away, still staring at her. 'Who *are* you?' he murmured.

'We've told you. She's staff,' said Freya, but Cain had a feeling there was more to Eliot's question than that.

'Come on, Eden. Take a seat and tell us what's been going on,' he said, his voice a great deal kinder than it had been a moment ago.

Dragging her gaze away from Eliot, she sat down and slowly, hesitantly, told them the story from the beginning. Cain could barely take it in.

'So, you're telling me, it was your fella who smashed me Roller?' he said eventually.

Freya tutted. 'Is that all you can say? A whole web of lies and deception, and you only care about your pathetic car. Typical. Do you realise how stupid she's made us look?'

'Who?' he said. 'Eden or Honey?'

'Both. They're as bad as each other.'

'Fair's fair, Freya. Seems to me Honey had Eden over a barrel. Little bleeder. She's one devious little git.' Cain leaned forward, touching Eden's hand. 'You should have told me. Are you really that scared of me? Did you really think I'd sack you over a car?'

'I wouldn't put it past you,' said Freya.

'You were in a real temper that day,' Eden pointed out. 'Honey and Freya had really wound you up. I didn't think you'd be in any mood to listen.'

He sighed. 'You're probably right. Sorry, darl. So you found yourself shunted off up here to play Mary Poppins to three kids who had nothing to do with you. Blimey.' He shook his head. 'That must have been some acting you did there.' He glanced up at Eliot, who stood, frozen, as he listened to the conversation. 'You said she was a proper madam, throwing her weight around and making some outrageous demands.'

Eliot seemed to come out of his trance. 'She was. She did.'

'Well, that's not Eden. Not at all. Honey, now, that's her to a tee.' He winked at Eden. 'Put on a proper show, didn't you?'

She gave him a weak smile, then looked round at Eliot. 'I'm so sorry,' she said.

'So, where is Honey now? You said she's in some holiday cottage?' Freya said.

'Yes. Just outside the village. But you needn't worry about her and Crispin any longer. Lavinia turned up and took him home. He and Honey are finished.'

'You're sure?' said Cain.

'Definitely. Apparently, Lavinia and Crispin have realised they love each other, after all. Honey was disgusted with him.'

'I'm more disgusted with Lavinia,' said Freya. 'Fancy taking him back, after all that. What a fool. Well, see how she feels the next time. It's Lucinda Farquhar all over again.'

'Let it go, Freya, for Christ's sake. That was donkey's years ago.' Cain turned back to Eden. 'So, is Honey still at the cottage?'

'Yes, but she's with some man. Apparently, she's been seeing him behind Crispin's back. But the odd thing is, he's the journalist who was at The Red Lion three years ago. Remember?'

Cain looked grim. 'Is he really? And our Honey's been seeing him? I don't know how much more of this I can take.'

'But there's something strange about him. Three years on, and he's still completely unprofessional. And why would he get the story, but tip off everyone involved instead of publishing? I don't think he's a journalist, at all.'

'And you left him there, alone with our Honey?'

'I'm sorry, but they seemed terribly fond of each other, and when Lavinia said she'd been here, I had to come back. I had to explain—' Her voice trailed off and she looked at Eliot beseechingly.

Freya and Cain followed her gaze. The farmer stood silently for a moment, then he shook his head. 'Get your things packed and go,' he said.

'Eliot!' Eden moved towards him, but the look on his face seemed to stop her in her tracks.

'There's nowt else to say. Just go, Honey, or Eden, or whatever the hell your name is. I don't know what kind of weird game you're all involved in, but this isn't me. This isn't what I want. I should have known. Been here before. Seems I never learn. Just, please, go back to wherever it is you came from and leave me be.'

Cain's voice was gentle, as he said, 'Do as he says, darl. Get your things, and we'll go and get Honey. See what the hell she's been up to now.'

He watched as Eden left the room, listening as she made her way slowly up the stairs, then turned to Eliot. 'Don't be too hard on her, mate. She's a good girl. I've gotta be honest, she's no match for Honey. I don't reckon she felt she had a choice.'

'She had the choice when she got here. She could have been honest with me, instead of pretending to be someone she wasn't. It seems to me that's all you lot are good for.' He glared at Freya as he said that, and she reared up, indignant, like some half-broken thoroughbred.

'Our lot? What do you mean by that?'

'Your family. Think you're something better than people like me, don't you?'

'He's got a point,' said Cain.

'Shut up. I don't know what your problem is. Whatever

this Eden did is nothing to do with me. Or Honey, for that matter. She has a mind of her own, doesn't she? It's hardly our fault if she chose the easy option, rather than face up to her crimes.'

'What bleeding crimes?' demanded Cain.

'Your Rolls Royce. Don't tell me you'd forgotten. Will wonders never cease? And I don't know why you're so keen to blame your own daughter for this mess. She had a more than willing accomplice, after all.'

'Oh, come off it, Freya,' said Cain. 'Who can stand up to Honey, once she makes up her mind?'

'She didn't have to lie to me,' said Eliot quietly. 'Eden, I mean. She could have told me the truth. All this play-acting and lying. She got my children to care about her, to love her. She means the world to—them.'

He broke off, and Cain narrowed his eyes. It seemed to him that Eden had come to mean the world to more than just the bloke's children. He wasn't wrong, he was certain. He'd seen it the moment Eden walked in—that mixture of rage and pain in his eyes. Eliot Harland loved Eden. Well, well.

They heard a bumping sound on the stairs as Eden struggled with her suitcases. Eliot glanced up for a moment then turned back to the window, as if forcing himself not to go to her aid. Cain went to help her, instead, and soon there was a whole collection of Honey's expensive luggage in the hallway, and two wide-eyed little girls standing at the top of the stairs, looking down with tears in their eyes.

'Do you have to go?' he heard one of them say. Something in her voice gave him a lump in his throat. Bleeding hell, he was getting soft in his old age.

'I'm sorry,' Eden replied, her voice thick with emotion and her eyes bright with tears.

The eldest child disappeared for a moment, then suddenly she rushed down the stairs, carrying a bag in her hand. 'You haven't opened Dad's present,' she said. 'He left it lying around, so I hid it in our room. You'd better have it now.'

'Present?'

'Dad went to Ravensbridge today,' the younger girl said. 'He got you those.'

Eden took the bag and opened it. As he watched, she lifted out a pair of black wellington boots with pink love hearts dotted all over them and trendy wedge heels. She gave a strangled moan and then salt water was spilling down her cheeks.

Cain couldn't bear it. He left them saying their goodbyes and returned to the kitchen.

'You sure about this?' he murmured to Eliot. 'Seems to me those kiddies' hearts will break when she leaves. And, if you ask me, she's breaking her heart right now. There's nothing for her to go home for, you know. Think about this.'

Eliot's jaw clenched. 'Close the door on your way out,' he managed eventually.

Cain sighed and motioned to Freya to follow him. At the front door, he saw Eden turn and glance down the hallway, but Eliot hadn't followed her.

Rubbing the tears from her cheeks, she picked up her holdall, tucked what looked suspiciously like a Shaun the Sheep soft toy under her arm, and left the farm—wellington boots included.

****

Teddy sipped his tea. 'It's really kind of you to make me a drink, Honey,' he said.

'Shut up,' said Honey.

Teddy sighed and waited a moment before speaking again. 'I'm really sorry.'

'For what?' Honey snapped. 'Tipping my father off that I was seeing Crispin? Telling Lavinia where to find us?

Taking those photos of me and Troy Troughton at The Red Lion, or—' She gulped. '—pretending to care about me, and having sex with me, just to get some wretched story?'

'Honey, I didn't! I didn't pretend!'

'Shut up.'

'But you have to believe me, I meant every word.'

'I said, shut up.'

'And it wasn't having sex. I made love to you, because I love you, Honey.'

Honey stood up and tipped her mug of tea over his knees.

He leapt up, squealing in pain. 'Fuck me, that's hot!'

'There'd have been no point, otherwise,' she said.

He put his mug down on the floor and frantically unbuckled his belt, pulling down his trousers and revealing an angry red patch on his upper legs.

Honey, in spite of herself, felt a twinge of guilt. 'You'd better do something about that,' she muttered.

He ran into the kitchen and grabbed a sponge, running it under the cold water tap and squeezing the water onto his legs. Soon, the kitchen floor was a mass of puddles. Teddy sank onto the floor. 'I think that should stop it blistering,' he said faintly.

Honey sat beside him, realising too late that she was sitting in a puddle. 'I'm sorry I scalded you,' she muttered eventually.

'I'm sorry I lied to you,' he said.

'So, you *did* lie!'

'Only about not knowing who you were. I meant all the other things I said. That day we spent together was the most perfect day of my life. I do love you, Honey. I always have.'

'What do you mean, you always have? We only met a couple of weeks ago.'

At a sudden commotion, Honey leapt to her feet. 'What

now?' She held out her hand and helped Teddy stand, then jumped in fright when her mother's voice cut through the air like a scythe.

'Good grief, Honey. So, there *were* two of them on the go at once. Talk about greedy.'

'What the bleeding hell's going on here?' Cain entered the kitchen behind his ex-wife, and Honey found herself stifling a sob.

'Oh, Daddy!'

'Eh?' For a moment, he seemed rigid with shock, as Honey hurled herself against him and his soaking wet jacket, then he wrapped his arms around her and held her close, patting her back and murmuring, 'There, there, darls. It's all right. It's all right.'

'What the hell have you done to her?' Freya demanded. 'She never behaves like this. Never! You monster!'

'It's not his fault,' sniffed Honey. 'Well, not all of it.' She pulled away from her father, who seemed very reluctant to let her go, and dabbed at her eyes with the sleeve of her very expensive top from Jigsaw. Looking up, she caught sight of Eden. 'Good grief, what's up with you?'

Eden shrugged. 'Nothing.'

Honey peered at her. 'You've been crying. What's happened?'

Her father looked at her, anxiety in his eyes. 'What's happened to you, Honey? Why are you being all caring and nice? It's all wrong. You're freaking me out.'

'It's this journalist,' said Freya, slapping Teddy on the arm. 'What are you doing with your trousers down? Have you been manhandling my daughter?'

'Oh, Mother, for God's sake!' Honey sounded much more like her old self, to her father's apparent relief. 'I poured boiling tea over him, and he had to sponge his legs with cold water, if you must know.'

'Serves him right,' said Freya coldly. 'How dare you

spy on my daughter? You—you pervert.'

Teddy looked mortified, but Cain was staring hard at him. 'I know you, don't I?'

'Of course you don't know him,' said Honey. 'You didn't see him that night at The Red Lion, any more than I did.'

Cain rubbed his forehead. 'No, I do know him. He's very familiar. He's—well, fuck me!'

'Not for a million pounds.' Freya shuddered.

'Theodore! Theodore Scotman!'

'What?' Freya and Honey gaped at Teddy.

'Who?' said Eden.

'The son of Cain's nemesis, Rex Scotman,' said Freya, apparently so astonished she forgot to ignore the staff. 'I don't get it. I thought you were working for Rex's charitable institution? When did you train as a journalist?'

'The charity work!' Honey clutched the edge of the worktop for support. 'You weren't lying.'

'No,' said Teddy. 'I wasn't.'

'I'm buggered if I know what's going on,' Cain said. 'Can we all sit down and start again?'

'And do pull your trousers up,' added Freya.

Teddy obeyed, and the five of them moved into the tiny sitting room and sat on the sofas facing each other.

'I thought you were in Africa,' said Freya. 'Don't you run your father's musical academy?'

'I did,' said Teddy. 'He sent me over there for three years. I didn't want to go, but he insisted.'

'Wanted to make a man of you,' said Freya.

'Wanted to get me away from Honey,' Teddy confessed.

Honey looked up, startled. 'Me? What have I got to do with anything?'

'Everything. Oh, Honey, where do I start?'

'How about you tell me why you were taking photos of my daughter at The Red Lion?' suggested Cain.

Teddy sighed. 'I wanted evidence to show you, Mr Carmichael. I knew she was seeing Troy Troughton, and I wanted her to stop. I thought, perhaps, if you knew about it, you'd put an end to it.'

'How did you know?' demanded Honey. 'No one knew.'

'I—oh, dear.' Teddy's face turned scarlet. 'I'd been following you for months, ever since we first met.'

'We met before?' Honey shook her head. 'I don't remember that.'

'No, well, I don't think I made that much of an impression on you. We were at that charity auction at Hoverton Hall. My father made sure we avoided your father—' He gave Cain an apologetic look, '—but I soon realised who you were. I was taking our glasses back to the bar, and you came over and asked me to get you a mineral water.'

'Oh, gosh.' Honey bit her lip. 'I must have assumed you were a waiter.'

'Obviously.' Teddy gave her a rueful smile. 'It didn't matter. I brought you the drink, and you gave me the most beautiful smile and thanked me.'

'Did I?'

'Did she?'

All four of them sounded amazed at that revelation, but Teddy nodded. 'Yes, and that was that. I was in love, and have been ever since. Of course, knowing how our fathers feel about each other, I knew it was going to be difficult, but that didn't stop me dreaming and hoping. So I started to find out all I could about you, and I—well, I started to follow you. Not to hurt you, or do anything creepy, just to see you. That was all. But then I realised you were seeing Troy Troughton, and I knew he'd break your heart, so I thought I'd better stop it before that could happen.'

'Gosh,' said Honey.

'That's downright creepy,' said Freya.

'But then, you say, your dad sent you to Africa?' Cain said.

'Yes, he found out what was going on and he was furious. He said I'd end up in jail, or something, and said I was to go away until I learned some sense.'

'I always did like Rex,' said Freya.

'Anyway, I stayed in Africa for three years,' said Teddy. 'Then Dad agreed I could come home and start working for the Foundation from this end. Of course, he assumed I'd got over Honey.'

'But you hadn't?' Cain asked.

'Of course not! Look at her.' Teddy looked dumbfounded that anyone could think that even possible.

In spite of her anger, Honey felt herself softening.

'So you started following her again.'

'I didn't intend to! I saw her, quite by accident, in a queue at some traffic lights. She's noticeable, especially in that cute yellow car when the roof's down. I couldn't resist going after her. I meant to talk to her, introduce myself properly, but she met up with *him*.' He looked disgusted. 'What could I do? I knew Cavendish's reputation. I knew he'd break her heart. I had to stop it before she got too involved.'

'Control freak,' said Freya.

'So you messaged me on Facebook,' said Cain, 'calling yourself Romeo Lovegod.'

'Hmm. Sorry about that. I made a shortlist and drew names out of a hat. It was that or Ferdy Feelgood, and I wasn't sure you'd take that seriously.'

'Oh, well, God forbid you'd choose anything stupid,' said Cain.

Teddy evidently missed the sarcasm. 'Anyway, nothing happened for ages, and I was beginning to despair. Then she went off radar completely for days. Not a sign of her, or the yellow car. I was worried sick, so I changed tactics and started following Cavendish instead. Saw his wife head off to the airport and realised something could be happening very soon, so I stuck close. Sure enough, he met up with Honey and her,' he said, nodding at Eden, 'in a layby. I didn't know what was going on. Honey got in his car, and *she* got back in the Beetle, and then he drove off, so I had to follow. I had no idea I'd be driving for so long. Ended up in bloody Dorset. Didn't even have any luggage with me.'

'The red Mini,' said Eden and Honey in unison.

'I'm so sorry, Honey,' he said miserably.

'I should hope you are. Bleeding deceitful,' said Cain. 'And have you any idea how much bother it caused, you taking them photos of her and that bloody awful singer?'

'It's not only deceitful,' said Freya. 'It's creepy, stalkerish, and weird. I think you want locking up, or at the very least, aversion therapy.'

'I think that's the most romantic thing I've ever heard,' said Honey with a sigh.

Teddy's face lit up, as she rushed over to him and threw her arms around him.

'So you did mean it that day in bed? All the things you said.'

'What bloody day in bed?' Cain demanded. 'Christ, this gets worse and worse.'

'If you stay with that man, you deserve everything you get,' Freya warned.

'Shut up, Mother,' said Honey. 'I love him.'

'Oh, Honey!' said Teddy with a devoted sigh.

'Cain, this is entirely your fault,' said Freya. 'I blame you for the way she's turned out. She's had such a poor male role model, she's got nothing to aspire to. Take me home immediately, you sorry excuse for a man.'

'It will be my pleasure, you frigid old bat,' said Cain.

Honey stopped listening at that point. She had far more important things to think about, and if her parents didn't have the decency to look the other way, that was their look out.

CHAPTER THIRTY-ONE

'You can't mean it? After everything we've been through? After everything Honey put you through?' Cain shook his head, obviously baffled. 'I don't get it Eden. What you wanna go and resign for?'

Eden wrapped her arms around herself and stared out of the window. Even through the rapidly approaching darkness, she could see that the garden was already changing colour—the summer green leaves turning to shades of autumn gold and russet. September was almost over. There was a distinct chill in the air, and in her heart. 'You don't need me now, and neither does Honey.'

'We'll find something for you to do. There's always some job needs doing, you know that. Besides, you're part of the family.'

It was possibly the loveliest thing Cain had ever said to her, but it wasn't enough. Not anymore. Honey didn't need a babysitter. She was so loved up with Teddy that she was rarely at home. To Cain's dismay, she had visited the Scotman family home and thoroughly charmed Rex, against all odds. She'd even started to take an interest in the Scotman Foundation, asking Teddy about his work, and telling Eden all about it with so much pride, it was as if she had started the damn charity herself.

Cain had reluctantly accepted an invitation—which had been no doubt issued with just as much reluctance—from Rex Scotman, to take part in the concert, after all. He'd been in two minds about accepting, but he'd admitted that the thought of Honey's tantrums, if he refused, was too much for him to cope with.

'Besides,' he said gleefully to Eden one evening, 'that will really infuriate Freya. Proper pissed on her bonfire, ain't I?'

He had finished with Roxy, who had cried for all of

ten minutes, until he presented her with a cheque and the keys to a rather fabulous Audi. He'd also—unbeknown to Roxy—paid off her sister with similar gifts.

'You can't put a price on a quiet life,' he told Eden. 'To be honest, I'm done in. Can't be bothered with women and all this romance stuff. Reckon I've had me fair share. Time to concentrate on me kids.'

To everyone's astonishment—including his own—he'd finally gone to his daughter's wedding in America and had a wonderful time. He'd since begun *putting out feelers* to see if he could help his son's musical career, and the two were in constant contact. He'd even gone to visit Marcus and spent some days with his grandson, although when he tried to teach the child to play his biggest hit, *Satan in Stilettos*, on the recorder, stern words had been exchanged. Emerald, he confessed, was a lost cause. At least for now. She was too busy *looking for herself* to waste time finding her father, but that was okay.

'In her own good time,' he'd said comfortably, and Eden got the impression that his middle child could take all the time she needed. He was in no hurry.

The Carmichael family seemed happier and more settled than it had ever been. It was time for Eden to move on.

'But The Red Lion! It's such a dump. You're too good for the place.'

'It's only temporary until I find something else. It will do me good to get back to cooking professionally, and at least I'll get a reference.'

'I can give you a reference! A bloody good one. You don't need to go back to that bleeding dive.'

'Thanks, Cain, but I need a reference that's about my ability in the kitchen. Not my ability to sit in a shop, staring at a wall for hours on end.' *Or lying, cheating, and deceiving the kindest man you could ever possibly wish to meet*, she thought bitterly. That had been one thing she'd proved exceptionally good at, and didn't she know it.

'This is about the farmer, ain't it?' Cain sighed, as she hung her head. 'You got it real bad, bless you. Why don't you call him? Talk to him. He must have got over his sulk by now.'

'Sulk?' Eden gave a hollow laugh. 'I think it's a lot more than that, Cain. You really don't understand.'

'Well, tell me.'

'It's complicated.'

'I got all day. Look, darl, just 'cos I've given up on all that romantic tosh, don't mean I don't remember what it felt like. And it don't mean I don't recognise true love when I see it.'

Eden sighed. 'Am I that obvious?'

'Not you I'm talking about.'

'What do you mean?'

'When I was at that farm, I saw the look in that bloke's eyes. He's got it real bad, too. He loves you, Eden.'

'You think?' She felt a momentary spark of hope, but it refused to ignite, like a wet match. 'It's too late. He may have been developing feelings for me, but finding out I was lying all that time, well, it would have killed off any chance we had.'

'I don't see why. If you love someone, it's amazing what crap you put up with.'

'Oh? What did *you* put up with?'

He shook his head. 'Not me. I was talking about my wives. Proper shit husband, me. They took it all. Mind you, I reckon the size of me bank balance had a lot to do with that. Don't apply in your case. You're both pretty skint, from where I'm standing. Match made in heaven.' He laughed, but Eden said nothing. Cain sighed. 'Come on, darl. This isn't like you. If you can put up with me and Honey and our shenanigans, I'm sure you can take on a farmer who needs putting straight about a few things. Or am I missing something?'

'It's because of Jemima,' she said eventually.

'You mean his dead wife? Are you saying he still loves her? Well, fair enough. You never get over someone you truly love, no matter how long it is since they snuffed it. You can live with that, can't you? Point is, he can still move on and make a new life with you. It ain't disloyal to his wife.'

'It's not that!' She stood up, fastening her jacket. 'I'm sorry, Cain. I appreciate you trying to help, but I can't stay. I'm going back to The Red Lion. Time to get my life sorted out.'

'Aw, Eden. I'm sorry.' He stood, too, and she held out her hand to shake. He stared at it for a moment, then pulled her into a warm embrace. 'You're a diamond, you really are. I'm sorry we gave you such a hard time of it. I really hope things work out for you. I'll miss you, darl.'

She stifled a sob and pulled away from him. 'Thanks, Cain.'

'There'll be a bonus and a reference for you. Promise. And Eden …' he added, as she opened the door of the den.

She turned. 'Yes?'

'Don't be a stranger, eh? You're welcome here, any time.'

Eden nodded, unable to say another word.

****

Eliot kissed the girls and walked slowly towards the bedroom door.

'You can read for half an hour,' he said softly, 'but make sure you're quiet. Don't want to wake George up, do we? No talking or giggling.'

He wondered why he'd even said such a thing. The two little faces looking solemnly at him showed no signs of wanting to giggle. They hadn't shown any sign for weeks. In fact, he would give anything to hear their laughter right then, even if it did mean they woke George up. What did it matter, anyway? It wasn't as if he wanted to be alone for the evening, was it?

'Goodnight, Dad,' murmured Libby.

'Night, love.'

He started to close the bedroom door, when Ophelia's voice cut through the silence. 'Dad, have you heard from her?'

He halted on the landing, pressing his hand to his forehead and willing himself to sound normal. 'No, love. Night now.'

'But, Dad, are you sure? Maybe she's been trying to ring us, but you've been working and we've been at school and George has been with Mrs Thompson. She wouldn't know that, would she? Why don't you ring her and talk to her?'

'Stop it, Ophelia.' Libby's voice came to him, sounding urgent.

'But she'd want to know about Gideon, wouldn't she? She'd be so excited that he sold for such a lot of money.'

He swallowed as he heard Libby hissing at her sister, 'Shut *up*, Ophelia!'

'But why?' Ophelia hissed back. '*You* said you missed her, too. Why can't I mention her?'

'It upsets him. You know it does.'

'So, I have to keep quiet about Honey as well as Mummy? Is there anyone I *can* talk about?'

'She's not Honey, she's Eden. And you know Dad can't cope hearing about Mummy. Just behave yourself.'

Eliot clapped his hand over his mouth to stifle the sob. He should go in there right now. He should sit beside them on the bed and explain everything to them, about Eden and about Jemima. Well, not everything about Jemima. There were some things he couldn't tell them, at least not yet. Maybe one day, when they were old enough to understand. He hoped they would understand. He hoped they would forgive. But that day was a long way away. Right now, they were young children, and they were confused, and he should do something, anything, to make things better for them. He just couldn't do it while he had no idea how to make things better for himself.

Hating himself, he crept downstairs and straight to the whisky in the kitchen cupboard. He rarely drank, and on the occasions he did, it was usually beer. A couple of weeks ago, though, when the loneliness had been pressing down on him and he couldn't face the thought of another night alone, he'd gone to the shop in Beckthwaite and bought himself a bottle. That had raised eyebrows, for sure. They'd looked stunned when he went back a few days later and bought another two bottles. He knew they were talking about him, discussing his odd behaviour. He wondered how much they knew. Then he realised he didn't care. Let them talk. What did it matter, anyway?

After pouring himself a glass of the warming liquid that he didn't particularly like the taste of, he took a mouthful, shuddered in disgust, and finished the drink. He poured another and carried the glass, and the bottle, back into the living room. He shouldn't do this. He had to be up early the following morning, not to mention the small matter of being in charge of three young children. He would only have three, though. No more. He would put the bottle away after that.

He downed the second glass, finding it wasn't as foul as the first one. Or maybe his mouth had gone numb. He poured a third glass. One more and that was it. He found himself pouring a larger measure that time—almost to the brim, before he screwed the cap back on the bottle. That was his lot. He'd better savour this one.

Picking up the glass, he leaned against the back of the sofa and closed his eyes. He took small sips, trying to make it last. It had become a comfort blanket, and he knew he would have to be careful. He couldn't let drinking become a habit. He had responsibilities. He couldn't let his children down.

Funny, he thought, staring into the amber liquid in fascination, how he hadn't even turned to drink when Jemima died. If anything was going to make him drink, it should have been that. Yet, it had taken a woman whose name wasn't even her own, and who he knew absolutely nothing about, to make him feel that, just maybe, he'd taken all he could stand, and it was time to surrender.

He took a large gulp of the whisky and stared around him at the empty living room. Funny how all those familiar things looked so bleak and pointless to him now. He missed her. He missed her so much he could barely breathe. He missed her smile. He missed the look she gave him when he was being grumpy. He missed the sight of her standing by the oven when he walked into the kitchen after work. He missed the way she giggled with the girls, or bounced George up and down on her knee, the way she so obviously cared about them and their welfare. He missed the smell of her perfume, the sight of her ridiculously impractical shoes next to his boots in the boot room. He missed the way she looked at him sometimes, the emotion in her eyes, the slight parting of her lips. He missed the way she made him feel—the way his heart pounded when she was close to him, the longing he'd felt to reach out and touch her, the scent of her skin when she was nearby, the feel of her hair as he'd twisted it through his fingers.

Eden. At first it had seemed alien, strange. But as he'd thought more and more about her over the last few weeks, he'd realised it suited her. And it was appropriate, after all. Eden, so beautiful, so heavenly, yet filled with temptation. And he'd succumbed to that temptation, hadn't he? All was lost. If she'd only told him the truth.

He gulped down more whisky, desperate to rid himself of her image. *Why, my love? Why?*

Was that a tap on the door? He wasn't sure at first, and

didn't much care, anyway. He took another sip of whisky, aware that the glass was almost empty and he mustn't pour himself another. Then the sound came again, louder that time. Cursing, he put down the glass and heaved himself off the sofa. The room swung slightly and he stood for a moment, trying to steady himself, before he went through the hallway and opened the front door.

He stared at the woman in shock for a moment. He couldn't remember the last time she'd visited the farm. Then he recalled the exact moment, and misery overwhelmed him yet again. 'Beth. Come in, why don't you?'

She followed him into the hall, her eyes anxious. 'Eliot, are you all right?'

He forced a smile, closing the door behind them. 'I'm absolutely fine. Are you?'

She stared at him, obviously shocked. 'So, it's true! You *have* been drinking.'

'Just a whisky, or three. It's a day for celebrations, after all! You wouldn't begrudge me that, would you? So, what can I do for you, Beth? This is a rare pleasure, I must say.'

'Oh, Eliot.' Her voice was loaded with pity. He couldn't stand it.

Tears sprang into his eyes, and he turned away, stumbling back into the living room. She followed him and stood there, as he fell onto the sofa, looking down in dismay at the half empty whisky bottle and the glass with just a drop of liquid left at the bottom.

'Since when do you drink whisky?' she demanded, putting down her bag and unbuttoning her coat.

He shook his head, having no energy to reply.

She picked up the bottle and glass and carried them through into the kitchen. A moment later, she returned. 'That's that poured down the sink,' she announced.

He glared up at her. 'Who said you could do that?'

'No one. I made an executive decision. For God's sake,

Eliot, you have children upstairs, and a bloody farm to run. What the hell do you think you're playing at?'

He opened his mouth to speak, but couldn't think of an answer. He shut it again and hung his head, suddenly ashamed. His kids. They could have come down at any moment. What would they have thought if they'd seen him like this? They'd have been so scared. What if something had happened to one of them? He wouldn't even have been able to help them. He was in no fit state. He was a disgrace. 'I'm sorry,' he murmured.

She sat beside him on the sofa, quiet for a moment. Then she took hold of one of his hands and squeezed it. Unknowingly, she'd lit the touch paper. Horrified, he watched as her image became blurred, distorted. Dear God, he was crying. He was actually crying. He hadn't let the tears fall since —

'Jemima,' he murmured, and Beth put her arms around him, and he found he was sobbing onto her shoulder and couldn't stop.

She said nothing, stroking his hair and letting him cry, until there seemed to be no tears left. Then she kissed him softly on the forehead, stood up and disappeared into the kitchen. He sat there for a moment, wiping his face and wondering what the hell had happened. Bloody whisky. He'd never touch the stuff again, that was for sure. He was mortified with shame.

Beth returned, carrying two steaming mugs. 'Coffee. Black. Drink.'

He took a sip and pulled a face. Bloody hell, it was almost as vile as the whisky.

She grinned at him. 'Serves you right.'

'Aye,' he acknowledged. 'Reckon it does.'

She put her mug on the coffee table. 'Right, Eliot. I don't care whether you want to, or not. Tonight, you and me are going to talk all this through, once and for all. Time to get it out in the open, don't you think?'

He put his own mug down and ran a tired hand across his forehead. 'Maybe you're right, Beth. I don't think—' He broke off and swallowed hard, blinking away fresh tears, '—I don't think I can carry on like this much longer. I need your help. I need to make sense of it all. And the one thing I need to know more than anything is, was it my fault? Did I kill my wife?'

CHAPTER THIRTY-TWO

'Is this what it's all been about, Eliot? You seriously believe you're responsible for Jemima's death?' Beth took hold of his hands and studied his face carefully. 'You do, don't you? My God!'

'Well, what else am I to think? We drove her mad that last day. We lied to her and tipped her over the edge. She took off in that bloody car like a bat out of hell, and look what happened. It was my fault. You can't deny it.'

'Well …' Beth shook her head. '… if it was your fault, it was just as much mine. I was standing right there beside you, telling the same lies, remember? You can't blame yourself and not me.'

'You had good cause. You'd been driven half mad.'

'Oh, and you hadn't? Look, Eliot, the simple fact is, she did it to herself. She was besotted with James, and she wanted him. Worse than that, she wanted to hurt you—as if she hadn't already hurt you enough. She was driving too fast that day out of spite. No other reason. She wanted to get to Kirkby Skimmer as soon as she possibly could, to make it all official and break your fucking heart. She was a cruel bitch, and that's that.' She bit her lip. 'I'm sorry. I know you loved her.'

He laughed suddenly. 'Loved her? Oh, no. That died way before she did, Beth. Trust me on that score.'

Her eyes met his. 'But I thought—'

'I know what you thought. I know what everyone thought. Poor Eliot. Lost the love of his life. Heartbroken. How will he ever recover? You see what a bloody hypocrite I am, Beth? I let them believe that. I let everyone think I was grieving for my dead wife. But the truth is, if she was still alive, we'd have divorced a long time ago, and you know it. I'd have lost my kids. All of them. Fact is, it worked out better for me, her dying. Not that I wanted it. Not that I don't hate myself every single day for driving her to speed off in that damn car. Not that I don't wish, every time I look at my children's faces, that their mother was here for them—even if it meant only seeing them once a month, or so.'

After a moment, she said, 'She was my best friend, Eliot, but that day, I wished her dead. I admit it. It's funny, there are times when I remember the laughs we used to have, and I miss her. Really miss her. It's like I can almost forget she was sleeping with my husband behind my back. Even—' She broke off, looking away.

He squeezed her hand. 'You can say it. You know it, and I know it. That's what caused this whole mess in the first place, after all.'

She sighed. 'Even that she had my husband's child.' She looked into his eyes, and he saw his own pain reflected back at him.

'It's becoming more obvious every day,' he said softly. 'For a long time, he was pure Jemima. I could see her in George's little face every time I looked at him. But lately, I can see James. The odd expression, the shape of his chin. There's no mistaking it.'

'Will it— ' Beth swallowed. 'Will it affect how you feel about him?'

Eliot shook his head vehemently. 'Of course not. I knew he wasn't mine from the start. Didn't stop me loving him. When she died, I had to be there for him, and he needed me. I love that bairn. I'm his dad, and nothing will change that.'

'You were always sure, weren't you?'

'Oh, aye.' He rubbed his forehead. 'She tried her best to convince me we'd got together that night we celebrated Roger's sale. I know I was a bit drunk, but not so drunk I couldn't remember everything that happened. And I know I never went near her. We hadn't slept together for months. Why would that night be any different, particularly as she spent the entire time flirting with James?'

'I remember that night.' Beth blushed suddenly. 'I kissed you. I still feel bad about it.'

He shook his head. 'You were upset, and no bloody wonder. You needed some comfort, Beth. No one could blame you for it, least of all me. I knew it was James you were wanting. Don't let it bother you.'

They sat quietly for a moment. Eliot remembered the day Jemima died so vividly. She'd been brazening it out for weeks, even going so far as to point out to every visitor who'd come to bring cards and presents for the new baby how like Eliot George was. He hadn't been able to stand it, and had made a point of getting out of the house every time someone came to coo over the little boy. He and Beth had discussed it regularly. He'd been reluctant to tell her the truth, but she'd guessed and wanted—needed—confirmation. Eventually, he'd admitted there was no way the baby could be his, and Beth had finally had to face up to the fact that her husband and best friend had been having an affair behind her back—something Eliot had realised more than a year earlier.

After that, Beth had begun to unravel fast. Her own inability to get pregnant had made the situation even more fraught for her, and, weirdly enough, she actually loved James. Eliot had never fathomed out why. She was a lovely woman and deserved better than that. There was no accounting for taste, he supposed. Look at him. He'd loved Jemima once, with a passion.

When Beth had arrived at the farm that afternoon, she was tearful and on the verge of hysteria. Luckily, Eliot had found her before she reached the house and taken her to the barn to calm down a bit. Gradually, she'd stopped crying, and he'd agreed with her that things couldn't go on. Playing the game was getting them nowhere. It was time Jemima knew they were both aware of the truth. The girls were at school. James had gone into Kirkby Skimmer to see his solicitor about a business deal. They had to get it over with.

They'd expected Jemima to deny it, but she'd actually laughed at them. As Eliot watched Beth crumble, his wife had put her hands on her hips and demanded to know what they were going to do about it.

'More to the point,' he'd heard himself saying, 'what are *you* going to do about it?'

She'd shrugged, looking from one to the other. 'I'll probably leave here now. There's no point in staying, and God knows, I've served my time. James loves me and wants me. I shall take the children and move into Thwaite Park. I'm afraid you,' she said, nodding at Beth, 'will have to search for alternative accommodation.'

He didn't know where the lie had come from. He supposed, looking back, he'd wanted to wipe the smug look off her face and defend Beth, who seemed unable to defend herself. 'Funny that.'

'What's funny?' she demanded. 'Don't even try to stop me from taking the children. The girls will be far better off with me than stuck out here in this dump, and we all know you have no rights over George at all.'

'It's funny, because James doesn't want them,' he said, trying to keep his voice calm. It was taking every ounce of his strength not to trash her precious kitchen and throw her out into the yard. He drew in a deep breath. He had to stay focused.

Jemima looked from him to Beth. 'Don't be ridiculous. Of course he wants them. We've discussed it, many times.'

'He doesn't.' Beth seemed to have found new strength. She faced her former best friend with cold eyes. 'He regrets the whole thing. It seems the reality of having an actual baby to look at has brought it all home to him. He confessed your affair to me this morning and asked for my forgiveness.'

'I don't believe you.' But there had been doubt in Jemima's eyes. Eliot saw it, and had seized on it.

'He wants nowt more to do with you. He's chosen Beth. He doesn't want to play father to his own bairn, never mind two of mine. Reckon you've had it, love.'

He'd wanted to hurt her. He had no idea what he had thought would come of it. Eventually, Jemima would have found James, and he would have denied the story, and that would have been that. But at that moment, he was so angry and so hurt for Beth that he didn't care.

'I'll call him,' said Jemima, hurrying towards the hallway.

'Don't bother,' said Beth. 'His phone is switched off. He's in a meeting.'

Jemima had tried, anyway, but her face told Eliot that Beth was right.

Panic filled Jemima's eyes. 'I'm going to see him,' she said, her face white. 'Where are my car keys?'

She'd run into the living room, and they'd followed her. When she moved towards George's carry cot in the corner of the room, Eliot had stopped her. 'No you don't. You're not trailing this little one all over the place, while you go looking for lover boy.'

'You can't stop me,' she said, fury in her eyes. 'He's nothing to do with you.'

'He stays here,' said Eliot.

She stared at him for a moment, pure hatred in her expression. Then she grabbed her car keys off the coffee table. 'Right, he can stay here, for now. I'm going into Kirkby Skimmer. I'm going to find James, then we're going to the registrar's. Together. And we'll register George's birth, naming James as the father.' At the horror she must have seen in their faces, she laughed. 'Yeah, not so clever now, are you?'

'James doesn't want to have anything to do with George,' said Beth, shakily. 'He'll never agree.'

'Well, if that's the case, I'll leave the father's name blank,' said Jemima. 'Either way, you won't be his father, Eliot Harland. I can promise you that. And when I leave here, I'll be taking all three children with me. I swear to you, I'll do everything in my power to make sure you only see them once in a blue moon.'

He'd almost lost it then. If Beth hadn't been there, pulling on his arm, he dreaded to think what he might have done. As it was, he let her leave. Thank God, at least, that he'd stopped her from taking the baby with her. But when the police had arrived at the farm, less than an hour later, he'd known he'd driven her to her death. He'd sunk to the floor in grief and shock and guilt. The tears had started and hadn't stopped for days. It was only when Beth told him that James had, indeed, confessed the affair to her and admitted he didn't want to take on the children, that he'd stopped wallowing and started thinking about the three little people who needed him. The irony of it didn't escape him. The lie they'd told had come true. James wanted no part in George's upbringing, and that baby needed a father.

Trying not to think about the implications of lying on an official document, he'd registered George as his own child and stepped up for the little boy. He'd been George's daddy ever since.

The fear that James would one day change his mind had never left him, though. He couldn't stand the sight of the man and tried his best to keep his children—particularly George—away from him. He knew it had hurt Beth. She loved the girls and had been close to them, but Beth came as a package with the man she still, unbelievably, loved. By choosing to stay with him, she had forced Eliot to keep her away from the children, too. He was sorry for that, but he couldn't risk James Fuller bonding with his son. He loved George. He couldn't lose him. Not now.

Beth stood and went to the window. 'James is taking me away, Eliot. We're going on a cruise. We'll be gone for a couple of months. Then we may, or may not, return for Christmas. I don't know. I've always fancied spending Christmas in New York.'

'What's brought this on?'

She turned to face him. 'You. You didn't turn up at the market. The biggest, most important sale of the year, and you didn't show up. You sent your champion tup with Mickey. I went into the village earlier to buy some milk and everyone was talking about it. Then Granny Allen collared me.' She wrinkled her nose. 'It wasn't a pleasant experience, but I'm still glad she did. She told me you'd been buying bottles of whisky. She was worried about you.'

He couldn't help smiling. 'Bless her. She's a funny old stick, but heart of gold.'

'She was of the firm opinion that it was because you were pining for *that nice little blonde lass*.'

His smile faded. 'Daft old bugger.'

Beth laughed and came to sit beside him again. 'I couldn't believe you were drinking whisky. I had to check it out for myself, so I told James I was coming to see you this evening.'

'Huh. Bet he loved that.'

'No, he didn't. Not at all. But I was adamant, and I told him why.'

'Oh, great. So now he thinks I'm a drunk. What if—'

'Eliot, trust me.' She patted his arm. 'I know what's been hanging over you, but it's not going to happen. We had a long talk this afternoon. Lots of things came out that we hadn't discussed before—not properly, anyway. James admitted to me that he knows you've been a wonderful father to George. He couldn't do better. He has no intention of trying to take him away from you. He's—he's ashamed of the affair. He wishes it had never happened.

There were reasons. Jemima was—'

'I know what Jemima was. Downright miserable and bitterly resentful that she'd landed herself with a farmer with no money to spare for fancy clothes and holidays abroad. I wish I could have made her happy, but I couldn't. I should never have married her. Reckon she thought, with James, she'd found one of her own, and she'd be welcomed back into the family fold.'

'Probably,' Beth admitted. 'As for James—well, she was beautiful. Hard to resist. And we were struggling. Every month it was the same devastation of no baby. I suppose it wasn't much of a life for him.'

'Don't reckon it were a picnic for you, either,' said Eliot wryly.

'No. And I'm not making excuses for him. What he did was wrong, but he knows that, and he has been trying to put things right. He feels especially bad that I lost touch with the girls. He wanted to make it up to me, so he ...' She looked at him, nervously.

He raised an eyebrow. 'He did what? Go on, Beth.'

She took a deep breath. 'He was blackmailing Eden.'

'You what?'

'I'm sorry, Eliot. He was only doing it for me. He told me this afternoon. He realised pretty quickly that she wasn't the real Honey Carmichael, and he told her, if she didn't make sure I got to see the girls now and then, he'd have no hesitation telling you the truth.'

'My God.' Eliot could hardly take it in. So, that was why she'd taken them to the open day. Poor Eden. 'First Honey and then James. She must have been under so much pressure,' he murmured.

'Absolutely.'

'But she never gave any sign. I mean, she were so good with the kids, and she brightened up this place no end. You'd never have known.'

'Is Granny Allen right, Eliot? Is this really all about

Jemima, or is it Eden you're so upset about?'

He hesitated before finally admitting it to himself. 'I suppose it's both. Losing Eden, well, it brought all the other stuff to a head.'

'Losing her? So, you care for her? I mean, more than as a friend?' He said nothing, and she sighed. 'Eliot, come on. We said we'd get everything out in the open, didn't we? Time for honesty.'

He shrugged. 'I suppose so. Yes, I cared for her.'

She rested her chin on her hand. 'How much?'

There was a long pause, then he said quietly, 'I suppose I fell in love with her. Or I thought I did. But how could I? I don't even know who she was, not really. I thought she was Honey, and that terrified the life out of me, because the last thing I wanted was to fall for someone like Jemima all over again. But I couldn't help myself. She made everything *good* again. I tried to stop it, I swear I did, but she won me over. I kept thinking, what if she turns out the same? What if it ends the way it did with Jemima? What if I'm not good enough for her one day?'

'But Eden wasn't Honey. She fitted in here, the whole village knows that. If Mickey and Granny Allen think she belongs here with you, it must be true. So what's the problem?'

He looked at her as if she was mad. 'She *lied* to me, Beth! She could have told me who she really was, but she didn't. She deceived me, and she deceived my kids. How can I ever trust her?'

She sighed. 'Sometimes we have to get over it, if we love someone enough.'

'Don't compare her with James,' Eliot said, indignant.

She smiled. 'I'm not. Seems you are, though.'

'What do you mean?'

'Eden didn't intend to have a relationship with you, Eliot. She didn't intend for you to fall in love with her.

She came here because she had no choice. She deceived you because she was being blackmailed—first by Honey, then James. She must have wondered what the hell she was caught up in. Yet, she still did her best to make your children happy, and to take care of you all. Imagine how terrifying it must have been for her, wondering how and when to tell you the truth, wondering if you'd be able to forgive her. And she's not the only one who's been living a lie, is she? I shouldn't imagine you've told her you're not really George's father. Or am I mistaken?'

'No,' he mumbled. 'I haven't.'

'Sometimes, we tell lies. We don't mean to, but we have to. Then we have to live with them. I should think she suffered every single day, knowing she was deceiving you. If Mickey is to be believed—and I do believe him, because I saw it for myself that day at the show—she'd fallen head over heels for you ages ago, so she must have been hurting for a long time. Eden's not Jemima, Eliot. Don't make her pay for Jemima's crimes. And don't—please don't—make yourself pay any longer. You've suffered enough. Jemima died because she was driving recklessly. She wanted to punish you. It wasn't your fault. Let the past go and look to the future. Find Eden. Let yourself be happy.' She stood, picking up her bag. 'I must go. I've stayed here long enough, when I have a lot to organise. We leave at the weekend.'

'Will you be all right?' he asked, getting to his feet. 'You and James, I mean? Are you sure you can be happy, after everything that's happened?'

'I honestly don't know,' she admitted. 'Things aren't great, but I know he wants to make it up to me, and for now, I'll let him try. Who knows how it will end? I just know we've suffered in silence for long enough. Time to start again. Make or break.'

'Good luck, Beth.'

She kissed him softly on the cheek. 'Give my love to

the children.'

'I will. Maybe—maybe when you get back, you can come round more. See them when you like.'

She smiled, delighted. 'I'd love that.'

He showed her to the door and she stepped out into the yard, turning to face him. 'Eliot, don't put it off any longer. Call Eden. Promise?'

He nodded and waved her off, then shut the door and rested against it for a moment. His gaze fell on the telephone, and he thought, just for a moment, about picking up the receiver. Then he shook his head. He couldn't and wouldn't call her.

He headed back into the kitchen. He needed another coffee. He had a lot of thinking to do.

CHAPTER THIRTY-THREE

'Is this the same place?' Eden gaped at the gleaming kitchen of The Red Lion. The stainless steel shone, reflecting her astonished expression back at her and urging her to close her mouth, which she hastily did. 'What's happened? Are we expecting Environmental Health?'

She'd been dreading going back, after two days off. Usually, she walked into a room that looked as if it had been in the middle of the Blitz. Gavin wasn't good at keeping on top of things, and first days back at work after any kind of break were usually spent scrubbing and disinfecting as if her life depended on it—after all, customers' lives really could depend on it. Someone had to ensure basic hygiene standards were met, and it wouldn't be Gavin.

'There's a party booked,' said Fiona. 'Some special do. Gavin was under strict instructions that the place had to be immaculate, or he wouldn't get paid.'

'Crikey. When's the party?'

Fiona glanced at her watch. 'In about four hours.'

'Four hours!' Eden looked at her, horrified. 'How am I supposed to get everything ready in four hours?'

'I'll help, and you don't have to make a cake, or anything. That's being provided by the clients.'

'But what do they want? A meal, a buffet? Are there any vegetarians? Oh, God, a party should take days of planning! This is going to be a nightmare.'

'Just wing it and enjoy,' advised Fiona. 'I don't think anyone will care.'

'But why such short notice?' Eden puzzled. 'When did they book it?'

'A week ago.' Gavin staggered wearily into the kitchen, looking as if he were about to have a coronary. 'That's the toilets done. Remind me to employ a cleaner. I've been on my hands and knees for hours. I'm done in.'

'A week ago? Well, why didn't you tell me?'

'Forgot.' He shrugged. 'Anyway, what's the problem? We've got a well-stocked kitchen—me and Fiona made sure you've got everything you need. The place is clean as a whistle. I've got two extra bar staff coming in to serve drinks. All you have to do is put your pinny on and stick a few sausages on sticks, for Christ's sake.'

'A few sausages on sticks?' Eden could have stamped her foot in pure Honey style. 'Are we having a nineteen-seventies theme, or something?'

Gavin looked delighted. 'How the hell did you know that? Client specifically requested it. Knock up some sandwiches, some prawn cocktails, some vol-au-vents and sausage rolls, and the like. Great minds, eh, Eden?'

'Don't be ridiculous.' Eden wondered if Gavin had gone mad while she'd been off. 'No one would want that nowadays.'

'Shows how much you know. Oh, speak of the devil,' he added, as his mobile phone rang. He disappeared into the bar, and Eden turned to Fiona. 'What's going on? Has he finally lost the plot?'

'You know Gavin,' said Fiona. 'A law unto himself. Look, don't worry about this. I'll help you out.'

'But I'll have dinners to cook, and you'll have to serve. When am I going to get the time?'

'Pub's closed to the general public all day,' said Fiona. 'We've got nothing to worry about but the party, so let's get cracking.'

'Gavin's closed the pub? Bloody hell.'

Her employer returned within minutes, beaming from ear to ear. His obvious joy was unnerving, to say the least. 'The bloke's really looking forward to this. Wants the lot! Throw in a few quiches, there's a good girl, and them Ritz crackers. Oh, and can you do a few bowls of Angel

Delight and jelly?'

'Angel Delight and jelly? Have you gone barmy?' Eden shook her head, then suddenly the penny dropped. 'Oh, my God. This is for Cain Carmichael, isn't it? No one else is stuck in the seventies like he is, and he loves Angel Delight! Is this party for Cain?'

'No. It's not.'

'Really? You're sure?'

'Cross my heart. Now, can we get on please, 'cos we haven't got much time, you know.'

'You think?' Eden rolled up her sleeves, fastened her apron, and went to wash her hands. 'Right. Let's crack on. Although, you'll have to go to the shop for Angel Delight. Funnily enough, we don't have any in stock.'

****

A large cake was wheeled in by two men. It was a chocolate extravaganza and must have cost a fortune. Eden peered at it, then glanced around at the room, which was almost unrecognisable. When she'd clocked off her shift two days ago, she'd left behind a dingy looking barroom with a beer-soaked carpet, and a layer of grime on every surface. Today, the place looked bright and clean. Everything had been highly polished and was sparkling. Gavin had even hired an industrial carpet cleaner, who'd brought years of dirt up, leaving a carpet that looked almost as good as new. Even the tables had no ring marks or beer stains on them. There was decent, soft toilet roll in the toilets, too, the soap dispensers were full, and there were paper towels. The toilets had a curious smell—a sort of mix of disinfectant and pot pourri. It was odd, but an infinite improvement on the usual smell that lingered in them.

In keeping with the seventies theme, Gavin had stocked up on alcoholic drinks that had apparently been popular back in that decade. The room was decorated with balloons and paper streamers and *Congratulations on your engagement* banners. So, it was an engagement party. She'd be face-to-face with a happy couple, flushed with love and looking forward to a future together. Great.

She wandered back into the kitchen and stood looking out of the window over the back yard of the pub. For a moment, she wondered what Eliot was doing. Did he ever think of her? Or had he pushed all thoughts of her from his mind, the way she'd tried to banish him from hers? Cuddling up to Shaun the Sheep every night in bed hadn't helped her forget, either, but she couldn't bring herself to throw it away. It was all she had left of the man she loved, after all. She hoped Eliot had been more successful at moving on than she had. He deserved peace of mind, and happiness. Maybe, with her gone, he'd find it with Daisy.

Realising the yard was a blur, she blinked away the tears. No time for wallowing. She had a party to get on with, and the guests would start arriving in a few minutes. The two extra barmen had turned up, and they helped Eden and Fiona carry the plates of food to the tables, which had been covered in immaculate white cloths. Gavin must have bought them specially. Whoever the clients were, they must have paid well to warrant such attention.

'Looks good.' Gavin nodded in approval, looking so excited, anyone would have thought it was his party. He kept glancing at the door while shuffling from foot to foot, like a child waiting for permission to open his Christmas presents.

'What's up with him?' Eden said, as she and Fiona headed back into the kitchen to finish washing and clearing up.

'Who knows?' Fiona smiled at her. 'Just relax and forget about it. Let's have a cup of tea, eh?'

Eden thought she could use something a bit stronger than tea. She felt a bit weird and a little strung out. Her nerves were jangling, but she couldn't imagine why. She supposed it was because she'd staked her reputation on bowls of Angel Delight and jelly, and a table full of seventies-type snacks. If the clients didn't approve, that could be her career up the spout.

A buzz of conversation started up in the bar, followed by some shrieks of laughter, and as the music began, they hurriedly finished their tea. Gavin would want them behind the bar any moment.

Sure enough, he popped his head round the door. Raising his voice over the blast of Suzi Quatro, he said, 'Do I pay you to sit on your arses, or what?'

'Bloody cheek,' muttered Eden.

Fiona winked at her, to her bemusement. Fiona was usually the first to moan about Gavin, but she looked as if his comment hadn't even touched her.

She followed her colleague through into the bar, but stopped dead in shock. 'Oh, my God!'

The room was like a Who's Who of seventies rock music. The good, the bad, and the downright ugly were happily tucking into her ham and tomato sandwiches, cocktail sausages, cheese and pineapple chunks on sticks, and Ritz crackers with soft cheese. They looked blissfully happy, as if they were right back in the good old days.

'Eden, my favourite girl who ain't related to me!' Cain threw his arms around her, his straw-like hair lacquered to within an inch of its life, and his eyes rimmed with kohl and layers of black mascara. He wore black leather trousers and a white shirt that would have looked good on a pirate but did nothing for his scrawny physique. 'How are you, my darlin'? You ain't bin to see me for ages!'

Eden returned his hug, glancing over his shoulder at Gavin, who gazed adoringly at his idol. 'I thought you said this party wasn't for Cain?' she said accusingly.

He beamed at her and waved his hand in the direction of the happy couple, who were chatting to none other than

Rex Scotman. 'It's not. It's for these two,' he said.

Eden broke away from Cain and stared at them in amazement. 'Honey and Teddy! They're engaged?'

'They are,' said Cain, putting his arm around her. 'Who'd have believed it, eh? Ain't never seen nuffink like it. True love that is, right there. Devoted to each other.'

'I'm amazed. I thought this would have all blown over by now,' admitted Eden.

'Me, an' all, truth to tell, but no. It's gone from strength to strength. You won't believe what's happening next. He's only taking Honey out to Africa, to see that bleeding music school in all its glory. Can you imagine Honey in Africa?'

'No,' said Eden bluntly. 'I can't.'

'Me neither, but she's up for it. I dunno, Eden. Seems like this charity thing has really caught her interest. She's planning all sorts of fundraisers. 'Course, Rex thinks the sun shines out of her arse, but she'll always be my baby, won't she? I mean, she's not his and never will be.'

'Of course not, Cain,' said Eden. 'Honey loves you. In her own sweet way.'

'Yeah. I realised that, that day at the cottage. She were that cut up about everything, when she thought Teddy had been lying to her, and all she wanted was her old dad. Just goes to show you.'

'Mm.' Eden didn't want to remember that day. She didn't want to think about Yorkshire at all. 'And are things between you and Rex any better? The concert was amazing, by the way. You were great.'

He had been, too, surprisingly. She could almost imagine why young girls in the seventies had thrown themselves at him. Soft lighting and makeup had worked a miracle. His voice had been strong, though, she'd give him that.

'Aw, thanks, darls. Let's just say, me and Rex have called a truce, for the sake of our kids. Wants me to go to

Africa with him next year, see the place for meself.'

'But you won't?' Eden thought he'd terrify the life out of the little children over there. He looked like a walking scarecrow half the time.

'I'm thinking about it. I'll see what Honey makes of it first. If she can`cope, I can. Got to admit, it wouldn't do my chances of a knighthood any harm, would it?'

'No. I suppose not.'

'Eden!' To her astonishment, she was enveloped in a huge hug from Honey. Well, that was a first. Honey had never been affectionate with her before. Would wonders never cease? 'How are you? I've missed you!'

'Have you?' Eden thought she might have to sit down. 'Er, well, thanks. I've missed you, too.'

She actually had. In her own weird way, Honey had wormed her way into Eden's affections, after all. How strange.

'What do you think?' said Honey, waggling her left hand in Eden's face, so she could see the huge rock sparkling on its third finger. 'Isn't it gorgeous? Teddy chose it. It was a surprise. I'm so happy.' She hugged Teddy to her, and Eden couldn't help smiling. Teddy looked at his fiancée so adoringly. It was funny how things turned out. One never knew what fate had in store.

'So, where's Freya?' Eden asked, not wanting to dwell on fate. It seemed to have dealt her a particularly cruel blow, and she couldn't think about what she'd lost, while Honey had gained so much.

'Pah! Freya.' Cain snarled. 'Too downmarket for her here. She was furious. She wanted a do in London, for God's sake. Told her, this was Honey's night and she could lump it. She's gone to some bloke's castle in the Highlands and won't be back until after the New Year now. Shame.'

'Well, to be fair, I would have expected you'd host this party somewhere a bit grander than the Red Lion,' admitted Eden. 'Why here? Of all places!'

Cain and Honey exchanged glances. 'Here is where everything started. Where Teddy came into my life, really,' said Honey.

'And where you came into our lives, too,' said Cain. 'I told Gavin, we'd happily pay a wad of cash, as long as he got the place sparkling. The slightest whiff of bacteria, and he wouldn't get a penny. And it had to be a secret, too.'

'But why?'

'To make sure you turned up, and so you didn't have time to think about things.'

'Things? What things?'

Cain winked at her. 'I'd best go and sort those two out,' he said, nodding over at one of his seventies bandmates, who was arguing with Snarler over the last bowl of Angel Delight. 'It will be handbags at dawn, otherwise.'

Honey kissed Eden on the cheek. 'I'll talk to you later, Eden. We'll have a proper catch up. I've got so much to tell you. I'm going to Africa, can you believe! I'm so excited. Anyway, I'm going to drag my husband-to-be onto the dance floor now, but I'll see you later.'

'Yeah, fine.' Eden stared hard at her. There was a definite air of mischief in Honey's eyes. What was she up to?

Turning, she headed back to the bar, thinking that today was like something out of a dream. She would never have believed what she'd be stepping into when she came into work a few hours ago. There was a long queue for drinks, and the two new barmen were obviously struggling. She stepped behind the bar and began to help.

'Er, Eden.' Fiona sidled up to her, flicking a cloth casually over the bar. 'Don't look now, but I think you've got a stalker.'

Eden frowned. 'What?'

'Don't look now, I said!' said Fiona, grabbing her arm.

'Very gorgeous chap, over by the door. Can't seem to take his eyes off you.'

'Huh. Very funny.' No doubt it was one of Cain's elderly cronies hoping to put another notch on his bedpost that night. Well, he could whistle for that.

'Ooh, he's coming over. Get ready. And remember, if you don't want him, send him in my direction.' Fiona winked at her and sidled off, a huge grin on her face.

Eden pulled a face and braced herself to fend off the ageing lothario's advances. As she looked up, she felt the ground begin to spin beneath her feet.

Eliot gave her an uncertain smile. 'Eden.'

It was the first time he'd called her by her real name. She clutched the bar for support and simply stared at him, unable to form a word.

He watched her nervously. 'Are—are you talking to me?'

She swallowed, then jumped as Gavin's voice bellowed in her ear. 'Two glasses of Blue Nun, Eden. Quick as you like.'

'Right. Yes.'

She poured the drinks, her mind whirling. Her hands shook so much, she was sure she'd given extra measures, but who cared?

What was Eliot doing here, of all places? And why tonight?

She handed Gavin the drinks, and he rushed off, no doubt to deliver them in person to one of his idols.

'How have you been?' Eliot's eyes burned into hers.

She wished she could read what was on his mind, but he was being very careful not to give much away. 'Oh, you know. Busy. You?'

'You know.'

She nodded and took someone else's order. A Babycham, two Cinzano and lemonades, two pints of lager and a Snowball. Wow, these people really knew how to embrace a theme. Unless they always drank the stuff, of course. Watching them bopping away to Wizzard's *See My Baby Jive*, it wouldn't have surprised her.

As she retrieved the glasses and reached for the bottles, she couldn't help noticing that a rather attractive redhead had sidled up to Eliot and was trying to engage him in conversation. There was no wonder, really. Dressed in black jeans, a black leather jacket and a checked shirt, he looked effortlessly sexy. His tousled curls were a stark contrast to the backcombed, lacquered styles that most of the other men were sporting, and he looked tall, lean, and exactly the sort of man that Eden would happily lock lips with until there was no breath left in either of them.

'I ordered a Snowball, too, remember,' said the customer, a sharp-nosed man, with two inches of black roots adding a fetching finishing touch to his platinum blonde mullet.

'Huh? Oh, yes. Sorry.' She quickly finished the order and took his money, trying not to smirk as she saw Eliot struggling to get away from the redhead. Small talk wasn't his strong point, and neither was flirting. At least, not intentionally.

'Did you want a drink?' she asked him, thinking he needed rescuing and she'd let him suffer long enough.

The redhead batted her eyelashes at him, obviously hoping he would ask her what she wanted, but Eliot wasn't playing.

'What?' He looked at Eden as if she was mad, then shook his head impatiently. 'No, no, of course I don't want a drink.'

The redhead looked disappointed, and after waiting a moment, she tutted and moved away.

Eden tapped her fingers on the bar. 'So, you don't want a drink. Crisps? Nuts?'

'Are you being funny?'

'Well, at least I'm speaking. It's more than you are.'

'You like working here?'

'It's a living. I used to work here before.'

'I know. Cain told me.'

'Did he indeed?' Eden raised an eyebrow. She'd be having words with Cain before the evening was over.

'Said you'd trained in catering and were a cracking cook. All them rubbish meals of sausage and chips you did us. Now, that's acting.'

'All right. Point taken.'

'We sold Gideon.'

'You did?' She clapped her hands. 'Good price?'

'Better than I could have hoped for.'

'That's brilliant news! It will be a massive help to you.'

'It won't solve all our problems, of course, but we've other irons in the fire now.'

'Oh?'

A young man dressed in a polyester shirt and corduroy flares lurched over to the bar. 'Excuse me, can I have a bag of pork scratchings?' he asked in a posh-sounding voice.

'Pork scratchings? Are you sure?'

'Oh, yah! Teddy says they're divine. This is a hoot, I must say. Never had a sausage on a stick before. Beats the dreadful dinner parties I usually have to endure.' He beamed at Eliot. 'Tremendous fun, isn't it?'

Eliot nodded. 'Oh, aye. Proper grand.'

'Proper grand!' The man grabbed the pork scratchings from Eden's hand and staggered off, laughing and repeating, 'Proper grand,' in a terrible attempt at a Yorkshire accent.

'Bloody hell,' Eliot murmured. He looked as if he couldn't believe what he was seeing at the party.

'What other irons in the fire?' said Eden impatiently.

'Eh? Oh, the barn thing. Your idea for bed and breakfasts.'

'You actually listened? You never said!'

'Aye, well. Just 'cos I don't say owt, doesn't mean I'm not thinking. We've been looking into it—well, Adey has. He reckons you're onto something, and with the money we made from the sales and a decent business plan, we should be able to get a bank loan to finance it. Adey's dad's cousin's an architect, and he's going to help us get planning permission.'

'Oh, Eliot, that's fabulous news!' Eden couldn't have been more delighted for him. She almost kissed him, but then she remembered that he still hadn't explained why he was there, and for all she knew he'd come to inform her he was marrying Daisy and intended to sue her for fraud. It wasn't likely, but she wasn't taking any chances.

'Aye. Suppose it is. Could use a cook.'

Could use a cook! Was that what he was here for? To offer her a bloody job? 'Well, I'm sure there are plenty of people who'd like to work in Skimmerdale. It's a great location, after all.'

'Mm.' He lapsed into silence again, and Eden served another three customers, while Eliot stood looking moody with his hands in his jacket pockets.

Eventually, her patience snapped. Handing the last customer his change, she leaned over the bar and confronted Eliot outright. 'So, what do you want?'

He looked a bit bemused, as if it was obvious. 'Well, what do you think?'

Eden shrugged. 'I have no idea. I'm assuming Cain invited you to Honey's and Teddy's engagement party. What else would you be doing here?'

'He did, yes.'

'Well, there you go.'

'But that's not why I'm here!' He must have spoken louder than he intended, because he looked around him, clearly embarrassed, before lowering his voice. 'You know why I'm here.'

Eden shook her head. 'That's just it, Eliot. I don't.'

'You're not going to make this easy for me, are you?'

'Eden, have we got any more pork pie in the back?' Gavin hollered at her in a most unprofessional manner. 'Plate's empty, and punters ain't happy.'

'Coming right up.' She rushed into the kitchen and stood for a moment, leaning against the door with her eyes closed. *Just breathe, Eden*, she thought. *Calm down.*

But what was he here for? The last time she'd seen him, he'd made it absolutely clear what he thought of her. Had he changed his mind? Then, why wasn't he telling her so? If he'd come all that way to offer her a job cooking breakfasts and serving cream teas in his new venture, she would shove the dratted pork pie somewhere so painful, he would have a permanent bloody glower.

Rummaging in the fridge, she removed what was left of the pie and cut it into slices. Her hands trembled by the time she pushed open the door and carried the plate through to the head table, not looking towards the bar.

'Pork pie, eh? Now you're talking. I don't believe we've met,' said an elderly man with long, dyed black hair, bloodshot eyes, and a tattoo of three teardrops on his cheek. He held out a hand adorned with a huge, ugly ring in the shape of a skull. 'Apparently, you're Eden, and you've done all this lovely grub yourself. I'm—'

'Rex Scotman,' she finished for him. 'Yes, I know. Pleased to meet you.'

'Sorry to interrupt,' came a voice in her ear, and before she could protest, a hand gripped her arm in a vice, and she was pulled away from the table and out of the pub.

'What are you doing?' she demanded, as Eliot led her into the car park towards a familiar vintage Rolls Royce.

'Cain's orders,' he said, rattling the car keys in her face. 'No arguments. You and me are going to sort this bloody mess out, once and for all.'

CHAPTER THIRTY-FOUR

'Well, I must say, this is riveting.' In truth, it was torture. Eden folded her arms and tried to quell the nervous churning in her stomach. They'd been sitting in Cain's car for five minutes, and neither of them had said a word. He'd come all the way from Skimmerdale for this?

Eliot smacked the steering wheel with the palm of his hand and turned to her, his eyes full of frustration. 'You know I'm no good at this stuff. What do you want me to say?'

'Excuse me? Look, I didn't make you come here, and I haven't asked you to say anything.'

'Sounds to me like you're not that bothered, anyway. Maybe coming here was a mistake.'

'Well, if you're just going to sit there and say nothing, maybe it was.'

'Do you mean that?' He searched her face, and she saw the anxiety in his eyes and crumpled.

'Of course I don't. I just—I just don't know what it is you want. Are you here for an apology? An explanation? Because I apologised that day, and I tried to explain. You didn't want to know.'

'I know. And no, I'm not here for an apology.' He shrugged. 'Mind you, if you want to say it again, I won't stop you.'

She glanced at him and saw the corners of his mouth turn up, just a touch. She unfolded her arms and took hold of his hand. 'Okay. I'm sorry. I'm really sorry, Eliot. I didn't want to deceive you, even before I arrived in Skimmerdale, but after I'd met you ...There wasn't a single day when I didn't hate what I was doing and wish I could come clean.'

'But why didn't you?' He twisted to fully face her, his expression deadly serious. 'Okay, I get that Honey left you with no choice, but once you'd got to the farm, once you'd met us, why didn't you tell me the truth then?'

'How could I? You were a total stranger. For all I knew, you'd be straight on the phone to Cain, and then I'd really be for it. If crashing his car wasn't bad enough—or at least, covering for the man who did—helping Honey make an idiot of him would have been the final straw.'

'I wouldn't have called him,' he muttered.

'Wouldn't you? Are you sure? Think about it, Eliot. I was being entrusted with your children. If I'd told you I was just an employee of Cain Carmichael, would you have felt able to leave me on my own with them? You only trusted Honey because she was a blood relative of Jemima's and you were desperate. Why would you trust someone who'd lied to you and was deceiving her own employer?'

After a quiet pause, he nodded. 'You're right. I wouldn't have trusted you. I'd have told Cain.'

She leaned back in the car seat and sighed. 'And then, once James Fuller started, I was in even deeper. He realised I wasn't Honey, and he—'

'Blackmailed you. Aye, I know. Beth told me.'

'Beth knew?'

'Not at the time, but she and Fuller have had a bit of a heart to heart apparently, and he confessed.'

'Oh.' Eden felt uneasy. She was on uncertain territory, talking about the Fullers. She didn't know what to say next.

'You must have been going through hell,' Eliot said eventually. 'First Honey, then Fuller. I'm sorry. I should never have thrown you out that day. I was just so churned up. Everything seemed to be coming at me all at once, and I didn't know what to do, or how to react.'

'You don't need to apologise,' she said. 'You had every right to be angry.'

'It wasn't so much anger,' he began, then his voice

trailed off. He thumped the car door and shook his head helplessly. 'I wish I could explain this stuff better. How I feel, I mean. I'm no good with words.'

He turned to face her again, his lips opening and closing as if he was figuring out what to say. When he suddenly pulled her to him, Eden dissolved into him, and he kissed her with a ferocity that proved he may not be good with words, but he knew exactly how to demonstrate his feelings.

'Crikey,' she breathed, when he finally released her.

'I know.'

They stared at each other for a moment. Eden trembled, as he took her hand and kissed it gently.

'That's what I'm trying to say, I reckon,' he said. 'I love you. There you go.'

'You old romantic,' she said, laughter in her voice. 'I love you, too, Eliot. You have no idea how much.'

'Really?'

'Of course, really. How could you doubt it?'

He hugged her tightly then kissed her again, cupping her face in his hands.

'Good job we got that cleared up,' Eden remarked, when he finally let her go. 'I dread to think which part of the car you'd have attacked next. Cain would have a fit, if he knew.' She lovingly stroked his face. 'I think you've made your point. If you ask me, actions speak louder than words, and I don't think there's any doubt that you're a man of action.'

'Well, it went better than I hoped,' he said, clearly relieved. 'Happen you've turned me into a proper romantic.'

'Hmm, you've made a start. Give me six months and you'll be bringing me flowers,' she said, nudging him.

'I'll give you meadows full of flowers,' he told her. 'Every summer, you'll have a carpet of buttercups, red clover, eyebright and globeflowers. It's all yours for the taking, Eden. Everything I have.'

She swallowed, her eyes suddenly swimming with tears. 'And you say you're no good with words. So,' she added, blinking furiously and sitting up straighter, 'what happens now?'

'Well, I were kind of hoping you'd want to come home,' he admitted. 'I mean to Fleetsthorpe. We all miss you. The kids are pining for you. Georgie won't settle, and the girls go on about you all the time.' He held up his hands in horror. 'That sounds all wrong. I don't mean that's why I'm here. Bloody hell, here I go, messing it up again. First telling you I'll need a cook, and now this. What I mean is, the kids do miss you, but I'm not interested in you because of them. Oh, Eden, please don't for one minute think I just want a mother figure for them. It's not that, at all. Oh, hell.'

'Eliot, if you just wanted a mother figure for your children, you could have had Daisy any time you wanted, and we both know it.'

He visibly relaxed. 'You knew that?'

'Of course I knew that. Anyone could see she was crazy about you. What happened that day at the show? She seemed really upset.'

He looked down at his lap. 'She was. Came to tell me her dad were going into a home, and she were free to move in with me. Told me she loved me.'

'Poor Daisy. How did you handle that?'

'Told her the truth. I'm fond of her and I'm grateful to her, but I don't love her. I could never love her.'

'Oh, gosh. How did she take it?'

'Told me I were a fool. Said I were going down the same path as I had with Jemima. Said you'd break my heart, just like Jemima had.' He squeezed her hand. 'That's what I meant when I said it weren't really anger that day. It were more fear. You see, it took a lot to admit to myself how I felt about you. I didn't want to love you. To me,

you were cut from the same cloth as Jemima, and I couldn't risk all that again. Somehow, though, I couldn't stop myself. When Daisy confronted me, I knew she were right. I loved you, and it were too late to stop it. So, that night, I took a gamble. I persuaded myself it could be different, that I could trust you. Then, when Cain and Freya turned up, and I realised you'd lied to me, like Jemima, I felt as if my worst nightmare were coming true. I panicked. I wanted you to go because I didn't trust my judgement anymore.'

'I can understand that,' Eden admitted. 'So, what changed your mind? What brought you here tonight?'

'I could never resist pork pie,' he said.

She nudged him in the ribs, and he laughed. 'All right, all right. If you must know, it were Beth. She came to see me. I were in a bit of a state, and she was worried about me. We had a long talk. There was a lot to discuss, to clear up. We had a lot of issues to resolve.'

'Something to do with why you wouldn't let the children near her?' Eden waited, wondering if he would confide in her, always supposing he knew the full truth.

He took a deep breath. 'When I said that Jemima had an affair, I didn't tell you who with. It was James Fuller.'

'Okay.'

'Thing is, it was much, much worse than an affair. Truth is, Fuller got her pregnant. George—George isn't mine.' When Eden said nothing, he looked at her, curious. 'You don't seem too surprised.'

It was her turn to confess. 'I'd guessed that.'

'What? How could you?'

'It was when I was sitting in the café with Fuller one day. There was something so familiar about his face, and I couldn't think what it was. Then, when I got home and George had gone missing ...When we found him, he gave us that smirk, and my blood ran cold. I realised who he reminded me of, and after that, it was obvious. I'm sorry,

Eliot, but he strongly resembles James Fuller.'

'Aye, he does. Beth and I can see it, too.'

'It must be awful for you, having to live with what happened every day. No wonder you didn't want them around to remind you.'

'There's more to it than that,' he said. 'For one thing, I was scared Fuller would claim George as his own and take him away from me. Beth's reassured me that won't happen, that Fuller's not interested. Apparently, he never was.'

'Well, that's good. Not that he'd be able to take him away now. You've brought Georgie up as your own. No court would drag him away from you.'

'You think? You don't know everything. You see, on the day Jemima died, Beth and I confronted her. We lied to her. Told her Fuller didn't want to know and had no intention of taking her or George on. It was a bluff, though ironically it turned out to be the truth. She were in a right state over it, and she shot off to Kirkby Skimmer to find him. Told me she were going to register George in his name.' His voice cracked, and he turned away, gazing out of the window toward the darkness of the car park. 'She never made it, and I've wondered, ever since, if I'd kept my mouth shut, if I hadn't lied to her that day, would she still be alive? Truth is, she probably would. She was rushing because I upset her. I've struggled with that knowledge ever since.'

'It was an accident! How could that be your fault? You weren't chasing after her. No one forced her to charge off at speed. You mustn't blame yourself for what happened, Eliot. For God's sake ...' Words failed her. He'd been living with all that guilt eating away at him, on top of the fear of losing George. What kind of man would take on a child, knowing his father was the man who'd betrayed him in the worst possible way? Only a man like Eliot. And he hadn't just taken George on, he'd loved him, cherished him. Eden didn't think it would be humanly possible to love this man any more than she did at that moment. 'I don't know what to say to you.'

'Thought it were me that were no good with words,' he said, half smiling through tears. 'I should also tell you I broke the law. I deliberately lied on a birth certificate. There was no way George could be mine, but I said I were his father.'

'I won't tell if you don't,' she said. 'Whatever any birth certificate says about the father, you're George's daddy. There's no mistaking that. So, you and Beth discussed all this at last?'

'Aye. I think we needed to. We'd barely spoken since the accident. I think we both wanted to clear the air. She made me see it were just a horrible twist of fate, and it were time to move on from the past and look to the future. Make a new start, like.'

'Sensible woman,' said Eden. 'And is that why you're here? Am I your new start?'

He wiped his eyes and grinned at her. 'Happen you might be, if you play your cards right.'

'I don't know how any woman could resist such a charming offer,' she said.

He reached out and gently brushed back a strand of her hair, looking at her with such wonder and devotion in his eyes that she felt as if her insides were melting. 'You're sure? It's not the life for everyone, you know. It can be tough. You've only seen it in the summer. Come the winter, we can be snowed in for days, even weeks.'

'Oh, I do hope so,' she said. 'Look, Eliot, you must know how I feel about the place. I feel at home there. The truth is, when I walked away that day, I left my heart behind. I guess you could call it hefting.'

He grinned at her, understanding what she was trying to say.

'I love Skimmerdale. I love the farm. I love the

children. Most of all, I love you. There's nowhere else I want to be, and there's no one else I want to be with.'

He took a deep breath. 'Thank God for that,' he said. 'Now, can we get out of this bloody Rolls Royce so I can kiss you properly?'

They scrambled out of the car, and Eden rushed round to stand beside him. His lips softly brushed hers, dusting them with light, butterfly kisses—almost as if he was afraid the moment wasn't real, or that she'd change her mind. His fingers twisted in her hair, and she put her arms around him, pulling him closer to her. She heard him catch his breath, then suddenly he was kissing her with a hunger that she returned in full.

Completely lost in the moment, Eden didn't notice that the pub door had opened, until she heard Cain's voice calling to them. 'About sodding time. Have you got me keys? I'm freezing me tits off here.'

With obvious reluctance, Eliot released Eden and fumbled in his pockets. Finding the keys, he threw them in the general direction of the pub, and Eden heard them land with a clatter somewhere on the ground.

Cain growled. 'Bleeding hell. Where's me lighter? Can't see a thing.'

'The Land Rover's parked just over there,' whispered Eliot. 'Do you want to go inside and say goodbye, or—'

Eden took his hand. 'I'll call them all later,' she said. 'And of course, you'll have to meet my mum and dad soon, but right now—'

'Aye?'

She looked into his dark eyes, smiling at the twinkle of mischief she found in them. Somehow, she was pretty sure his glowering days were behind him—unless, of course, she could think of a few ways to annoy him enough to ensure they resumed. Just now and then. She would miss them if they disappeared entirely.

'Right now, what?' he said.

'Right now, I just want to go back to Fleetsthorpe and wake up in the morning in our bed, with three beautiful children waiting for me to cook their breakfast. I've already been away too long.'

He put his arm around her and led her across the car park. 'Come on, my love. Let's go home.'

The End

Acknowledgements

Writing is a scary business. Confidence has never been my thing, and without support and encouragement, I doubt I could put myself through this. My husband is always certain I can achieve anything, and so my first thank you is to him. Steve, your words of encouragement and your constant belief in me mean more to me than I can ever adequately explain. Thank you. You're my rock, and I don't think I could manage without you.

I'm extremely fortunate, because I have nine other voices chipping away at me, nudging me into action, demanding that I keep the faith. Without my fellow Write Romantics, I don't know where I'd be, so a massive thank you to Alex Weston, Deirdre Palmer, Helen Phifer, Helen J Rolfe, Jackie Ladbury, Jo Bartlett, Julie Heslington, Lynne Davidson and Rachael Thomas. You're always there for me when I need you the most. You're all superstars.

To Jo, as always, thank you for all your practical help, and for the time you've given over to me. I know how busy you are, so don't for one minute think that all your efforts aren't appreciated. They are HUGELY appreciated. Thanks must also go to my beta readers, whose comments and suggestions made such a difference. Alex, Julie, Jo, Liz and Rachael, I am so grateful for your help. Massive thanks to JB Editing Services for a "grand" job with editing and proofreading. Thoroughly professional, friendly and efficient, I would highly recommend you to anyone.

I must thank Rachael and Alex for helping me in my quest to learn more about sheep and farming. As if being a very talented writer for Mills and Boon, while helping to manage a dairy farm, isn't keeping Rachael busy enough, she took the time to send me snippets about farming life and routine. Having once also kept sheep, she was kind enough to give me details about sheep farming and showing, and cast a critical eye over my farming scenes, pointing out to me some things that needed tweaking. Who knew farmers drank so many cups of tea? I could never have tackled it on my own, so thank you, Rachael. Alex accompanied me to a fabulous talk in Malton, given by authors Neil Hanson (*The Inn at the Top*) and Amanda Owen (*The Yorkshire Shepherdess*). Not only were these talks interesting and highly entertaining, they were full of useful pointers which enabled me to rethink aspects of Eliot's personality, and get a better idea of how Dalesmen think and act. It was a great evening, and I probably wouldn't have had the nerve to go along on my own, so thank you so much, Alex, for volunteering.

Thank you, as always, to my friends and family for your patience and support. Where would I be without you? Thanks for caring and for showing such interest. To those of you who have been nagging me for the next book—especially Caz, Karen and Sarah, my cheerleaders—I hope it's been worth the wait.

Finally, thank you to everyone who has bought *There Must Be an Angel*, *A Kiss from a Rose*, or *This Other Eden*. I am so grateful to every one of you. Thank you if you've left reviews for the first two books, and if you would consider leaving a review for this one, it would be much appreciated. It really does make a difference.

Sharon

xxx

Also Available by Sharon Booth

There Must Be an Angel

"This lovely book tugged at every heart-string. A treat from start to finish. I loved it!" Valerie-Anne Baglietto.

When Eliza Jarvis discovers her property show presenter husband, Harry, has been expanding his portfolio with tabloid darling Melody Bird, her perfect life crumbles around her ears.

Before you can say *Pensioner Barbie* she's in a stolen car, heading to the North Yorkshire coastal village of Kearton Bay in search of the father she never knew, with only her three-year-old daughter and a family-sized bag of Maltesers for company.

Ignoring the pleas of her uncle, chat show presenter Joe Hollingsworth, Eliza determines to find the man who abandoned her mother and discover the reason he left them to their fate. All she has to go on is his name – Raphael – but in such a small place there can't be more than one angel, can there?

Gabriel Bailey may have the name of an angel but he's not feeling very blessed. In fact, the way his life's been going he doesn't see how things can get much worse. Then Eliza arrives with her flash car and designer clothes, reminding him of things he'd rather forget, and he realises that if he's to have any kind of peace she's one person he must avoid at all costs.

But with the help of beautiful Wiccan landlady, Rhiannon, and quirky pink-haired café owner, Rose, Eliza is soon on the trail of her missing angel, and her investigations lead her straight into Gabriel's path. As her search takes her deeper into the heart of his family, Eliza begins to realise that she's in danger of hurting those she cares about deeply. Is her quest worth it?
And is the angel she's seeking really the one she's meant to find?

A Kiss from a Rose

Flynn Pennington-Rhys is the quiet man of Kearton Bay, so when he finds himself entangled in the chaotic life of Rose MacLean, his whole world turns upside down.

Rose is at a low ebb. With one daughter clearly harbouring a secret, another who has morphed overnight from Shirley Temple into Miley Cyrus, and a mother hell-bent on reliving her misspent youth with her childhood sweetheart, Alec, AKA Red rum, it's no wonder her self-esteem is at rock bottom. But when, on top of all this, her best friend goes on ovulation alert, and her slimming club leader has a meltdown, Rose needs someone she can rely on.

It seems, though, that Flynn has his own secret, and as events take an unexpected turn, it's no longer certain that he can be counted on. Will the quiet man come through for her? Will her daughters ever sort themselves out? And will her mother ever move on, or is Rose really doomed to years of sleeping in the bath tub?

Coming Soon

Once Upon a Long Ago

Lexi Bailey doesn't do love. Having seen the war zone that was her parents' marriage, she has no interest in venturing into a relationship, and thinks romance is for fairy tales. As far as she's concerned, there's no such thing as happy ever after, and she's not looking for a handsome prince.

For Will Boden-Kean, that's probably a good thing. He hardly qualifies as a handsome prince, after all. He may be the son of a baronet, and live in a stately home, but he's not known for his good looks. What he *is* known for, among the residents of Kearton Bay, is his kind heart, his determination to fund Kearton Hall — and his unrequited love for Lexi.

While Lexi gazes at the portrait of the Third Earl of Kearton, and dreams of finding the treasure that is reputed to be hidden somewhere in the house, Will is working hard to ensure that his home survives and thrives. When he goes against Lexi's wishes and employs the most unpopular man in the village, she begins to wonder if he's under a spell. Will would never upset her. What could possibly have happened to him?

As plans take shape for a grand ball, Lexi's life is in turmoil. With a secret from Will's past revealed, a witch who is far too beautiful for Lexi's peace of mind, and a new enchantress on the scene, things are changing rapidly at Kearton Hall. Add to that a big, bad wolf of a work colleague, a stepmother in denial, and a father who is most definitely up to no good, and it's no wonder she decides to make a new start somewhere else.

Then she makes a discovery that changes everything — but time is running out for her. Is it too late to find her happy ending? Will Lexi make it to the ball? Will Buttons save the day? And where on earth did that handsome prince come from?

15891702R00240

Printed in Great Britain
by Amazon